IN THE
KEY
OF
13

An anthology of
music and murder

by the Mesdames of Mayhem

Editor: Donna Carrick
Copy –editor: Ed Piwowarczyk
Project Manager: M.H. Callway

In the Key of 13

An anthology of music and murder

by the Mesdames of Mayhem

Copyright Mesdames of Mayhem 2019
Copyright Carrick Publishing 2019

Editor: Donna Carrick

Copy-editor: Ed Piwowarczyk

Project Manager: M.H. Callway

Cover Art by Sara Carrick

Carrick Publishing

Print Edition 2019

ISBN 13: 978-1-77242-111-8

Praise for 13 Claws

"A great mix of shuddery dark and tongue-in-cheek funny. What devious minds all these nice women have. (Murdog liked the stories as well.)"

~ *Maureen Jennings, author of Murdoch Mysteries, the Tom Tyler series and Christine Morris Books.*

Contents:

Dedication

On behalf of the Canadian Crime writing community, the Mesdames of Mayhem would like to dedicate this anthology to the memory of Howard Engel CM, (April 2, 1931 – July 16, 2019).

The award-winning author of the Benny Cooperman detective series, co-founder of the Crime Writers of Canada and honorary member of Sisters in Crime, Toronto Chapter, Engel was known to many as an extraordinary novelist, teacher, friend and gentleman.

In 2000, Engel suffered a stroke that robbed him of his ability to read, a cruel outcome for a prolific and passionate author. His dedication in re-training himself to read and write after this trauma will stand as an inspiration to all who knew him, especially those of us who share his passion for the written word.

Rest in peace, Howard. We stand with Canadian authors from coast to coast in thanking you for your contribution to Canadian Crime.

Foreword

By Donna Carrick

In 2012, Madeleine (M.H.) Harris-Callway had an idea: Why not form a collective of like-minded crime authors, with a view to sharing this journey of writing, promotion and the general hilarity of struggling to succeed in the crime fiction industry?

What followed has been an exuberant roller-coaster ride of creativity, passion, dedication and above all, friendship.

From inception to realization, our collective has produced four stellar crime anthologies: *Thirteen*, *13 O'Clock*, *13 Claws*, and our latest, *In the Key of 13*. These works have been met with both critical acclaim and industry recognition.

As a team, the *Mesdames of Mayhem* have attended and hosted countless workshops, presentations and events related to the art and business of genre fiction.

It's been seven years since we took our first tentative steps toward realizing Madeleine's vision. With the imminent release of *In the Key of 13*, I find myself reflecting on our shared journey, on the comradeship we've enjoyed and the fun we've had working toward a common goal. I cannot help but believe we have been truly blessed in this calling.

To my fellow *Mesdames* and *Messieurs*, I am honored to call myself your friend. Alex and I wish to thank you, one and all, for bringing us your best stories and for allowing us to present your work to readers.

And to our readers, without whom even our most dedicated efforts would be meaningless, we thank you for your long tradition of loving the stories we share. Your readership is that thing we treasure above all else.

We wish each of you a long and healthy life, filled with countless glittering words.

Donna and Alex Carrick
Carrick Publishing
August, 2019

Nice descriptions
Not enough motive
Silly tidy ending

THE *MOONLIGHT SONATA*

By Caro Soles

I have never lived in such an elegant place as this. It's like being in another world here, with the gold-braided doorman and echoing black-marble vestibule. Up we go, Mother and I, in the golden cage to the fourth floor where more marble awaits. Two large vases stand on either side of the entrance, holding huge ostrich plumes more suited to be waved in front of some Egyptian pharaoh like Tutankhamen. There's even a second floor inside the apartment, with wide banisters and a curving stairway with shallow carpeted steps. The red runner has brass rods holding it in place. I stare at them sometimes, almost hypnotized. The rooms here are large and filled with shadows, the long windows hung with heavy lace and velvet drapery. There are oil paintings, suspended by long ropes, on the walls.

Of course, this isn't our apartment. We could never aspire to anything this grand. It belongs to my Aunt Esmé and Uncle Robert. We're just the poor relations. When Mother ran away with an Italian musician years ago, she was disowned, but now that he's dead in the war and I am

3

so good at what I do, it seems much can be forgiven, if not forgotten. "If only he had been an officer, like Robert," Aunt Esmé would say, "you would have been taken care of." Everyone knows Uncle Robert was never anywhere near the front, but Mother says nothing, just bites her lip the way she does and then changes the subject. Mother swallows her grief for me, so that I can perform during their musical evenings. Perhaps someone will notice and remember me, and take me away to study and perform elsewhere. And bring her with me. I spend a lot of time practicing on the square grand piano my aunt and uncle are so proud of. It is lovely to look at with its mother-of-pearl inlay, but its tone leaves something to be desired, a fact I keep to myself. It is, Mother says, the ship that will sail us out of bondage. She says things like that sometimes.

Today Aunt Esmé swept out the door in a formidable velvet hat with a tassel hanging down on one side like a bell pull. Mother thought her dress shockingly short, halfway to her knees, but Aunt Esmé says this is the fashion now. She is meeting her lord and master for lunch at The Club. At least that's what she says. I followed her one time a few weeks ago when she said the same thing and found out The Club was not her true destination. But I digress. Mother went out as well on some errand or other for my aunt, so there is no one here but the maid and Cook. My shoulders gradually relax as I start up the stairs.

The grandfather clock in the marble foyer wheezed into its job of striking the hours and was followed in short order by the French clock on the mantel in the main salon, the Ivan Mezgin Russian monstrosity and all the other lunatic timepieces so beloved of Uncle Robert. The man was obsessed with time, or perhaps only with timepieces, since he hired a clockmaker to come once a week to look after them all. Amusingly, he claims not to have the time himself, but I think he does not have the patience. I was upstairs and out through the French doors onto the terrace before the clamor ceased.

Out here, the extravagant blooms have died in their cement urns, trailing skeletal remains over the edges. No one has come to clean the dead leaves from the stone floor. I walk through them to the low railing, leaning over to greet the leering gargoyle I can just make out over the entry. If I lean over far enough, I can see into the neighbor's apartment that joins this corner, forming the small courtyard. They're new here, having moved in with all their goods and chattels a mere few weeks ago. I had watched as every settee and sideboard, hamper full of crockery and roll of Persian rug, Tiffany lamp and pier glass made its way inside. Last, but not least, came the grand piano, a real Bösendorfer. A girl began to practice on it the very next day.

She was lovely, this girl, with long dark-gold hair almost to her waist, held back from her face with a huge hair ribbon that never seemed to go limp. She was like an illustration in an old book. I watched her every move avidly, drinking in her grace, the dimple in one cheek, the way she tossed back her hair with one hand as she played. She came to the window one time, and I saw she had eyes the color of lavender. Her mouth smiled, as if she saw me and liked what she saw.

I soon discovered that I could see and hear her even better from our music room if I pulled the drapes way back and opened the window. I began to spend a lot more time there. No one but the maid ever came into the music room, so no one but Mother noticed. When I heard her at the door today, I jumped down from the wide window seat and slid onto the piano stool.

"A little chilly in here, isn't it?" Mother closed the window and pulled the drapes closer together, the brass rings rattling like a rebuke to my ears. "We don't want them complaining about the heating." She sat down on the ottoman near me and folded her hands. I noticed she was wearing one of Aunt Esmé's old dresses, which she must have altered, since she was smaller than her big-boned sister.

"I know things are not easy for you here," she began, and I tensed. "You must study and practice and do well, my dearest. It is our only chance of getting away from here. You are my lodestar, my hope." She looked at me in that intent way she had, and I felt my insides turn over and my heart swell with love.

"I will," I promised, tears in my throat.

"Esmé is having a big dinner party next week, and she wants you to play beforehand. Nothing too modern, mind."

"Don't worry. No Russians, I promise." I grinned, trying to make her smile.

"Thank you, dear." She reached over and patted my hand. "Now I must go. Esmé wants me to help with the flowers."

I sat there for a long time after she left, thinking about how things used to be, in our small walk-up apartment that was always full of music and laughter. No one here laughed much, I noticed, and the only music was provided by me. And that wonderful girl next door. I got up and opened the window again.

At once the flowing strains of the *Moonlight Sonata* filled the dim room. I laid my head against the wooden casement of the window and pulled my legs up to my chin. The melody was like a balm to my heart, although her technique was far from perfect. Somehow, the erratic slowing of the chords or speeding up when she felt more confident was endearing. "What is your name?" I wondered.

When she stopped, I closed the window again and began to practice. At first, just for fun, I played the *Moonlight Sonata*, like a distant echo of the girl across the way, only slightly faster as it should be, and I played the whole thing. Then I began to practice in earnest, thinking hard about what pieces I should choose for next week. Beethoven? Chopin? Perhaps just a little Scarlatti for a change of pace? A lot depended on who would be there, so I decided to prepare enough that I could choose seemingly on the spur of the moment—opting for technical difficulty, feeling, interpretation, depending on the audience.

I kept pestering Mother to find out who was invited, but she was not very forthcoming. So, I waited, and practiced, and watched for another appearance of my golden muse. I dreamed about her sometimes. In the dreams, we were playing duets and laughing together. In reality, it nearly happened one day when I left the window open as usual and she was playing Für Elise. I joined in and we finished together, but in truth, I'm not sure she was even aware of our shared performance.

The days passed, and I was getting anxious. I had performed for these parties before, but Mother said this one was special. For one thing, it was bigger than usual. For another, Aunt Esmé had started calling it a musical soirée, which was a bit alarming. It meant there might be other performers. It also meant there might finally be someone important in the audience who might mentor me.

At last Mother confessed. She had been in charge of writing most of the invitations, so she had added three of the musical luminaries of the city: Godfrey Rider the

7

impresario; James Untermeyer, the music critic for the *Herald*; and Carlo Sanders, the talent agent.

"What will you say to Aunt and Uncle if they come?" I asked.

"That they were friends of your father. After all, he did play in the orchestra in several theaters Rider does bookings for. And he did meet Sanders one time."

"They won't come," I said glumly.

She smiled at me knowingly. "I think they will," she said. "I enclosed a short note in each one."

I stared at her, but she refused to tell me what was in the notes.

"Don't be nervous," she said, just as she was leaving. "The others are just amateurs, and you are my star." She blew me a kiss.

The next day, she appeared again to reassure me about the competition. "Cousin Sally will sing, I'm sure, and the Samson brothers will do their clever patter songs. Fred Lynley will recite some amusing drivel, just as usual. But you will have a chance to really shine in front of some people who matter."

I breathed a sigh of relief. The more amateurish the others were, the better I would sound.

The day came. The house began to fill with flowers and the chatter of extra housemaids preparing the silver and dishes. The kitchen was a steamy place of mouthwatering magic, and Cook chased me out with a shout. Although I'm sure she had done this many times before we arrived, Aunt Esmé seemed to need Mother by her side at every turn. It occurred to me for the first time that Mother had been used to all this as a girl, that she had arranged flowers and ordered the maids about, inspected the laying of the table and sparkle of the crystal. She had loved my father, Francesco Martino, enough to leave all this luxurious servitude behind her. And she expected another Martino, me, to take her away from it all again. Maybe even tonight.

I straightened my shoulders and went to inspect my new clothes. I don't really enjoy dressing up as many do, but admit it does make one feel that the event is more of an occasion. And this event truly was. Even as I finished getting dressed, I could hear the tinkle of glasses, the scrape of chairs as the guests took their places, the buzz of conversation, the bass tones of the men droning an accompaniment to the lighter voices of the women.

I went down the stairs slowly, gathering my thoughts. They had moved the piano into the grand salon, where all the tuxedoed men in their sparkling patent leather shoes and satin striped trousers sat with their ladies, strings of pearls draped over their chests and feathers in their bobbed hair. I was glad Mother had not given in to this latest style and still had all her lovely long hair that Father used to love to brush when he came home from a job late at night and they thought I was asleep.

As I walked through the door, I almost stumbled. There she was. My dream girl. My muse. Standing in the front row, leaning against a stylishly flat-chested woman I assumed to be her mother, her long pale mauve dress with the wide, low sash echoing the color of her eyes. She was even more beautiful close-up than seated at her piano 30 feet away.

No one paid any attention to me as I hung back in the shadows. I had meant to take an inventory of the crowd, look carefully to see if any of the three people of importance to me had actually come, but seeing her there had thrown me. I suppose it was sensible to invite the new neighbors. My aunt and uncle might even have known them before they moved here, for all I knew. They might even be great friends. I hadn't thought of that. I never thought of her in relation to anyone but me. When I saw her, she was always alone, with only occasionally the shadow of her music teacher in the background.

The evening proceeded along the lines that Mother had predicted, people chatting together softly during the singing and recitations, the occasional laugh smothered by a lady's hand, until Aunt Esmé stood up and introduced me, "without whom no musical evening would be complete." That was warming, but the fact she used an anglicized version of my last name was not. I was not Martin, but Martino! I glanced at Mother as I stood by the piano, but she gave a slight shake of her head and her eyes warned me to ignore the slight. *Carry on*, they said. *You are my star.*

I sat down, shook out the tension from my hands and swept into the Scarlatti, my fingers rippling along the runs, bringing out the brilliance of the melody. After that, I had planned on Chopin, Nocturne Opus 9—much slower, with a depth of feeling to show I was not all technique.

I stood to acknowledge the applause, caught Mother's eye and saw she was smiling a genuine smile that made my heart sing. Then I saw the smile fade as Aunt Esmé rose to her feet.

"Very lovely, but before you go on, I would like to invite our young neighbor Lillian to sing something for us. Her mother tells me she is quite talented musically. You could accompany her, if you will?"

I smiled and sat down again, glad that I at least still had control of the piano. She would sing, and then I would continue.

Lillian seemed quite self-possessed as she came to the piano and asked me if I knew "Annie Laurie." I tried not to look insulted and asked her what key. That gave her pause but only for a moment.

"The right key for me," she said, and her dimples flashed.

I felt a flash of annoyance, but everyone else was laughing so I smiled back and made a stab at what I thought it might be. I had heard her sing it, after all. As it turned out, I was right, and she sang it with a purity of tone that was quite lovely. The audience was very enthusiastic, more than her rendition deserved, I thought, but she was very sweet and pretty.

I was flexing my fingers to continue with my program, when she spoke up, her voice high and childish, carrying to the back of the room.

"I would love to play the opening of the *Moonlight Sonata* for you, too," she said, her childish hands pushed against her flat chest. Even before she had finished speaking, she was moving around to the keyboard, looking at me pointedly, expecting me to move.

What could I do? "That would be lovely," I said, getting to my feet. But I did not move far.

"Lillian is preparing for a recital soon," her mother said, smiling indulgently.

I gritted my teeth as she began the opening, much too slowly. In her excitement, she seemed to have forgotten it was supposed to be *pianissimo*. None of the first movement ought to be more than *piano*. It was a poem that should linger in the mind, but this interpretation should be forgotten as quickly as possible. I noticed the tip of her tongue appear between her sharp little teeth in concentration as the piece went on, her hands slowing even more from time to time as she focused on reaching the right notes. I sat down against the wall and looked at the audience. They were all smiling tolerantly. I sighed. At least this travesty wouldn't take long. I had never heard her play the whole first movement all the way through and suspected her teacher, that shadowy presence I had never seen, had suggested the cuts.

When she finished, the whole room stood up and applauded, led by my aunt and uncle. Of course, Mother had to stand as well. What would it look like if she had not? I stood, too, and moved my hands as if I were clapping, but I made no noise. My hands did not even touch. She was doing a pretty curtsy now, her cheeks unusually pink from pleasure.

My hands clenched. Lillian had, in effect, stolen my night. She had a recital coming, to which her family would invite all the swells and cognoscenti in the world who might help her. This was supposed to be my night! My mother had connived and even lied (if only a few little white lies) to get three people here who might help me. Me. Someone who had no wealthy parents to pay for a musical debut, no influence to put me on any program where I might be seen and hired. I had this one night. She had stolen it.

Everyone was chatting now, taking champagne from the maids passing though the room, the ladies using their fans to punctuate their conversations and flirt. Lillian stood alone, still by the piano.

"Were you very nervous?" I asked, moving to her side.

She nodded. "I was. I really was. But you know, I was also really happy at the same time." She looked straight into my eyes. "Isn't that strange?"

"I think we feel the most happiness when we're doing something really difficult, and doing it well," I added, giving her what she would deem a compliment.

Sure enough, she blushed in pleasure.

"I've been listening to you play for a while now, you know," I said, watching her.

"No," she said. "You can't have."

"But I have. Do you want to see how?"

She nodded and took the hand I extended to her.

We went up the stairs side by side, leaving the chattering and laughter behind us. I was only a little taller than she was, I noted. I felt so very much older that this discovery was a surprise.

"You have a terrace," she exclaimed as I opened the door and the cool breeze touched our faces. "We have a balcony but it's over the street. Funny, I never noticed this."

I suspected she was not one to notice anything that had no relationship to her.

"Look," I said, leading her to the low stone balustrade. "See?" I pointed to the window of the room where her beautiful piano sat in the shadows.

"Is that the right room? Really?"

Above us the moon slid into view, sending a shaft of moonlight into the courtyard, where the shadow of the gargoyle crept into sight.

"There! Now you can see." I slid my arm around her waist as she bent over, her long blond hair falling over one shoulder.

"Yes! I see it now! And your window is just kitty-corner?"

"Lean over a bit more. There. See?"

"Yes, but—let me go!"

And I did.

As she slid into the night below, the moon ducked back behind the clouds. I left the terrace door open a crack and went back downstairs. I noticed that people had moved around, some changing their seats to sit beside another friend. They were settling down now, almost ready to listen again. Mother still sat in her place. She nodded to me, her

13

smile gone. *Your time is running out*, her nod said. *You are going to lose them.*

I sat down at the piano and quickly scanned the room. I still couldn't tell if the big three were here. It didn't matter. I would play for them anyway. For them and for my mother. As soon as there came a brief lull in the conversation, my hands crashed down on the keys, and I rushed headlong into the last movement of the *Moonlight Sonata*. The one filled with passion and dark fire and breathless hope. The one Lillian could never play.

FAREWELL TO THE KING

By Rosemary McCracken

When the news broke that the King of Rock 'n' Roll had died, we were beyond consolation. We knew the words to every song the King had recorded. We'd lost our dearest friend.

The four of us gathered at Toni's apartment that morning. Elvis was singing "Are You Lonesome Tonight?" on the record player when I arrived.

"There'll never be another like him," Mai-Lei wailed. "Elvis was the King. He was ours!" Her pretty face was wet with tears.

"We should hold a wake," Cécile said. "Stay up all night to show how much we miss him."

I lowered myself onto the sofa with Robbie strapped to my chest in his Snugli. "Sleep tonight, my friends," I told them. "Tomorrow, we go to the King's funeral."

They stopped what they were doing and stared at me.

Toni, jiggling little Gabriella on her hip, was the first to speak. "The funeral is in Memphis, Paula. And in case you don't know, Memphis is south of the border. In the U.S. of A."

15

"Toni's right," Mai-Lei said. "There's no way we can get from Montreal to Memphis for the funeral tomorrow afternoon."

I waved off their protests. "Bon Voyage Travel is offering a charter flight to Elvis Presley's funeral. The first 150 people who put their money down will leave Dorval Airport at 7:30 tomorrow morning."

They stared at me with wide eyes and open mouths.

"A bus will take us to the Elvis sites in Memphis," I told them. "And we'll be back in Montreal tomorrow night. What do you say?"

"What would that cost us?" Mai-Lei asked.

"One hundred and sixty-five dollars each."

"*Mon dieu!*" Cécile cried.

"And a babysitter on top of that?" Mai-Lei said. "Dream on."

"It's not impossible," I told them. "One hundred and sixty-five dollars is five dollars a week for the next 33 weeks. We'll give up smoking for Elvis. And we all know someone we can leave our kids with for a day."

"Might work for the three of you," Toni said. "You're not breastfeeding." She looked down at Gabriella.

"Pierre would let you go to Memphis?" Cécile asked me.

"Pierre can't stop me," I said. "The cops nailed him in a raid last week. He's doin' the 'Jailhouse Rock.'"

The girls giggled uneasily.

"We have to do this," I told them. "For *us*. We can tell our kids we were at Elvis Presley's funeral in 1977."

"We'd need the money today," Mai-Lei said. "That won't be easy."

But we managed to get it. Toni raided the joint bank account she had with Rocco, her husband. Cécile wheedled it out of her horny father-in-law. Mai-Lei dipped into the till at her brother's restaurant. And I cleaned out the emergency fund I'd created by squirreling away money from Pierre's grocery allowance.

That afternoon, we took the Métro to Bon Voyage Travel and bought our tickets.

As soon as I got home, I made the call. "Change of plans," I said. "Gonna say farewell to the King in Memphis. I'll be behind the buses outside Forest Hill Cemetery."

"Suspicious Minds" was on the radio when I hung up. Elvis was singing about being caught in a trap. I was determined to get out of mine.

***

Toni arrived at the airport with Gabriella the next morning.

"You gotta be kidding, Antonia," Cécile said, rolling her eyes.

"I'm breastfeeding and Gaby won't take a bottle. I can't go without her," Toni said. "But she'll be no trouble. All she does is sleep and feed and poop."

"You'd better be right," Mai-Lei grumbled.

Toni looked down at my feet. "Blue suede shoes, Paula?"

I shrugged. "They were good enough for Elvis."

Mai-Lei pulled a camera out of her backpack. "We gotta have a group shot with Paula's blue suede shoes in the middle."

"*Monsieur*," I called out to a man in a business suit, "would you take our photo?"

We posed for several shots. Then we remembered why we were at the airport and scrambled to make our flight. We found ourselves breathless in the departure lounge with dozens of other women. Many were in their 20s like us, but there were several teenagers, and a good number of older women. They wore Elvis T-shirts and

Elvis ball caps and Elvis badges. Many of them were in tears.

The King was crooning "It's Now or Never" over the sound system as we filed into the airplane.

I sank into my window seat and tried to relax.

"If I died today, my life would be complete," Cécile moaned when she sat down beside me. "I'll be with him this afternoon in Memphis."

"I've never felt so close to him," I heard Mai-Lei tell Toni in front of us.

Gaby, we soon learned, did more than sleep and feed and poop. She screamed at the top of her lungs. As the plane climbed into the sky, she started to howl and she didn't let up.

"Shut that damn kid up!" a woman shouted across the aisle.

"Yeah, shut her up," Cécile muttered beside me.

"Air pressure in her ears," I called out to Toni. "Nurse her to make her swallow."

Was I ever glad I'd left Robbie with my landlady.

The airline provided coffee and pop, and we'd brought peanut-butter-and-banana sandwiches, Elvis's favorite. "Hey, it's not fancy," Cécile said when we'd shared our cookies and Rice Krispies squares, "but I'd rather be eating lunch here with Elvis than in the fanciest restaurant in the world."

Mai-Lei heaved a sigh. "I can't believe he'll never release another record."

"Don't be cruel," Toni said with a groan, and moved Gaby to her other boob.

Cécile stopped munching her sandwich. "It's over. The King is gone."

***

After four and a half hours in the air, we landed at Memphis International. The airport was a circus, packed with fans carrying Elvis posters, waving Elvis banners, wearing Elvis caps and T-shirts and rhinestone jumpsuits.

But going through customs was a breeze. "How long will you be in the United States?" the frazzled agent asked me.

"Just a few hours," I said, my heart hammering in my ears. "We're going to Elvis Presley's funeral, then flying home."

"Tell me something new," he muttered and waved me through.

No one asked to look in my handbag.

Outside the terminal building, the heat and humidity nearly bowled us over. Mai-Lei snapped photos of us hamming it up with the Elvis Forever sign I'd made. I took the camera and got a few shots of her.

Then we boarded our air-conditioned bus. "Cool in here and there's a toilet at the back," Cécile said, nabbing a window seat behind Toni and Mai-Lei. "We could stay on this bus until it's time to fly home."

I took the aisle seat beside her.

"Why didn't we ever see Elvis in concert?" she asked, her brown eyes filled with tears.

"Because he only came to Canada back in 1957, and we were in in kindergarten then."

"We should have gone to see him in the States. The one trip we ever took for him was to his funeral."

I reached over and patted her hand.

"I'm Virgil, your driver this afternoon," the bus driver announced. "Welcome to Memphis, the city that gave the world the Holiday Inns. And Elvis Aaron Presley, the King of Rock 'n' Roll."

Elvis's name was greeted by whoops and cheers and clapping. Mai-Lei turned in the seat in front of us and gave Cécile and me a thumbs-up.

"All flags in Memphis are at half-mast," Virgil continued as he maneuvered the bus through the airport parking lot. "And traffic's the worst I ever seen. Thousands of people from all over the world are here to say goodbye to the King, same as you. On top of that, 16,000 Shriners are in town for their convention. Good thing you folks fly out tonight. There's not a hotel room to be had in all of Memphis."

We merged into the city traffic. "We'll be spending the afternoon in the suburb of Whitehaven," Virgil said. "Whitehaven is 12 miles south of downtown Memphis, and its best-known landmark is Graceland, the King's home."

We responded with more whoops and cheers. Gaby let out a wail, and Toni did her best to pacify her.

We crawled through the streets. About 20 minutes later, we managed to merge onto a major thoroughfare where traffic was almost at a standstill. "Elvis Presley Boulevard," Virgil said. "In 1971, the City of Memphis changed the name of this stretch of Highway 51 in honor of the King."

Creeping north on Elvis Presley Boulevard, we passed a Denny's restaurant with a gigantic flower arrangement in the shape of a guitar, a muffler shop with a hound-dog floral display, and a car dealership with Rest In Peace Elvis on its neon billboard. At a traffic light, a uniformed police officer crossed the boulevard in front of our bus holding a young woman in his arms. She must have passed out from the heat, or maybe from the excitement.

Then we were in front of Graceland's famous metal gates with their musical notes. Police officers were holding fans back. Down the drive, I glimpsed the white mansion fronted by four pillars and two stone lions.

"Graceland, the King's home," Virgil said.

"C'est extraordinaire!" Cécile's voice was filled with reverence.

The bus went completely silent for several moments. Until Gaby started to scream.

"Damn kid!" someone shouted.

Elvis's "Love Me Tender" wafted over the sound system, and Gaby quieted right down.

"When the King bought Graceland back in 1957," Virgil said when the song was over, "this was way out in the country. But this area's grown up in the past 20 years."

"Can we get off and take photos at the gates?" Mai-Lei called out.

"No, ma'am," Virgil said. "Private funeral service starts in there in 10 minutes. You shoulda been here yesterday. Thousands went in to pay their respects. They were lined up for blocks down the street."

"I don't care," Toni shouted back to us. "I'm livin' my dream just seeing Graceland."

"I can feel Elvis all around me," Mai-Lei yelled over her. "He lived and died in there."

Beside me, a sobbing Cécile leaned back in her seat, clutching her heart. In front of her, Mai-Lei snapped photos through the window.

People were standing and sitting on the branches of the trees beside Graceland Christian Church, Elvis's neighbor to the north, trying to see beyond the rock wall. The church grounds were littered with pop cans and fast-food wrappers.

We crawled north on Elvis Presley Boulevard. Crowds thronged the sides of the street, wooden barricades holding them back from the traffic. At Forest Hill

Cemetery's main gates, we pulled into a parking lot filled with rows of buses.

"We can watch the funeral procession go into the cemetery from here," Virgil said. "Only invited guests are allowed in there, but you folks can get off the bus and walk around. We'll wait here until the procession leaves the cemetery."

We followed Virgil into the heat outside. He joined a group of drivers having a smoke. We stood fanning ourselves in the shade of a tree at the edge of the parking lot.

"Seems this is as good as it gets," I said to the girls. "It's a downer that we can't go into Graceland or the cemetery."

"That would've been out of sight," Toni said, "but it's enough for me just to be in Memphis. Elvis knows we're here for him. And Gaby's happy here too." She patted her sleeping infant's head.

"Careful," Mai-Lei said. "Don't wake her up."

I lit a cigarette, and Toni waved me away. "Don't smoke near my baby."

We watched the procession come up the boulevard. It was led by a silver Cadillac, followed by a white Cadillac hearse and 17 white Cadillac limousines. A helicopter hovered overhead. People on the sides of the road reached out their arms as the hearse drove by.

"He's in there!" Cécile cried as the hearse approached us. She started to run towards it.

Mai-Lei and I held her back, and she collapsed, sobbing, in our arms. But she pulled herself together a few moments later. "Let's hold hands," she said, her eyes on the procession.

The four of us gripped one another's hands as the vehicles turned into Forest Hill Cemetery. Then we hugged and pledged our eternal love for Elvis.

Mai-Lei pulled a portable tape recorder from her pack. "I need to hear his voice."

"We can hold a vigil in the bus while he's put into the ground," Toni said.

"Not in the ground, Toni," Cécile chided. "In the Presley family vault."

"Let's do it," Mai-Lei said, and they turned towards the bus.

"I'll be with you in a few minutes," I called after them. "I need another smoke."

I took a homemade badge out of my handbag proclaiming that Montreal Loves Elvis and pinned it on my blouse. Then I lit a cigarette and headed behind the buses. No one seemed to be following me.

I jumped when I felt a tap on my shoulder. A woman of about my age with a mane of teased black hair stood behind me. She looked like a tough, street-smart version of Priscilla Presley.

She glanced down at my badge, then scrutinized my face. "Montreal blonde who loves Elvis. You must be Paula."

I nodded, and she pointed to the badge she was wearing: Knoxville Loves Elvis. "I'm Larissa. Come with me."

I looked around nervously. Other than the two of us, there was no one behind the buses. I followed her.

She pulled up in front of the wire fence. I looked around again. We were completely alone. I reached into my handbag and removed a packet from the false bottom. Larissa quickly slid it into her shoulder bag, and pulled out a small, fat envelope. She showed me that it was filled with large American bills. I slipped it into my handbag, and she sauntered off, disappearing between two buses.

By this time, hundreds, maybe thousands of people had congregated outside the cemetery. I crossed the road, and glimpsed a sea of flowers beyond the gates. I chatted with a police officer doing crowd control. He'd been a year behind Elvis at Humes High School, and had seen the King perform at the annual talent show shortly before he graduated in 1953. "He put a foot on a chair, strummed his guitar and sang his heart out. For me, that's when rock 'n' roll was born."

At a sidewalk souvenir stand, I bought four black T-shirts stamped with Elvis's face and the words Love Me Tender, four Elvis coffee mugs and four Elvis baby bibs. I put my Montreal Loves Elvis badge back in my handbag and ran for the bus. My blouse was drenched with sweat and sticking to my skin.

"We been waitin' for you," Virgil said as I climbed aboard. "Funeral procession left five minutes ago."

I smiled and thanked him. Back in my seat, I handed out my Elvis gifts to my friends. "Let's wear our Elvis shirts back to Canada," I said. I needed to change out of my sweaty blouse.

We took turns in the washroom at the back of the bus. "This has been the best day in my entire life," Mai-Lei said when she returned to her seat.

Outside the airport, Mai-Lei took a photo of Virgil in his driver's seat. Inside the terminal, she snapped photos of us in our new T-shirts.

On the plane, we listened to Elvis and dozed a bit. A few people complained to Toni that Gaby's disposables were stinking up the washroom. I told her not to pay them any mind.

Cécile placed a gentle hand on my arm. "*Merci*, Paula," she said. "I can tell my grandkids I was at Elvis's funeral."

She pulled the baby bib from her bag. "And they can wear this!"

***

"They're searching bags and purses," Cécile whispered in the lineup for Canadian customs.

My heart slammed into my throat.

"It's gonna take forever to get through here," Toni whined, "and Gaby's diaper needs changing."

Gaby let out a howl.

"Phew!" Mai-Lei wrinkled her nose. "I can smell it."

Toni's eyes flashed daggers at Mai-Lei. "Your kid don't poop?"

"He poops at home, which is where yours should be, Antonia. We've had to put up with Gaby all day."

Toni moved closer to Mai-Lei, but Cécile edged between them. "*Arrêtez, vous deux!* Let it go. We've had a long day, and we're all tired and cranky." She whispered something to Mai-Lei, and steered her ahead of her in line.

"I'll take the baby for a while," I said to Toni. When I had the Snugli strapped in place, I motioned for Toni to walk ahead of me. I slipped the envelope of cash into the Snugli, pushing it down into Gaby's diaper.

My gut was twisting as we neared the customs counter. "You'd better take Gaby now," I said to Toni when we were almost at the front of the line.

"Anything to declare?" the Canadian customs officer asked as he searched my handbag. He had a bad case of acne and looked like he was still in high school.

My heart hammered as I held up my Elvis mug. Out of the corner of my eye, I saw another officer going through Toni's diaper bag at the counter beside us. Gaby was screaming in her Snugli. The officer waved Toni on.

"And this T-shirt," I added, thrusting out my chest for my officer. "I was at Elvis Presley's funeral."

"Far out!" he said, ogling my breasts. He didn't bother looking in the handbag that I held wide open for him.

In the ladies' room, Toni slipped the Snugli's straps off her shoulders. "Hold Gaby while I take a leak." She thrust the baby into my arms and went into a cubicle.

I reached into the Snugli and pulled out the envelope. I wrapped it in a paper towel and stuffed it in my handbag.

"Thanks, Paula," Toni said, when she took Gaby from me. "What would we do without you?"

***

I hugged my handbag to my chest as we headed into the city on the airport bus. "Thank you, Elvis," I whispered. "You made it work."

The money from Pierre's drug stash would mean a fresh start for me and Robbie, away from Pierre and his fists. I would miss Montreal and my friends, but that couldn't be helped.

And I would always have Memphis.

A CONTRAPUNTAL DUET

By Blair Keetch Pretentions

Even as the music fades and I look back through the years, I wonder if the chime of the triangle had, in fact, been a warning bell.

It was early March when I first met Jeanie, on a day when the beauty of winter had long passed, snowbanks were high, and most city sidewalks were impassable.

I'd been wandering the basement corridors of Koerner Hall, looking for a former teacher who'd generously offered me a spare ticket to a concert that evening. I walked past rehearsal rooms and studios, some large enough to hold a small orchestra.

In the hallway, exuberant students chatted, coats were piled outside open classroom doors, and larger musical cases, like those for cellos, performed sentry duty.

The teeming space belonged to Enid Fletcher, and a big oak desk dominating the far end of the room indicated her prestige and her influence. However, I never saw her sitting behind it. Rather, she'd be perched on the edge of it, or, typically, roaming the rehearsal room, weaving between chairs and deftly sidestepping instruments.

Along one wall ran a low row of bleachers that served as both a cheering stand and an informal gathering place for gossip and flirting.

This was the maelstrom into which I stepped—a cacophony of flutes and oboes, shouted taunts and jeers, dueling French horns, someone performing scales on an off-key xylophone and a girl with striking looks and green hair leading an impromptu chant of Queen's "We Will Rock You."

I searched in vain for Enid. Nervously, I cleared my throat. "Excuse me."

Everyone was oblivious to my presence. I was about to shout louder in an effort to get through when something strange—almost magical—occurred.

The wild-haired girl stopped mid-chant and held her triangle aloft before giving it a short tap.

I couldn't hear it above the din, but it was like a silent dog whistle audible only to her fellow students. The racket stopped abruptly.

The girl struck the triangle again, and a clear, delicate note reverberated through the classroom.

After a few seconds, I met her expectant gaze.

"The rest is silence," I said.

She rolled her eyes. "Oh, please, not Shakespeare." It was my first glimpse of her intelligence and petulance. "And you are?"

"Charles Soliqov." It was Enid Fletcher, returning to her class with a vanilla latte from Starbucks.

"Charles is a music critic with quite an esteemed reputation," Enid said. That was gracious, to say the least, especially since most of my early reviews had been published in community newspapers.

"A music critic?" The girl tossed her green hair back in exasperation. "Isn't that like a level below a high school teacher? I mean, like those who don't succeed, teach. Those who can't teach, criticize."

If that was a veiled insult at Enid, she ignored it. "In fact, Jeanie, Charles is a very accomplished bassoonist."

That has the same career value as a very accomplished eight-track repairman, but for a second it seemed to impress Jeanie.

"Oh, like *Boléro*?" she said breathlessly. Then, her voice dripping with disdain, she added, "Am I supposed to be impressed by a faggot player?"

Behind me in the bleachers, someone gasped at the political incorrectness of the word faggot, unaware that it was the medieval name for the bassoon.

"Actually, I'm impressed by your grasp of the idiophone," I replied.

Jeanie waited for a sarcastic comment.

"Like the bassoon, the triangle is underappreciated and not often given its proper due. Liszt's Piano Concerto No. 1 is a prime example." I paused, afraid of sounding any more pretentious.

To my surprise—and Jeanie was always full of surprises—she looked at Enid. "Any chance you have another spare ticket for tonight's concert?"

***

The concert turned out to be a hackneyed version of *The Mikado* that would have had Gilbert and Sullivan leaping to their deaths from the Gardiner Expressway had they been alive and visiting Toronto.

Yet to my amazement, Jeanie was surprisingly kind in her comments. "This is the type of music that brings laughter to so many no matter what the quality," she said during intermission while sipping third-rate wine in a plastic cup while I nursed a craft beer that I had dismissively called "IPA—Idiot Piss Ale."

We must have made a curious sight—an obvious free spirit in intense conversation with a buttoned-down introvert. It was the beginning of what Jeanie referred to as our contrapuntal romance—two separate tunes being sung at the same time, but making beautiful music nonetheless.

But that first night, I caught a glimpse of her mercurial personality.

When our conversation inevitably turned to classical music, her opinions were strong. "Mozart—overrated. Bach—truly a superstar. I love Johann. Don't you?" Her eyes dared me to disagree.

Even though it was a wintry night, we took the long route to her apartment, talking about a wide range of subjects—alternatives to Tim Hortons coffee, her parents' indifference to her love of music, her versatility in all things keyboard from organ to harpsichord, and even her dabbling in, yes, the triangle.

I'd chalked this up to an interesting one-off experience, but when we reached her apartment lobby, she suddenly grabbed me by the elbows and looked up at me with her blue eyes. "I think you should come upstairs and do bad things to me."

And so it began.

***

How do you measure the passage of years? By concert ticket stubs? By arguments won and lost? By career advancements?

Eight years later, Jeanie was still known by her trademark wild-colored hair, but now it was cut by a fancy stylist in Yorkville. She still gave it her well-known toss whenever she sat down for an organ recital or to play the harp, her bright red blouse showing off her impressive figure.

As for me, I became a superstar bassoonist, constantly touring the world. Well, not really—unless you counted occasional recitals in the local church basement.

The reality was more mundane yet much more profitable. I created and moderated an online forum called A Sour Note, providing music students the world over with virtual tutorials and instant feedback.

So, if I became a type of teacher, Jeanie never threw it in my face during one of our frequent arguments.

Probably because A Sour Note brought in an unexpected amount of income and helped her achieve a certain degree of online fame, more than her concert appearances provided.

The Sour Note revenue also allowed us to move from a cramped one-bedroom apartment to a house in Leslieville and to buy a small cottage near Bracebridge. And to receive tickets for more concerts than either of us cared to attend.

It was our third YouTube video on contrapuntal music—when we appeared together discussing, demonstrating and performing Bach's *The Well-Tempered Clavier*—that generated the online buzz.

Jeanie had been in full flirtatious mode, wearing striking colors that accentuated her womanly attributes, though it was her toned arms that aroused me the most.

The lesson had been loaded with double entendres, including more bad variations on *fugue* than I thought possible.

But it caught the public's imagination and set our course in life.

Maybe it also sealed our fate.

***

Our arguments often dwelled on the online videos. I felt they were too commercial, too comical and too common, while Jeanie adored the reckless nature of them.

Yet it was my online persona, perhaps not far from reality, of a straitlaced sidekick that led to my first affair. I was semifamous—not well-known in public and never pestered for autographs at the local supermarket, but recognized in chamber music halls.

Usually by earnest young women, university students who wore gray skirts and black tights and read poems by Leonard Cohen. Who never would have conceived of sleeping with a married man until he gently touched them in the darkness of a rehearsal hall and whispered, "You make my blood sing."

There was Freida, who always wanted the room pitch-black when we made love, and Esther, who loved to talk dirty once behind closed doors. They were all fun flings, but carried 10-month expiry dates.

The affairs would have gone on until Jeanie and I retired, settling in a home overlooking a golf course in Florida and attending orchestra concerts in Tampa.

That is, if I hadn't met Winnie.

***

I listened raptly as Winnie stood in front of a large screen with a projected manuscript. She had no notes and had been speaking for well over half an hour about Bach's *The Well-Tempered Clavier*. Despite her severe appearance—dark hair bluntly cut, primly dressed in a white blouse and windowpane suit—there was an underlying openness about her.

I was in the front row, conducting an informal audit of her novice lecturing abilities.

"Excuse me," interrupted a disheveled student. It was Scott, a talented violinist, who was caught up in a false image of his own sexiness and who, I suspected, was slipping into the party circuit. "I was watching Jeanie and

Chuck on YouTube, and they both stated Bach intended a well temperament as opposed to an equal temperament."

Not exactly true, but Jeanie, as usual, had overruled my opinion through the sheer force of her argument.

Winnie shook her head briskly. "An old debate that's now been dismissed by most worthwhile scholars. It no longer has any credence."

Scott mumbled a response, but Winnie cut him off. "Who do you trust? A buffoon bassoonist?"

The class erupted in laughter. At first, I flinched, thinking she was unaware of my presence. Then her eyes momentarily flicked in my direction. *I have met my equal*, I thought, and vowed at that moment to woo her.

***

My courtship carefully evolved over the next eight months. It began with chance encounters in rehearsal halls and striking up conversations about our mutual love of Vivaldi, Handel and Bach.

The bantering, intellectual respect and cordiality I experienced with Winnie but rarely with Jeanie were addictive. Even so, I bided my time.

I was on the verge of giving up when one day Winnie suggested having coffee.

"Sorry, I can't." I said. "Busy this afternoon." I paused, then continued as if a thought had just occurred to me. "But hey, I'm free tomorrow night. Jeanie has a concert that I really don't want to attend. How about we have dinner? I know a cute little French café nearby."

She hesitated, but I stared back innocently. The acknowledgment of my wife and my nonchalant attitude all worked in my favor. It became the first of many meals that slowly transitioned from casual café to candlelit dinners.

Over time, it became clear that Winnie had feelings for me, and I confess I returned them equally, if not more strongly. Her intelligence, calmness and stability were elements missing from my life.

But there was a catch. "Rule Number One," she informed me. "I don't sleep with married men."

"And if I wasn't married?" My tone was playful.

"Then torrid nights of passion would be yours." She gave me a soft but sad smile. "But you'll probably never know."

***

What if I wasn't married? I thought. *Not divorced. But what if my wife was no longer an issue?*

Divorce was not an option. I knew Jeanie would not only expect her half of our marital assets, but also demand more. She'd claim she was the "one with the personality, the charisma and the loyal fan following," known as the Sourettes.

What Jeanie didn't know was that the *BBC* was considering a more serious version of A Sour Note. Why shouldn't I provide them with a more dignified forum and increase my status as a music expert?

Yet I never considered any other options until Garth came on the scene. The unruly and disheveled composer had a "bad boy" reputation, even though he was easily in his 50s. He appeared rumpled, with untamed hair and nicotine-stained fingers that stood out in contrast to the white of his conductor's baton. He had a self-inflated ego and scorn for most people, including his long-suffering wife, Martha, a minor but respected opera singer. His comments on her weight and her failure to reach greater heights were well documented.

I thought all of this would have repelled Jeanie, but, on the contrary, they decided to collaborate on a quartet composition.

Many nights, she'd come home smelling of second-hand smoke and detail Garth's sarcastic comments toward his spouse.

"Then why work with him?" I asked.

"Because for all of his faults, he is actually a genius," Jeanie admitted. "And he wants to showcase my talents."

***

It might have gone on like this for another few months, perhaps even years, had I not found out about their affair.

I usually respected Jeanie's scattered files, and never gave them a second glance. But I was searching for one of my music essays with her scribbled notes and had to burrow through her papers.

In the mess of half-finished scores, old correspondence and unopened junk mail, I found a loyalty statement from a hotel chain with a convention location across from the concert hall.

A statement detailing weekly stays—at a special day rate, no less—every Wednesday. The time of her supposed collaboration with Garth.

All the more reason for me to start over and find out if Winne would be true to her promise of nights of endless passion.

***

Figuring out how to kill Jeanie was surprisingly simple. Poison wasn't practical; staging an accident would involve too much scrutiny.

However, a pedestrian death, an all-too-common occurrence in Toronto, would receive lots of media coverage, and maybe even mean double the insurance payout. And it likely would keep the focus away from me.

A hit-and-run—Jeanie struck by a car on her nightly walk home from rehearsal—would be perfect. I would arrange an ideal alibi, play the part of the grief-stricken husband and inherit Jeanie's estate.

As for the driver, who better than Scott? He had dropped out of music school and was, by all accounts, a slave to opioids and likely open to anything to maintain his habit.

And if that left a loose end, it was nothing I couldn't tidy up afterward. Who would think twice about a fentanyl overdose, or even a fatal beating? A drug deal gone wrong. Part and parcel of such a risky lifestyle.

"You want something to happen to Jeanie?" Scott greedily accepted my offer even before I had finished outlining my proposal.

Everything was set for the following Tuesday.

***

"Remember 'Prelude and Fugue in B Minor'?" Jeanie asked over breakfast.

I smiled. "How could I forget? It was our first real concert together—after *The Mikado*, of course."

"I even get a little turned on hearing it now," Jeanie said. "We still make great music together." She kissed me passionately on the lips and for a moment, I felt that old familiar thrill.

"See you, tonight," Jeanie said. "And I expect you to be awake. Practice, practice, practice."

I nodded dutifully. Another church recital was on the horizon and I'd been neglecting my bassoon.

"Promise!" I called as she went out the door.

***

The day ticked by ever so slowly.

My internet tutorials dragged on, an endless shuffle of painful auditions with students blind to their lack of talent.

Over lunch, Winnie was preoccupied. I gently prodded her until she burst out, "Maybe I should date again. Go online. Sign up for Prelude, that dating Web site for musicians."

"Whoa, whoa," I said. "What brings this on?"

"You. Us," she lamented. "Where are we going? What am I doing with my life?"

We'd had this conversation before, but today she seemed even more intense.

"Just give me more time," I said.

"More time for what? I know you're never going to divorce your wife."

No, but I've made arrangements to kill her. Instead, I said, "Give me another month, two at most. I promise things will be different shortly."

In fact, I had no idea how Winnie would react to my plans, so I lied. "We had a candid talk this morning, and I think Jeanie's come to certain realizations."

Winne looked slightly mollified. "Okay, two more months, but absolutely no more. You know once I make up my mind, there's no going back."

I only nodded. Winnie was just as iron-willed as Jeanie, but in a more agreeable way.

***

Half an hour remained before Jeanie usually arrived home. I was waiting expectantly for the sound of sirens, or maybe even a police car with two somber officers clambering out to break the devastating news.

Yet the only sound was the distant ticking of a metronome on top of the piano in another room. I thought longingly of a bottle of Scotch in the den, but didn't want to be anything but completely sober when I heard the tragic news.

I was pacing back and forth when I noticed my double reed soaking in a glass of water where Jeanie had left it on the dining room table. I was totally out of practice, so perhaps this was a way to soothe my nerves. I reassembled my bassoon and fixed the reed to the bocal when I heard a disturbance outside.

Opening the door, I found Garth, underneath his usual plume of smoke, furiously stuffing sheets of music into our mailbox.

"Garth! To what do I owe this pleasure?"

He glared up at me. "You can give that unfaithful slut of a wife this mess of a music score. This is derivative and badly cribbed crap. I refuse to continue this charade any further."

"After all this work, all those evenings spent together, you're giving up?"

"What work? She comes over two nights a week, spends 15 minutes with me, then heads out the door with Martha. I warned her before, I can't collaborate via e-mail."

I thought I heard a vague chime of a triangle, but I continued on. "I thought Wednesdays were devoted to working on the chamber piece."

"Wednesdays?" Garth looked perplexed. "No, Wednesday is my day to go to Stratford to visit my mom at that retirement hellhole."

"Give me that," I hissed and grabbed the sheets from Garth's hands. "Go home and leave me alone."

He stared at me, searching for the perfect retort, but gave up and stamped off into the snowy night.

***

Back inside, I glanced at the clock. Jeanie was now more than 45 minutes late. I imagined a crowd of people huddled around her prone body. Or maybe she was in some hospital corridor with a sheet draped over her face.

I smoothed the crumpled music score in my hand and took a closer look. The words *bassoon intro* were scribbled on the first lines of the notes.

I smiled. What better image of a dedicated husband than to be playing his wife's composition when notified of her death?

I picked up the bassoon and started to play. I paused briefly. I was so out of practice even the reed tasted strange.

I wet my lips, made a minor adjustment to the strap and resumed playing. After four minutes, I stopped. Garth was right. It was an uneasy mash-up of styles. Overall, a melodic mess.

I tried again, in case my first impression was overly harsh, but, if anything, it was worse the second time I played it. Plus, I kept slipping off the hand rest.

My phone buzzed on a nearby music stand announcing the arrival of a text. A message from Scott's burner phone: *Sorry. Missed opportunity. Will try tmrw.*

A missed opportunity, or a drug deal too good to pass up? I wondered.

And if it was a missed opportunity, where was Jeanie?

As if in answer to my thoughts, a floorboard creaked.

"Jeanie?" I called.

"No, it's me. The fat lady sings." Martha stepped into the light, her eyes intently searching my face. Jeanie followed right behind her.

"Ladies." I smiled in welcome, but my face felt lopsided. "What brings you here?"

"Charles," Jeanie said. "I did mean it this morning when I said I loved you. Once."

A wave of tiredness swept over me. When I tried to stand, my legs were as numb as my lips had become.

Jeanie saw me look toward my bassoon, which had slid to the ground. "That's right, Charles. Your reed was poisoned. But don't worry. All traces of it will be gone by the time we dump you into the lake."

Martha and Jeanie exchanged glances.

"What a tragedy," Martha said. "A second-rate musician has too much to drink. Goes for a moonlit walk at his cottage and gets disoriented."

"Falls through the ice," Jeanie finished.

"Too bad we couldn't figure out a way for Garth to join you," Martha added. "But don't worry, he's our project for next season."

I looked searchingly at Jeanie.

"What's the matter, my love? Cat got your tongue?" She laughed softly. "What do you want to ask me? How long Martha and I have been together? Far longer than you can imagine. You men and your egos. So wrapped up in your own little worlds and your own tawdry affairs. Yes, I know all about them, Charles."

In my last moments, I realized that despite her irrational ways and our roller-coaster life, I still loved her— even though she was intent on killing me. I struggled to warn her. "Scott," I finally mumbled.

"What's that? Yes, I think we will be scot-free. This has been carefully planned. I'm not as impetuous as everyone thinks I am."

***

As the music fades, I wonder if she will be walking home tomorrow. If Scott will follow through on his pledge.

I'll never know, but perhaps even in death, we'll still be a contrapuntal duet.

HIT ME WITH YOUR PET SHARK

By Lisa de Nikolits

The day the music died, Dad came to mind.

"*Schtum*," he said. "Keep *schtum*. If you get into hot water, don't say a word."

So I stared at the cop and kept it zipped. I looked away from the bloodstained hoodie, I looked away from the butcher's knife, and I shrugged.

***

Rewind two weeks to the start of a holiday of a lifetime. Yup, cokehead loser me, up to my eyeballs in debt, there I was, living it up in Key West, thanks to my brand-new buddy Joe—who also happened to be my boss.

That was one strange interview. He didn't make eye contact the whole time. He stared over my shoulder, like he was eyeing the ghost of some dead relative, and he had a twist of a half smile that made me want to belt him across the face. But, whatever, he hired me, and I counted myself lucky. I was 24, with not too many prospects in life.

My dad, a small square man with a mashed-potato face and a heart of gold, died all of a sudden, leaving a great big hole in my life. Mum, and I use the word loosely, had, as Dad put it, scarpered off as soon as she got shot of me. She kicked the bucket a few years later, but I couldn't have cared less. Dad was all I needed, and then he was gone. And gone, too, were his love of punk rockers, the toasty tang of his unfiltered fags, his take-no-shit brandies that flowed like blood in his veins, his deep belly laugh, and a hug when I needed it most.

I couldn't keep the house because it turned out Dad wasn't so stellar with money. A garage mechanic with grease under his fingernails, he had a tendency to lose jobs more than he kept them, which is most likely where I got the gene. Peas in a pod, Dad and me.

Dad knew I liked to mix my science, as he put it. "But be Johnny Rotten," he said. "A survivor. Not Sid Vicious, poor mutt. You can get in too deep before you know it. Keep it to a minimum." Which I had to do anyway, since I was always skint. Teachers said I was clever enough. I was good with numbers and I aced accounting school but I just couldn't go to work every day. Dad understood. He told me not to be too hard on myself. We were free spirits, was all; it was the world that was out of whack, too demanding.

It was his dad, Gramps, who named me Christine Ellen, after Chrissie Hynde. The London punk rock scene in 1977, that was Gramps' heyday. He was only 19 when he fell for a Canadian girl, a punk rock groupie back when Malcolm McLaren and Vivienne Westwood were all the rage. Granny got into drugs when she was a teen, and her family sent her to an aunt in London to spend a summer and clean up her act—which worked on one level but not another.

When his sweetheart got a bun in the oven, Gramps married her and came to Canada with her to set up house in a small town just outside of Toronto. They built solid lives, with Gramps working in a factory and Gran a stay-at-home mum.

Gramps was as British as Bovril, though, and he never let us forget it; in turn, we copied his slang and whatnot. I knew people laughed at us, but we were proud of our British heritage. Gramps sounded like he came right out of *Lock, Stock and Two Smoking Barrels*, or vintage Michael Caine, saying no *bovver* and taking the piss. I thought talking like a Brit made me sound exotic, although it annoyed the crap out of my teachers. Which made it even more worthy.

As it does, history repeated itself, and Mum and Dad had me when Dad was only 19 himself. Mum was hardly 16, and she popped me out and ran off with a small-time pop rocker from Vancouver who was in town to play the Peach Festival. Mum died of a heroin overdose when I was seven, and the only proof I've got of her existence is a single faded Polaroid with her looking small and pale, with Cleopatra eyes and wild black hair. She was pretty while I got Dad's features, born looking like I'd been in a bare-knuckle fight in the womb. It wasn't fair. Mum was like a kitten, all tiny and fluffy and cuddly, and I could have hated her for that if I'd been bothered.

Dad was only 41 when he died. Too many fags, and a bad heart to start with. He said brandy kept his veins flowing clear, but it turned out he was dead wrong about that. He inherited his love of punk from Gramps. He said that while he had at least passed his love of music on to me, God only knew where my taste came from. ABBA? He said that must have come from some defective gene on my mother's side, but my love for Iggy Pop, the Sisters of

Mercy and T. Rex redeemed me. *Here comes Johnny here again, hey now, hey now now* and *sing a song, have a bong, get it on.* We listened to music together all the time, vinyl all the way.

Dad never called me Christine Ellen or Chrissie. He said I was his Christelle, but I hated that name. After Dad died, I told people to call me Ellie, which I thought was much more suave.

So anyway, the job at Joe's was a low-level affair, a piece of cake. And, bonus, I got to listen to my music all day, one playlist after another, no one cared. I had four iPods—a Touch, Shuffle, Nano and Mini—with thousands of songs, and earphones with extra bass. I filled spreadsheets on autopilot, working as a temp to log in expenses and such while the usual girl took a break. *A break from what?* I wondered, but no one said and I didn't ask. I thought a video production firm would be super glam and that they'd have hard candy lined up on the coffee table for us all to share, but no such luck. They were a bunch of geeks, and Joe was just about the geekiest of the lot.

At least I thought so, until I saw him in front of me in the lineup in the alley behind the local greasy spoon, and I don't mean him or me wanted coffee and pie. I was there to meet my dealer.

I wasn't overly surprised that Joe liked his candy, too. He looked horrified to see me and his pretty-boy face went this scarlet color, like a rash had suddenly covered him. But so what? I didn't care what he did in his spare time. If anything, he went up in my estimation.

If I was Joe, I would've left without making eye contact, but he let me do my business. Then he beckoned me over. He was my boss; I had to go.

I sat across from him in a booth inside the diner, with the little bag of blow in my pocket, wondering why I didn't feel happier. What with the promise of good times right there at my fingertips, I should've been. But I just felt lonely, like the weight of the world's sorrows were locked inside my chest. I couldn't breathe, and I closed my eyes, not caring what Joe thought. Then "Dancing Queen" came on the jukebox, and the solid gray rocks inside me burst apart as if they'd exploded in an old video game. I opened my eyes and looked squarely at Joe.

"I love ABBA," I said, and Joe twisted his half smile just that much more.

"Who doesn't?" he replied easily.

"What do you listen to?" I asked, feeling the need to try my hand at small talk.

Joe waved his hand around vaguely. "Hip-hop. Drake, Kanye, the usual suspects."

I shuddered. "You wouldn't like my playlists," I said. "I've got stacks of music, '80s stuff mainly. *See the beam on the tangerine, oh yeah!*" I sang out loud and Joe looked perplexed.

"Those aren't the words," he said.

What a dick.

I shrugged. "So what?" I forgot to be polite. "I sing what I like."

I shrug a lot. It used to drive the teachers nuts at school. I got detentions for shrugging, but since when is shrugging a crime? Dad told me I needed to learn to be more socially interactive. I told him the trouble with being socially interactive was that it made me want to hit people. Dad didn't know what to say to that.

"You enjoying work?" Joe asked.

I started to shrug, but I forced myself to be more socially interactive and told him it was okay. "Dancing Queen" ended and some rap shit came on about a guy eating sushi from Japan and wanting to kick Jackie Chan.

45

Like that's music. I suppose it was the kind of crap that Joe liked.

Joe looked at me steadily and didn't say anything. I picked at my fingernails. He was wasting my time when I could be getting high. I started to get up, but Joe picked up his phone. "Hang on a moment," he said to me, and he waved me back down.

I zoned out while he talked. "More Than a Feeling" by Boston came on. I love that song. *More than a feeling, I keep believing, I see my love leaving...* I heard Joe say, "There's someone you'd like to meet, for what we were talking about." Then he put down his phone, and I dragged my focus back to him.

"You want to come to a party?" he asked.

I was startled. "I'm not so great at parties."

Joe gestured to our mutual dealer, who was sitting across the room eating a cheeseburger. "That kind of party."

"Oh. Okay, yeah, sure."

I followed him outside to a brand-new Mini Cooper. I got in and breathed the scent of fresh leather.

"Nice," I said. "Straight out of the box."

I was twittering like a budgie because I was really nervous, saying stuff about how great the car was and how I could fix it if something went wrong, I was good with cars, even the new ones. Joe gave me a strange look; I shut up and stared out the window.

We got to a shiny new skyscraper and we rode up 56 floors to Joe's condo in silence, with me trying not to look at my reflection in the floor-to-ceiling mirrors. Only rich and thin people want mirrors in their elevators. I'm happier with scratched beige plywood and graffiti like Patti Licks Kim.

Joe opened the front door, and I tried to hide how impressed I was by the black leather, the glass, the steel, the wood and the marble. But I froze. I didn't belong here. The sun was low, and the city glittered below us, a stretch of cubic zirconia in the hot summer haze. Dad had always said I was like a little magpie, addicted to sparkle, but this was too much, even for me.

Joe held out his hand. "Give me one of your iPods."

I shook my head. "People laugh at my music."

Joe laughed. He had a weird laugh, like Beavis and Butthead put together. He kept his hand outstretched. I sighed and dug out an iPod, and he plugged it into his Surround Sound Bose system.

The bass notes of Bananarama's "Venus" remix thudded in the room, and Joe looked startled.

"I told you," I said.

"I like it," he protested. "Come on, let's get this party started."

He laid out a few lines and helped himself. Then he gestured to me, and I dived right in. He cracked open a bottle of vodka, and we each had a shot. Hot peace hit my veins, and I helped myself to another shot, filled to the brim.

"Paranoid" by Black Sabbath was up next, and it seemed that Joe and I had found common ground. We started dancing. He looked like a skinny kangaroo trying to keep time that made sense only to him, and I thought that maybe he wasn't so bad after all.

Then the doorbell rang. Joe went to get it while I was pogoing around and singing *aye yi yi yi whoa! M-m-m-m-my Carona* to the Knack at the top of my voice.

I spun around and stopped dead. Talk about humiliating. I stared at the floor, sneaking glances and pulling down my ratty old hoodie, hating Joe for letting a girl like that see me like this. This girl was Bambi in see-through white chiffon, her black bra and panties like the shadows of a wet dream. She sparkled, from her dangling earrings down to her silver high-heeled strappy sandals. Looking at her was like staring into the sun.

Joe waved his hand to make the introductions. "Ellie, meet Emma. Emma, Ellie."

I grunted, rooted in place.

Emma flashed a ridiculously perfect smile in my direction and floated to lean over the glass table. She had a perfect round apple of a bum. I forced myself to look away.

"Who's That Girl" by the Eurythmics wailed through the speakers, hitting the nail on the head. *I'm tongue-tied and twisted, there's a price I'll have to pay.*

Emma patted the sofa and beckoned to me. I was still standing there, the village idiot. I forced myself to move, a muddy moth drawn to a golden flame.

Emma reached up and pulled me down next to her. I lost my balance, nearly falling on top of her. An electric current jolted me. Flushing with embarrassment, I tried to shift to a more graceful position. She handed me the snorter, and I took it with trembling fingers. I vacuumed a line; Joe handed me another shot, and I threw it back.

Thank God for Goldfrapp's "Strict Machine." Thud, thud, thud. The bass helped calm me a bit, but I was a cornered mouse. I saw Joe watching me, and there was a look in his lizard eyes that told me to run away, run as fast as I could. But cool fingertips brushed my neck, and I closed my eyes, trapped by pleasure, a dumb creature unable to move. The sofa took the weight of another body, and I opened my eyes to see Emma rubbing Joe's balls. I thought okay, so that's how it's going to be.

When I woke up hours later, there was silence and darkness and the soft sounds of Joe and Emma passed out or asleep. I knew not to push my luck. Dad always told me the smartest thing you can do is know when to walk away. I grabbed my iPod and snuck out of the apartment.

Monday came, and Joe wasn't any different to me in front of the others. I was back to being invisible Ellie, just there to crunch numbers. But Tuesday rolled round and he texted me to come to his office.

"Want to come to Key West with Emma and me?"

My mouth dropped open. I thought he was going to fire me.

"In two weeks, for two weeks. I'm the boss here, vacay's no prob."

I leapt at the chance before Joe could change his mind. "Yeah, that would be cool, sure."

"Your passport is good?"

"No. But I'll go get one now. I mean, please can I go now? Do you mind?"

Joe grinned. "Go. Pay extra, get it done."

***

I listened to Grace Jones' *Island Life* on the plane ride, sharing an earbud with Emma and smiling at her all the way through "Pull Up to the Bumper."

"My mother will be there," Emma had told me. "She parties in her own way. Valium, Xanax, codeine, booze. She likes to take the edge off. She doesn't care if I have fun. It's my father who's the asshole. *Slow down, Emma, go to rehab Emma, get a real job, grow up.* He stopped my allowance, can you believe that? What does he expect me to do? He's even cut me out of the will, the bastard. Well, screw him. But my mom's okay, you'll see. Something weird happened in my life and my family fell apart, so none of this is my fault."

I had no idea what she was talking about, and I didn't want to pry.

When I met her mother, it was 10 a.m. Marilyn was gripping a juice tumbler three-quarters filled with scotch—hold the rocks, hold the water. She was reclining on the sofa in a large satin chartreuse muumuu with animal prints. She extended her hand, like Marlon Brando in drag playing the Queen of England, holding court as Emma and Joe watched.

"You could get lost in this house, and no one would ever find you," I said to her, and she smiled.

"It's modeled on our family cottage in the Bruce Peninsula," she said with an accent that sounded strangely Southern. "My husband and I wanted identical places in both locales, right down to the décor. It was such fun, making little twin homes. Then we split up, and he got Canada and I took the Keys. We were never divorced," she said pointedly, although I didn't care. "I am, and always will be, his wife. He likes to forget it, but I'm the one with the money. He's lucky I didn't cut him right off. All the money he says he's made, he made on my money. He was nothing. He had nothing. He'd still be nothing, without me." She spat the words at me, her eyes watering and her chin wobbling, but her drinking hand remained steady.

"Don't bore Ellie with the intricacies of our family mess," Emma said. "But I think you two share the same taste in music. Get your iPod, Ellie, let's have some fun."

I plugged in a playlist. Pat Benatar blasted through the house, and Marilyn laughed and sat up straighter. "I like you, girlie," she said.

"Ellie's got her own lyrics," Emma said, and I thought I heard a mocking note in her voice. "What do you sing to this one? *Hit me with your pet shark, fry her fillet?*"

I blushed. "Something like that." I closed my hand around the tattoo on the inside of my wrist, a shark face, teeth bared, inside a red heart, with Dad Loves Me scripted in the scroll. I got it after Dad died because he loved this song, too, and sometimes he called me his little pet shark. He never got the words right either, and him and me would make up the craziest things, trying to outdo each other.

Joe shot a look at Emma, and she put her arm around me. "Only joking, sweetie pop. I think you're adorable."

Adorable. My heart burst like toffee exploding in my mouth.

Marilyn hauled herself off the sofa. "I'm going to soak in the hot tub outside," she said and she looked at me. "Come and join me, Bonnie."

"Ellie," I said. "Thank you, I'll go and put on my swimsuit."

I ran upstairs and when I came back down, I was shocked to see Joe and Emma freebasing coke. Freebasing? That was just stupid. Joe offered me the pipe, and I shook my head.

"I didn't know you two did that," I said, feeling stupid, just like all those other times at school when I got some fundamental principle wrong. And here I was again, alone and lost on the playground while the cool kids partied without me.

Joe took another deep drag and then he looked at me, his eyes unfocused.

Emma came over and pinched my nipple hard, the way she knows I like it.

"Don't you worry, baby girl," she said. "You don't have to do anything you don't want to."

"I do want to," I said. My groin felt hot and tight at the thought of something new and dangerous.

Joe fired up his lighter, held it under the pipe and passed it to me. I inhaled, and it was like all the lights in the world turned on at the same time.

"Holy shit," I said. "Well, okay."

Emma pulled me down onto the thick carpet, undoing the straps of my bikini, and Joe pulled off his shirt. I wondered about Marilyn, sitting in the hot tub, getting all mellow on her breakfast scotch, but I didn't think about her for very long.

Later, I ambled out to find Marilyn who was still in the tub.

"I hope you youngsters won't be too bored here," she said languidly and I noticed that she kept sliding down, her chin bobbing against the water and her eyes closing. I wondered what would happen if she dozed off. Would her survival instincts wake her, or would she drown?

"I think we'll be okay," I said, the drug and sex still tingling in my body. I sat in the tub with Marilyn for a while, but I already wanted another hit. I went back inside to share another pipe. Suddenly it was dark, and I lost track of time.

We moved the party to a huge sunken living room, sofas curving around the walls and a giant TV set up high. The room felt isolated from the rest of the house, and Marilyn was nowhere to be seen. It was like she wasn't even there.

"Welcome to paradise," Emma said. "We'll live here forever. Goodbye cruel world, goodbye! Find us a song, Ellie."

"Just Like Heaven" by the Cure was an easy choice, followed by "Damn I Wish I Was Your Lover" by Sophie B. Hawkins, "I Melt With You" by Modern English, "Hot Stuff" by the Pussycat Dolls, "Do You Love Me?" by Nick Cave and the Bad Seeds, "White Flag" by Dido, "Daddy Cool" by Boney M., "African Wake" by Johnnie Osbourne, "Fade Into You" by Mazzy Star, and "Bang Bang (My Baby Shot Me Down)" by Nancy Sinatra. I deejayed like there was no tomorrow, all my faves. It was like I had died and gone to heaven.

We partied for a couple of days. I never wanted to leave the house, but Emma got restless.

"Let's go into town for dinner," she said. I was happy to lie on the couch, ordering takeout, switching songs and doing exactly what we were doing, but Emma was the boss.

"Should we invite Marilyn?" I asked. We saw Marilyn from time to time, all of us soused in our own ways, no one questioning any of the others.

Emma shook her head. "She's happy out there in her tub."

We got gussied up and me, her and Joe walked into town. I loved it when Emma dressed me up. Before we left for the holiday, she'd got me a makeover, and I had an expensive hairdo, with highlights and lowlights and bangs that Emma told me were sexy. She told me I looked a bit like Sandra Bullock when she was super young, which was a good thing, but added that I could stand to lose 30 pounds and that she'd help me with that.

It wasn't far into town, but I wished we'd got a cab. My feet were killing me in those sparkly high heels, but I didn't want to make a fuss. I tried not to limp as blisters formed and the straps cut into my skin like red-hot steel wire. I was so happy when we got to the restaurant and I sank down into my chair.

We were out on the patio. Tiny lights, twinkling like stars, were looped on the beams overhead. "Hallo Spaceboy" by Bowie came through the speakers; I couldn't have picked a better song. Emma ordered a pitcher of margaritas and a platter of nachos. I was halfway through my second margarita when I heard Emma gasp and sit bolt upright.

"It's Julia." She nudged Joe so hard he swallowed his drink the wrong way. "I swear, it's Julia. Look, Joe."

Joe coughed and looked where she was pointing.

"Yeah, could be, maybe, who knows?"

They were both looking at a girl who was starting to walk away.

"I know it's her!" Emma pushed her chair back and rushed after the girl who had disappeared.

"Who's Julia?" I asked. I felt sick. Was she another lover?

"Julia is a story about statutory rape or true love, depending on your point of view," Joe said. "Julia was Emma's best friend. They were together from the time they were babies. Then, when Julia was 13, she and Emma's father fell in love. Emma doesn't know that, by the way, so don't tell her. I only know because Marilyn told me."

"Why would Marilyn tell you?"

"She was drunk one night, not that that's unusual, but she was also screwing me, something that she had done from time to time from when I was about 15."

"Eugh," I said, thinking of Marilyn's saggy wrinkles.

"She was way younger then," Joe said defensively.

"Then what happened?"

"Julia went to Marilyn and told her that she and Eddie were in love, and that they had been for two years. Julia was 15 by this time."

"And Emma had no idea?"

"No idea. Must have been half the fun, all the secrecy. Julia tells Marilyn that she and Eddie want to get married as soon as she's old enough. She says Eddie's afraid of Marilyn, that's why she had to tell her."

Joe poured himself another margarita. "So Marilyn threatens to have Eddie arrested for rape. She tells him she will never divorce him. They were high school sweethearts, and she said she would never let him leave her. And remember, the money was all hers. Her family was into home hardware. Millionaires."

"Why didn't she divorce him?"

"She didn't want him to be happy with Julia. Then Marilyn got Julia's parents involved. They weren't rich like Marilyn and Eddie, so they got paid off to move away. Emma was told that Julia's father had been transferred to Alaska, and Julia wrote a long letter to say she'd be in touch. But of course, she just disappeared. It really messed up Emma. Julia was suddenly gone, her mother came to live here, and her father was like the king of mope because he had lost his princess."

"Marilyn left Emma with her dad? But why?"

"She wanted to her to finish school. The thing is, Marilyn loved Eddie, right? She was heartbroken. She got rid of Julia but she had lost him, so she left."

"She couldn't have been that in love with him since she was banging you."

"That was just sex. Eddie loved Julia, Marilyn loved Eddie, and Emma loved Julia. It was all such a mess. Marilyn came here and camped out in the hot tub with her scotch and her tranqs and blew up like a whale. Emma waited for Julia to write, which never happened."

Joe ordered another pitcher and got me another platter of nachos. He had just picked at one nacho while I had somehow devoured the entire platter. I was furious with myself. I had been hoping that all the drugs would help me lose weight and to a degree, they had. I was smaller than before, but I was still about four times bigger than Emma. No wonder she wasn't in love with me. It was amazing that she even found me attractive.

Emma came back and slumped into her chair, out of breath and her eyes wide.

"You okay?" I asked. I wanted to put my arm around her, but she shrugged me off.

"A friend," she said. "I thought I saw my best friend. I ran all over the place trying to find her." She started crying and I topped up her drink and she downed it in one go.

"Are you sure it was her?" I asked, and Emma nodded.

"Let's go home," I said, but Joe shook his head.

"We need to go dancing," he said.

Emma agreed. "Yeah, right. Let's hit a club. Show Ellie a good time."

We shared a quick pipe in an alley, and then we hit the club, its name lit up in green and white lights—Heaven.

"All your kind of music," Emma said. She sounded annoyed, but I had no idea what I had done to piss her off. The club was great, but Emma was subdued. She hung back while I danced with Joe, who did his kangaroo thing to "Born Slippy" by Underworld. One of the best songs ever, but I was miserable to my bones and my feet were killing me.

But who cared about my feet? My heart was broken. I was head over heels in love with Emma, and sometimes I thought she didn't even like me.

All I wanted was to go back to the house, but Emma and Joe insisted we stay. I threw back shot after shot, and Emma and me did vast amounts of drugs in the washroom. I tried to make out with her, but she wasn't into it.

"I'm sorry," she said. "My libido's left the building but it'll come back, sweetie pop. I'm sorry."

I told her it wasn't a problem, but I was sure her lack of desire for me was because I had eaten all the nachos and was just a fat slob. I hated Julia, whoever she was, for ruining everything.

Then the music turned to hip-hop crap, which made me grumpy. No one was having a good time.

By the time we staggered out, it was dawn, and I couldn't think straight. None of us talked on the way home, and thank God we got a cab. Hard to imagine, but we were totally partied out and went straight to our rooms to crash. I face-planted into my pillow.

I was still wearing the silver strappy sandals. There was blood around my ankles and toes from the blisters that had rubbed raw, but I couldn't feel anything.

I was also still wearing the tight-fitting sequined dress that Emma had bought for me at Nordstrom Rack. It cost a fortune, but I didn't care.

I would've slept for a week if it wasn't for the screaming in my dream, the screaming that went on and on like a four-alarm fire on a Sunday. I pulled myself awake but the screaming didn't stop.

I got up, unsteady on those heels, my feet throbbing. I had to find out what was going on, and I had to hurry. There was no time to unstrap the brutal shoes I once loved with all my heart.

I kept my balance by holding on to the wall and moved toward that screaming.

I found Joe and Emma outside, next to the hot tub. By then, Emma's screams had dropped to a horrible moan.

Joe was standing there, his hands in his pockets, his expression blank. He was staring at Marilyn. Marilyn was facedown in the hot tub, buffeted back and forth by the swirling water, her hair somehow disgusting and pathetic at the same time, her pale scalp showing through.

I didn't know what to do. We probably all would've stood there forever, except that the cops arrived.

For a moment, there was only the swish and swirl of the water, and the bumping of Marilyn's body hitting the edge of the tub. Finally, one of the cops switched it off. The only sound left was the early-morning chirping of the birds.

An ambulance arrived and took Marilyn's body away. Then the cops interviewed us together in the living room. I was surprised they kept us together, but I was glad, too. The less I had to say, the better.

The questions went on for hours. Hundreds of questions. Yes, Marilyn had been alive when we left. I didn't remember checking in on her to say goodbye, but I said we had. It seemed important to the cops that we had left her alive. But we had been so wasted the whole time, who could remember?

"She was strangled," Mr. Plod said and I snapped to attention. He'd said it so casually that I nearly missed hearing him. Emma's jaw dropped, and even Joe sat up, shocked. He let go of Emma's hand.

"But who would kill my mother?" Emma asked.

"My question exactly," the detective said.

No one said anything for a while, and I chewed on my nails and wondered if anyone would mind if I took off my stupid high-heeled silver sandals.

Joe cleared his throat and leaned forward, scratching his head.

"Spit it out, laddie," the detective said. He had a Scottish accent and a weird scar on his face, as if someone had taken an ax to him. He looked at Joe like he wanted to turn him upside down and shake the answers out of him.

I would have shaken Joe myself if it would have got us out of there quicker. I was coming down fast, and it wasn't pleasant. I was cold as ice, sweating like a bag of peas taken out of the freezer and left on the counter. I hugged myself, trying to stop from shaking.

"Julia." Joe's voice was hoarse, and I could tell he was hurting, too.

Emma leaned forward to light a cigarette, inhaled, coughed and waved a hand through the smoke.

"Who?" the detective asked. "Oh, for God's sake son, just spit it out. We're all dying a slow death here."

"Julia," Joe said.

"Julia who?" the cop demanded.

"Julia Sherwin. Emma's former best friend. We saw her last night. Well, Em did."

"Yeah, I did." Emma nearly inhaled the cigarette to the butt.

I swung my foot to try to hurry everybody along. The pain of my blistered feet was a distraction from my withdrawal, and I bobbed my foot, cutting that strap in deeper. Move the pain, shift the focus. I took a cigarette, too, although I hated smoking.

"You saw this Julia last night?"

"Yes," Emma said. "We all saw her. I ran after her. But she disappeared."

"You people are driving me bloody mad," the detective said. He had said his name was McFaddish or something. "Joe, please tell us who Julia is and why she would want to kill Marilyn Hanlon. Only Joe is to talk. The rest of you, shut it."

"Julia was Emma's best friend," Joe said. "Julia had an affair with Emma's father when she was 13."

"WHAT?" Emma screamed. She jumped up and glared at Joe.

"Like I said," McFaddish, or whatever his name was, repeated, "*Joe* is talking. Sit down, Emma."

Emma sat down, but her face was a weird green color and her lips looked blue. I noticed that her hair was quite stringy, and she had somehow gone from slender to addict-skinny in the past week.

"Julia had an affair with your father," Joe said. He looked down, and his voice was a monotone. "I never told you. Your mother told me. Your parents paid off Julia and her parents to vanish, after Julia told your mother that she and your father were going to get married. Your mother threatened to have your father arrested for statutory rape. Julia hated your mother. And you said she was here. I saw her. I did. You were right. She would want to kill your mother because she was so in love with your father."

"And you saw this Julia and ran out after her?" McFaddish asked Emma.

Emma was still shaking her head in disbelief over what she heard. I could see her drag her thoughts away from the past and back to McFaddish.

She nodded.

"And how long were you gone, while you ran after her?"

Emma shook her head. "I don't know. I didn't wear a watch."

"Did you take note of the time?" McFaddish asked Joe and me, and we shook our heads.

"I wonder," McFaddish said, "if maybe you ran back home and strangled your mother, while pretending to be looking for this girl who ruined your parents' marriage."

"I didn't have time to come back here," Emma shouted at him. "Ask them. While I was gone, Ellie ate all the nachos. And she eats quickly, isn't that right, Ellie?"

I flushed beet-red. It seemed pretty darn rude of her to say that. I was aware of the rolls of fat straining at the sequined dress; I sat up straighter and sucked in my gut. I knew I shouldn't have eaten all that food. I had turned Emma off. It was my fault. I was just glad she didn't say I had eaten two whole platters. She was being kind, not saying that, and my heart warmed to her.

"Emma wasn't gone for long. There was a cruise ship in the harbor," Joe said, bringing me back to the moment. "You should look there. For Julia Sherwin, I mean."

"That had crossed my mind, laddie," McFaddish said drily. "And if you have any other gems to offer, feel free to let me know. What a tangle," he said. "But get to the bottom of it, I shall."

After he left, it was like we didn't know what to do. We fired up a pipe and got our immediate needs seen to.

Then I pulled off the shoes, yanking the bloodied straps out of my feet. "I am going to heat up a pizza," I said, and they nodded. I felt weird, like something was going on between them, and I was the odd man out. It was a horribly familiar feeling, and I didn't like it one bit.

I put the pizza in the oven and huddled near the door, trying to listen. I heard Emma laugh and say "my stomach dropped" and I was sure I was right—they were talking about me. I crept even closer.

"I did well," Emma said, "pretending not to know that Julia was screwing Dad." She laughed. "I deserve an Oscar. I just went back to when I heard it for the first time, and I channeled that."

"Listen, I know you've been carrying the load," I heard Joe say, "but wasn't I right about bringing Ellie along? She said she saw Julia. She backed us up. What a laugh."

"Yeah, the slug's a good alibi but I'm so sick of her. I wasted so much time and money on her. And the sex. Oh God, I don't even want to think about it."

The slug? I turned and threw up into the potted plant I was hiding behind. I didn't have much to throw up, just stomach bile. I tucked my body behind the plant and strained to hear more.

I heard Emma fire up the pipe again. I ached to join her and pretend I hadn't heard anything, pretend they hadn't called me the slug and used me from the start. It all made sense now. Of course, they would never have cared for a person like me. A slug like me.

"Where's the rest of the fentanyl?" Emma suddenly asked. Fentanyl? Was Emma into that, too?

"Hidden," Joe said. "Where's Ellie? She's taking a long time with that pizza. Come on, let's go and get her. We need her to be on board until we're in the clear."

"I'm not having sex with her anymore," Emma said.

"You may have to," Joe said.

"No. I'm too grief-stricken over my mother, and anyway, there's the Julia thing I can say I have to deal with. I am not in any emotional state to make out with the slug. No sex. I have more than enough excuses."

"Don't make her suspicious, though," Joe warned.

"She's too stupid to notice anything."

"She's in love with you. She'll notice if you suddenly go cold."

"I can't do it. *Hit me with your pet shark. Rock the cat's spa.* She thinks she frickin' hilarious with her messed-up lyrics but she's so friggin' stupid. I can't stand it. I hate her, and I hate her stupid music."

I was sucker punched. She couldn't have hurt me more. Not only was I ugly, I was ridiculous and stupid. I had trusted her, and she laughed at me. No, worse. She hated me.

But I wasn't as stupid as she thought. I tiptoed back into the kitchen and got the pizza out of the oven. I went back into the living room where they were still arguing and pretended not to notice anything.

"Here," I said to Emma, "eat something."

"Oh Ellie," Emma rushed over and hugged me. "You poor little thing." I stood still in her embrace and that's when I realized that no matter what she did, I would love her. And I would take whatever love she would give me, even if it was no more than the dregs of her filthy manipulations.

"Let's put another rock in the pipe," I said.

Emma laughed. "Sure, sweetie pop, sure."

***

A couple of days passed in a blur of drugs, booze, movies, fast food and cigarette smoke. I was vaguely aware of McFaddish, or whatever, coming by again. Thank God he hadn't been able to search the house, much to his chagrin. There wasn't enough evidence for him to get a search warrant.

Which seemed odd to me. Had he bought into the Julia story? I didn't think he had. But Emma had mentioned something about bringing the hotshot family lawyer into the picture, so maybe he had sorted it. I had no idea, and I wasn't worried. Emma and Joe had it all figured out.

I knew Emma didn't want to have sex with me. But I also knew she couldn't just go cold, like Joe said, and I worked that to my advantage. I still wanted her. What did I care if I knew she was faking? I wasn't, and in a way, I got off on knowing I had the upper hand, knowing what I knew. For the first time in my life, I felt powerful.

"Of course, if you're all innocent, then why not let us look?" McFaddish asked on one of his visits, and Emma laughed and closed the door in his face.

"We checked the cruise ship manifestos," McFaddish said when he came back yet again. "There was no one onboard called Julia Sherwin."

"Maybe she got a fake passport," Joe suggested.

63

McFaddish shrugged. "Possibly." He turned to Emma. "Your mother had a lethal amount of fentanyl in her system. What do you have to say about that?"

"Ask her doctor, not me," Emma replied.

"We did ask him."

"My mother was strangled," Emma said. "And if she took drugs, that's not on me."

McFaddish looked at her like he was waiting for her to confess, but she just let out a shrill, crazy laugh. He turned and left.

We still had a week to go on our so-called holiday, and I knew I didn't want to go back to my old life. Joe would stay here with my beautiful Emma, and I would be back in my brown-and-gray bachelor apartment, going to work and inputting expenses. I'd be all alone.

"I want to stay here with you two," I said suddenly.

Joe looked at me.

"Joe, you're not going back, are you?" I asked.

He looked at Emma, and neither of them said anything.

I sat up. "I know the truth. I heard what you said. You need me to alibi you."

"Oh, you little fool," Joe said, and he sounded affectionate. "And who is going to believe you?"

"They'll believe me." I stood up, my fists balled at my side. "McFaddish will believe me."

"You're *threatening* us, you slug?" Emma's face turned purple with rage. "And it's McFadden, not McFaddish, you friggin' moron."

I knew I had made a big mistake. I turned and ran out the French doors, out into the garden, past the tub and crawled under the hedge, wedging myself in tight. I heard Joe and Emma look for me halfheartedly.

"She won't go to McFadden," Joe said. "She's an addict. And who'll believe her? Come on, Em, let's go and take the edge off. What a day. Stupid little bitch."

I decided to wait until Joe and Emma had passed out, and then get my passport and leave. They were right; who would believe me? I had to get away, or they would kill me, too.

I waited for hours, shivering in the night. I finally went in through the back door and tiptoed through the kitchen. I grabbed a big knife and stood still, listening hard but there was nothing. They were asleep.

I crept down the hallway and nearly dropped the knife in fright when Emma suddenly appeared in front of me like some kind of evil zombie queen. I looked at her— her hair was wild, and she was gaunt and ragged and beautiful. I loved her completely.

But I didn't hesitate. I rushed at her and shoved the knife into her belly with all my might.

"I'll hit you with my pet shark," I whispered. "I loved you and you betrayed me." I yanked the knife upward, and my love and rage rose like vomit in my throat.

I looked her right in the eye while I killed her. I swear she looked more surprised than anything. She crumpled to the floor, and I stepped over the blood that puddled over the tiles.

I wiped the handle of the knife on my hoodie and went over to Joe, who was out cold, face-planted on the plush cream carpet. I put the knife in his hand and pressed his fingers around it. He didn't move a muscle.

I ripped off the hoodie and washed up as best I could. I ran into my bedroom and started stuffing things into my suitcase, all the lovely things Emma had bought me. Oddly enough, I found a scarf I thought I had lost—a white scarf with silver sequins—draped over a chair. I

65

looked at it for a moment, wondering how I could have missed seeing it when I searched for it the night we went out on the town—the night Marilyn was killed—and couldn't find it. Yet now, there it was. I stuffed it into my case. I was taking all my pretty things.

A thought occurred to me. I ran into the sunken living room and grabbed a big bag of rock. Then I raided Marilyn's washroom closet and scooped up her sleeping meds, tranqs and painkillers. I saw her jewelry box on her dressing table and told myself not to be greedy. I took a few gold necklaces, some earrings and a couple of diamond rings, but there was so much there, I hardly made a dent.

But then I stopped. If I left, they'd think I killed them all. If I ran, I looked guilty. I sat down on Marilyn's bedroom floor and tried to think. I was coming down, shaking like a rabbit having a fit. I ran back into the living room and took a hit off the pipe on the coffee table. Joe was still passed out.

My head cleared, and my nerves settled down. I had no choice. I had to call McFaddish now. I had to pretend I'd wasted no time in calling the cops, I was innocent. I'd been asleep and when I woke up, Joe had killed Emma before he passed out.

I ran back to my room and changed into a pair of pajamas that I hadn't bothered to pack. I grabbed my small suitcase and hid it in the laundry room, stacking it neatly behind the ironing board.

"Joe killed Emma," I told McFaddish when he arrived. "They are sick and evil, both of them. They killed Marilyn, too. Joe is passed out in the living room. I don't know why he would've killed Emma. Too many drugs, if you ask me. They're both crack addicts."

Cops swarmed the house, and I sat in the kitchen where McFaddish had taken me. A uniformed cop kept an eye on me. I was overcome with exhaustion and dozed off, my head on my arms folded on the table.

"Breaking news, kiddo. Joe is dead." McFaddish said, shaking me awake. "He overdosed. He died at least an hour before Emma did."

As these words sank in, I watched him hold out three clear plastic bags. One had my bloodied hoodie in it. The other had a tiny baggie. The third had the knife I used to kill Emma.

"Found the fentanyl in your room," he said. "And this hoodie in your suitcase, along with a lot of jewelry that I'm willing to bet isn't yours. And, since I'm a betting man, I'm betting this is Emma's blood on your hoodie. You killed Emma. The knife speaks for itself. Rest assured, we're going to check every item in your room and suitcase that you could have used to strangle Marilyn. My money's saying you killed her, too."

The scarf. I bet Emma used the scarf to kill her mother and planted it in my room. Joe and Emma were going to set me up, have me as the fall guy if it came down to it. Yet another reason to keep me around, so I could take the blame.

But would that have made sense to the cops? Why would I have killed Marilyn? Marilyn and her husband had separate wills, and Emma's father had cut her out. If anybody had reason to kill Marilyn, it was Emma, not me.

And Joe was along for the ride with Emma. He also had a motive, whereas I didn't. Marilyn and I liked each other. But no one knew that.

Thoughts were spinning around in my messed-up brain. Joe and Emma could've said anything to McFaddish, like Marilyn wanted me gone and so I killed her. They would've thought of a reason, and who'd believe me over them?

"Why you did it, I don't know," McFaddish continued. "And I don't even care. I'm not one of those motive-driven policemen who want to know why. It's always the same thing anyway. Drugs, money, sex. I just want to know who. And it was you. You got anything to say, girlie?"

"But when would I have killed Marilyn?" I managed. "I was with Joe the whole time in town. Emma was the one who left us. She went looking for Julia who I never saw. I saw a girl. Emma and Joe pointed to a girl they said was Julia, but I don't know who she was. They set me up."

McFaddish gave me something that passed for a smile. "You all lied. There wasn't any truth whatsoever to any of your stories. So none of that counts. What I've got are three dead bodies, and all the evidence points to you. Nice and tidy for me, so thanks for that."

I guess I was the one who got shark bit in the end. It was over. The day the music died. *Bye bye, your love was a lie.*

So I stared at the cop and didn't say a thing. I looked away from the bloodstained hoodie, and I looked away from the butcher's knife. I did what Dad would've told me to do. I shut it from that point and kept *schtum*. Not one more word.

I did, however, shrug.

REQUIEM

By Jane Petersen Burfield

Requiem *was runner-up for the 2005 Bony Pete Award, top prize in a short story competition at Bloody Words, a Canadian mystery conference. Originally published in the 2006 Bloody Words program book, it is reprinted here with the permission of Bloody Words' organizers.*

I first encountered death when I was not quite four. After our old dog, Blackie, was put down, my mother took me to the garage to see him lying collapsed in a wooden crate. I was sickened by a smell of damp cement and rotten fruit. I said a weepy goodbye, hugged my mom, and went up to my room to think. Children are far more capable of intense thought than most people believe. From that day on, I tried to protect those I loved from death.

Tradition became my comfort.

I work in an office in my family's home in midtown Toronto. I'm a dentist, like my father, grandfather and great-grandfather. I use modern dental tools and an ergonomic chair, but I practice dentistry in much the same ways as they did. I enjoy the precision of this profession.

After work, like my predecessors, I escape from my professional frustrations by being outdoors in the garden, surrounded by the scent of pink and purple double-headed lilacs in spring, by the protective weave of branches throughout the summer, and by the fragile beauty of nature's death in the fall.

As the sun disappears behind the trees, I sip gin and tonic, and listen to music as time and seasons make predictable changes around me. When light fails, I move indoors and enjoy the peace of my old house.

Tonight, while listening to Mozart, I thought about what happened over the past month and the unexpected opportunity to carry out a long-held wish. When it came to taking revenge on the murderer of my family, I didn't act the way I'd thought I would.

***

Even dentists have to suffer dental examinations. Lying back in the dreaded chair with mouth agape, pinned by the bright examination light, I fight my sense of vulnerability by putting on dark glasses and listening to music. I give my own patients these tools to block the sounds of dental work.

Listening to a Mozart concerto while in my dentist's chair a few weeks ago, I barely heard the whir of Mary's equipment inside my mouth, or her conversational forays into politics and the lamentable state of her marriage. I had the mental peace to think.

At last, Mary finished polishing my teeth and looked at the X-rays taken earlier. Through the dark glasses, I saw her signal me to turn off the music.

"We've got some trouble on this back molar," Mary said, tapping my tooth and making me wince. "Can you see the dark shadow on the X-ray?"

I took a moment to look at my teeth on the screen above the chair. "I've had some temperature sensitivity there, but not anything more than usual."

"I think we caught it early enough to save the tooth, but it needs an immediate root canal. I'll fit you into my calendar," Mary said, going to her desk.

I knew I would not have a good weekend thinking ahead to the procedure.

In my own dental practice, I have no assistant. When I can't answer the phone myself, an answering service books patients into preset time slots. On the e-mailed patient list I had read earlier that morning was a name I had spent years of therapy wrestling with. Perhaps it belonged to a patient who only shared the same name as the other man. If he was the man from my past—the man who took my past—then I wasn't sure what I would do. I had hoped never to hear about him again.

On the walk home, this man was all I could think about. Not even Beethoven on my office stereo made me feel better that afternoon.

When I called my therapist, Dr. Leslie Arris, she suggested I take a deep breath. "Bill Williams is a common name," she said. "It's not likely he's the killer. You still see threats everywhere." As usual, her pragmatism calmed me down. Then she told me she would be away for the next two weeks and I no longer felt as calm. I wrote down the number of her emergency replacement, but I knew I wouldn't call.

I locked up my office and walked down the stairs of my childhood home. A sense of peace began to return. This house evoked my past, my family's past. We have lived here for close to 100 years. Every morning, I went up to the office to organize my day. Through three seasons, I took my morning coffee outside on a patio near an old garden. Continuity soothed me.

Like the rest of the city, my North Toronto neighborhood had changed. Old houses were torn down and replaced with mansions. Young families had moved in, providing me with new patients and pleasant if not overly friendly neighbors. But my house, my world, was much the same as it had been all my life. I put Mozart's *Cosi fan tutte* on the stereo. I loved the lightness of spirit that overlaid the darkness beneath.

I knew I needed more contact with people. Maybe I wouldn't be so obsessive if I could channel my concerns outward to other people. I looked forward to seeing John so I could talk this situation through with him. I messaged him, asking if we could meet for coffee. Time with him was rare nowadays. In his troubled marriage, his wife was becoming more suspicious. When I checked an hour later, John's text said he couldn't meet me, so I took the chance of leaving an urgent message on his cell phone. I didn't hear back from him all weekend.

***

Monday began with bad weather; the house was as dark as my mood. I thought again about the Bill Williams who was coming that morning. Why had he chosen me, an obscure dentist with a little-known practice? I tried not to think of that day long ago when my life had been changed so horribly.

Why have I never moved out of this house? Dr. Arris claims I have unresolved issues to address before I can move on. I'm not sure I agree. I just feel comfortable here. After long sessions with Dr. Arris, I feel there are no lingering ghosts in the house, no dread corners in the middle of the night. I feel protected here, thanks to my grandparents. Many years of their love and care in this house have overlaid the darker memories.

Midmorning, I watched a heavy storm from underneath the patio awning while having my morning coffee. I went back into the house, my mind heavy with thoughts the wind couldn't blow away. On my way down the hall, I glanced at the little cupboard under the stairs. I had hidden in there to save myself. My thoughts about Williams brought back the memories.

***

On a sticky summer afternoon more than 20 years earlier, I had run home from a neighborhood game of tag to cool off with a Popsicle. As I opened the screen door, I sensed something was wrong. Music was playing loudly. The air in the house smelled like hot metal. I can't remember the rest clearly but I know I was afraid.

I had to hide. I ran to the little cupboard under the stairs, my refuge when I was hiding from my brother. I had just managed to get inside when I heard heavy footsteps above me. As they came closer, I heard ragged breathing and saw a man, his face distorted through the metal mesh of the grill in the cupboard door.

He looked angry, mean. His eyes were most frightening—wild, wide eyes looking down the hall and back.

He moved past the cupboard, and I heard the back door open and close. I shut my eyes and crouched tightly against the corner.

A very long time later, I quietly opened the little door and listened. Silence. I climbed out, but froze at the foot of the stairs. I called to my parents and brother. No answer. I crept up the stairs and turned left into my parents' bedroom. On the far side of the bed, next to the gauzy curtains, I saw them, their sprawled bodies covered in blood.

I remember screaming as I ran, hitting the stairs in a panicked hurdle. I must have fallen; I was found at the bottom landing with a concussion and no memory of recent events.

It took years of therapy for me to remember what happened that day. And when I could recall the face of the man—and his eyes—I wished I had never tried.

Those wild eyes have been in my dreams ever since. The man who I call The Monster was tried and convicted of murder. He was sentenced to prison for 25 years without chance of parole. That was 22 years ago; how could he be released without serving his full sentence?

After the trial, I stayed in the house with my grandparents. It took several years for me to feel comfortable, but gradually I lost some of my anxiety. They repainted throughout, and redecorated upstairs. Grandma used the under-the-stairs cupboard to store her preserves. Even though I was told the cupboard was safe, I hated to go near it. I also hated my parents' old room.

I've sometimes wondered why my grandparents chose to stay. Maybe they needed the comfort of their old memories, too.

Eventually, I glossed over my terror with new memories. The grim association of the music I heard that day was another element I worked on with my therapist. She told me Mozart's *Requiem* had been playing when I heard the intruder. Perhaps that's why he didn't hear me come in.

Leslie used that music to help me recover memory. Now I associate the piece with inevitable death, and with the sweetness of life about to be lost.

And I think about the divine justice that might come after.

***

I was grateful that my afternoon appointments distracted me from my thoughts. After listening to my three o'clock patient slur as he extolled the value of midget hockey and after I strongly urged my 3:45 to floss, I closed up the office and went downstairs to make a cool drink.

Patrolling the garden, I noticed some serious weed growth as a result of recent heavy rain and looked in the toolshed for an herbicide.

Like many older homes, mine contains remedies now considered dangerous: lye, carbolic acid, malathion, arsenic, warfarin. In my storage room upstairs, I have a drawer full of old dental remedies that now would be considered toxic. I really hated to get rid of the old cures for so many problems. I keep them secured, but I suppose someday soon I'll have to clear the clutter.

After dinner, I had coffee in the den as I listened to a favorite part of the *Requiem*, "Dies Irae." At the computer, I worked on my journal, recording my thoughts, trying to sort out how I felt. My diary was one way to explore my ideas when I had no one to talk to. After sending a quick e-mail to John, asking him to phone me tomorrow, I went to bed.

Sleep eluded me. Not even listening to Eine Kleine Nachtmusik helped to turn my thoughts off. One of my clearest memories of my mother was her winding up my Mozart music box to help me get to sleep. My grandmother had done the same. Tonight, nothing helped. I wished Dr. Arris was not away. I wished I had someone to share my fears and memories with.

I took a sleeping pill, but the bad dreams still came.

75

***

My first patient arrived promptly at 9:00 the next morning, and I started a routine checkup. At 10:00, my second patient had no problems thanks to regular flossing and brushing. I always tell them just to floss the teeth they want to keep. While I was working on her, she mumbled about her sons' behavior. Duct tape and a mesh bag would take care of those problems. It's probably good I've never wanted children. During her chatter, I watched the wall clock. Time moved like molasses. I dismissed her after booking her next appointment and sterilized the instruments.

Nervously, I tidied the treatment room and waited for Williams. Some quiet Mozart calmed me. At 11:05, I heard footsteps on the stairs, footsteps that didn't sound like the ones I had heard years before. They were slow, hesitant, weary.

An old man came into the waiting room and sat down heavily. As he filled in the new patient questionnaire, I studied him. His face, lined and colorless, framed heavy eyes that seemed both older and smaller than the ones I remembered. Uncut, straggly hair covered his neck. He had a teardrop tattooed under his right eye, and shoulders that had rounded in ill health. More than 20 years had blurred my memories; I couldn't be sure whether this man was the one.

Williams asked me how long I'd been practicing dentistry in this house. As I led him into the examination room, I lied and said I'd bought the practice from another dentist a few years earlier. He settled back in the chair and opened his mouth. His teeth and gums were in appalling shape. I looked at his medical history and saw that he had leukemia and some heart problems, which helped explain his poor dental condition. When I said he would need to have quite a bit of dental work, he said he just wanted to get the painful teeth fixed now. If he had some time later, he would have the others done.

X-rays showed two upper molars had deep decay beneath old amalgam fillings. After we discussed treatment options, he decided to have a root canal and asked if I could do the work. I suggested Dr. Glassman, a renowned endodontist, but Williams said he didn't trust modern doctors. "That's why I found you," he said. "A small practice in an old home."

I shrugged and passed him the dark glasses and the iPod loaded with Mozart. The glasses meant I couldn't quite see his eyes, and he would have trouble seeing mine. And while his mind was filled with music, I would have some peace.

After a careful cleaning, I booked an appointment to drill out the decay and two longer appointments to work on the two upper teeth. Both needed to have the roots removed, the space packed with gutta-percha, and the tooth rebuilt before a crown could be put on.

I didn't know how I would feel being close to him for that long. Again, I suggested the specialist but he wanted me to do the work. I don't know why, but I agreed.

Before he left, I needed to find out more about him.

"Have you moved to Toronto recently?" I asked.

"A few weeks ago," he said. "I wanted to see the neighborhood again. I remember this dental practice and your house from my walk to school."

His voice was soft, weak. I wondered how ill he was. Even with just hazy memories, I knew he was the one, The Monster. What had brought him back into my life?

***

After I helped him down the stairs and out the door, I went into my grandparents' old bedroom and unlocked

77

the drawer where they had kept the file on my family's murder. They had protected me from hearing about the trial when I was a child, but after they passed, I found a collection of newspaper clippings and photos.

Bill Williams had been arrested a few days after Matthew and Betty Jones and their son, Chris, had been found murdered. One article said he had been looking for drugs and cash, and another reported he had become angry when he couldn't force the locked door of the practice. A third article said the son had been killed when he arrived home early from day camp. Constance, the daughter, survived and would be in the care of her grandparents. The final article reported Williams had received the maximum sentence. How strange it was to read about my family as if we were disembodied text.

I looked for pictures of Williams. Old newsprint is not clear, but the man I saw in three photos could be a younger version of my new patient. It was his eyes.

I contacted the Toronto newspapers to see if they had information on Williams' release from prison. No news. Google brought up a small item about Williams being released a few weeks earlier on compassionate medical grounds.

I decided not to phone the substitute shrink. Instead, I left an urgent message on Dr. Arris' service. Pouring myself a hefty drink, I sat down to think. Beethoven, rather than Mozart, was the music needed. I chose the Violin Concerto in D Major.

***

Revenge seems sweet when you don't have the opportunity to enact it. I had dreamed of encountering him again, of putting his face in some focus so I could try to understand what he had done. I had believed that if I could confront Williams, the horror would lessen.

Thoughts of confrontation and revenge became a leitmotif in my life. Kill the killer. Avenge my family. It didn't fit with my traditional and respectable lifestyle, but I'd harbored this hidden passion for a long time.

If I decided to kill him, I knew I could do it easily. Less than 75 years ago, arsenic had been temporarily packed into root canals to kill off the root before the tooth was flushed, packed and crowned. I had a willing victim with two teeth ready for treatment. I had more than enough space in the root cavities to pack in arsenic for slow absorption into his body. I could give him an arsenic-laced rinse to swish through his mouth. Oil of cloves in the temporary filling would cover any peculiarity of taste or the garlic smell. Given his physical condition, by the time I took out the temporary fillings and rebuilt the teeth, Williams would be a much sicker man. Putting crowns on a few days later, with arsenical mouthwash to soothe the gums, would cap it, so to speak. I could do it, but would I?

Dr. Arris was truly out of touch. I didn't hear back from her. I couldn't think of anyone else I could talk it over with except for John. I left another quick message on his cell, asking him to call me.

***

The night passed slowly. Williams was due back the next day. I'm not sure, the next morning, whether Williams or I looked grayer.

He came on time, mounting the stairs slowly. He smiled tentatively as he settled into the chair. I explained the procedure and gave him the iPod to listen to. I hadn't yet made up my mind, but an idea was forming about a comfortable way to get revenge.

As I was drilling, he seemed to relax. I was careful not to startle him. I worked at getting the decayed tissue out of the first frozen tooth and applying a soothing compound to reduce inflammation before putting in the temporary filling. I then froze and began work on the other tooth. It was unusual to work on both sides of his mouth on the same day, but I thought it would be easier on him.

With dark glasses firmly in place, he fell asleep. I was glad I was wearing my mask, as his breath was putrid.

At the end of the treatment, I woke him and asked how he was doing. He said he was okay, but his jaw was sore. We set the next appointment for Friday.

Williams staggered a bit getting out of the chair, but made it down the stairs and out the door.

I had one more day to decide.

***

That night I went through the newspaper file again. Before I did anything, I had to confirm he was the same Williams. I phoned my lawyer at home and asked him to check with the prison authorities and parole board in the morning. He sounded shocked that Williams had been let out and said he would phone back. I didn't tell him I was treating Williams.

John finally called me but said he had no time to talk. He was at home and didn't want to risk his wife overhearing. We didn't discuss my problems, only his. I knew I looked for uninvolved relationships, but I was getting fed up with John's detachment.

I took out Williams' chart and saw he was staying in an apartment on Yonge near my home. Why had he chosen to live there? Did he know who I was? Had he chosen my dental practice because it was close to his rental apartment? I found it hard to concentrate. Mozart's "Agnus Dei" didn't soothe me as it usually did. My mind kept going over what I should do.

I had dreamed of revenge, of letting The Monster know how much pain he had caused. They were childhood dreams. Back then, by thinking I could do something about him, I felt I could have some control over my life.

I had fantasized about having him in my chair. I would give him an injection and wait for him to fall asleep. I would bind his hands and feet with duct tape. When he awoke, I would tell him who I was and what I was going to do to him.

My shrink thought this fantasy encouraged me to find a way to get him out of my life. Sometimes, I just wanted to shove her.

I mulled over what I would do to him. I could use an old bottle of arsenic I found in a locked cabinet upstairs to kill him. But that seemed a little too quick. I dismissed causing excessive pan by drilling his teeth systematically. That was just crude. I wanted more finesse.

After dinner, while drinking my second brandy, I decided what I would do. I celebrated with the Three Tenors. Puccini's "Nessun Dorma" sounded sublime.

***

On Friday morning, Williams arrived right on time.

I explained what the next part of the root canal procedure would involve. He winced a little when I described how I would file out his roots. Local anesthesia and music would help prevent discomfort, I told him. I thought about using the old-fashioned arsenic method, but it would take too long. I wasn't worried. I knew I could get arsenic into him when I wanted.

After a visit to the bathroom, Williams got settled in the chair and I handed him the dark glasses and iPod. He asked me to choose something soothing. I wondered if he remembered Mozart's *Requiem* from that day so long ago.

I spent the next hour filing, measuring and flushing. I was pleased to see my hands were steady. Williams had four canals in the first tooth, but one was so calcified, I could only find three. After filing, I filled the canals with my selected substance and covered the tooth with a clove-enhanced temporary filling.

I woke Williams up and asked how he was. He hadn't felt a thing.

Williams came back Saturday morning, and we got to work on the other molar. He said he had had a difficult night with stomach issues. He listened to the *Requiem* while I drilled the four canals, packed them, and finished with a temporary filling. We set the next appointment for Monday.

***

I looked forward to time off, albeit a shortened weekend.

Working Saturday morning on Williams meant I had much less time to relax and to talk with John. We met for a late lunch on the Danforth, well away from our neighborhood, and sat inside at a back table.

I needed this time to relax; John had a different agenda. He told me his wife had found out he was seeing someone and was worried she might find out it was me. We had been so discreet that I doubted it. I tried to tell him what was going on in my life, but he was too distracted to listen.

First, Dr. Arris, and now John. I went to bed early and alone.

Sunday, I cleared out the toolshed. I gathered up questionable old bottles and boxes and put them in a plastic container awaiting a trip to the waste depot. The little bottle of arsenic from the top shelf was quite beautiful. It had a glass stopper, a label still legible in spite of the years, and visible contents. The skull-and-crossbones warning looked ominous. I took it up to my bathroom where I cleaned it.

***

On Monday, Williams came late and complained of ongoing stomach problems. He looked pasty, and his gums were quite swollen, but that was not unusual for the amount I work I had done.

I carried on with the procedure while he listened to Mozart. His eyes, through the dark glasses, glanced about the office and stopped at the old-fashioned bottle of arsenic on the shelf beside me. He asked about it, and I explained about the old treatment method. He couldn't say much, so he just shut his eyes again. I let him wonder just what I might have done.

I took impressions for the final caps and rebuilt the teeth. After cementing temporary caps on, I tapped him on the shoulder. Opening his eyes, he looked at me searchingly for a long time. I smiled and asked him to book his final appointment in two weeks' time when the caps would be ready. He staggered a bit as he got out of the chair, and I steadied him.

Williams went into the bathroom for some time. When he came out, he looked grayer.

"This leukemia treatment is difficult," he said. "I inject arsenic trioxide, and it makes me feel sick. They think it may give me some more time."

I nodded, not knowing what to say.

"They let me out of prison for treatment and to put my affairs in order."

I nodded again.

"I don't think I'll last long," he continued.

"Why are you doing all this dentistry?" I asked. "Why spend your time on that?"

"I wanted to meet you, and I didn't think you would see me."

I stayed silent, when I could have sworn at him for the pain he'd caused me. I wouldn't give him any kind of closure. But I was satisfied that he didn't know what I might have done to take away his last bit of life.

I waited for his color to normalize somewhat and saw him down the stairs. He looked at the cupboard under the stairs as he passed it, and then back at me. I gave no sign of recognition and was glad to see him out the front door.

I could have gotten away with it. The arsenic in his system would have been explained by his treatment. I doubt the coroner would have even questioned his death.

But I discovered I simply couldn't kill in real life as I could in my dreams.

***

Over the next few days, I looked at the sparseness of my own life with a new perspective. I decided to clean out the house. I would do some pruning in the garden. I thought about getting a dog, phoning old friends and getting a little more plugged into the world.

And I thought of John, poor John, who had been so conflicted about meeting me when I so needed him. John needed to work out his own priorities, and I didn't want anyone else's problems right now. I needed to sort out my own life. I decided to break off with him.

The next week, I returned to Mary to have my root canal finished. She seemed a little anxious. Mary had booked a two-hour appointment to do the endodontic part of the procedure. She cleaned out the old amalgam fillings and drilled out the decay. Then she began to work on the roots.

Mary has always liked to chat. She told me she wanted to renovate her home but couldn't until her personal life cleared up a bit. I heard about her kids, her parents, their cottage, scandal at the church and other drivel. As Mary filed and swabbed, flushed and dried, I wanted to block her out with my Mozart. After plugging in earphones, I lay back and drifted off behind my protective dark glasses. When I woke up, I saw Mary putting aside a small bottle marked with what looked like a skull-and-crossbones label. I looked at her questioningly.

"I found your messages on John's cell phone and e-mail, Connie. I suspected for a while, and now I know."

"I'm not interested in John anymore, Mary. We won't be seeing each other again. I'm sorry if you were hurt."

She just looked at me, and I left.

I have decided to change dentists as well as lovers. After several days of stomach trouble and a growing sense of malaise, I had the temporary fillings removed, and the procedure finished by my new dentist. When I phoned Mary to tell her I would not be back, she wondered why a personal problem would affect our professional relationship.

I will not listen to the *Requiem* again until I've sorted through my thoughts. I'll put all Mozart aside until I am ready to think about my legacy, my mortality and, hopefully, my redemption. For now, I'm looking forward to getting a new dog and naming him Blackie, and to continue being traditional in my family home.

I can only hope, for his sake, that Williams does not come back.

Cum Sanctis tuis in aeternum Quia pius es.

(As with Your Saints in eternity, because You are merciful.)

UNDER THE LAMPLIGHT

By Kevin P. Thornton

Later, Armstrong remembered the broken sequence of events.

There was the request for Canadians of German background. Nothing official, all word of mouth. But everyone knew what it was—spying—which Armstrong despised. In his world, if you confronted a criminal, you did it face-to-face. Spying seemed like cheating, and he would have no truck with it.

He spoke some German, thanks to his Bavarian mother. Not enough, but even if he had been fluent, he wouldn't have volunteered. Sergeant George Armstrong did everything by the book. Even the other members of the detachment joked that Armstrong slept at attention, ramrod straight. Honorable, upright, the epitome of a Mountie.

Still, when one of their own had applied, Armstrong had supported his request, despite his professional and personal misgivings. He had been encouraging, even enthusiastic. They had worked together, the two of them, trying to fill in the parts where the military briefings seemed sparse. Privately, Armstrong thought the idea was a bit amateurish, and he worried his constable was being cast into the unknown, with no means of escape.

"It's a good career move," he'd said. "And after, who knows?"

"It's dangerous," Armstrong had replied. "You can't afford to make a mistake."

"You worry too much. I'll be fine. My German is near perfect. I've been completely briefed, and I think I can do this. Before you know it, I'll be in and out, and life will be back to normal. We'll be keeping the peace, wearing the red serge and always getting our man."

***

They had tried to prepare him thoroughly, but there were so many unknowns. They'd told him, "Your back story is the best our intelligence can create. Your papers belong to a real soldier killed on D-day plus one. He was chosen because he came from a small German village wiped out in a bombing raid, five miles from your family's original home. Your accent won't give you away, and there's no one in the camp who will know you. You will be safe."

***

The telegram from Edmonton had asked Armstrong to attend to the death of a policeman at a POW camp. It also said: "There's a strong suggestion it's Rudy." So he'd been prepared, as prepared as one could be.

His body was lying in the mortuary attached to the clinic. Prisoner of War Camp 139, Fort Clearwater, Alberta. It was January 12, 1945. Inside, the room was clinical and cold. Outside, it was -40°F, and the wind was picking up.

Armstrong looked at the corpse on the table. He lifted the clipboard. Name and rank: *Unteroffizier* Rudi Hertzen. Date of birth: February 25, 1920. Died: January 11, 1945. Age at time of death: 24. Cause of death: exsanguination by way of a neck injury. There was more, and George read it all, absorbing the details, numbing himself to the reality.

He looked at the paperwork again, anything to avoid looking at the body. Rudi Hertzen. They'd let him keep his first name, at least, as they'd funneled him into his undercover role. Of course, they'd changed the spelling, using the German Rudi instead of Rudy. Armstrong hadn't known where they had sent him, had imagined he was overseas. What a horrible irony that he had ended up here, at Camp 139, so close to home.

***

The coroner's report seemed competent and professional. The words on the official government forms had been carefully chosen. The coroner would have been cautious. Sometimes a death in a camp wasn't treated the same as a civilian murder. They were prisoners of war, after all, the enemy. This one was different. The victim was one of their own. And there was only one suspect.

"Where is the prisoner?" Armstrong asked.

"In the guardroom," a corporal replied. None of the officers had escorted him, a lowly sergeant in the RCMP. Armstrong was used to the tension between the services. In any event, he preferred the company of the corporal, a member of the Veterans Guards and likely a First World War soldier.

"Where did you serve?"

"I was at the Somme," the corporal said.

"You were lucky, then," said Armstrong, "to have survived. My dad served, as well."

"Where?"

"Ypres first, then Amiens."

"Was he lucky, too?" the corporal asked.

"No. He never came home."

The corporal nodded, then seemed to be about to put his hand on Armstrong's shoulder. Armstrong would have liked that.

Instead, the corporal drew himself to attention. "Where to now, sir?" The sir was unnecessary, but it had the weight of the untouched shoulder in it, and Armstrong was momentarily comforted.

"Let's meet the suspect," he said.

***

The wind had died down, so the cold didn't slice through his body. Instead it settled on him, weighing him down, permeating his clothes and feeding on exposed skin.

The camp had been built in 1943, as the tides of war shifted. It was five miles outside Fort Clearwater, and was about as far north as one could go before Alberta became the Northern Territories.

As Armstrong and the corporal walked across the parade ground, they passed the main hall, and Armstrong could hear singing. It was a familiar tune, muffled by the cold.

"What's that?" he asked.

"The prisoners' choir," the corporal answered. "They're really rather good actually, they even stretch to a bit of Wagner and Mozart when the mood takes them. That's one of their favorites, though. 'Lili Marlene,' it's called. It's very popular with the soldiers on both sides."

"I recognize it," Armstrong said. "It's been on the radio."

Which may have been true, but it was the recording by English singer Anne Shelton he remembered. They had borrowed it from the radio station after some bright spark from the army sent a telegram suggesting that learning the words to the song would be useful for the cover story they were creating for Rudy.

Armstrong had been angry at the sheer amateurishness of the command. "Where in the hell does he think we are going to get that in northern bloody Alberta? Does he think German sheet music just grows on trees?"

Along with the recording, they had commandeered a German-English dictionary from the school. They sat in front of the detachment gramophone, transcribing the words from the song before translating them into German. Armstrong had thought it a waste of time, but he had been carried along by his constable's enthusiasm.

The holding cell was small, fronted by an even smaller office. Armstrong stopped there first, taking off his layers, exposing his uniform. The lieutenant at the desk looked like a teenager, newly promoted, trying to fill out his uniform. He had large owlish glasses with thick lenses that told Armstrong why he wasn't serving in a more active role.

Armstrong picked up the paperwork, glancing over it. Feldwebel Pieter Schmid, the suspect, having lost part of his foot, had been captured in Normandy in July 1944, and shipped back to the prisoner of war camps in North America. There wasn't a lot of information about him; prisoners were only obliged to give their name, rank and service number. Schmid had been in the camp for only a month, which raised questions in Armstrong's mind. Even with his injury, why had it taken six months for Schmid to get here, and where had he been?

As Armstrong walked back to the cell, he heard the lieutenant pick up the phone and dial.

Feldwebel Schmid lounged on a cot in the cell, smoking a cigarette. It was a standard military folding cot, the same ones they used at police training. If you knew where to kick it, the cot's legs would collapse. Armstrong did so, and Schmid fell to the floor, his dignity and cigarettes scattered.

"Next time I walk into your cell, you stand to attention," Armstrong said in German.

Schmid looked surprised, then said, "I speak English."

"Good. Then tell me why you killed Hertzen."

"What makes you think I did?" Schmid said. There was a slight air of confidence about him, unwarranted given the report Armstrong had read.

"You were seen by one of the guards." Armstrong looked at his notes. "Tower 7 has an excellent view of the only door to the building. Prisoner Rudi Hertzen was seen entering the entertainment storeroom at 16:30 hours. It was snowing, and his were the only footprints into the building until 16:48, when you went in. You came out again at 16:52, leaving your fresh prints in the snow. At 17:14, the guard realized he hadn't seen Hertzen leave the building, so he raised the alarm. They found Hertzen, dead, stabbed in the throat. They arrested you 47 minutes later. Any questions?"

"They couldn't identify anyone from Tower 7," Schmid said. "It was dark."

"There's a lamp above the door. You were recognized."

"By a retired soldier from 80 yards away? They can't even see beyond their noses."

"There are only a handful of prisoners with authorized access," Armstrong said, "and you are the only one with a pronounced limp." He closed his notes. "I'd like your written confession, if only to save you the embarrassment of telling the court how incompetent you were. In all my years as a policeman, I have never seen such a ham-fisted murder. You really thought you could get away with this in one of the most closely guarded camps in the country?"

Still looking surly, Schmid remained silent.

Armstrong was angry, angrier than he had ever been. He wanted to knock the sullenness off Schmid's face. It was a rage he had never before felt on the job. He clenched his fists. *No, that's not the way. The book. Do things by the book.*

"The good news is that you will be tried for murder in Fort Clearwater and not in a military court, so it will be quick. No hiding behind the Geneva convention for you."

"And the bad news?" Schmid said.

"He's a hanging judge, so whichever way this war ends, you won't be around to see it."

Armstrong had the satisfaction of seeing the terror on Schmid's face. Then he felt guilty about that satisfaction, as if he had not maintained police procedural standards of impartiality.

He was also confused by Schmid's behavior. It was as if Schmid had believed, up until that moment, that he was going to get away with it. But how? It was the easiest murder case Armstrong had ever had to handle. He had no doubt that Schmid would see the gallows before summer.

"Sergeant!"

Armstrong turned at the voice behind him. It was the duty lieutenant.

"Sergeant, the colonel wishes to see you immediately."

***

The same corporal led him to the commanding officer's building.

Judging from his ribbons, Colonel Drummond was a veteran of several wars. They were a proud record of Drummond's service, and a storyboard that Armstrong could read as well as any soldier. In addition to medals from the First World War and other campaigns, Drummond had the Queen's South Africa Medal for service in the Second Boer War. That had ended in 1902, so this was a man with nearly 50 years in uniform. Armstrong was impressed.

"Did he do it?" the colonel asked.

"You know that I don't have to share the results of my investigation with you."

"Indeed. How far do you think you are going to get in this camp—my camp—without my permission?"

Armstrong bristled, but the colonel went on. "Come, come," Drummond said. "Sit down. And please, answer my question. It is of the utmost importance."

"Very well," Armstrong said. "Feldwebel Schmid may be the dumbest murderer I have ever met. He is the only suspect and until I told him he'd likely be hanged by July, he seemed to be oblivious to his situation. If I cared enough, I would say he is mentally incapacitated."

"In some ways, it's worse than that," Drummond said. "Here, read this missive from HQ. It will explain everything, including Schmid's hubris."

It was a short message. Armstrong read it in silence, horror mounting within him. He flung it at the colonel and raced for the door, running through the cold to the guardroom.

***

"Tell me who you are."

"Feldwebel Pieter Schmid, service number—"

Armstrong turned to the lieutenant. "Get out. This interview is now classified."

"But—"

"Get out now or so help me I will throw you out the window."

The lieutenant left as rapidly as his dignity would allow.

"Now," Armstrong said, "Tell me who you really are."

"My name isn't important, but I'm a captain, undercover, from U.S. Army Intelligence. I was injured during the invasion, sent home and given this assignment."

"Hence the limp," Armstrong said. The injury also explained Schmid's whereabouts since D-day.

"It's less of a hindrance here than in the infantry."

"And your mission?"

"You are not cleared for that."

"I am cleared for anything I want," Armstrong said. "Even though our countries are allies, you are a foreign spy dressed in enemy uniform. You have no legal protection under the Geneva Convention, and you have just murdered a Canadian policeman."

Armstrong wasn't sure about that last detail, but he bet that Schmid knew even less about international law than he did.

"*Unteroffizier* Rudi Hertzen was actually RCMP Constable Rudy Becker, a colleague and a friend," Armstrong said. "I should shoot you myself, save the hangman's time. Now, I'll ask you once again. What was your mission?"

"Can I sit down, at least?"

Armstrong dragged two chairs into the cell.

"I was given my cover last year," Schmid said, "and inserted into the prisoner system along with about a dozen others. We were all German-Americans, and we didn't know where we were going, I swear it. We were all supposed to be in the States. Six hundred prisoner of war camps on this side of the Atlantic. What are the odds I'd end up in Canada? Typical military SNAFU."

95

"What's a SNAFU?"

"Military slang. Situation normal, all, er, all fouled up."

"The mission," Armstrong said. "Get to the mission."

"Nazi hunting. We're trying to identify who the Nazis are."

"Why?"

"There are stories coming out of Europe of atrocities being committed. Really bad stuff, like you couldn't even imagine," Schmid said. "The war is going to end soon, this year definitely, and the high command doesn't want the Nazis getting away. There's talk of trials after the war for murder and even worse. They are calling them war crimes. The Germans have been trying to exterminate all the Jews in Europe, as well as gypsies, homosexuals, the insane, socialists and many more."

Schmid paused to take a drag from his cigarette. His raspy voice gave credence to his story. "We don't want any of them to get away, and it's not just us. The Brits started infiltrating their own people into their camps nearly two years ago, and I guess Hertzen was part of the same for you guys."

"And?" Armstrong prodded him.

"And it was working for me. I grew up speaking German. I'm from Little Germany on the Lower East Side. So I sound the part, and my cover story was good. When I arrived, I joined the choir as members get special privileges. They can move around the camp easier, they have access to all the prisoners.

"In just over a month, I've identified a hundred men who are hard-core Nazis, and I have names and details. These records are going to be important. I kept notes of the things they said, where they'd served, their organizations, the work they had done. They trusted me, thought I was one of them. I was doing well. I had the evidence to nail them. And then Hertzen arrived."

"What happened?"

"He stuck out like a sore thumb. Whoever briefed him…"

Schmid paused, wiping his brow with the back of his hand. He looked at Armstrong, half-sad, half-defiant.

"I'm Jewish. Half my family is German, but on my Mother's side they're Ukrainian, and her family escaped the pogroms in Russia. I've heard all the stories from back then, but what the Nazis are doing to the Jews now is far beyond anything this world has ever seen. Which makes this work vital. My notes are needed. After the war, they have to be held accountable.

"So when Hertzen blundered in, looking like a Boy Scout, it didn't take long before people started getting suspicious. Not just of him, of anyone who seemed too friendly."

Schmid paused to light another cigarette. He was chain-smoking now, the rhythm of his actions punctuating his story.

"It was at choir practice yesterday. I heard some of them, the Nazis, talking about Hertzen. They said they knew he was a spy, and they were going to get him during the night, make him talk. After practice, I watched him go to the storeroom and followed him in. I told him what they were saying, what they were threatening to do to him. He didn't believe me, and he attacked me with a shank."

"He attacked you?" Armstrong didn't believe Schmid, could sense the cover-up starting to fall into place. Schmid had been protecting himself. He hadn't cared who Rudy was.

"He attacked me. I defended myself. He died."

"Where is the shank?"

"Somewhere out there in the snow. I don't know where."

His story rang false in Armstrong's ears, but it was good enough to keep Schmid from ever seeing the inside of a courtroom. The Canadian government would not risk the wrath of the Americans by putting one of theirs on trial.

***

Armstrong stood, defeated. He was never going to be allowed to arrest Schmid, regardless of what he'd done. He would try, but he knew how this would play out. They'd escort him off the base, he'd write a report, send it to RCMP headquarters in Edmonton along with his findings. And it would be buried, or maybe returned with a recommendation that Sergeant Armstrong be posted to Tuktoyaktuk.

"Just one last question. How did they discover he was a spy?"

Schmid laughed. "I told you he hadn't been prepared. During choir practice, he started singing the wrong words to 'Lili Marlene.'"

"What do you mean?"

"Hertzen didn't know the German lyrics. It sounded like he was singing a translation of the English words. I tell ya, the Nazis were near killing themselves laughing at how incompetent he was."

***

Armstrong saw Drummond before he left. He wanted to tell him that a good man had died, and he would do all within his power to have Schmid arrested.

Drummond allowed him to rage on for two minutes before he stopped him.

"We are at war," Drummond said. "I don't know why the undercover American killed the undercover Canadian, nor do I care. The reason why I don't care is there is nothing I can do. This is a Grade A first-class mess. We should have known the American was here. If we had we could have separated them so they didn't get in each other's way."

He sighed and rubbed his hand over his bald head, as if to erase the memory of it all.

"The Americans will never admit they made a mistake, and by the time you get back to Fort Clearwater and write your report, I'll wager that Schmid will be on his way home," Drummond said. "I'm sorry for your loss, as well as the loss to the RCMP. Any man who is prepared to do what Constable Rudy Becker volunteered for is a brave man."

"Yes," Armstrong said. "He was very brave."

***

The wind started up again as he rode back to town. He had Rudy's personal effects strapped to the motorcycle and he could feel the box nudging against his back.

At the detachment, he sat in the cabin he'd shared with Rudy. As a sergeant, he'd rated separate accommodation, and it had been logical for Rudy, as the senior constable, to use the other bedroom.

Armstrong walked into the room. It was sparse, Rudy had never owned much. In the morning, he would pack it all up and send it to the family. Rudy had a younger sister. She was engaged to a mining engineer in Calgary and had been planning a summer wedding. Rudy had wanted Armstrong to go down with him to the wedding.

"You'll like her," he'd said, "and they'll like you."

The side table next to the bed held some papers. Armstrong picked them up. They were the translation of "Lili Marlene" they'd worked on together.

"This is on me," Armstrong said aloud. "This is all on me. Oh Rudy, my Rudy. What will I do?"

Then he started to cry and sat down on the bed in Rudy's room, the bed they'd never slept in because Armstrong's room had more space and his bed was bigger.

He cried for his loss, his heart-wrenching loss, and he cried because he felt responsible for Rudy's death. Rudy, so brave yet so foolish.

Mostly though, he cried because this was the only place he could.

"Oh, Rudy. My poor Rudy."

SOUL BEHIND THE FACE

By Madona Skaff

The Great Leonard sat motionless on the wooden chair. Shoulders back, his arms rested comfortably on the Plexiglas table before him. He controlled his breathing and the relentless need to scratch at the electrodes attached to his chest and scalp. He resisted the urge to fiddle with the oxygen monitor on his left index finger. The four researchers, wearing intense expressions, watched him from outside the glass-enclosed booth.

He closed his eyes and tried hard not to laugh.

After 10 years of pretending to be a psychic, life was good. Profitable. Comfortable. And boring.

So when he heard about a northern university's research study to verify psychic abilities scientifically, he volunteered to be a test subject.

Leonard pictured the headline: Psychic Is Real Deal, Scientific Tests Show. He'd be famous—and filthy rich.

He'd fooled the eggheads for three days, graduating to today's final, most rigorous stage.

Late at night, when he'd first arrived, he'd sat in his car in the parking lot to hack into their computers to download the tests. This one consisted of a series of numbers he'd have to "see." With so many sets of numbers and no way to tell which he'd be assigned, he'd memorized them all, thanks to his only legitimate talent—a great memory.

It took four to five numbers before he knew which set the researchers were using. He threw in random wrong answers to make his "vision" seem legit. He smiled inwardly. Took a dramatic deep breath for the last answer.

"Fifty-nine!"

He opened his eyes, expecting to see expressions of surprise and awe.

You didn't need to be a psychic to realize that something was horribly wrong. The techs stood there, staring at him. Finally, the head technician, Stanley, came into Leonard's booth, holding something behind his back.

"The Great Leonard," Stanley mocked. "Proud of how well you did?"

Leonard's eyes narrowed slightly "Yes."

"You really sailed through every test. Even passed this last one. My personal favorite."

Then with a magician's stage-show flourish, Stanley revealed a laptop hidden behind his back. He tossed it onto the table. It bounced once.

Leonard's mouth went dry. He recognized the computer as his.

"Look at the great confused psychic," Stanley gloated. "Halfway through this test, I switched to a new set of numbers. But you happily continued on the first." He leaned forward on the table and tapped the computer with his index finger. "You really should lock your car."

With a laugh bordering on maniacal, Stanley left. Another technician came in to remove the electrodes. Leonard winced as a couple of chest hairs were yanked off in the process.

Leonard stood, buttoned his shirt and squared his shoulders. His face calm, he slipped his laptop under his arm and, with head held high, left the lab. He ignored the cackles behind him.

Stiff-legged, Leonard returned to the parking lot, opened the door of his navy Mercedes and pitched the laptop onto the backseat. Then he collapsed into the driver's seat, panting with suppressed anger.

What a way to end a lucrative career. Debunked by a bunch of geeks. Maybe it was time for The Great Leonard to return to plain Lennie. Life had been simpler then.

All he wanted right now was the quickest route out of this place, but of course the GPS was useless out here. He tossed his cell onto the passenger seat and pulled out a map.

With the car's tires squealing, he roared out of the university parking lot. Within minutes, he was on a washboard gravel road with occasional potholes. The unnaturally straight thoroughfare and its flanking trees created a claustrophobic tunnel effect. That, along with the groans of his Mercedes shuddering over the rough surface, soon irritated him. He turned on the radio hoping for some distraction. Static. Damn stupid northern town. Did anything work here? He punched Autoscan.

Then something up ahead that wasn't a tree caught his attention. A roadside memorial. He'd always zipped past those shrines on his way somewhere. He didn't have to be anywhere now, so he pulled over.

The memorial was a wooden cross, about three feet high, with pots of brilliant flowers at the base. There was a simple inscription on the cross: OCT. 4. No name. No year.

Today was Oct. 2.

He shut off the engine and got out for a closer look. As he came around the car, he doubled over with intense nausea. He gagged and leaned against the car, managing to stay on his feet. He swallowed the acrid taste in his mouth.

Lennie had felt like this once before—when he was nine at his grandfather's funeral. As he walked deeper into the cemetery, he'd felt a bit dizzy and queasy. Without warning, the air thickened, forcing itself down his throat and into his lungs. He sputtered as if he were drowning. Fists of pain had pounded on his chest. Knocked him to the ground. He'd come to and saw his mother's tear-streaked face looking at him. His parents had described it as a seizure. The doctors had agreed.

He'd never set foot in a cemetery again.

The stress of being unmasked today and being strung out on too much coffee had triggered the memory. Nothing more, he told himself as he wiped sweat from his forehead with the back of his hand. Enough sightseeing. He just wanted to get home and set up his next scam. He returned to the driver's side and pulled on the door handle.

Locked. With the keys in the ignition. Damn! He punched the roof of the car with both fists. He rested his head on his fists and closed his eyes to hold back burning tears of frustration.

He heard a loud rustling in the woods, jerked his head and scanned the forest in wide-eyed panic. With his luck, it would be a bear. He'd bought the gun a few years earlier, after receiving threats from the furious husband of the woman who'd been cheating on him. Lennie had that gun with him now—safely guarding the glove compartment.

When nothing arrived to eat him, he relaxed and reached for his cell to call for roadside assistance. Then he laughed bitterly; his cell sat on the passenger seat. He'd have to walk back to the main road and civilization, such as it was. This was the last place where he'd want to be walking in the dark. He looked up to see the sun hugging the treetops. Best to get moving.

After walking for a while, he got tired of his brisk pace and glanced at his watch. Only 3:30? He squinted, searching for the turnoff in the distance. How fast had he been driving to get so far? He glanced over his shoulder and saw...

His car! A few yards away. Impossible. He'd been walking for...how long, only to be back to where he'd started?

He turned to face the vehicle as thick, humid air rushed into his lungs. Pressure pounded on his chest. A heart attack! Here? All alone? With all his strength, he sucked in long, deep breaths. The pain eased.

Time to get the hell out of here. Now! He rushed to his car and yanked on the door handle.

"Damn!" He punched the roof of his car. "Calm down, Lennie. Relax. Think!"

Locked car? No problem, with the universal key. What he needed was a rock. The only ones big enough were holding up the cross.

"Sorry." He picked one up. "I'll bring it right back."

A shadow hovered over him, and he spun around. He lost his footing and fell back, knocking the cross over and breaking several flower pots. He cried out in pain as a sharp piece of ceramic pierced his hip. He held up his arms to shield his face, expecting to be attacked by some animal. He was alone.

He checked the wound and removed the fragment. He'd live. He started to get up, but was pushed back down by some unseen force.

Brain racing, he lay still. It felt like a hand was pressing on his chest. He gasped as a shadow moved overhead. Nothing there. He tried to sit up and was forced

105

down again. Less gently. Another attempt. This time, a powerful punch to the chest knocked him flat. He lay on the destroyed shrine as images and sounds enveloped him. He shut his eyes, but couldn't block out the vision.

Lennie holds a beautiful, dark-haired woman in a loving embrace before driving away. Turns onto a dark road. This road. An oncoming car. It pulls over. Lennie makes a U-turn and stops behind the other car.

The scene faded as Lennie sat up.

Rubbing his chest with the heel of his hand, he stumbled back to his car. He tugged on the door handle and didn't question why it was unlocked. He got in and revved up the engine to get the hell out of there.

That's when he saw a wallet lying among the crushed flowers. He checked his pants' side pocket. "Damn it!"

He got out and braced against the urge to puke as he picked up his wallet.

A blow to the middle of his back dropped him face-first into the flower pots. Through the blinding pain he heard...

A gunshot.

Lennie falls sideways onto the front seat, and his arm hits the car stereo. Rock music blares from the speakers. How can she listen to that crap?

Ears still ringing from the blast, he looks up to make eye contact with a man staring at him through the open car window. There is a blurred movement. He closes his eyes and through the loud music he hears the echo of a second...

Gunshot.

Lennie rubbed his temple to relieve the lingering pain as the vision faded. He was sitting in his car with the engine running. His clothes were clean. The shrine undamaged.

He checked the time. Three-thirty. Peering through the windshield, he was relieved to see the sun still hovering over the treetops.

God, he'd never fallen asleep at the wheel before. He rested his head on the steering wheel, grateful that he'd pulled over in time. Loud music startled him fully awake. Autoscan had found a station playing a song by the Scorpions.

"How can she listen to that crap?" He clicked off the radio.

Surprised by his comment, he laughed at how vivid the dream had been. He actually liked "Soul Behind the Face" and reached to turn the radio back on when the air gradually thickened around him. He remained calm as the images drifted back and finished the story.

After the vision faded, Lennie looked at the cross. He understood now. Armed with the date and the face of the man who had looked in through the driver's side window, Lennie drove back to the university library.

***

Lennie used the library's WiFi to search the Internet for local news stories. Within moments, he found a newspaper article dated Oct. 4 of last year. The headline read:

Prominent Businessman Franklin Boyd Commits Suicide.

The article had the usual obituary-type details. Boyd had enjoyed a successful career in accounting. Coworkers and friends were heartbroken and couldn't imagine why he'd taken his life. "Because it wasn't suicide," Lennie whispered to the computer screen.

He had to tell someone. But who? Stanley, the technician? He could still hear the guy laughing. The police?

They'd lock him up for sure when he mentioned the visions.

He thought about his grandfather's funeral and in the calm of the library he remembered forgotten details. As he'd walked through the cemetery, images from each grave had conjured up a different, horrifying scene. Violent deaths, lonely deaths, lingering deaths. He remembered the pain had become unbearable the more he'd tried to block out the images.

So many years lying about being a psychic—he could only laugh at the irony.

He looked at the article. He couldn't let Franklin Boyd's killer get away with murder.

"Lennie..." a voice whispered behind him.

He spun around, but no one was there. Damn his overactive imagination. He turned back to the computer in time to see his fingers on the trackpad clicking through several Web pages on their own. He yanked his hand away.

Great. Not only was he stressed and depressed about his crumbling life, now he had to deal with hallucinations.

Loud rock music cracked through the silence, then faded away. Looking behind him, Lennie shook his head at the person he presumed was playing the music. How ignorant and inconsiderate to be doing that in a library. But the staff and students seemed to pay no heed.

Funny that it was the same Scorpions' song that had been playing on his car radio. It must be a local favorite, he decided as he turned back to resume his search.

His eyes widened, lips parted as though to speak. He'd found the killer in a photo on the back page. It showed people handing out balloons to children at a charity fundraiser. He checked the names in the cutline and smiled.

Dan Kabala worked at the same accounting office as Boyd had.

***

Lennie checked into a hotel on the outskirts of town. The key to any good scam was preparation. He spent Saturday searching for information on both men and the accounting firm where they'd worked. From what he understood of human nature, the best time to confront the murderer would be on the anniversary of the crime— tomorrow, Oct. 4.

On Sunday, Lennie showed up unannounced at Dan Kabala's apartment just before 3:30, when the murder had been committed. His lame excuse of being Franklin's college buddy got him inside the plush three-bedroom condominium.

Dan was a gracious host. Anything for Franklin's old college buddy. Over coffee, he chatted freely about how nice Franklin had been, how his friends and coworkers missed him.

"Terrible how Franklin died," Lennie interjected.

"Yes." Dan's voice was sombre.

"It was early morning, right?"

"No, 3:30 in the afternoon." Dan swallowed hard and stood abruptly. "How about some more coffee?"

"Thanks."

Dan picked up both mugs and started for the kitchen.

Lennie hadn't seen a reference to music at the murder scene in any of the news reports. That was a detail only the killer would know, he concluded. He decided to egg Dan on.

"It must have been terrible for him to lie dying, listening to music he hated," Lennie observed.

Dan turned around, still carrying the mugs. "W-what are you talking about? What m-music?"

Lennie sensed Dan's hesitancy and pressed ahead. "Wasn't there a CD playing hard rock?"

Dan stared at him, shook his head and started to turn away. "Look, Lennie, I'm sorry but I have some work to do."

"Working on the weekend? What a shame," Lennie said mockingly. "I guess that's ironic, too."

"What?"

"Well, if Franklin had gone to work on a weekday rather than a Saturday, there would have been people around. They might have noticed he was…well, you know…suicidal."

Dan's hands trembled so much that he barely got the mugs back to the table. He collapsed into the armchair and ran his fingers through his hair, making it stand on end.

The image of a folder flashed before Lennie's eyes. "I guess he went in to pick up the Trelaine file."

Dan's face blanched. His eyes moistened.

Lennie continued, "He probably stopped on the side of the road to either talk to or help someone and they shot him. Close range, so it's no wonder the police thought it was suicide."

"Stop it!" Dan screamed as he jumped to his feet.

Startled, Lennie reached inside his windbreaker for the gun he'd brought with him. Dan stopped his advance as he leaned his hands on his knees for support. Lennie released his grip on the weapon.

"It was an accident. I swear!" Dan's voice was shrill, and tears streamed down his cheeks.

Lennie helped Dan sit down. "Tell me what happened."

"I was on my way home from work when I saw Franklin coming the other way. He signaled me to pull over. Asked why I was at work on a Saturday. When I told him I was picking up some files with irregularities, like the Trelaine file, he freaked out. Yelled something about refusing to be blackmailed anymore. Then he pulled a gun on me!

"I grabbed his wrist, but the gun went off. He fell over. I ran. I could hear rock music. I didn't know where it came from. But I got back in my car. Left. Left him there." He sobbed once. "When the morning news called it suicide, I kept quiet."

"Yeah, right," Lennie cut him off. A faint image of a gun in a gloved hand came to him.

"It was an accident, Lennie, I swear. My God, he tried to kill *me*. I couldn't take the chance the police wouldn't believe me. You can understand how I felt, can't you?"

Lennie was angry. "You let his family think he committed suicide?"

"He's never been close to any of them." Dan frantically fingered his hair. "I needed to do something, so I placed a cross at the spot. Every day I stop to make sure the flowers are doing fine, watering them, replacing them."

"Very touching. Showing everyone what a grieving friend you are."

"No one knows that I do it. With those potholes, hardly anyone uses that road. I make sure the shrine's never without a flower tribute, so I can't even take holidays. My wife wants me to pay attention to the living. I think she's going to leave me soon. But I *have* to do this."

Lennie had brought his gun with him because he'd expected to meet a greedy, cold-blooded killer—not a sniveling, pathetic shard of a man slumped in an armchair.

Lennie heard the condo door open. He started at the sudden blare of that same Scorpions' song. The music stopped abruptly when the door closed.

"Dan, I'm back!" a woman called from the entrance, then walked into the living room. "Wait until you see the dresses I—" she broke off as she saw Lennie. "I'm sorry, I didn't know you had company."

She tilted her head, giving him an approving look and a seductive smile. Instead of being flattered, he felt like a caged animal.

"Hi, sweetheart," Dan wiped his eyes with the heel of his hand, then went to greet her with a peck on the cheek. "Angela, this is Lennie, Franklin's friend from college."

Lennie didn't miss that Angela never noticed her husband's red eyes, strained smile or trembling voice.

When Lennie reached out to shake her hand, the air in his lungs thickened. He stayed calm. He felt Franklin's presence in the room. This time, the information flowed freely.

This was the dark-haired woman in the loving embrace.

"You were there," Lennie whispered. "You were having an affair with him. You were there."

"You hired a private eye?" she screeched at Dan. "Our marriage is in trouble because of *your* problems. Don't start inventing affairs!"

"Honey, no...I didn't...this...he isn't..."

"You were blackmailing him," Lennie said to Angela. "You were partners at first. You gave Franklin your husband's computer codes to access the clients' investments and liberate a tiny amount of their profits—too small to be noticed. But when he started having second thoughts, you blackmailed him to keep going."

"Are you going to let him talk to me like that?" she screamed at Dan.

"That last day," Lennie continued, "after you'd made love, you guessed that Franklin was going to work to cover his tracks. Maybe you were worried he'd make sure you got all the blame. Or that he'd implicate your husband, which meant you'd lose this cushy lifestyle. Whatever the reason, you followed Franklin. Took advantage of the scene on the side of the road."

Lennie turned to Dan. "*You* didn't kill him. The bullet missed and went out the open passenger window. He was just stunned by the sound of the gunshot. When he fell over, his hand hit the car stereo. She kept her CDs in his car."

He turned back to Angela. "He hated rock but put up with it for you. As he lay dazed and helpless on the seat, *you* came by and picked up the gun. You wore gloves, so no prints."

Lennie watched her expression change from denial to amazement to fear and finally to anger. Then a disturbing coldness swept over her eyes.

"Quite a nice story you've cooked up." She dropped her shopping bags on the sofa and reached into her purse. "Too bad no one else will hear it!"

She turned, holding a gun leveled at Lennie's chest, only to come face to face with the weapon in Lennie's hand.

Her eyes opened wide and her lips parted as Lennie's finger pulled the trigger.

Lennie's heart pounded, threatening to rip open his chest. He watched as, in movie-style slow motion, she fell backward, her startled eyes staring at him. Blood and brain matter formed a halo around her head. Somewhere beyond the sound of blood rushing in his ears, Lennie could hear Dan screaming her name.

She lay on the floor, her blood pooling on white marble. Lennie's mouth opened in a silent cry. He hadn't meant to fire. The adrenaline rush of seeing a gun in her hand had made his finger squeeze the trigger. He wanted to drop the gun before it went off again. He willed his fingers to open. They refused.

Lennie managed to shift his focus from the body to Dan. The man was huddled on the floor in the corner, rocking himself as he sobbed Angela's name over and over again.

He wanted to go to Dan and make him understand—before the police arrived—that it had been an accident. He tried to move, but his feet felt leaden.

A tremor rippled through Lennie's body as a thick rush of air moved through him. With a jolt, he realized Franklin wasn't after justice; he was intent on revenge. A voice echoed in Lennie's head.

I had to endure Dan's sniveling each and every day. Knowing that he took my clients. Made money that should have been mine. No one else stopped on that road. Until you, Lennie.

Lennie felt his hand start to rise. No, he screamed silently. He wouldn't kill. Not again.

Why let that useless bastard live and enjoy a life that is rightfully mine?

Lennie grabbed at the gun with his free hand, but only managed to flail at it pathetically. The gun was aimed at Dan, who paled and pressed himself into the corner, trying to escape.

Lennie's heart pounded as he braced for the inevitable deafening blast. Sweat trickled down his back as he helplessly watched his finger begin to squeeze the trigger.

He refused to take another life. "Stop!" he cried, but his hand ignored him. He gulped in mouthfuls of air and slowed the thickening in his lungs by a will born of panic. He heard the Scorpions' song grow louder, but he forced himself to ignore it.

"No!" Lennie shouted at his hand. It lowered the gun.

No, *he* had lowered the gun. With a sharp sense of relief, he realized he was finally strong enough to keep Franklin under control.

Dan stared at him with wide eyes and stood up.

Lennie said, "It's okay. Don't be afraid." What must the poor man be thinking as he watched the ravings of a lunatic? Lennie gave him a comforting smile and added gently, "It's all right, Dan. I'm in control now."

Dan shook his head. Then, with halting, almost robotic steps, he approached Lennie with his hand extended. He spoke calmly. Too calmly, Lennie thought.

"Just give me the gun," Dan said. "I know you didn't want to shoot her. Give me the gun. It'll be okay."

Lennie nodded and handed over the weapon. He realized that Dan's calm voice was just an act to get the gun safely away from him. Which was just fine with him.

Taking the gun, Dan studied it carefully. Then he draped an arm around Lennie's shoulders. Pulled him close and stared into his eyes. When he smiled, Lennie felt a shiver run down his back.

"Lennie, it'll be okay," Dan said gently, wrapping his arm tighter around Lennie in a brotherly embrace. "I'll tell the police it was self-defense."

The faint music echoed in Lennie's head from a distance, as though he were listening to it coming from another room. He looked closer into Dan's eyes.

"Franklin?"

WINONA AND THE CHUM CHART

By Catherine Dunphy

Tuesday morning was brisk, the kind of weather that telegraphed winter was coming, damn it. But Winona didn't mind as she swept aside some leaves on the park path behind the Millartown Library. She loved Tuesdays, her day to open the old building located in the treed dip near Main Street. She loved its early morning serenity and silence, and that's why she always paused when she entered the library's back door before flicking on the series of switches that illuminated her workplace in a magical flash.

She let out a satisfied breath. She twirled on her toes, arms outstretched; this was all hers. She had 90 minutes alone, alone, alone until 8:15, when her boss arrived. She hustled into the staff room, tossing her shaggy cape over her office chair. In the '70s, another plus-sized woman had cherished that alpaca cape. Winona believed its somewhat mangled state made it all the more worthy of her own Size 18 love.

With a practiced swoop, she gathered her colleagues' used coffee mugs and lunch dishes, dropped them into the antiquated, extremely noisy dishwasher and turned it on.

The racket was, as expected, excruciating. Wincing, Winona wiped the counter and filled and set the coffee machine to start 10 minutes before the others were due to arrive. They'd be happy to have coffee freshly brewed for a change. Usually she'd bash the button right away for her own morning hit, but for some reason, she had gone off coffee.

Whatever. It was time for her favorite part of Tuesday. She hurried out to the main area of the library and hauled the book return bin inside the windowless front doors back to the staff room, kicking its door shut behind her. She emptied the contents onto a long table and sat down. Here be treasures.

Winona almost rubbed her hands in glee. She still had more than an hour to go through the bin's contents and remove all the pressed flowers, bobby pins, $20 bills—yes, it had happened to her—love letters and gas bills with which people marked their places in books. The library never threw anything out. Well, maybe the bobby pins. Winona had seen women weeping over reclaimed mementos they'd thought gone forever, and agitated men breathing more easily when that white envelope containing a large cheque was handed back to them. What people leave in library books never ceased to astound—and sometimes disgust—her. Like finding a condom. And that desiccated pizza slice.

She eagerly fanned the pages of the book at the top of the pile, then another and another. Just bus transfers today. She ignored the dishwasher's squeals and shrieks as she worked steadily, flipping open the cases of the CD and DVD discs to ensure they hadn't been returned empty and checking the children's picture books for torn pages. She kept Scotch tape handy for that.

Hang on. Winona picked up her library's only copy of *The Library Book*. In fact, Susan Orleans' latest best seller was the library's newest acquisition, dropped into circulation just the day before. People were clamoring for it. And here it was back already. It was 336 pages; someone read it that fast? Winona picked up the book and automatically fanned it. Its binding cracked. The book hadn't been opened. It hadn't been read. But there was something in it. She turned the book pages down and shook. A piece of yellowed paper fluttered onto the table.

Winona picked it up gingerly.

It was an odd shape, almost but not quite square. It said chum30 in a weird puffy lowercase typeface she recognized from her posters of '60s psychedelic concerts. It was a CHUM chart for the week ending September 14, 1974.

Winona swooned. This was retro gold, the real thing from a time when one of Toronto's —hell, Canada's— biggest and brashest Top 40 hit-playing radio stations gave them away every week. She knew that most CHUM charts were small and folded, the kind you stuffed in the big back pocket of your jeans and opened up to read. This one was different. One page, front and back. Interesting, she thought. Likely a short-lived experiment before they reverted to the tried-and-true pocket-sized version. Bet there weren't many of these around.

There were streaks on it, and she had to look closely to see that "I Shot the Sheriff" by Eric Clapton was at the top for the second week in a row, beating out songs by Elton John, Paul Anka, Donny and Marie Osmond— Winona shook her head in disgust—but also Guess Who and, yes, ABBA.

Wow. This was so cool. There was no way she was adding this to their lost-and-found file. And the chart really was a mess. The brownish red streaks almost obliterated the top album listings. She removed her turquoise cat's-eye glasses for a quick clean before holding the paper up to the light so she could make out the famous names: *Endless Summer* by the Beach Boys; *Band on the Run*, that would be McCartney. She peered closer. Who or what was Golden Earring?

A door slammed. Winona dropped the paper, which fell to the floor; she knew she hadn't unlocked the front door yet.

Then the door to the staff room swung open so forcefully it hit the wall. It was her boss. Roseann Mills was usually elegant and pulled together, but this morning her hair was falling out of a messy ponytail and she'd thrown a ratty black cardigan over workout clothes. And there was a man close behind her.

"This will disrupt our entire week. People count on the library being open." Winona had never heard Ms. Mills sound as upset. "And I don't appreciate your people putting that yellow tape all over the place."

A look of annoyance flashed across the man's face, then vanished.

"Well, it is a crime scene," he replied.

Winona rocked back in her chair. "What the—" she gasped. "What happened?"

"A woman died on your doorstep," came the laconic reply. "Jogger found her. Beaten to death." He sat down opposite Winona and shoved a business card across the table. It said he was a detective named Hendricks. His calculating eyes said he meant business.

"What time you did you get here this morning?"

Winona glanced over at her boss, who was leaning against the wall looking very worried.

"Winona gets in around seven o'clock on Tuesdays," she said. "By the back door, right?"

Winona nodded, unable to speak.

"You didn't go around to the front? See anything unusual? I don't know, maybe like a dead body?" The detective didn't look like he was joking.

"I got here before seven o'clock," she finally managed to squeak. "But I didn't open the front door or anything. I've been inside, right here working."

The cop raised an eyebrow.

"Lady, you've already had two police officers and an ambulance at your front door this morning. But you didn't hear anything."

"For goodness' sake!" Ms. Mills strode to the dishwasher and shut it off mid groan. "How could she hear anything over that?"

Winona came to life. "You mean someone was killed when I was here?" She grabbed the edge of the table.

The policeman relented. "A woman. Late 30s. Maybe early 40s. We think the time of death might have been earlier this morning. Much earlier."

"And I didn't even know." Winona felt sick to her stomach.

"I think Winona needs to go home now, Officer," Ms. Mills said, gesturing to the man to follow her into her office. "She has your card."

The man nodded at Winona and got up. "I'll be in touch."

The door to Ms. Mills' office closed behind them with a click. Still Winona didn't move. Couldn't. Finally managing to get up from the table, she slowly retrieved her cape and bag, and stumbled over the CHUM chart. She bent down to retrieve it and shoved it into her bag.

***

Jason was leaning on the kitchen counter, drinking coffee and deep into his computer when she walked into their kitchen.

"Knew you'd be back," he exclaimed. "A woman found dead at the library's front door. F—king amazing. It's breaking news all over the Net." He was so excited that his dark goatee was vibrating. "Guess we get the day off."

Winona threw off her cape for the second time that morning. Jason was not the library's most dedicated employee. He didn't need to be. He was heir to the fortunes of the richest family in town. But he shouldn't be treating this like something on Netflix.

"Jason, for God's sake. The police say she was murdered." Winona dropped into the chair beside him.

Jason stopped tapping on his laptop, his lanky, six-foot-six frame suddenly taut.

"Murdered. It didn't say that on the news." His voice was a whisper. "You okay?"

Winona took off her Princess Leia hairband and toyed with it before answering. "Yeah, I guess. I didn't see her. It was outside at the front, and I went in by the back, the way I always do. The detective said it probably happened way before I got into work."

Jason wrapped an arm around her. "Still, you might have been in danger."

Winona smiled at him. "I wasn't. Ever."

They sat silently until she suddenly had a thought. "I think I might be able to find out who she was."

"How?" Intrigued, Jason turned back to his laptop and fired up his search engine. "Did you see something?"

Winona reached into her Peruvian woven shoulder bag and withdrew the yellowed brochure.

"I found this old CHUM chart today in the returns."

"Grooovy," Jason drawled as he picked it up. "Maybe it's one of the more valuable ones. You can get $10, $20 for some of 'em. The ones that had coupons you tore out and mailed in are really rare—"

He stopped. "What's this stuff on it?"

Winona sighed. Deep down she'd always known what the reddish-brown streaks were. That lingering metallic smell. The aura of violence and despair.

"Blood," she said, more to herself than to her live-in. "And it's got something to do with that woman's murder."

Jason raised an eyebrow as Winona went into the living room to retrieve her own computer. As the library's IT specialist, it was easy for her to find who had taken out *The Library Book.* A few swipes and she was looking at the library profile of a Susan Dalgleish, who lived at 29 Rummer Road—definitely not the best part of town anymore. Winona scanned the extensive history of the books Susan had borrowed. She certainly had read a lot.

And lately Susan had been reading about Canadian and Californian pop culture.

"Jason," she called out. "I think I might have known her."

He was by her side in a flash. "Phone the cops."

Winona said nothing, remembering the woman she'd recently helped find old touring schedules for bands, current Web sites for aging rock stars and more. Although grateful for Winona's help, she'd been so diffident, always hiding behind her curtain of dull, dark blond hair. She could have been 20; she could have been 40. Winona had noted with approval her clothes were thrift-shop finds, not her own retro punk'd style but from the classic tweed era. And with her lean frame, she rocked the look. Once Winona had tried to tell her that but the woman had immediately retreated, flushed and flustered. Winona had kept it purely professional from then on.

"Phone the cops," Jason repeated.

Winona shook her head. She thought of Susan and how desperately she had been to receive whatever Winona could locate for her. She thought of Detective Hendricks and his cool assessing eyes. "Not yet."

Then, before Jason could stop her or even ask where she was going, she grabbed her cape and bag, and ran out of their apartment.

***

The house at 29 Rummer Road had once been beautiful. No, Winona thought. With its curved front window, ornate iron railing, stone stairs and burnished oak door, it had once been grand.

Now it was tired and divided into flats. Small flats, Winona thought, looking at the double row of buzzers. She pushed the ones on either side of the button labelled Dalgleish, hoping for a friendly neighbor. No response. Then she pushed the buttons of all the ground-floor flats, hoping for a nosy neighbor. And got lucky.

"Hello?" The voice was rusty from age and lack of use.

"I'm a friend of Susan Dalgleish." Winona rationalized that she wasn't lying; she would have been her friend had the woman allowed it. "May I speak to you about her?"

The woman didn't reply, but the door buzzed and Winona walked in. The musty hall was dim, save for a streak of light at the end coming from an open door. The tall white-haired woman standing there was gesturing to Winona.

"I knew she was in trouble," the woman proclaimed as Winona found herself in a surprisingly large but empty room. Winona realized it had not always been so. She could see the outline of ornate settees and large paintings on the faded wallpaper. "I just knew she would come to a bad end after that awful man kept coming by."

Winona's head swirled. So she was right. The dead woman was Susan Dalgleish. And the police had already talked to this woman. But what awful man?

"I told those police officers about him," the woman said as if reading Winona's mind—or perhaps the look on her face. This woman was alert and shrewd. "Not that they paid any heed. You know, the ramblings of another rattled old woman."

Her clear gaze swept over Winona. "But you might be different," she said, turning away. "Although I know you were not her friend."

Winona flushed.

The woman waved away Winona's embarrassment. "She didn't have any friends. Didn't want any, either."

Winona followed her through beveled French doors to another grand room centered on a carved alabaster fireplace, made golden from the morning sunlight filtering through stained glass windows. A single chair and matching sofa were the only furnishings in a room designed for entertaining.

The woman opened a side door to an office, no, a magnificent library. Bookshelves lining three walls were interrupted only by a massive rolltop desk, at which the woman sat herself. She seemed to have regained her composure; in fact, she was positively regal. This was where she belonged.

"My name is Alice Hornsby and my family has lived in this house for more than 150 years," she stated as her fingers stroked the desk's burnished wood. "I live on the main floor. All of it. The other buzzers are there to keep people away."

Her upraised hand cut off any comment.

"I take in one or two paying guests who live on the second floor. Quite comfortably, I might say. They are all carefully vetted. I insist they be quiet and cultured. Susan has—had—been with me for the past two years."

Ms. Hornsby commanded Winona to a chair by the desk. "And now, you will tell me how you really know Susan."

So Winona told her about helping Susan in the library. But not about what she held in her purse. The woman listened impatiently, as if waiting for something specific, but also for something Winona wasn't saying. Two spots of color appeared on the woman's patrician cheeks.

"There's something I think you should see," she announced.

She unlocked the rolltop and unveiled thick piles of plastic files. CHUM charts. Hundreds of them.

Winona gawked.

"It's a complete set. Worth something. A good something." Alice Hornsby had noted Winona's reaction and seemed satisfied by it. Her eyes bore into her. "He wanted these. I know he did. He wanted them from Susan."

***

"Yeah, like I would kill for another CHUM chart? She's batty." Morty was as miserable and grimy as his namesake hole-in-the-wall music memorabilia shop in the far end of Old Town. "I can't give away the ones I have."

Jason had easily tracked down Susan Dalgleish's mystery man. Millartown wasn't home to that many guys with salt-and-pepper, waist-length beards, still dressing as if it were the tie-dyed '60s, a fashion decade Winona loathed. After Jason had let her know how he felt about her running

off, he had calmed down enough to insist he go to see
Morty with her. As the library was still closed and they both
had the day off, Winona couldn't see a way out of it.

"You're not the only one who gets to play detective,"
Jason had said as they hoofed it across town. Winona had
pulled a face but now she was glad Jason was here, because
Morty wasn't looking her in the eye.

Winona knew he was lying. She just didn't know what
he was lying about.

She decided to find out.

"Look," she said, laying aside an armload of old
newspapers so she could sit. She almost regretted it when
the chair swayed and tilted under her weight. She fought a
wave of vertigo by keeping both feet on the floor for
balance. Then she took out the stained CHUM chart from
her purse.

Morty recoiled.

"It's ruined! How could you—let me see." He
reached toward her.

"Not so fast." Jason put an arm between Winona and
the grasping dealer. "I happen to know that some of
Canada's most famous people collect these charts. Mike
Myers. Martin Short."

Morty snorted. "Been reading up online, have you?"

"So what if I have?" Jason countered. "It's a gold
mine of information. Speaking of gold..." He gently took
the chart from Winona.

Morty exhaled. "Give it to me, and maybe I can tell
you what you want to know."

Jason relented and handed it over. Winona noted
Morty's sudden grace and care as he turned the CHUM
chart from front to back, frowning in concentration.

Then a start. A double take. Wonder crossed his face.

"What is it? What's there?" Winona wanted to know. She could feel Jason grow tense next to her.

Morty removed his mug of cold coffee from the vicinity before lovingly placing the chart in its place. His shrug was forced.

"Nothing," he said. "For a minute, I thought—but no, it's just one more CHUM chart that's been disrespected. Where did you get it?"

His rheumy eyes followed the chart as Winona very carefully put it back in her bag and got up to leave.

"The library," she said. "Where I work."

***

A phone message from Roseann Mills was waiting for her when they got home. It was back to work tomorrow. The library was re-opening. The yellow tape was gone. So were the police.

The police. Oh God. Winona sank onto a chair, stomach roiling. The CHUM chart somehow held the key to solving Susan Dalgleish's murder. She should never have kept it; she should have handed it over to that cop then and there, but it was too late now.

She could be charged with obstruction of justice. Maybe Jason, too. And that mustn't happen. Not to him. He was the good guy in this. It was up to her—not him— to find out why Susan had hidden the CHUM chart in the book. Then she'd tell the police everything.

But first, she'd talk to Alice Hornsby. The older woman would know.

***

The library was busy all day—crowded with gawkers checking out the scene of the crime and those who made sure to lodge their complaints at being inconvenienced by the closure. Winona was exhausted at the end of it, but needed a word with her boss before heading home.

Ms. Mills looked equally worn out. Winona glimpsed Hendricks' card on her desk.

"Any word from the police?' Winona asked.

Ms. Mills shook her head.

"I know who she was." Winona plunged ahead. "Susan Dalgleish. She was in here a lot recently looking things up."

Winona was not going to say that she'd done some looking up herself to find that out. And that inside her Peruvian shoulder bag she had stashed some of the heavy library books Susan had been using for references. Maybe tonight at home she could figure out what the dead woman might have found in them.

Ms. Mills reached for the card and picked up the phone. "Thanks."

Winona felt better, much better, as she left the library. Of course, the police had already identified Susan even if they hadn't made it public, otherwise why would they be talking to Alice Hornsby? But Winona wanted the cops to think she was helpful.

And Ms. Mills hadn't asked her how she knew it was Susan. Finally, some luck. She straightened her shoulders and shifted her heavy bag as she crossed into the park. Tomorrow she didn't start work until noon, so there'd be time to drop in on Alice Hornsby again. Winona had a gut feeling that the woman could help her shake the truth out of Morty.

"Hey. You. Stop." A hand gripped Winona's shoulder from behind.

"Let go of me," she yelled, whirling to face her attacker, ready to swing her purse strategically.

It was Morty, holding up both hands in surrender.

"I just wanted to talk with you," he whinged, as if she were the aggressor.

Winona willed her heart to stop racing.

"You said you worked at the library. I waited for you to come out."

Winona gazed at him with disgust. To think she'd been frightened of this weasel. *Steady there,* she told herself. *Proceed carefully.* Susan Dalgleish probably had thought the same thing about this weird guy with his strange eyes and crumb-filled beard. And he might be carrying a weapon in his canvas army bag.

"What do you want to talk about?"

He looked around him. Office workers were filling the street at the end of their work day. "Not here."

Winona thought fast. "The CHUM chart."

"You have it with you?" Decades dropped from his voice in his eagerness.

Winona drew her bag closer to her. "Come with me."

They walked in silence until they turned onto Rummer Road. Morty jerked to a stop as Winona had known he would. She was ready with a lie.

"Just moved in here. You know the place?"

"Nope."

You lying scumbag.

Winona stepped between him and the door, and used her Peruvian bag to cover up the fact she was pushing Alice Hornsby's buzzer, not unlocking the door to her phantom flat. The door clicked open. Morty reluctantly followed Winona down the hall to where Alice Hornsby stood.

The woman's cool eyes went past Winona to Morty. A tilt of her head indicated they were to follow her. Winona grabbed Morty by the arm, practically dragging him through the empty room into the room with the fireplace and the only places to sit. Alice Hornsby strode to the armchair beside the darkened hearth, leaving Winona and Morty no choice but to sit on the sofa.

Something didn't feel right, Winona thought as she tried to make as much space as possible between her and Morty. *I'm supposed to be on her side, not his.*

She tried to catch Alice Hornsby's eye. Failed.

"So, you've come to your senses?" Alice said to Morty. Her voice sneered. Her face twisted into cruelty. Winona tightened up, confused. Her thoughts spun out of control.

"Hand it to me." Alice snapped her fingers.

"She has it." A shaking Morty indicated Winona beside him.

The already dim room seemed to darken more as Alice turned to Winona. Her long arm reached out, and strong fingers wrapped themselves around the fire poker.

Alice knocked the poker against the fire stand and glared at Winona. "I suppose you are going to tell me that Susan—your very good friend—gave it to you?" Her voice oozed scorn.

She rose from her chair. "You stole it." She crossed the floor to the sofa in two swift steps. "I would like it back."

Winona shrank into the couch, instinctively holding her bag against her.

"It's there," Alice cried. "You have it in your bag."

Winona saw the madness in those furious eyes before the first blow of the poker connected with her body. She felt waves of pain. She heard her own screams. Her arm covered her head, trying to block the trajectory of the iron weapon. Morty was screaming, "Stop! Stop! I'm calling the police." But the blows kept coming to her arm, shoulders and ribs. Hard metal. Somebody pulled at her bag. Now there was nothing to protect her. A voice urged her to turn fast, turn her back to the blows. Protect. She must protect.

A thud, gasp and it stopped. The beating stopped.

"You okay? You okay? Tell me you're okay." Morty's rasping voice sounded far away. Winona shuddered, then turned.

A panting Morty was holding her bulging purse over the figure on the floor. Alice Hornsby had been felled by a blow of her Peruvian bag containing Susan's reference books. The fire poker lay on the floor near her outstretched hand.

Then the door burst open.

"Hands up where we can see them."

The police. They were here. Winona was safe. But they were arresting Morty.

Winona recognized Detective Hendricks. "Not him. She—"

Hendricks held up a hand. "We need an ambulance," he said into a phone.

***

"Ready to tell me now?"

Winona squinted at the police officer standing at the end of her bed. Then remembered. Hendricks. His name was Hendricks.

She sighed, then winced. She'd been in the hospital for two days. Her broken left arm was in a cast, and her fractured ribs made it hurt to breathe, let alone talk. Other than that, everything was fine.

"Tell you what?"

The cop echoed Winona's sigh as he pulled up a chair by her bedside.

"Let me catch you up on things," he said, leaning forward. "Alice Hornsby has decided to talk. Now that she no longer has a complete set of these CHUM charts—it had been desecrated is how she put it—she doesn't care. She won't get the money and she can't hang on to her house so she's lost the fight. As well as her grandniece, but she doesn't seem as upset about that."

He was watching Winona carefully as he spoke. "Susan Dalgleish was her grandniece. Her only relative."

Winona's eyes widened.

"Seems she didn't bother to tell you that."

Winona shook her head.

"Susan was the only other person who knew about the collection." Hendricks became very still. "Besides Taubman."

Winona frowned. Taubman?

Hendricks tilted the chair back onto two legs. "I believe you know him as Morty. He says that a complete set of CHUM charts—like that one—was worth a lot of money. Quarter, half a million maybe."

That was a crazy amount of money for something they used to give away, Winona thought. But in a way, it made sense. Otherwise, none of this would have happened, and Susan Dalgleish might still be coming to the library.

"The girl—well she wasn't a girl, she was 41—knew it too. She used to drop by Taubman's shop. Pick his brain." Hendricks cleared his throat. "Even took him to her place once to show him what she had. Seems Susan figured the collection was hers because it used to belong to her mother, not Alice Hornsby."

Hendricks' upended chair legs hit the floor.

"Susan's mother died when she was a girl. Just 12. Seems that Ms. Hornsby swooped in and took everything—except Susan. She had to go into child care."

Winona let out a sigh. What a cruel thing to do to a kid.

Hendricks cleared his throat. "She moved into Rummer Road with Hornsby last year. She told Taubman her aunt needed her rent money because she was too proud to rent rooms to just anybody."

That jibed, Winona thought. But Susan also may have been plotting the whole time to get back at the aunt who didn't want to raise her. Wrecking a complete set of charts would do that, nicely.

"So here's where you might fit in," Hendricks said. "Hornsby has said she saw Susan filch one of the charts and stick it in a library book. Who knows why? Maybe revenge is sweeter if just one thing is missing from an otherwise perfect set. Maybe she wants the soon-to-be-missing chart to be somewhere safe, like a library. Maybe she thinks it's easy to get it back. Or maybe she thinks it's gone forever when she pushes it through the Returns slot.

"We'll never know because Hornsby picked up that poker from her fireplace set—I think you've had a nodding acquaintance with it—and followed her. Tried to stop her when she figured out Susan was dumping the chart off and, well, we know what happened next." Hendricks stood by the bed. "We think Susan got the book into the library somehow—even while she was being bludgeoned to death."

He stopped. Let the silence unsettle her. "We think you may have found the missing CHUM chart that morning at work. Do you have it?"

For a moment, just one moment, Winona was tempted to tell the truth.

But the cops had their confession. They didn't need the CHUM chart and they didn't need to know she had it. Or that she'd had it from the beginning.

"No," she said.

***

It was late afternoon, hours after the detective had left, and Jason was slumped by her bedside. His go-to grin was replaced by worry and exhaustion. Winona reached for him.

Yesterday, after they had run tests, taken X-rays, assessed all the damage Alice Hornsby had inflicted, long after she'd been cleaned and bandaged and attached to intravenous tubing, a beaming nurse had appeared by her side.

"Your baby is fine," she'd said.

Winona had cried happy tears and reached for the phone to call Jason to tell him she now knew why the floor sometimes tilted and coffee tasted strange. But the nurse removed the receiver from her hand, reminding her it was 3 a.m.

Now she took his hand.

Jason was insisting on Spock for a name, be it boy or girl, when Winona spotted a droopy figure at her doorway. Morty Taubman looked so hangdog his beard was close to brushing his knees. He thrust a bouquet of grocery-store daisies at her, which Jason deftly intercepted as he stood to escort him out of the hospital room.

"No, let him stay," Winona said. "I think Morty saved my life."

Morty looked sheepish. "Whacked her with your bag. Sorry for grabbing it. Got her right on the head. Good thing you had those books in it. Thought she was really going to kill you."

"Touchdown," Jason pumped the man's hand and gave him the seat by the bed. Morty lowered himself carefully onto it.

"Sorry," he said again, waving a floppy hand at her cast, tubing and the rest of the medical paraphernalia.

"Yeah," Winona grimaced. "All this. For a CHUM chart?"

Morty looked away.

"What's the deal with it anyway?" she asked. "Was it worth dying for?"

A weak smile. "That's the $64,000 question," he said. "Actually, I guess it's now more like a quarter-of-a-million-dollar question."

Winona got the reference to one of television's first game shows, all right—except she still didn't get it.

"But why?"

"First of all, it was a complete set. That's big. And that chart—the one with the streaks, the one that's missing—turns out it was pretty special, too."

Jason and Winona exchanged a look. "Why?" they both asked.

Morty looked at his rapt audience. "Because of Golden Earring. A Dutch band. Had a big single called 'Radar Love' and the No. 6 album that week."

"And?"

He sighed elaborately. "There are a lot of people out there who dig this stuff, ya know." A look of cunning crossed his face. "People with money."

Winona signaled Jason to hand over her Peruvian bag hanging on the back of the door.

"Look, Morty," she said, fishing out and holding up the CHUM chart with her good arm. "Why this chart? You better tell me right now."

Morty went pale. "I thought it was gone."

Winona waved it impatiently. "It's not."

"Here." Morty reached towards the chart and pointed at the bottom of the page, where Winona now saw there was a scrawled signature, numbers that looked like a date and the letters *S.M.* "That proves it."

"What?" Jason and Winona asked at the same time.

"That Golden Earring really did play Santa Monica on September 19 in '74. Santa Monica. S.M. See? And that signature. Band founder. And look. Nine. Nineteen. Seventy-four. Month, day, year. The way Europeans write dates. Americans do it the other way—day, month. People have been arguing about whether this concert actually happened for a long time. Check the Net."

"So that's what Susan found out in the library," Winona said. "That this CHUM chart was valuable on its own."

"Filching it would ruin her aunt's collection, but it would also make her some money? A CHUM chart?" Jason sounded as if he couldn't believe it.

Morty nodded. "Okay, not nearly as much as a complete set of CHUM charts. But I know some people who'd pay just to see this, let alone own it."

He eyes lost focus as he looked past them out the hospital room window.

Like you, Winona thought to herself.

She held out the chart to Morty.

"Take it."

"You don't want it?" Morty was gobsmacked.

She could never look herself in the mirror if she cashed in on Susan's death.

"Morty," she said. "You saved my life. I'm here because of you."

He looked embarrassed.

"Now go," Winona said.

He sped out the door.

"Maybe he thought you were going to change your mind," Jason said with a smirk.

For yet one more time that day, Winona rested her hand on her stomach. Slowed her breathing.

"I think I can feel something."

Jason loped to her bedside and put his hand over hers.

"Me, too," he said.

BRAINWORM

By M.H. Callway

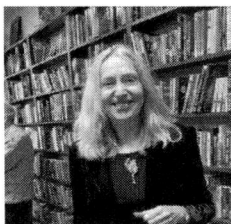

Sur le pont d'Avignon, l'on y danse, l'on y danse...

Fiona huddled over her rapidly cooling coffee. *Maman's* damn tune wouldn't stop. Even shock and awe couldn't blast it from her mind. Her heart still hammered like a drum.

The accident kept playing over and over in her mind. Halfway out of Toronto, to survive the blizzard, she'd fled Highway 403 for the relative safety of the service road. Driving blind, she'd sought shelter behind a transport truck, but it crawled along at 20 klicks below the speed limit. Cars stormed past her in the passing lane. She was losing time. She had to make sure *Maman* was all right.

For God's sake, grow a pair. Find a hole in the traffic. Move! That's what her brother, Bertie shouted at her, the few times he deigned to be a passenger in her Honda. But it had taken miles—miles and miles and miles—to work up her nerve. Then right by the Royal Botanical Gardens, the transport's brake lights flashed on, forcing her into the oncoming lane.

Out of nowhere, a white ghost slammed into her side.

"That SUV—I could be dead right now!"

"Terrible," said the lady behind the counter, whose name tag read Linda. "But they didn't hit you or nothing, right?"

"No, no, of course not." In truth, Fiona remembered only fragments: a flicker in her peripheral vision, blaring horns, the flash image of the white SUV fishtailing behind her, her hands shaking on the steering wheel.

They were shaking even now. She should have cleared the salt and dirt off her windows, she knew she should have.

Breathless, she'd pulled into the first doughnut shop she saw. Climbing out into the teeth of the howling wind, she hadn't dared to check for damage.

Did the SUV driver get her license plate?

She gripped her coffee mug. Outside the shuddering plate glass window of the Tim Hortons, gusts of snow swirled across the deserted parking lot.

"White is such a stupid color for a car," Fiona said. "I mean, Canada isn't Florida."

"You got that right." Linda tugged on her pink cardigan. "You know the first rule of winter driving, don't ya? If you don't need to go out, don't."

"I don't have a choice. Chérie, my stepmother, she's elderly." Fiona fumbled in her purse for her cell phone and tried Chérie again. Still a busy signal. She slammed her phone down on the counter.

"Problems?"

"*Maman* leaves her phone off the hook. Or she just lets it ring and ring, then claims she can't hear it."

Unless Dora Mason phones. Chérie always answers *her* calls.

"Hey, I can relate. My dad drove us crazy." Linda topped up Fiona's mug without asking. "Finally got him a phone from Walmart with real big numbers and a super loud ring."

Fiona pulled a face. She'd given Chérie a similar phone, but to no avail. "Sometimes I think she's ignoring me deliberately. Playing games with me."

"Terrible." Linda shook her head in sympathy.

Fiona seized her phone and punched in Bertie's number. Three rings and his voice mail kicked in. As usual.

Forget it! She'd deal with Chérie on her own. Like every other time.

She forced a polite smile and waved off another offer of coffee from Linda. "Funny thing, I just remembered. My trendy little brother drives a white car. A Jeep."

***

Back outside, Fiona dashed for her Honda, the wind tearing through her coat and hair. This time, she couldn't ignore the silver gleam of fresh metal in the long scrape down the driver's side. Or the sizable dent in the back fender.

Heart beating, she climbed in behind the wheel. *I don't need this,* she thought. *Please, I don't need more trouble.* Her breath coated the inside of the windshield.

Sitting there, she remembered her first glimpse of Bertie's new Jeep Cherokee. She'd turned into the driveway of his Oakville home and pulled up beside it. Light streamed down from the full moon overhead, lighting the Jeep almost theatrically. How glossy its paintwork looked, as smooth as rich cream. How perfect, how moneyed, how impregnable…just like her trim, immaculately dressed little brother.

Probably the only reason he'd asked her over. To show it off.

Mind you, Bertie never grew to be tall. He probably couldn't see over the steering wheel of his oversized piece of bling.

She shook herself back to reality and summoned up Google Maps on her phone. What was the fastest way home—to Chérie and Dad's house rather? There! She could circle back to the Royal Botanical Gardens, cut over to Limestone Road and then head up Hamilton Mountain, though that meant using that nasty, narrow road up the face of the escarpment.

She glanced back at the Tim Hortons. Linda was watching her through the plate glass window.

She managed a jaunty wave and backed out of the ice-encrusted parking space. *That was dumb,* she thought, pulling out onto the main road. Venting to Linda, a perfect stranger. She really was losing it.

Sur le pont d'Avignon, l'on y danse, l'on y danse.

Damn that tune! Even 30 years later, she still hated it!

It was Chérie's favorite ditty. She'd made all her students sing it in French class, to encourage an appreciation of *l'histoire et la culture de France*. Fiona, who had no ear for languages, tried her best to keep up but only provoked both Chérie's and her classmates' laughter when she chanted: "*Sur le pont d'Artagnan, lorry doh-sa, lorry doh-sa.*"

Chérie entered Dad's life a short year after Mother had died. All Fiona's friends raved about their new French teacher, who'd left the lights of Paris to teach in the boring backwater of Hamilton. Imagine!

She had thick black hair, smoothed into a chignon. Her egg-yellow jacket, red shoes and clanking costume jewelry added *le punch* to her wardrobe, as she put it to the class. Nothing, though, struck Fiona as more profoundly stupid than the name Chérie called herself: Madelle. A witty contraction of *madame* and *mademoiselle*, the French version of "Ms." *Très chic, non?*

Fiona soon began to hate French class. Chérie liked to single her out, posing questions about tricky French spellings with a twist to her cherry-red lips. She lingered beside Fiona's desk, scanning her work before departing with a small tap-tap of her fingers on Fiona's notebook. That Dad would consider dating her, let alone marry her, was unthinkable.

But he had.

Time, though, erodes everything. Dad and Chérie's 30-year marriage, with its ups and downs, foreign travels and family festivities, had faded into memory. Their only son, Bertie was now 29 years old, a sought-after data base analyst. And Chérie was no longer a glamorous 40; she'd dwindled into a frail shadow of her younger self.

Fiona forced her eyes back onto the road. The weather had deteriorated. Clouds of blowing snow wrapped everything in a haze; oncoming headlights loomed toward her like the dull, yellow eyes of beasts. She slowed to a crawl, terrified she might need to swerve or brake.

The Royal Botanical Gardens were barely recognizable under the heavy shroud of snow. She inched past them.

It's like the ice age has come again, she thought. *Grinding human civilization, our history, our lives into nothing.*

By the time she reached the escarpment, she was sweating in her down coat despite her broken car heater. The road ahead looked icy, treacherous. She thought of the deeply cracked asphalt underneath her wheels, imagining great sections hiving off, tossing her car down hundreds of feet into the gardens of the stone mansions below.

Halfway up, her car phone system shrilled to life. "Bertrand White here." His voice startled her. He almost never returned her phone calls, especially when she needed to talk to him.

"Oh, Bertie, thank God, you called me back."

"Bertrand." He pronounced his name the French way.

She ignored his automatic correction, concentrated on steering. "I've been trying to reach *Maman* all day. She isn't picking up."

"Oh, for God's sake. She's probably gone for a walk."

"In the middle of a snowstorm?"

"Well, if you're worried, get the two Julies to check on her." That was Bertie's favorite epithet for Chérie's next-door neighbors, Julian and his husband, Jules.

"No! I've asked them too many times. Besides, I'm already here. Driving up Escarpment Road."

"What, now? You're supposed to be looking for a job."

"I *am* looking! And for the last three years, *Maman* has been my job. It's because of her, the insurance company fired me!" A slip of the back tires sent her heart racing. She took a deep breath. "*Maman's* bank manager called me. She said it's urgent. Do you know what it's about?"

"It's nothing. Dora can handle it."

"No, Dora *cannot* handle it. I'm the one with power of attorney."

"*Joint* power of attorney. With me," Bertie reminded her. "Look here, since you called, Dora asked me for the Singer. I said she could have it."

"Wh-what?" The road curved back on itself, a hairpin turn. She negotiated the curve at a snail's pace. Singer?

What was Bertie talking about? The old Singer sewing machine in Dad's study that Chérie used as a plant stand? But that was hers, and Bertie knew it! The Singer belonged to Mother, her real mother before Dad married Chérie.

"No, Dora cannot have the Singer."

"Why do you care? You never use it. It's just taking up space. Besides, it isn't worth a damn thing."

Trust money-minded Bertie to know that. "I said no. And don't change the subject. What is going on with *Maman's* bank?"

"I have no idea. Can we discuss this later? I have a meeting."

"You always have a meeting. Why is everything always up to me? Bertie? Bertie?"

The car phone had fallen silent. Once again, her little brother had cut her off.

***

Her car crested the hill. Here at the top of the escarpment, the winds blew much harder, buffeting her Honda left and right. Only a few more streets to Dad's house, she told herself. She could do this.

The way was familiar now: a long straight run past the brick Victorians perched along the edge of the escarpment, followed by a sharp curve north. At this point, the boulevard gave onto a dull street lined with substantially more modest homes. Bungalows from the 1960s in the style of Frank Lloyd Wrong, Dad would joke. Even better, he relished the street's absurdly inappropriate name: Upper Paradise.

"Where's Lower Paradise then?" he'd say. "Ah, right, it's The Other Place. Our street, Hell Street."

He meant Hill—not Hell—Street, the road she turned onto now—a street as bland as its name. She pulled up in front of an equally bland yet achingly familiar split-level. Its peeling white paint made her sad, but to her it was home. Always home, even though she was now 43 and had lived in Toronto for more than 25 years.

She paused getting out of the car, gathering strength to brave Chérie's latest caprice. Last week, a strong odor of mildew had led her downstairs to the basement laundry next to her old teenage bedroom. There she'd discovered a moldering wet load of Dad's old underwear in the washing machine. What was Chérie thinking? Dad had died more than three years ago.

And what had Chérie done when she'd confronted her? Stood there giggling at the top of the basement stairs while she, Fiona, scrubbed out the machine with bleach. But when she tried to shovel the reeking mass of laundry into the garbage can outside, Chérie turned into a wildcat, shrieking insults at her, pummeling her, clawing through the garbage can, desperate to retrieve everything.

Thank God, the two Julies intervened. They managed to calm Chérie down and lead her back into the kitchen. By the time Fiona returned from dragging the garbage can out to the curb for pickup, Chérie was all smiles, humming to herself over a cup of tea.

Sur le pont d'Avignon, l'on y danse, l'on y danse.

The curtains in the windows facing the street were still drawn. No lights on inside. Was Chérie still in bed? She'd been sleeping in more and more lately.

Fiona got out of her car and trudged through the deep snow covering the driveway. The concrete steps leading up to the front porch were thick with snow and ice. No one had cleared them since her last visit.

Damn that kid, Dora's nephew! She hated being right all the time.

A week ago, she'd been going through Chérie's bank statement at the kitchen table when she found the canceled cheque Bertie had made out to Dora.

"Fifteen hundred dollars, Bertie? For snow clearing?" she'd shouted after he finally answered his phone. "Dora's 73. Are you out of your mind?"

"Oh, for God's sake, I made it out to Dora to give to her nephew. The kid needs a job."

"Jules and Julian have always cleared *Maman's* snow. For nothing, for friendship. We don't know anything about Dora's nephew. Have you even met this kid?"

"Dora swears he won't leave a snowflake for Chérie to trip over. I trust Dora completely. She's *Maman's* best friend."

"Since when are they best friends? They never saw much of each other until six months ago. And when they worked together at our high school, *Maman* used to call Dora *déclassé*. Don't you remember?"

"You're imagining things."

"Dora didn't even come to Dad's funeral!"

"Of course, she was there." And at this point, true to form, Bertie hung up on her.

Damn those stairs! If Chérie ventured out, she'd fall. Break a bone or worse.

Fiona gripped the rusty wrought-iron railing and hauled herself up, one slippery step at a time. Safely at the top, by the front door, she dug through her coat pocket for her key chain.

Funny how the overcast sky and blowing snow cast a strange light. The brass bolt lock seemed to glow against the faded red paint of the front door.

She pushed her tarnished house key into the lock. It wouldn't turn. Had she made a mistake?

She yanked out her key and stared at it. Of course, she had the right key! She'd used the same key since high school.

She tried again, wiggling the key, coaxing the lock. Still nothing.

Was the lock frozen? Had Chérie's furnace gone out? Was she lying on the floor, dead or dying of hypothermia?

"Chérie!" She banged on the door. "Open up. It's me, Fiona!"

No answer. She pressed her ear against the door, listening for Chérie's light footsteps. Not a sound.

She hammered the door again. Shouted again, screamed in fact.

"Fiona!" Julian, a burly Englishman in his 60s, called from his porch next door. "Anything the matter?"

"Chérie isn't answering. I can't open the door. My key refuses to work," Fiona called back.

"I'll bring our key. Be right over." He ducked back inside his house and reappeared a moment later dressed in boots and a tweed overcoat.

Fiona watched him lumber through the snow over to the bottom of the steps leading up to Chérie's porch.

"Bloody hell, look at those steps," Julian said. "You really should have let Jules, The Lad, look after them. I told Bertie it's no trouble for us." He balanced his way up the steps to join her. "Right, here's our key. Let's have a go."

He tried the door. The lock still wouldn't budge.

"That's odd." Julian banged on the front door. "Chérie, it's Julian from next door. Open up, please. Fiona's worried about you."

Still nothing.

"Let's give it one last old school try, shall we?" Julian twisted his key again with some force.

"Julian, stop!" Fiona cried. "You'll break it off!"

"Oh, that's what I said to him last night." Jules, The Lad, stood at the bottom of the stairs. He was much younger and slimmer than his husband and wore a fashionable green parka.

"Time to call the police, my lad. Break Chérie's bloody door down. Make sure she's all right," Julian said.

"NO! Not the police!" Fiona cried. The scrapes on her car, the white SUV...

"But Chérie went out!" Jules, The Lad, broke in. "She left hours ago. With that Dora-saurus creature."

"Out?" Julian echoed. "You might have told me."

"How could you miss Dora and her black behemoth of a pickup truck? Roaring in here like Godzilla while we were trying to sleep. You're right. You *are* getting deaf."

"But today's Monday," Fiona said. "Dora takes *Maman* out for fish and chips at the mall on Thursdays. At least, that's what Bertie told me." Fiona watched Julian and The Lad exchange glances.

"Oh, no, Dora-saurus is here all the time, sweetie," The Lad said. "Nearly every day, isn't that right, Julian?"

"Spying on the neighbors again, are we?" Julian said.

"Well, somebody has to." The Lad flashed a grin at Fiona.

Julian cleared his throat. "Right. Look here, Fiona, why don't you come over and have a nice cup of tea? The Lad and I, well, we've been wanting to speak to you about Chérie. We're a bit concerned about her, you see."

"Wait! Look over there!" Jules, The Lad, pointed through the snowstorm.

Far up the road, through the billowing snow, Fiona spotted a faint gray shape, stopping, starting, staggering a little.

"It's *her*, it's Chérie," Jules, The Lad, said.

"Good Lord, he's right," Julian said. "Stay here, Fiona." He picked his way down the icy steps. Together, he and The Lad plowed over the snow-covered lawn and headed up the sidewalk.

A swath of flurries obscured them from her view. A heartbeat later, they reappeared on either side of a tiny person, helping her along.

Oh, my God, it is her! It's Chérie!

Julian and Jules led Chérie up to the porch. She had on her long silver mink coat, its sleeves drooping over her hands. Her dyed black hair, scraped back in a thin imitation of her signature chignon, was dotted with snow. But Chérie seemed oblivious to the bitter cold. In fact, through the wind, Fiona could her singing: "*Sur le pont d'Avignon, l'on y danse, l'on y danse...*"

"Where the hell have you been?" Fiona shouted. "What are you doing out in this weather with no hat? Look at your coat. There's ice all around the hem from your dragging it through the snow. Have you even got boots on?"

Chérie tossed her head. "I have been out. Out! I am not your prisoner, no, not at all. So Dorrie says." She threw Julian a flirtatious smile. "I have been doing business. *À la banque*. From Dorrie, I am learning A-T-M. Which," she shook a crooked bare index finger at Fiona, "you refuse to teach me."

"That is not true! You told me you hate ATMs," Fiona said.

"Okay, time for Julian and me to leave, I think," Jules, The Lad intervened.

"Not until we get her inside, out of this wind," Julian said. "Bit of a problem, Chérie. Your lock's broken. Why don't we call the locksmith for you?"

"No! He has already been here." And with surprising speed, Chérie crouched down and clambered swiftly up the steps on all fours.

"Oh, my God, did you see that? Just like a monkey!" Jules, The Lad, said.

"You heard Julian," Fiona said to Chérie beside her. "My key doesn't work, and neither does his."

"Oh, that." Chérie pursed her thin lips. She pulled a shiny new key from the side pocket of her coat and thrust it into the lock.

The front door opened smoothly.

"Where did you get that key?" Fiona demanded.

Chérie threw her a sly smile. "Dorrie gave it to me. For my new lock." She shoved past Fiona and disappeared inside.

"Right then, we'll be off," Julian called up to Fiona. "Get your mum settled, then come over. We really do need to talk."

Talk? Fiona thought. *As if words would help.*

***

Fiona shut the front door against the weather. The dark inside felt oppressive. She could barely make out the white trail of snow Chérie had tracked through the entryway. But there on the tiles she spotted Chérie's shiny new house key. The old fool must have dropped it. She snatched it up and shoved it in her pocket.

She couldn't take any more of her damn nonsense, she really couldn't.

A clatter of pots and pans rose from the back of the house. Chérie was messing about in the kitchen, occupied for the moment, thank God.

Fiona kept her coat and boots on. The air felt chill. Peering through the dim light of the entryway, she saw that someone had set the wall thermostat to 15°C. Madness!

Chérie and Dad had always been thrifty, but never to the point of suffering.

She pushed the thermostat back up to 20°. Light, she needed light.

The house had a traditional split-level layout: L-shaped living room and dining room to the right of the entranceway; a cramped, narrow kitchen at the back overlooking the garden. A short set of stairs on the left led up to the bedrooms. Immediately next to them, another set of stairs led down to the laundry and her old room in the basement.

How she'd hated living down there in that dark, dank space! But the house had only two bedrooms, and baby Bertie was on the way. As always, she was the one who had to make the sacrifice.

"It's only for a short time, old girl," Dad had assured her. "You'll be off to university in a few years. Grown up, married, with a place of your own."

Five long years in the basement, as it turned out. And her marriage hadn't lasted.

She groped her way through the gloom of the living room over to the front windows and yanked open the drapes. Daylight streamed in past sun-bleached, green velvet curtains to reveal an avalanche of newspapers spilled over the beige sofa and worn broadloom. More papers littered the seat of Dad's brown plaid armchair in its usual place by the stone fireplace.

Fiona swore. Six months ago, out of the blue, Chérie had refused to throw out her old newspapers. Only Dora could persuade her to put them out for collection in the blue recycling bin. Part of Dora's regular Thursday visit now. When Fiona had stopped the newspaper to do an end run round the problem, Bertie had promptly restarted it. His rationale: "The newspaper makes *Maman* happy."

The damn blue box lay tipped on its side beside the maple coffee table. Fiona righted it. Now she had to clean up this mess. Why was it always up to her?

She grabbed the nearest piece of newspaper, the Better Living section as it happened. Something fluttered down to the floor. A slip of paper? She held up the newspaper and shook it: another paper fell out. Then another and yet another. She blinked. Not pieces of paper, but money! Four $50 bills, almost invisible against the orange-brown carpeting.

She scooped up the bills. Tossed them onto the coffee table. She pawed through the few newspapers left in the blue box. More bills, fifties and twenties. She gathered up the papers scattered throughout the room, combing through them page by page. By the time she'd finished and all the newspapers were safely back in the box, she'd recovered $800.

So that was it! Chérie was using the blue box as her piggy bank, hiding her cash in the newspapers for safekeeping.

No wonder Dora-saurus faithfully took Chérie out for fish and chips every Thursday, before Hamilton's recycling day on Friday. She must have retrieved hundreds of dollars a week that way—the conniving old bitch!

And now she'd taught Chérie how to use the ATM. Even worse, Jules had said that she was turning up here every day.

So that's why the bank had called. Dora must be draining Chérie's bank account. If she hadn't emptied it already.

Back in the kitchen, Chérie's atonal singing drilled through Fiona's ears: *Sur le pont d'Avignon, l'on y danse, l'on y danse.*

She stood up slowly, her knees protesting. With shaking hands, she gathered Chérie's money together. How could Bertie have trusted Dora? He wasn't naive.

Knowing her brother, he wasn't blind to Dora's venality, he was merely indifferent to it. Because more than anything, Bertie hated to be bothered. And for him, $800 would be mere pocket change. As a skilled data base analyst, he made more money in a year than Dad and Chérie's life savings put together. Besides, he'd probably crunched the numbers to prove that Dora's pilfering cost less than hiring a caregiver for Chérie.

And what about her, Fiona? For three years, ever since Dad died, she'd looked after Chérie, as she promised him she would. She'd never taken a dime. Now she was broke and out of a job, thanks to Chérie. They owed her: both Chérie and her precious son.

The urge to stuff the $800 into her coat pocket felt overwhelming. She stepped into the dining room. Little had changed since the day Chérie moved in 30 years earlier, from the Normandy lace tablecloth covering the maple dining room table to the ridiculous, oversized rabbit soup tureen squatting at its centre—Dad's long-standing family joke.

She smiled. Dad had won it at their church's Christmas fair, just after Mother died. He'd dubbed the white ceramic rabbit, crouching in a sea of violets, Sir Peter Tacky-Bunny. Later on, he maintained that the violets reminded him of Chérie's favorite perfume, *Goutal la Violette*. That mild bit of flattery had pleased Chérie enough to allow him to keep it.

Fiona reached across the table for the lid of the tureen. She'd slip the $800 inside Sir Peter for now.

"What are you doing?" Chérie, imperious, stood in the doorway between the dining room and the kitchen.

Fiona fumbled with the lid, straightened it. "What *are* you doing dressed like that?" she shot back.

For Chérie was wearing a threadbare magenta cardigan over her striped pink pajamas. She'd tossed her mink coat onto the kitchen floor, but kept on her winter boots.

"Look at yourself," Fiona went on. "Did Dora take you out to the mall dressed like that?"

"Dora looks after me. Not like you."

"Really? Dora *dumped* you at the mall. She let you walk home alone in a snowstorm dressed like—like a street person."

Chérie's pinched, wrinkled face contorted. "Give me my money! Give it to me!" She lunged across the table.

"No!" Fiona held the bills out of her reach. "You're out of your mind. Hiding $800 in a bunch of old newspapers! I'm putting this money back in the bank. And putting a stop on your account. You can't handle money anymore."

Fiona slipped the bills into her pocket.

Chérie's purplish lips made a thin line. "You are a thief. I shall tell Dorrie."

"Me, a thief? Dora's the thief! How much did she get you to take out of the ATM today?"

The front door lock clunked open. A blast of cold air, followed by heavy steps in the entranceway.

"Coo-ee! Where are you, my turtle dove, my love?" Dora Mason's loud voice echoed through the house. Her broad Cockney accent had always struck Fiona as unbearably fake. But perhaps her comedy-theatre persona went along with being a retired drama teacher.

"We're in here," Fiona said.

Dora stomped into the living room, not bothering to remove her heavy winter boots and down coat. She was a large woman, taller than Fiona and much broader and sturdier. She pulled off her maple-leaf-patterned toque, shoved it into her shopping bag and fluffed her short gray curls.

"Put on the kettle, my love, my turtle dove." She bustled into the dining room without acknowledging Fiona's presence. "Let's make ourselves a nice cuppa Rosie Lee."

"You've got a nerve showing up here," Fiona said. "You let *Maman* walk home in the snow. Alone."

"I did not, did I, my turtle dove?" Dora said to Chérie who dipped her head and smiled. "Come and give us a proper hit and miss, French way." The two of them embraced, air kissing each other's cheeks.

"Julian saw. And Jules did, too," Fiona said.

Dora's mouth twisted. "Oh, them two ginger beers. Queers." She winked at Chérie who tittered.

"And you changed the lock on the front door," Fiona went on. "Without telling me. You're deliberately coming between Chérie and her family."

"Never!" Dora drew herself up. "I was looking out for Chérie's safety. Yesterday I found her wandering about the mall all by her lonesome. Lost her key, she had. Couldn't get home, couldn't get back in the house. I did what any decent person would've done and called the locksmith. Got your mum back home nice and cozy. I'd say you owe me thanks."

"Why didn't you call me?"

"Because you're always so rude to me. Isn't she, my turtle dove?"

"Oh, yes," Chérie piped up.

"And you fly in here whenever it pleases you," Dora went on. "I'm the one here every day looking after her. Just like she was me own mum."

"You're 73 and she's 70!" Fiona said. "Who paid for the locksmith? You or *Maman*?"

A shrewd light crept into Dora's small black eyes. She turned her back on Fiona and shepherded Chérie into the kitchen.

"I am making *ratatouille*," Chérie announced. "Rat Tart, my Harry's favorite."

"Rat Tart. Aren't you smart?" Dora snatched up Chérie's mink coat from the floor and made a grand display of brushing it off.

Fiona ran back through the living room and retreated up the stairs to relative privacy of the upper level. The air here felt so close, she could hardly breathe. She had to talk to Bertie!

On her left, facing the street, lay the master bedroom which Dad had shared with Mother and afterwards with Chérie. As a child, Fiona had spent many hours there sitting with Mother, reading to her during her last illness. Everything changed, though, after Dad remarried. Chérie made it abundantly clear that Fiona must never intrude. Never, ever. Even now Chérie guarded her room like a hound from hell. Fiona hadn't ventured inside it for years.

Down in the kitchen, the tea kettle whistled. Dora's non-stop prattling rose above the clatter of dishes.

Fiona ducked into the safety of the second bedroom, opposite Chérie's *sanctum sanctorum*. Air, she needed air. She marched over to back window and wrenched it open. Icy air rushed in from the garden. She breathed in deeply.

Her old bedroom, changed so many times. Funny how for many years after Bertie moved out, Chérie had preserved his bedroom untouched, no doubt hoping that he'd find a nice girl and start a family. But as time passed and both he and Fiona proved to be skilled only at divorce or bad relationships, Chérie had surrendered the room to Dad for his study.

Little had changed since Dad died: his desk and worn leather chair stood in their usual places, his history texts still lined the bookcases along the walls. Not a trace of her childhood remained, except for the framed photo on the desk showing Dad, Mother and herself as a solemn 12-year-old.

She slumped down in his chair and stared at the old photo. If only Mother hadn't died!

A short year after Mother passed away, she came home from Girl Guides to find Dad and Chérie together in the kitchen. Chérie wore a clingy, white wool dress and an enameled yellow bracelet that clacked when she moved her arm. She laughed brightly at something Dad said. And he was smiling, too, moving about the kitchen with an energy that lit up the place.

"I've invited your French teacher to dinner," he told her.

Having Chérie invade their home felt wrong. School and home existed in two separate worlds. Parents went to school to talk to teachers; teachers never came to a student's house. Never mind that Dad taught history at her school and that he and Chérie worked together.

That day, Dad didn't cook; Chérie did. She made chicken with a creamy, lemon-flavored sauce over rice and a green salad on the side. They sat around the dining room table to eat, not at the kitchen table where she and Dad usually ate. Then Dad produced a bottle of wine from an ice bucket on the sideboard and set it on the table.

Fiona stared in horror. Alcohol! She had never seen Dad and Mother take a drink, not ever. The wine bottle was a beautiful dark green color, its label white and gold with words on it in flowing, old-fashioned handwriting. Chérie opened the bottle and poured out small portions into three tumblers.

The wine looked like apple juice. Fiona still remembered its pungent, sweet-sour smell as she pushed her glass away.

"It's all right, Fiona." Chérie held up a placating hand. "In France, we start drinking wine at age six."

"No!"

"Fiona…"

"*Non, merci.*"

"That's better." Dad took a sip of the wine and made a sound that meant he liked it.

Fiona picked up her fork and glowered at him. Chérie's food tasted much better than the boiled British stuff she and Dad typically ate. She watched the level of wine in the bottle go down and down. After dinner, she retreated to her room, burying herself in a book for what seemed like ages until Dad and Chérie knocked at her door, both wearing their overcoats.

"I'm walking Chérie home, old girl. Back in five."

"You are so funny." Chérie reached out to stroke Fiona's hair off her face. "Like a little middle-aged woman. I shall make you *chic*." Tap-tap: her lacquered red nails danced along Fiona's arm.

And then they were gone.

She rushed to look out Dad's bedroom window. The night was dark, the streetlamps like pearls. She watched them stroll together from one pool of light to the other. Dad was holding Chérie's hand as they leaned against the wind.

The wind tore through the maple trees along their street. Bright yellow leaves swirled down the middle of the road, littering the sidewalk, covering the parked cars, coating the landscape, claiming everything for their own.

***

Fiona shivered in the wintry air blowing in from the study window. Chérie had never made her *chic. It suited Chérie's purpose to keep me frumpy,* Fiona thought. After all, she was Dad's child from his first marriage and thus past history, while Chérie was the sparkling present. Many times she'd introduce Fiona to strangers as her sister. Even at age 60, she'd done it. And Dad maintained Chérie loved her. She'd fooled him all right.

Fiona slammed the window shut. *Look at Chérie now,* she thought. She could introduce her as her grandmother and no one would doubt it.

Mother's old Singer sewing machine, tucked away in its maple cabinet, rested, as it always had, under the window. Glancing down, Fiona noticed a white water stain marring its surface. Chérie's African violet houseplant was gone.

Who had removed it? Dora, of course.

What else had that sticky-fingered old bat taken? Fiona tore open the desk drawers, one by one. Nothing seemed to be missing: Dad's fountain pen and the Nazi dagger he used as a letter opener were still there. Perhaps Dora had pinched a valuable book from Dad's collection. She scanned the bookshelves, but found no gaps to indicate a missing volume. Besides, she told herself, no one bought old books anymore, especially tomes on dreary, overresearched World War II.

Damn Dora to hell! How she'd love to catch her thieving red-handed!

She eased open the study door. Down in the kitchen, Chérie was droning: *"Sur le pont d'Avignon, l'on y danse, l'on y danse..."*

She stared at Chérie's bedroom door across the hall. How long since she'd peeked inside? A year, maybe longer. Damn it, this was her house, too. It was now or never.

She slipped across the hall. A quick turn of Chérie's doorknob and she was in.

Her breath caught in her throat. The double bed was a riot of filthy sheets and laundry. Stalactites of dust and cobwebs dangled from the ceiling. And the faded blue carpet was so encrusted with dirt it seemed to be coated in kitty litter.

Oh, God, she was going to be sick.

How could Chérie live this way, she who once had been so fastidious? Fiona rubbed her nose against the stale odor. What had she hoped to find in here, treasure? Forget it!

She turned to leave. In the detritus of jewelry and used tissues littering the dresser, she spotted a white, unblemished letter. She snatched it up. The envelope was addressed to Bertie, not to his home in Oakville, but here to this address. To Hill Street.

What had her little brother been up to?

Someone had already slit open the envelope. She yanked out the single-page letter. Dated two weeks previously, it had been sent from an auction house in London, England.

"Dear Mr. White:

"My apologies in offering my condolences to you and your mother at this late date, but I only recently learned through a fellow military enthusiast of the passing of your father, Harry White.

"As you know, over the last several years I was able to assist Harry in the sale of a number of WWII military decorations and assorted memorabilia, which brings me to the secondary purpose of this letter. At long last, an interested party has approached our firm about your father's Singer.

"Might I inquire if the Singer is still in your family's possession? Given its rarity and historic value, I estimate that it should fetch a price of £50,000 or between C$85,000 and C$100,000.

"Should you and your mother, as Harry's presumptive heirs, agree to the sale, our firm would be happy to provide guidance in completing the necessary paperwork for customs, shipping and insurance.

"Sincerely yours,
"James Gibson, Auctions and Private Sales"

Singer? Surely not Mother's sewing machine. No, "the Singer" must be something else entirely. But what?

She crumpled the letter. It didn't matter what "the Singer" was. Bertie and Chérie were *cheating* her—cutting her out of her rightful share of $100,000! As Harry's oldest child, she was as much Harry's "presumptive heir" as they were.

She leaned against the bedroom door, heart racing. Three years looking after Chérie because she'd promised Dad she would. A lifetime enduring Chérie's thinly veiled insults and petty games, not to mention losing her job at the insurance company, the overdue mortgage payments on her condo and her maxed-out credit cards.

She needed that money! Where in hell was that damn Singer?

Her hands shook as she smoothed out the letter and read it through again. After retiring, Dad had become so obsessed with World War II that Chérie, with amused tolerance, named his study Harry's *L'Abri de Guerre* or Harry's War Room. At the time Fiona reasoned that Dad was trying to discover more details about his father's death at Dunkirk. But apparently that hadn't been his plan at all. No, ever practical, he'd been buying and selling the medals and memorabilia of Second World War soldiers. The clever old fox!

Why had Dad never told her about his sideline? Judging by James Gibson's letter, Chérie and Bertie knew all about it.

But when she thought back, she recalled his frequent trips to the post office and his constant complaints about mailing costs. How he'd bragged about the Nazi dagger he'd bought off an old veteran down at the Legion! And of course, his favorite dinner story—endlessly repeated—about the Hamilton woman who found a Victoria Cross while clearing out her late aunt's house, a medal worth $100,000.

So that was it! The Singer must be a war medal, a decoration worth as much as the prized Victoria Cross. Somewhere, somehow it had fallen into Dad's possession.

But why hadn't Dad mentioned the Singer in his will?

Fiona frowned. Dad hadn't mentioned it, because he didn't have to. Because Chérie already knew about the medal—and Dad's will left everything to her, the house and *all* his possessions.

163

And Bertie? Chérie must have told her little darling about the Singer like she did everything else.

Or had she?

What if Bertie wasn't aware of the Singer's existence? What if he had never read James Gibson's letter?

But someone had opened the letter, slit open the envelope ever so neatly. Not Chérie, who these days tore letters in half to open them or tossed them into the garbage unread. No, Chérie hadn't read Gibson's letter.

That left only one other person: Dora!

So that's why Dora had asked Bertie for Mother's Singer sewing machine. She needed to remove it to cover her tracks—in case Chérie blurted out to Bertie that Dora had taken "the Singer."

Old age and cunning indeed! Bertie the high-flying IT genius, outsmarted by a scheming, greedy pensioner.

But dear Dorrie had made a mistake: she hadn't destroyed James Gibson's letter. She'd placed it on the bedroom dresser where Chérie, in her distracted state, might have dropped it. By the time Bertie found and read the letter, or James Gibson wrote him again, the medal would be long gone, spirited out of the house in Dora's scruffy shopping bag.

So why was Dora still hanging around? Selling the medal would yield her more money than years spent rifling through Chérie's recycling box.

There was one staggeringly simple explanation. Fiona couldn't help smiling. Dora hadn't found it.

And Chérie could have stashed the medal anywhere. Dora must be desperate to prise the Singer's hiding place from the labyrinthine maze of Chérie's dementia. Well, the best of British luck to her!

Fiona thrust the letter into her pocket next to Chérie's money. That $800 was going to be payback for putting up with *Maman*. And the Singer medal, too. But where to start looking?

Her phone shrilled in her pocket. She yanked it out to silence it. The bank again. Damn!

What if they'd heard her phone downstairs? If they found her here in the master bedroom, Chérie would go crazy. Scratch her, strike her. The way she did last week after the washing machine incident. And what would Dora do? Cheerfully stoke Chérie's hysterics. Probably join in the attack.

She crept back out into the hall, but not quickly enough.

"What the hell's going on?" Dora stood at the bottom of the stairs, a large apron tied over her bulky wool sweater and jeans. "What do you think you're doing, snooping around in Chérie's room?"

"How dare you talk to me like that?" Fiona shouted. "This is my house, my home, you interfering old bitch."

Dora chuckled. "You see how she behaves to me, my turtle dove. And me the one that looks after you, the only one who cares."

In the kitchen, Chérie sang tunelessly: *"Sur le pont d'Avignon, l'on y danse, l'on y danse."*

Fiona started down the stairs; she mustn't show fear. "That was *Maman's* bank calling. To tell me how much money you've stolen from her down to the penny. I'm going there now."

Dora's beefy face darkened. Her thick hands curled into fists.

She's going to hurt me, she's really going to hurt me!

"Fiona?" The front door swung open. "Julian and I are waiting for you to come over." Jules, The Lad, stepped into the entryway.

"I'm up here!" Fiona's voice had faded to a squeak.

Dora uttered a snort, but she blocked Fiona's way.

"Julian's getting antsy," The Lad said, holding the front door open.

"Get out of my way, Dora!"

Dora eased her bulk to one side, leaving barely enough room for Fiona to squeeze by.

Fiona rushed outside. By the time she was standing on the front porch next to Jules, her breath was coming in gasps. Her heart pounded all the way down the stairs.

"What was that all about?" Jules asked when they reached the bottom.

"I don't know!" Fiona ran a hand through her windblown hair. "I-I think she meant to kill me."

"Oh, come on, people don't murder each other on Hill Street, sweetie. Dora's just a puffed-up old paper dragon. Don't let her scare you."

Sure, Fiona thought. "Jules, sorry, I can't do tea. *Maman's* bank called again. With everything that's happened, I forgot they wanted to see me. I have to drive up there now before they close."

She moved toward her car but hesitated. Jules used to work at Sotheby's, he knew about antiques. "Did you know that Dad was buying and selling war medals?"

"Of course I did. He bored us to death chatting about it over the garden fence." Jules waved a hand. "But war trophies are *so* not my thing. I mean, why would anyone *want* a Nazi dagger letter opener? A murder weapon for heaven's sake! I told Harry if it were up to me, I'd gather up all that old war stuff, burn it and bury the ashes."

Unless it was worth $100,000, Fiona thought. "Did Dad ever tell you about his Singer medal?"

"You mean like the sewing machine?" Jules frowned. "No, he didn't. I've never heard of a Singer medal before. Tell you what, though, Julian might know. He's the history buff in the family."

Her phone vibrated in her pocket—yet another text from the bank. Bertie had arrived for the meeting. They were waiting for her.

Bertie? What was he doing here in Hamilton?

***

Chérie's bank lay in a half-derelict shopping mall at the far end of Upper Paradise Road. Fiona churned up the snow-covered street in her Honda, not caring if she ran into the curb or even a bus. The mall's parking lot was almost deserted; the weather had driven the few remaining customers away. Plenty of empty spaces over by the entrance to Chérie's bank.

She parked next to a large white Jeep. Bertie's Jeep.

She scrambled out of her car. Bertie's prized possession sported a blue scrape along the right front fender. She bent down to examine it. The blue paint matched the colour of her Honda.

The white SUV was swerving toward her, a stealth missile through the snowstorm…not an SUV, a Jeep.

He tried to kill me! Bertie tried to kill me! He wants me to die! They all want me to die! Her legs refused to move. In the end, rage and the cold wind drove her into the mall.

***

Maxine Woods, Chérie's bank manager, was a tiny woman, her skin and hair so pale that she reminded Fiona of a wax doll. Her deep, throaty voice made such a startling contrast to her appearance that Bertie nicknamed her "The

Bride of Chuckie," a demon-doll character from a horror movie.

Fiona stumbled through the bank manager's open office door. Maxine's loud bark—"Wipe your feet!"—made her jump.

"Hello to you, too," Fiona said. She squeezed into the cramped office, slamming the door behind her. She refused to knock the snow off her boots.

Bertie was sitting in one of the two visitors' chairs opposite Maxine's desk, his thin fingers fiddling with a half-empty cup of the bank's execrable coffee. So he'd been there a while. No doubt filling Maxine's head with lies, the sneaky little shit.

"Aren't you going to say hello to me?" she asked Bertie.

A flush rose above his shirt collar, but he refused to glance at her. As usual, he looked impeccable, his fair hair combed smooth, his thin moustache perfectly trimmed. His red parka, draped over the back of his chair, probably cost more than her entire wardrobe.

She crashed down into the empty visitor's chair, zipping open her worn down coat. "I had to make sure *Maman* was all right, that's why I'm late. Because Dora brought her here to the bank, then let her wander off alone. To get lost in this blizzard, in her pajamas!"

"That's ridiculous!" Bertie said.

"It's true! Ask the two Julies," Fiona shot back.

"Excuse me." Maxine cleared her throat. She looked like a child in the large leather chair behind her desk. "Your sister's right, Mr. White. Your mother did visit our branch this morning with another woman." She checked the sticky note on the folder in front of her. "A Mrs. Dora Mason."

"Yes, yes," Bertie said. "Dora looks after my mother."

"I look after *Maman*," Fiona put in.

"Be that as it may," Maxine said. "Mrs. White was unhappy when we wouldn't increase her $500 ATM limit. She then tried to cash a cheque for a large amount of money."

"How...how much did she want?" Fiona asked.

"Ten thousand dollars." In the ensuing silence, Maxine asked: "Is there a reason your mother requires this much cash?"

"Absolutely not!" Fiona said.

Bertie said nothing, but his flush deepened.

"The teller tried to explain to her that we don't keep this much cash on hand. Besides, she noticed a problem." Maxine drew a cheque from the folder in front of her and turned it so that Fiona and Bertie could read it. "This is not your mother's signature."

The signature bore no resemblance to Chérie's tremulous scrawl. It was a rounded hand, the loops of the letters executed with flourish.

"Dora signed that," Fiona said. "She forged *Maman's* signature. Admit that, Bertie!"

Bertie shrugged his shoulders in reply.

"Well, not exactly," Maxine said. "Dora Mason presented us with this document." She pulled a legal-looking form from her folder. "It appears to grant Power of Attorney, or POA, to Mrs. Mason—and to you, Mr. White."

Fiona could not breathe. She recognized the broad strokes of Bertie's signature and sure enough, the loopy signature belonged to Dora Mason. But in the space for her signature, Chérie had only made a spidery X.

"That's a forgery," Fiona said. "Bertie and I have joint POA for *Maman*."

Maxine wrinkled her forehead. "This would appear to supersede your joint POA. It was drawn up by the legal firm here at the mall. Yesterday, as a matter of fact."

"But *Maman* didn't sign it. She just made an *X*," Fiona said.

"Her mark was witnessed at the lawyer's office. See here." Maxine held out the document and pointed to two signatures beside the *X*, neither of them familiar.

"I-I don't understand," Fiona began.

"Frankly, neither do I. Is that your signature, Mr. White?" Maxine asked.

"Well, I…well, it's for the best." Bertie's words poured out in a rush. "Mrs. Mason is a close friend of my mother's. She lives nearby, she's devoted to *Maman*. Fiona lives in Toronto. It's too far away."

"But I'm family," Fiona cried. "I'm your sister."

Bertie turned on her. "You are not my sister!"

"What do you mean I'm not your sister? Dad, Harry, was our father!"

"Mr. White?" Maxine was staring at Bertie. "Is Fiona your sister or not?"

A small muscle in his jaw twitched, a sign he was cornered.

"My half sister, then." He looked furious.

"Whatever problems you and your half sister have between you, I must ask you to reconsider this POA," Maxine said. "Your mother is clearly not in her right mind. And Mrs. Mason was very aggressive with my staff demanding the $10,000. I question whether she has your mother's best interests at heart."

"How dare you!" Bertie said. "That POA is legal. It's what I want and what *Maman* wants. You don't have a choice. You challenge me and I'll go over your head. I'm personal friends with your vice president. I'll have you fired."

He scrambled out of his seat and tore his parka off the back of the chair. He tripped over Fiona's feet in his haste to get out of Maxine's office.

Fiona stood up. "You can't let him get away with this."

"I'm sorry, there's nothing I can do. The POA appears to be legal," Maxine said. "Of course, you could always challenge it in court."

"I don't have money for lawyers!"

Maxine stood up. "Then my hands are tied. I truly am sorry, Fiona."

Fiona tore out of Maxine's office. She caught up with Bertie in the tiled corridor between the bank and the exit to the parking lot.

"You conniving little toad!" she screamed.

He kept moving, but she grabbed his parka hood and hung on. She'd always been bigger and stronger than he was, and now she had the advantage of surprise.

"Let go of me!" He wrenched himself free. She threw herself in front of him. "Get out of my way."

"You tried to kill me on the highway. You rammed my car."

"Serendipity driving here." He smiled. "An opportunity."

She hit him. His face felt meaty under her fist. His mouth made a perfect *O* of surprise.

She felt glorious. She hit him again, a heavy slap across the cheek that echoed through the deserted hallway.

He caught her wrist before she could hit him a third time. His strength surprised her.

"You foul monster," he said. "Screech and beat on me all you want. Nothing you can do will stop me. Nothing!"

"Just watch me!"

He shoved her away. "You've always had an inflated ego. Just look at you, a frumpy nobody like *Maman* always said. You can't hang on to a job or a husband. You're such a loser."

"And you're a pussy." She crashed into him with her full body weight. He staggered back against the tiled wall. "Driving around in that honking big Jeep to prove you're a macho man. You're nothing but a tiny swinging dick. Like that." She held up the tip of her little finger.

Bertie straightened his coat. "Fuck you, Fiona."

She turned and ran for the exit doors. Slipping and sliding on the snow-covered pavement outside, she rushed over to her car. Her heart hammered as she waited for the wipers to beat the snow off her windshield.

Bertie was coming out of the mall.

She reversed madly, not caring if anything or anyone stood behind her. For a mad moment, she wanted to ram Bertie's Jeep, slam into it again and again, until it collapsed in a heap of bolts and twisted metal.

But self-preservation took over. She revved out of the parking lot and skidded onto Upper Paradise. An atavistic instinct propelled her back to Hill Street.

How could she have been so stupid? Obviously Bertie and Dora had been colluding for months. When Dora had asked for the Singer sewing machine, she hadn't meant to mislead Bertie, but her, Fiona.

Chérie was overdue for the nursing home. Bertie didn't need her, Fiona and her free labor, anymore. He wanted to be rid of her. To grab everything for himself. And for money, Dora had been his willing tool.

Fiona pulled up in front of the house. Dora's truck was still in the driveway. Bertie would only be seconds behind her.

She gripped the steering wheel, her mind reeling. How could she fight the three of them?

A rap on the passenger window made her cry out. But the dark shape wasn't Dora or Bertie, but Julian.

"Are you quite all right?" he asked as she struggled out of her car. Snow dotted his scarf and tweed overcoat.

"No! No, I'm not all right." She swallowed. "There were problems at the bank. Big problems."

Julian looked troubled. "Look here, Fiona. I don't want to add to your burden, but this is vitally important. The Lad told me you're looking for your father's Singer."

"Yes, yes, the Singer." She wished Julian would go away. She needed to get back in the house. Protect what was hers.

"I thought he sold the bloody thing years ago. I told him he mustn't store it at home, but he was so damn proud of it. The find of a lifetime, he told me. Singer only manufactured 500 of them during World War II."

Fiona blinked. "Singer only made 500 medals?"

"No, my dear girl, you misunderstand. The Singer isn't a medal. The Singer is a gun."

"A-a gun," Fiona echoed.

"Yes, the U.S. army believed that sewing machine companies could easily convert their operations to manufacture handguns. They commissioned Singer to design a.45 calibre pistol. Singer came up with the Model 1911A1, a remarkable prototype, but for various reasons, it never went into production. A piece of history to be sure, but still a gun and therefore dangerous. You do see my concern."

"I-I've never seen a gun in the house."

"Good, very good. If you do find it, call the police immediately. Promise me you'll do that, Fiona."

Fiona nodded. Her body had gone numb.

She left Julian standing on the driveway, staggered up the ice-covered stairs, unlocked the front door and let herself in.

The house was in motion. Chérie was flitting about the living room, tossing newspapers in the air, chanting: "She took it. She stole from me."

Dora stood in front of the dining room table, her broad back to Fiona. She was stuffing a large and heavy object into her shopping bag.

She's stealing Sir Peter Tacky-Bunny! He's mine!

Fiona charged into the living room. Chérie barred her way, arms flapping. Fiona grabbed the old woman's hideous cardigan and tossed her aside like a rag doll. Saw her twirl and fall. Stumble over Dad's easy chair.

A loud crack as her head hit the stone fireplace.

Dora turned toward them, her back to the dining room table, the rabbit tureen clutched in her thick arms. The gleam in her black eyes was not fear, but triumph. "I saw that, as God's my witness. You assaulted your mum. You're going to jail, and I, for one, will be singing hallelujah."

Fiona flew at Dora, fingers grappling for that fleshy throat. But though old, Dora possessed a brute strength. She crashed the tureen into Fiona's side, making her cry out in pain.

But fury burned away agony. Fiona struggled to get a grip on her precious rabbit, her hands slipping on the ceramic. For a moment, they wrestled in an absurd tug-of-war. And then the bottom of the tureen fell free and shattered against the stone fireplace.

The noise was like an explosion. For a moment, they paused in shock. There, in the violet, sharp-edged fragments, lay a dark shape.

The gun, the Singer.

Fiona snatched it up.

Dora's fingers gripped the rabbit lid. She heaved it at Fiona's head. In slow motion, the rabbit sailed serenely toward her, glancing off her shoulder, banging into her chin.

An ear-shattering blast. The room was full of blue smoke. And snowflakes. Big, puffy snowflakes.

Not snow, but feathers. Spilling from the huge hole in Dora's down coat.

Dora toppled to the ground. Blood puddled in the hole, like ice melting in spring. She lay there gasping, her eyes full of disbelief.

"You didn't know it was loaded, did you?" Fiona stared down at her. "Neither did I. Lucky me."

She watched the light in Dora's eyes fade and die.

Behind her, Chérie moaned. She tried to sit up. Blood poured down the back of her neck. Fiona went over to her, gun in hand.

"What's happening?" Chérie's voice was plaintive. "What was that noise?"

"Shut up!"

"Where is Dorrie?" She began to whimper, plucking at her sweater.

"SHUT UP!"

A bright set of headlights arced through the window. Fiona watched Bertie's Jeep pull up and park on the street.

She sat down heavily on the edge of the fireplace. She grabbed Chérie by her cardigan and dragged her over so that the old woman sat, flopped over, between her knees. They both faced the entryway.

175

"Why are you shouting? Where is Dorrie?" Chérie whined.

"She's dead. Because you killed her, you stupid, horrid old witch. You grabbed Dad's gun. Because your brain is mush, you fussed with it. It went off and killed your Turtle Dove." She forced Chérie's thin hands onto the pistol grip. "I tried to get the gun away from you. You fell and hit your head."

Chérie moaned and struggled, but Fiona clamped her frail hands to the gun. "What are we doing? What are we doing?"

Fiona felt her heart grow cold as the stone beneath her. "Why, *Maman*, we're going to sing. Come along now. *Sur le pont d'Avignon, l'on y danse, l'on y danse.*"

"I don't want to sing." Chérie's eyes were wide with terror.

"You ARE going to sing." Fiona heard Bertie swear as he slipped on the steps. The front door creaked open.

"*Maman*? What the hell's going on?"

"Sing, damn it!"

"*Non, non.*"

"*Oui, oui. Sur le pont d'Avignon, l'on y danse, l'on y danse.*"

Bertie came into the living room. His face went pale with shock.

"Now we're going to shoot your precious Bertie. Straight through the heart."

She squeezed Chérie's finger on the trigger.

THE BEETHOVEN DISASTER

By Rosemary Aubert

To be successful in any endeavor, you have to do three key things: You have to focus. You have to make sure that the person or people you are working with are 100% reliable. And you have to stick to what you yourself know best.

If I had not forgotten these things, I would not be incarcerated today.

It started when I was six and in the first grade. It was art class, and the teacher told me that being an artist of any sort meant that you got an idea and used that idea to make something that other people would want to experience.

Well, that was okay. And I knew how to make things. What I didn't have was any idea of what to make.

So I watched the other kids, and I saw that they had lots of ideas. I soon realized that all I had to do to work on my project was to copy one of theirs.

I decided on a portrait of a puppy. There were 20 kids in our class. I was pretty sure that meant quite a number of puppy pictures. I just kept my eye out for the one I needed—big enough to see all the details clearly, but little enough to not take up too much paper, crayon or time.

I hit it lucky. I saw that there were a lot of kids who didn't seem satisfied with their early attempts. They kept drawing picture after picture until they got it right. And the versions of their masterpieces that they rejected got thrown out one way or another—crumpled up in the garbage, lying underfoot on the floor, even just abandoned in little piles on their desks.

All I had to do was to take one.

I had lots of crayons and pencils, and even a paint box. My mother had given me these nice things in the hope that they would encourage me to work on my school art projects.

Well, they did. I carefully traced the best puppy picture I found in the garbage. I made sure that I didn't miss any detail. The picture showed that the puppy had a nice furry coat with spots. He had black eyes and what looked like a swishy tail. I didn't know why anyone would throw away such a nice picture, but someone had. As I wrote my own name in the corner, I thought that if anybody said anything about the picture maybe not really being by me, I would say that yes it was and anybody who said differently was just a liar.

Never happened. The teacher gave me an A for the assignment. And when I brought the picture home, my mother said that she had always known that I could do good drawings and that as a reward, she was going to give me more advanced art supplies: paint in tubes and brushes and even a palette.

Well, it didn't take me long to master the use of these items. At first, everything I did was what today would be labelled abstract. I enjoyed working with the paints— dabbing them onto the palette in what I learned was a certain prescribed order every time, mixing them to make new colors. But when it came to using them to make an actual picture of something, I was stumped.

Then I had the good luck of going to the public library one day and discovering the art section.

It was many years before I was good enough to make my first copy. It was a Mondrian. Lots of colored squares and black lines. Easy. And what made it even better was the fact that my mother's sister, my aunt, told me that she loved the painting and wanted to buy it. She offered me $10.

I was on my way. I copied more complex modern paintings: Chagall, Picasso. My mother and her friends and relatives found them amazingly well done and very charming. Before too long, I had a little business going. The fact that nothing I sold was ever really "by" me, didn't seem to bother anybody, least of all me.

"You should really go to art school," a lot of people said, and one day I decided they were right.

I suppose you could say that art school was where I discovered my "true self" as an artist. Because there, my awkward abstracts were somehow considered innovative, and I also learned how important it was to be pleasant and persuasive if you're trying to convince someone of something. Like when I convinced my teachers and my fellow students that I could do a traditional painting if I wanted to, but preferred to experiment, to reveal myself in my art.

Of course at art school, I got a couple of years of experience at learning to identify the techniques and materials that various artists used. In class, I carefully did all the technical exercises until I could pretty much get any effect I wanted. At night, I studied books that were full of pictures of the paintings of the masters. I was always trying to figure out how they could make a picture look so real.

I seemed to do fine in art school. My abstracts were accepted for assignments and appeared in the annual art show every year, often selling—to my amazement—to strangers.

But every time I had to do an exercise or an assignment that depended on a realistic picture of an actual person or object, I failed.

Until luck seemed to give gave me an answer to my problem.

The Art College decided that to be "responsible citizens," it wasn't enough just to work on our own projects. A committee was set up to recommend things we could all do to "help" our brothers and sisters in the community. I got chosen to be a mentor to a boy who was only a little younger than me, but who had already been in trouble with the police and had already spent time in detention. When the teachers there had been handing out assignments around the city for students, this boy got picked to take night courses at the Art College. "He's always drawing something," his parole officer said.

And for some reason, it seemed natural to my own teacher to assign him to me. "You are a good, diligent worker with excellent technical skills," the teacher told me. "You can share your knowledge."

At first, I was a little afraid of being assigned a student who had, as I understood it, already spent time in jail. But I had no choice. Besides, who was I to look down on a fellow "artist" when I had spent pretty much my whole life copying the work of other people and pretending it was my own?

I showed him how to copy pictures. I explained to him that a successful copy (I never used the word *forgery*.

Not then. Not ever.) had to be the same, but different. I also showed him how the changes he was making in the copies had to be consistent so that every copy that purported to be a picture done by me, for example, had to have certain characteristics, certain consistencies that marked the painting as "mine."

With his skill and his dedication, I graduated from Art College with the highest honors, with a gallery eager to represent me and with the offer of a teaching position at the art school.

Of course, I had to turn down the teaching position. But my "assistant" and I put together a gallery show that brought in several thousand dollars which we split 50-50.

Those were the beginning years of my life as a realist painter. First, works "by" me and before too long, undiscovered works by artists far more famous. Until, between the two of us, we learned how to fake everything: the special pigments of every age whose works we "duplicated," the paper, canvas, board, linen. Between us, we learned about provenance—the history of a work, usually the history of its ownership.

We figured out how to copy signatures with total accuracy and when we couldn't copy one, we created it.

If it bothered me that we were liars and thieves, I suppressed the thought, and my assistant was always eager to look upon us as top-notch artists in our own right rather than as defilers and deceivers.

So it all went well, financially and reputationwise, until the day the assistant convinced me that it was time that, as he put it, we should "branch out." That was the day he precipitated the Beethoven Disaster.

And because I let myself forget my three principles, our fate was my fault.

"Manuscripts," he said to me one day as we sat in our studio discussing whose work was currently marketable enough and currently obscure enough with reference to its history that we could work on it safely and profitably.

"What are you talking about? What manuscripts?" I had just read a fascinating account of the long and complicated provenance of the Voynich manuscript, an illustrated work purportedly from the 16th century that some considered a complex and beautiful fraud. Whether it was real or fake, the manuscript had to have taken years to construct and had never been proven real or fake. Eventually, it landed in a university library, whether as a donation or a purchase, I didn't know, but I could easily see that all the trouble it had taken some real or imaginary person to create it could not have netted the profit all that work deserved.

"The easiest, I think," the assistant answered, "would be music."

I stared at him in wonderment. We had a good operation going. We had now worked together for years. We knew exactly how to create "lost" works by old famous artists, by recently deceased modern artists, by promising but never-before-seen artists. Why in heaven's name should we be changing our product? I knew it always bothered the assistant when I referred to our works as products. But clearly they were, and like all successful products they had a market that it would be totally foolish to meddle with.

"What do we know about manuscripts?" I asked him, trying to control my frustration. "Why should we switch to something we know nothing about when we've been so successful at things we are experts at?"

He was strangely silent. He had always been an enthusiastic partner in everything we had done, so his sudden reticence struck me as odd—even as dangerous.

"Well," he finally said, "I think we have to be a bit more careful than we've been."

"Why?"

"The market's a bit—I don't know—sensitive at the moment."

I should have listened. I should have taken this as a warning. Though he had been my "assistant" over the years, he had often demonstrated that he knew more than me in some areas, areas having to do not with the production of artworks per se, but with sales and making contacts and establishing the fake history of every piece that we had produced.

"Is someone on to us?" I asked with alarm.

His answer made perfect sense. "We've been at this for five years," he said. "In that time, we've 'discovered' just as many 'masterpieces' of art. Sooner or later, it's going to occur to someone that our record is too high to be accidental. Too high, period. The time to quit is now before anyone questions us. I think we should consider music."

"Music? What do we know about music?"

"Only that a historic manuscript is no different from a painting. Lines and circles and curves and dots. Here," he said, "take a look at this…"

I didn't wonder about his having "proof" of his theory. He always had some object, some document handy to prove his point. It was, after all, an important part of his "trade" to prove things just in case somebody thought of questioning him.

What he showed me on his phone was a web page from a site about Beethoven. It depicted several pages of music manuscripts written at different times in the composer's career. There was quite a difference in the appearance of the works over time. I could see at once that anyone attempting to forge a music manuscript, especially one by a famous composer, would have to have quite a precise and accurate knowledge of each stage of that composer's musical trajectory over exact periods of time.

"We don't know anything about music," I repeated. "At least, I don't."

"We don't have to know anything about music. Look, look at these pictures I got off the Internet."

He moved to my computer and pressed a few keys. Within seconds, he handed me a paper copy of part of a musical score for a study that Beethoven had written in his later years. Of course, the master himself had never heard the notes written there. Perhaps no one had. A lost bit of paper like this had surely never been "performed," though it was impossible to think that no one had ever "tried it out."

The online photo was remarkably clear. I could see at once how it could be copied by hand on the right paper in just a matter of hours. I could also see how lucrative it might be for a skilled forger to produce what were basically scraps of paper and small splashes of ink and then "dispose" of them for hundreds of thousands of dollars.

"There is one big problem, though," my assistant admitted. He was never the type to declare a challenge without also declaring that he knew of a viable solution.

"What?"

"Paper."

"What?"

"It's just the same as canvas or board or linen. We have to have the exact paper for the exact date of Beethoven's execution of whatever we decide to copy."

"Really? And just how are we going to get that?"

"The same way that we are going to get the right ink. The same way that we are going to age the ink. The same way that we are going to get the information necessary to have every square centimeter of our little piece of Beethoven 100% authentic." He stopped and stayed silent for a moment. "The same way," he said, "that we have done our work every single time."

I was unconvinced, but I had worked with him now for several years and I was aware that he always knew what he was talking about. Had I not been thoroughly convinced of that at all times, I would never have been able to work with him, not only in the techniques he shared with me in creating the "copied" pictures, but in creating their provenance as well.

"Leave it with me," he said, and he disappeared, as he had often disappeared for weeks, even months, to bury himself in the arcane research necessary for our craft.

Three weeks later, he showed up at our studio unannounced and carrying one of the countless portfolios he possessed. This one was new, simple, slim, shiny leather with a small handle and a closure that was a snap rather than the zipper that sealed his larger portfolios. I knew the minute I saw it that it contained things I'd not seen him toting around before.

"What's this?"

"What we need—for a start…"

He pushed aside some papers and a coffee cup on my desk and opened his little portfolio. He carefully extracted a paper envelope the size of a letter. I stood over his shoulder, overcome by curiosity, but pretty certain that I knew what was inside the pristine envelope.

I wasn't at all surprised when he reached inside a pocket in the portfolio and pulled out a pair of plastic gloves, like those worn by a nurse or a dentist. He also had a plastic sheet in the pocket and he carefully unfolded it so that whatever he was about to take out of that envelope would not touch anything on the desk.

I had figured out what I was about to see. What I had not figured out was how he had gotten what he was about to show me. I almost held my breath as he tipped the envelope and allowed its contents to spill out onto the sheet.

There were at least 10 pieces of fragile, stained, sometimes water-damaged paper, identifiable instantly as something very old, very rare.

Each piece of paper was worn and sometimes ragged on the edge of one side. But in every case, the edge on the opposite side was smooth and clean. I knew at once this meant that we had crossed a line, that we were in immediate danger of being caught, not only for our preliminary preparations to fabricate a Beethoven manuscript, but also for all the work we'd done over the years.

"How could you do this? How could you be so careless? Do you realize what you've done?"

He shrugged as if the crime he had committed was no big deal.

"You've been at the music library these past weeks, haven't you?" I demanded to know, though the answer was clear. "You've been cutting up manuscripts. You've been defacing precious documents to get paper for the Beethoven project."

He would possibly have answered, I suppose. But it was too late. It was already too late.

He turned abruptly toward the door. He tried to scoop up his collection of stolen paper pieces. But his hands were shaking, and there was nowhere to hide them or himself. And nowhere for me to hide, either.

The footsteps on the stairs were heavy, determined— as determined as the slam of the door to the studio, as determined as the cops who handcuffed us both, who pushed us down the stairs into the two waiting cruisers.

It's too long and disturbing a tale to tell again after all the times we had to tell it to lawyers, to judges, to art dealers and museums and even to universities.

Too disturbing to admit to ourselves—and I suppose to each other, had we ever spoken again—was that we had been thieves for a long time, that what we had stolen—the ideas, the execution—had been precious until we got our hands on them and ruined their meaning, their pristine refinement, their unique existence.

Of course, being the kind of criminals we were, we never damaged real art, never damaged anything real until the Beethoven disaster.

We got long sentences, and the day the judge handed them down was the last day we ever saw each other.

Now, in the solitude of my incarceration, having been found guilty of a nonviolent offence, being an aging man, I am separated from real criminals. Ironically, I have been chosen to work in the prison library.

It doesn't matter that there is nothing worth copying—or even reading, actually. The only thing I've ever used is the collection of vintage recordings. Once in a while, I listen to a little piece by Beethoven—a sonatina, a bagatelle.

As I listen, I can almost see the notes on the page. Dots, swirls, neat lines and sometimes crooked lines, written as though in a hurry.

Ideas. Someone else's ideas made mine for a moment in time.

For unending moments in time.

HER PERFUME

By Marilyn Kay

Despite the bright August sun, a chill wind swept through the ruined castle's grounds and ruffled Julie's chestnut hair. Shivering, she hugged her denim jacket close and moved next to the low stone wall rimming the promontory's brink. There, she drank in the panorama of the silty brown river snaking its way through the Wye Valley. For a moment, Julie let her imagination soar, spinning a scene of Earl Roger and his lady wife tipping wine goblets to their lips while looking out over the river from their private balcony.

Before long, though, Julie's thoughts strayed back to Dima. Today was the six-month anniversary of her husband's death. For a brief year, she, a diplomat's daughter, and he, a dashing young attaché, had dazzled London's social scene. Her heart cried out: *Oh my love, we had so little time together.* They had not even allowed her to mourn at his grave. Instead, they whisked her away from London to this small Welsh town of Chepstow. They said she had to hide farther afield and fast, especially after what had happened in Salisbury. Wales would be safer. Even with the tourist lure of a Norman castle, no one would think of searching for her here.

The muffled tapping of rubber-soled shoes on the stairs behind her interrupted her grief. Julie lifted her sunglasses and wiped at a wayward tear trailing down her cheek. A tall, wiry blond man in jeans and a navy hoodie came to a halt at the far side of the parapet. She watched him contemplate the sky, the river and the surrounding countryside. After a while, he took his iPhone from his hoodie pouch and proceeded to photograph the view from different angles. Once he'd finished, he turned to her and in an American accent said, "Quite a view, wouldn't you say?"

She bobbed her head. "Yes."

He plucked a daisy-like pink flower from the ivy on the wall. Raising his shades to reveal a puckish twinkle in his blue eyes, he sniffed the flower and twirled it between thumb and forefinger before presenting it to her with a bow. "My Lady."

Charmed, she mimed "For me?" and laughed. Accepting the flower, she pretended to lift a voluminous skirt, placed her right foot behind her left and curtsied. "Thank you, Sir Knight." She sniffed the flower before tucking the stem into a buttonhole in her jacket.

Smiling coyly, she turned on her heel and descended the stairs to admire the vaulted ceiling of the wine cellar. From there, she could hear his trainers pattering up the steps. Then the sound stopped. He must have wandered onto the grass and over to Marten's Tower. She went back upstairs to loiter in the kitchen and other service rooms within the remnants of the building known as the earl's Gloriette, and then meandered into the Middle Bailey area to see if their paths might cross again.

He happened on her while she was snapping a photo of the exterior of the Great Tower. Julie perched her sunglasses atop her head and flicked her hair over her shoulder. "Ah, we meet again, Sir Knight."

He bowed and gestured forward. "Shall we explore the tower together, My Lady?"

"I don't even know your name."

"Gareth. Gareth Evans." He put his hand on his heart. "I am but a lonely errant knight who has crossed a continent and an ocean on my quest to discover this fair 'Land of My Fathers.'"

She half smiled at his allusions to knights errant and to the Welsh national anthem "Hen Wlad fy Nhadau." He was definitely trying. If she were honest with herself, maybe she was, too.

"How about you? You sound like you're neither from the mountains of Snowdonia—" Gareth assumed the sonorous tones of North Wales, pitching his voice in an exaggerated singsong "—nor from the green *vallees* of the south."

She skipped a beat before answering him. "I'm Julie. And Monmouthshire is quite…Anglo-Welsh."

"I see. I…didn't mean to cause you offense."

"I'm not offended. Come on. I'll give you a tour of the Great Tower and the rest of the castle. It'll give me practice for my class's history field trip next week. How long have you been in Wales?"

"Going on three weeks. I'm doing the castle circuit, with a bit of hiking and other sightseeing thrown in." He winked, but made no effort to get closer.

Julie soon found Gareth eagerly immersed in the history and architectural and sculptural details of the castle—almost as much as she was. What's more, he was a fun companion, with no ring on his left finger and California surfer-guy looks as an added bonus.

***

"I should've had you for the whole circuit. I've learned more from you than from all the guidebooks and apps I've tried at the other castles. Thanks, Julie, for giving me so much of your time." Gareth checked his phone. "It's nearly six. They'll be kicking us out soon. What say I buy you an early dinner to give you a proper thank-you? Or would you rather go home and I pick you up later for dinner? There's got to be a nice place to eat in town."

Julie considered his offer. She hadn't had such a lovely afternoon since Dima's death. "There's the Riverside Wine Bar. That's pretty good. Are you staying in a B and B, or at the Two Rivers?"

"I got a deal with the B and B across from the castle. It's quaint, but only serves breakfast and Sunday roast. You got your car here?"

"No, I walked. I just live on the hill south of the castle off Welsh Street, the road which borders the Castle Dell." She still hesitated.

"Look, my car is in the lot. Why don't I run you up to your place and pick you up at around 7:30? That'll give us both time to change into something other than jeans and a T-shirt. What do you say?" He flipped through his phone. "I can make a reservation at the Riverside Wine Bar. For one or two people?"

She breathed in, exhaled and nodded. "Two, please."

***

Julie stepped out of the shower, refreshed and tingling. Other than with a few mates she'd met at her gym classes, she hadn't gone out on a date for six months. She clicked on Rag'n'Bone Man's "Perfume" from her Spotify playlist and proceeded to get ready.

Eschewing her usual light citrusy Jo Malone scent, she spritzed Dima's favorite, Dior's sexy Pure Poison, on her collarbone, in the crook of her elbows and behind her knees and ears, letting some of the spray fall on her hair.

Rummaging through her clothes, she grabbed a lacy, black knit bodycon dress, pulled it on and admired her silhouette. Nope. Far too forward and too London.

After trying on several other outfits, she opted for a floral skater, one she'd bought at Ted Baker for a silly flower-themed hen party last year.

As she buckled the dress's skinny belt around her slim waist, a sharp yearning for friends and her old life engulfed her. Did they miss her as she missed them? Did they ever wonder about her? Or were they too lost in London's rush to care? She hugged herself, trying to squeeze all the pain into a small ball deep inside her.

***

A frisson of delight rippled down her skin when she opened the door. Gareth appeared decked out in a blue-and-white checked shirt, khaki chinos, navy blazer and chocolate-brown leather loafers. His widened eyes and huge grin told her that she'd made an impression on him.

As they drove through the arch of the crenelated tower of the medieval town gate on High Street, Julie counted her breaths in an effort to calm the quickened pulsing of her heart. Excitement like that wasn't supposed to happen when you were still in mourning.

When they swung into Middle Street, Julie sensed a certain nervousness about Gareth, too, and wondered if he was also feeling the buzz. Or maybe he was stressed by the haphazard parking of cars on this narrow single-lane street.

"It's tricky getting to the restaurant all the way by car," she said. "We're better off using the Castle Dell car park. Besides, it's only a short walk down to the Old Wye Bridge."

Gareth relaxed. "My car seems to spend more time in that lot than on the road. Good thing parking is free there."

As they sauntered toward the river, Gareth suddenly grasped Julie's arm and guided her through a gate leading to another restaurant.

She tried to back away. "No. This is the wrong place!"

His grip on her arm tightened; his voice was low. "Be quiet and keep walking." He swung open the door and pushed her and himself inside.

"What are you doing?" She shook her arm from his grasp.

He held a finger to his lips. "Wait."

The heady aroma of Italian herbs and garlic wafted around Julie, whetting her appetite and her fear. She hunched in the corner, her heart pounding while cold perspiration dripped down her neck. A young couple came through the open doorway and walked past them. Gareth peered out the window. "Okay, we can go now."

"What was that all about?"

"Sorry. Some nasty people I met along the way I'd rather not encounter again."

Julie rubbed her arm.

"I didn't hurt you, did I? Shit! I did. I'm so sorry."

"I'll survive." He had seemed like such a nice guy. Now she wasn't so sure. "Who were they?"

"Two English guys who tried to run me off the road in Snowdonia. I encountered them in a pub where they were harassing a young lady. I bought her a beer and told them to piss off. I didn't think I'd ever see them again, but there they were poking around that building yard. Satisfied?" He glanced at his Apple Watch. "Hey! We've got a reservation for quarter to eight. You lead the way."

Julie strode down the street without glancing back. She was already berating herself for crumpling in fear. Where were those lightning reflexes she had cultivated for the past six months at the mixed martial arts gym? Why had she let him take command of her, when she had worked so hard to empower herself?

He let her take off by herself, only walking beside her when they reached the bridge. They stood together, but not touching, to admire the limestone cliffs and the Regency cast-iron bridge.

Across the river perched the Gloucestershire village of Tutshill, where J. K. Rowling had lived from the age of nine to 18. Tutshill was also the location of the school where Julie would begin her teaching career on Monday.

On the Chepstow side, a tree-lined groomed path ran along the river where several boats were moored.

The wine bar's willow trees shaded a row of picnic tables, each mounted with an umbrella. Set back from the tables was a white stuccoed, two-storey building housing the restaurant.

Inside was an eclectic mix of red and white walls, curtains and floral wallpaper. Dark wood tables and chairs filled the restaurant seating area, while the bar boasted leather settees and barrel chairs.

"It's kind of warm and homely, wouldn't you say?"

Gareth turned to Julie and grinned. "Did you say *homely* or *homey*?"

Julie grimaced at Gareth's try at a witticism.

"Okay. It seems, uh, funky. Like a place for real fusion cooking."

"Well, it's British meets Spanish. I hope you'll like it."

"I can already taste the garlic and chorizo. Of course, I'll like it."

Julie noticed Gareth's raised eyebrow to the waiter as they were escorted to a romantic table for two with a view of the river. "Did you especially arrange for this table?"

He winked and began perusing the wine list. "Hmm, only one California wine and it's sweet. Would you like to choose the wine? I'm having the steak."

"I want the prawns. How about we get a bottle of Prosecco?"

"Prosecco? There's champagne on the list. Why don't we go all out and order a bottle?"

"You sure?"

"Of course. I think I saw a Bollinger on the list."

As they leisurely sipped and chewed their way through the feast, conviviality replaced the evening's earlier tension. Gareth gave up trying to tease Julie into talking more about herself and regaled her with tales of his travels. His story about using his iPhone GPS for hiking and nearly getting lost in a bog outside of Tregaron made her clutch the table to keep from laughing hysterically.

"There was no cell coverage. Just me, the rain and the sheep," he deadpanned. "I was soaked to the bone, squelching in shoes that were getting sucked downward with every step I took. Eventually, I heard a whistle and madly whistled back. Next thing I knew, a black-and-white collie was herding me and the sheep to greener pastures. The farmer took me to his home."

Gareth locked eyes with Julie before continuing his saga, "Then, over tea and Welsh cakes, I got the third degree about my family origins. Only after he and his wife were satisfied they'd wrung every bit of family history from me and fed me dinner, did he drive me back to my car....I haven't shared that episode on Facebook yet."

They both broke out laughing.

"So what do you do when you're not tilting at white dragons or getting lost in a bog?" Julie asked.

Gareth raised questioning eyebrows before grinning like a Cheshire cat. "I work at Facebook."

Her voice tart, she said, "At least you don't bite the hand that feeds you."

"That was a low blow."

"Sorry. I didn't mean to be—"

"Catty?"

Julie's face grew hot. She sat up straight, arms crossed in front of her chest and glared.

Gareth licked his lower lip and closed his eyes. When he opened them, they were wide and glistening. "Look, I know Facebook has gotten a bad rap lately. I'm not saying it doesn't deserve it. But I wasn't part of the Cambridge Analytica fiasco, fake news or Russian hacking."

Julie flinched at the word *Russian*.

"I work in the user experience area. You know—live videos, emoticons, birthdays, fun backgrounds for posts—things like that."

Gareth searched her eyes. "You're not on Facebook, are you?"

She shook her head. "No. As a teacher, I…I…don't want my students stalking me."

Gareth tucked his chin into his hand and rocked his body slightly. "I figured as much." He picked up the second bottle of champagne and gestured toward Julie's glass. "Shall we finish it?"

Julie dropped her arms and dipped her chin to indicate yes.

He apportioned the remains between the two glasses and lifted his up to her. She took a sip, and he did the same. They each took another sip in silence, his eyes penetrating into the depths of her soul. Then he leaned over and reached out his hand to her. She clasped his.

The waiter interrupted their mute colloquy to offer them dessert. Neither was interested. Neither wanted to break the spell.

Once the waiter had left to tally up the bill, Gareth asked, "Care for a stroll by the river?"

"I think I'd better get back home."

***

At the door to her semidetached house in The Mount gated community, Julie surprised herself by asking Gareth in for coffee. They never got to the coffee. Gareth's kisses softened Julie's stiffened lips, and his caresses were like warm water lapping over and into every crevice of her body. Like everything he'd done that day, he did it with care, sensing when to relinquish to her the lead in their lovemaking. They fell asleep locked in each other's arms.

Sometime after midnight, she shifted onto her other side. But when her arm stretched back to touch him, her hand landed on an empty duvet. Had it all been a dream? She lay there alone, listening for his movements, too afraid to open her eyes to emptiness, too crushed that he hadn't wanted to stay the night with her. As she began to doze off, Gareth slid back into bed. He buried his head in her hair and nibbled her ear, cooing, "Your perfume is driving me wild."

The next morning over a breakfast of poached eggs on toast with tomatoes and mushrooms, Julie asked Gareth, "Where were you last night?"

He sucked in his lips and, with narrowed eyes, considered her and his words. Then, tapping the table, he said, "Sorry. I didn't want to worry you. I heard strange noises around your house and went to investigate. I didn't find anything, though. I guess those two guys spooked me last night…. You want to go to Tintern with me today?"

Julie considered. Today was Wednesday. Her lesson plans were completed; she'd still have plenty of time to prepare her classroom for Monday. Besides, she couldn't bear the thought of never seeing him again. "I've got a gym class at eleven. Maybe we could go after lunch?"

"There's that coffee-and-sandwich place, Coffee Something? We could meet there for lunch, say one o'clock?"

***

The sun shone. A few cottony clouds, buoyed by a light breeze, drifted in the azure-blue sky. Julie left her car at the house and walked into town. Her phone pinged as she approached the Town Gate. She stopped to read the text: a message from Sir William Barr, code name B. Dima used to say, "B for bastard." Dima had warned her never to trust Sir William, who, on more than one occasion, had tried to grope her.

Yet Sir William had just assumed management of her relocation here. B*olo 2 men black ford fiesta hatchback.* Be on the lookout for two men. The two men Gareth had seen? Julie glanced around, inhaled and let her breath out slowly, then walked through the arched gate.

Set into the hillside sloping northeast toward the Wye River and the train station, Beaufort Square was the last remnant of the large central town square dating from medieval times. On the higher west side was Bank Street, while the town's retail High Street ran along its east side. The square featured the Chepstow Cenotaph war memorial, benches and a series of several stone staircases leading down to High Street.

Coffee #1 was situated at the corner of High Street opposite Beaufort Square in an attractive white, two-storey building.

As she waited for the light to turn green, she glimpsed Gareth bounding down the stairs from the square toward her and waved. He arrived at the intersection just as the light turned green for her. Thwarted, he threw up his hands. Julie motioned she would cross over and wait for him at the corner, then blithely stepped into the intersection.

Out of the blue, a black hatchback barreled from the hidden side road at the bottom of the hill and accelerated up Beaufort Square Street. Gareth called out to Julie. Then, darting between moving cars, he sprinted toward her. She was halfway across before she realized the speeding car was aimed straight at her. Gareth leapt and snatched her out of the car's track, flipping her on top of him onto the asphalt. Meanwhile, the car squealed around the curve and continued away from the square.

"Fuck! What was that?" Gareth extracted himself from under Julie. Still panting from the close call, he hoisted her up.

Several teens sitting at one of the outdoor tables came over to help. "Are you and the wife okay?"

"Yeah, thanks."

With his arm around her waist, Gareth guided Julie to one of the outdoor tables and sat her down. He knelt beside her and hugged her until she stopped trembling. One of the teens went into the shop and came out with two glasses of water.

"Thanks."

"No problem, mate. We're off now. You need anything else?"

Julie shook her head and mumbled, "No."

"I think we're all right, but thanks again, you guys." Gareth settled on a chair next to her. "Do you want me to take you inside while I run and get the car? I can drive you home."

"No. I'm fine. How are you?"

He shrugged. "Good."

"Then let's go to Tintern. We can eat there." She paused. "Were those the two from last night trying to run you down?"

Gareth blew out a long breath. "Julie, whoever was in that car was gunning for you."

"But I don't understand."

Shaking his head, he said, "Neither do I, Julie. Neither do I."

***

Their Tintern Abbey outing proved to be nigh perfect.

Set among the pine-covered hills of the Wye Valley and manicured lawns dotted by yellow daisies, the ruins of Tintern Abbey rose in all their magical mystical majesty.

After enjoying soup and sandwiches at the White Monk, they entered the abbey. They spent the rest of the afternoon exploring the remains of the abbey and admiring the full and partial stone walls, monumental pillars, graceful arches and the intricate framework of gothic windows of the abbey church.

Feeling playful, Julie tickled Gareth as he crouched and lay down on the grass, in his attempt to capture every angle in his photos. He countered by insisting she pose against the dramatic backdrops among the ruins. She consented only if he promised not to post any photos of her on Facebook.

Afterward, in spite of her protests, he bought Julie a silk scarf and earrings, and a tapestry and wool blanket for his mother in the abbey gift shop.

When they returned to her place, Julie flung open the door and announced, "We're having Nigella's 'Curry in a Hurry' and I'm cooking."

Gareth swept her off her feet and carried her over the threshold, declaring, "I'm crazy about you, Julie." Her feet grazed an envelope on the entryway stand, knocking it to the floor. Gareth put her down and picked up the letter before she could snatch it away. He read the name on the envelope, "Julie Ball," then replaced the letter on the stand and shut the door. "Do you want me to chop? Or open a bottle of wine?" He nuzzled her neck and shoulders before heading to the kitchen.

That night in bed, the two sat propped against the pillows. Julie leaned against him, and he wrapped his arm around her shoulders. "I promised my mother I'd visit Raglan Castle. I was thinking I'd go up there tomorrow morning. That will be my last castle before going home."

Julie tugged his arm closer around her. "When do you leave?"

"Saturday afternoon from Heathrow. I'd planned to drive to London from Raglan and spend the rest of the time there. I'm thinking I'd like to spend it with you instead. But it means my finding another place to stay in Chepstow."

"Stay with me, Gareth."

"You sure about that?"

"Yes. Yes," she said in a breathy voice. "I'll fix up my classroom while you're at Raglan. Then we can have the rest of the time together."

"Julie?"

"Yes?"

"Will you be okay while I'm at Raglan? After what happened yesterday afternoon, I'm worried. I mean, what's going on with you? You're so secretive. You wouldn't even tell me your last name."

"You know it now. And nothing is up with me. I…I know it'll all be over with us in a few days. That's all."

"Then let's make the most of our time." He drew her down under the duvet and buried his head in her hair. "What's that perfume again?"

"Pure Poison."

He jerked upright. "You're kidding?"

She began to chuckle and hauled him down beside her. "No, I'll show you the bottle in the morning."

***

Gareth had already left by the time Julie loaded her car with items for her classroom. She had everything but the heavy-duty knife she needed to trim her foam-core posters. She dashed back into the house and popped the knife into her purse.

Her phone pinged. Sir William had sent a series of three question marks. She had not yet answered yesterday's text about the black car incident. She couldn't get it out of her mind that there was something fishy about Sir William's texting her right before the men had driven their car at her. A chill crept down her spine. What if the sounds Gareth had heard the other night were those men?

Gareth arrived soon after she returned from the school. She threw her arms around him and kissed him as soon as he dropped his bags at the entryway.

He cupped her face in his hands and gazed into the wells of her dark brown eyes before kissing her long and deep. "I feel like I've come home."

She clung to him a moment more and murmured, "You have." Afterward, she let him settle in the spare room upstairs while she made lunch.

While they finished their coffee at the kitchen table, Julie reassured Gareth once again that she'd neither seen nor heard anything untoward when she had gone to work at the school. "But I need to do some grocery shopping. I thought I'd wait to see what you wanted for dinner tonight first."

"Good idea. Let's make a list and get some wine, too. There's a Norman church by that Tesco Superstore. I wanted to take a peek at it. I thought I heard the bells ring yesterday morning."

Julie's jaw dropped, and her pulse quickened. She stammered, "S-s-saint Mary's Priory?"

Gareth smacked his forehead, his face full of contrition. "I'm so sorry. I didn't mean to suggest we go near Beaufort Square again."

Julie swallowed before saying, "That's okay. There's more selection at Tesco anyway." To make her point, she grabbed a pad and searched for a pen in her purse. Frustrated at not finding one, she disappeared for a few moments and came back with a pen, the one Dima had stored in the desk she had insisted on moving with her from London.

Eyes wide, Gareth stared at it. "Nice pen. May I see it?"

"It was given to me by a…dear friend. I don't usually use it."

He didn't press any further.

With the list completed, Julie dropped the paper in her purse and headed out of the kitchen. A minute later, she stood at the door and called back to Gareth, "Shall we go now? We can use my car if you like?"

"Let's take my rental."

Julie clutched the car seat when Gareth turned down Beaufort and concentrated on navigating him into the Tesco car park. The plan was to leave the car there and make a dash over to see the church.

As they walked back to Tesco, Gareth kept his arm around Julie's shoulder, his eyes constantly scanning the walk and the parking lot. "Let's do our shopping and get out of here."

The corner of her right eye began to twitch. Julie surveyed the car park and moved her body closer to Gareth's, but neither saw anyone suspicious either outside or inside the store.

Gareth flashed his wallet and insisted that Julie stock up with groceries for the rest of the week and the beginning of the school term. "Frankly, I don't know why you Brits shop every day."

"It's called small fridges and freshness."

Gareth, laden with three heavy bags, halted. Twisting around toward the store, he said in a low tense voice, "Julie, go back into the store. Once they're gone, I'll bring the car around to the entrance and pick you and the bags up there."

The hair on her arms and the back of her neck prickled. A scruffy, dark-haired, bearded man was getting into a black Ford Fiesta hatchback about 15 feet away from Gareth's car. She backed away, turned and, with one quick glance back, scrambled on shaky legs to the store entrance.

***

The tension of unspoken words reverberated throughout Julie's house. After helping her put away the groceries, Gareth retreated into the living room and turned on the telly. Julie sat at the kitchen table and fetched her phone from her purse. Sir William had texted her several times that agents had her under surveillance. In the meantime, she was to lie low.

Reality hit. She was putting Gareth's life in danger. It was time to explain her situation to him. But something else was nagging her. Were the men in the car also tracking him? And why? Was the altercation they'd had in the pub with Gareth a coincidence or part of a larger plot?

Silence. Gareth had switched off the box and loomed in the kitchen doorway. Julie dropped her phone into her purse.

"Okay, Julie Ball, suppose you tell me what's going on?"

A melancholic sigh slipped from Julie's mouth, but she remained tongue-tied. Gareth seated himself opposite her. Propping an elbow on the table, he nested his chin in his palm, locked eyes with hers and waited.

"Six months ago, I lost someone very dear to me. I came here to forget."

Gareth remained silent, willing her to continue with his steady gaze.

Her anger and frustration boiled over. "Why do you care? You'll be gone soon and we'll never see each other again." Julie slapped the table and spluttered, "I feel like I'm stuck in a bloody interrogation room."

Gareth sucked in his breath and pushed back his chair. "I feel like I'm attached to a walking bomb. You want me to leave?"

Julie reached out. "No! Please stay, Gareth."

Planting his fingertips on the table, he leaned in to glower at her tear-streaked face. "Just a few seconds ago, you lashed out at me. Now you want me to protect you? Surely you have other friends to hold your hand."

Then his voice softened. "Julie?" He dropped down beside her and sheltered her in his arms. Lifting her, he carried her up the stairs.

***

Julie woke to the sharp aroma of coffee curling up her nose. She could hear Gareth whistling in the kitchen. By the time she came down the stairs, the smell of fried bacon and eggs mingled with the coffee. He greeted her with a huge grin and a plate of bacon, eggs, sausages, tomatoes and mushrooms. He'd even filled the rack with toast.

After breakfast, Gareth went up to the spare bedroom to make phone calls and pack for tomorrow's trip. In the meantime, Julie organized an ecowash cycle for the clothes he'd be wearing home. In a little goodbye ritual of her own, she threw in his underwear and socks. Next, she hugged in succession his jeans, red T-shirt and navy hoodie before placing each into her washer/dryer.

A pall of sadness engulfed Julie and riveted her focus on the sudsy water submerging and agitating away the traces of their time together.

Raised voices outside and the slam of her neighbor's front door broke the trance. She remembered Gareth had promised to set her phone and computer up on WhatsApp so they could stay in touch, and she needed to make adjustments to next week's teaching plans. Squaring her shoulders, she headed to her office to boot up her computer.

Somehow her office looked amiss. The top page of the papers she'd neatly stacked on the left side of her computer was out of kilter. She also found the pages were out of order.

Her heart pounding, she punched the combination to unlock the desk drawer where Dima had kept his pen. The contents of the drawer appeared more jumbled than usual. She touched a hidden button and a secret compartment sprang up. The pen was still there. She breathed a sigh of relief and shut the drawer.

Taking big gulps of air and exhaling slowly, she plunked herself down on her desk chair and rotated around to do another scan of the office.

The intercom crackled and a gruff baritone voice with an Estuary English accent announced, "B sent us."

She'd forgotten about Sir William's agents, and now they were at her door. But how did they get through the gate?

She squinted into the one-way window they had installed in her door. Two dark-haired men, one with a beard, stood there: the men she and Gareth had eluded at the Tesco car park. She gasped, then remembered her mixed martial arts training: stay calm and move fast. She called out, "I'll be there in a minute," grabbed her purse and went back into the office.

Retrieving her pen, she dropped it into a pocket in her bag. When she looked up, Gareth, in jeans and a gray hoodie, was standing in the doorway. "What's up?"

She seized his hand and dragged him toward the kitchen. "We're going out the back door. I'll tell you later." She pointed to the band of hedges and trees surrounding the communal garden. "Are you game to tackle those boxwoods?"

Gareth shrugged. "For you, anything."

Julie had already started to race toward the hedges. The two clambered over them, and she pointed toward the road. "Let's head to town."

At Welsh Street, Julie took the crosswalk over to the Dell Primary School. "They may have parked here." She scanned the car park and spotted a black Ford Fiesta hatchback. "Gareth, is that the car?"

He compared the license plate to the one he had on his iPhone. "Yes."

Julie fished the skill knife from her purse and slashed the car's tires, while Gareth gawked in disbelief. She retracted the blade and returned it to her bag. "That should do it. Shall we cut through the Dell?"

"Anything you say."

As they strode down the trail to the castle, Julie's words poured out in a fast staccato. "I should have told you sooner. My husband was an attaché to the Ukrainian ambassador. My father was counsellor for political affairs there before he retired. He and my mother returned home to Kiev. I fell in love and stayed. I don't know all the details, but the UK secret service believed Dima was murdered and moved me here."

She paused to collect her thoughts. "This morning, I discovered that my office had been rifled. Then those two guys showed up at my front door." She halted and fixed Gareth with dark piercing eyes. "What do you know about these men? You said you met them in Harlech?"

He dropped his head, avoiding her gaze, and scuffed his right trainer on the beaten dirt path. A group of noisy kids crowded by on their way to the Dell playground. "Yuliya Baiul, let's tour the castle for old times' sake." He beckoned to her with his outstretched hand.

At the sound of her name, she stopped cold.

"Come on. Your disappearance was public knowledge. Why are you surprised I know your name?"

"I...just hadn't heard it said for a long time." Julie placed her hand in his.

Once they were out of earshot, Gareth resumed his narrative. "MI6 was right to be concerned. The GRU thought Dmitry—your Dima— might be a useful idiot; instead he turned mole for MI6." He squeezed Julie's hand. "Of course, GRU has its own mole in MI6."

Julie croaked, "Sir William?"

Ignoring her, Gareth continued, "A mole whose name is all over the last packet of information Dmitry received, and not just about operations in Crimea and Ukraine. There's money laundering that not only implicates Mr. B, but also several UK financiers and high-ranking government officials. That's why Mr. B got involved." He swung around to face her and clasped both her hands. "I'm so sorry, Julie. They botched the job with Dmitry."

She covered her face. "Those men?"

"Likely the ones who killed your Dima."

Once inside the Gloriette, Gareth said, "Let's go to that balcony where we first met. The tide's in, so we'll have the vista minus the mudflats. It'll also be quiet there."

Gareth's suggestion spawned a sensation of spiders crawling over Julie's back, yet she let him lead her up the stairs to the promontory.

Julie stood farther from the balcony's low semicircular enclosure wall, but each stood in positions similar to those they were in when they had first met and admired the view. But when she turned her head to Gareth, his twinkly blue eyes had morphed into a steely glint. He carefully withdrew a clear plastic zip bag holding a bottle of Pure Poison perfume from his hoodie pouch. "In Raglan, I was given this, courtesy of the GRU, to be your goodbye gift. I won't open the bag. The poison is real."

The lump in Julie's throat choked off any words she struggled to blurt out.

"Yuliya, Julie. I was given until today to get Dmitry's camera pen from you. I've tried to fend off the goons, but if I don't have that pen now, Mr. B's agents will force it from you."

Julie finally managed to swallow. "Is everything about you a lie? Are you even American?"

Gareth blew a long breath through his teeth. "I haven't lied to you. My mother is American with Welsh roots. My father? You know of him. Konstantin Firtash is a crony of Viktor Yanukovych. Right now, Kostya's in big trouble for fraud in Russia. A handler from the GRU approached me at Facebook and gave me an ultimatum: get Dmitry's pen or else. Julie, Kostya is not a good man, but he's my father. When I was small, he loved me. And I don't want to see him murdered or frozen in Siberia.

"Look, I never wanted our relationship to end this way. I never wanted it to end at all. I meant it when I said I'm crazy about you. Truth be told, my heart's desire would be to run away with you to some place in Canada, but even there, they would hunt us down."

"Like you hunted me?"

"They knew you lived near a castle, but only recently did Mr. B learn which one. For Christ's sake, just give me the pen. I promise to call off the dogs. You can go free, and I won't end up like your Dima did."

Julie plucked the pen from her purse and waved it around. "What if I throw it in the river?"

"Don't be stupid, Julie. What would that accomplish?"

She knew he was right. The pen needed to be handed over to the Ukrainian ambassador or to a reliable authority in the British intelligence service. But still she prevaricated. "It would go out to sea and all the secrets with it. Surely, Russia doesn't need a copy of the plans. And there'd be no *kompromat* for Sir William and the rest of his sort to worry about."

Heavy footsteps pounded up the stairs. Gareth's features projected danger, as a dark-haired, beardless face popped through the archway.

Her reflexes kicked in. She clutched the pen hard, like a knife. Wedging her thumb tightly against the pen's top, she tucked her fist into her left armpit and spun to meet the man as he and Darkbeard piled out of the archway.

Beardless moved in to grab her throat, and she lashed out like a cat at his. She moved in closer and grabbed a wad of his shirt at the neckline, while jabbing and slicing his face with the pen. A rapid knee to the groin and she stabbed his cheeks again.

Gareth ripped the perfume bottle out of the bag. Darkbeard charged Gareth and was met by jet after jet of Pure Poison sprayed into his eyes and gaping mouth.

Gareth then turned to Julie's opponent. "Move away, Julie!" he shouted and sprayed the other man's bleeding face.

Coughing and sputtering from the spray of bergamot, gardenia and other floral notes laced with Novichok, Darkbeard suddenly realized his fate. With a grunt, he lifted Gareth and flung him against the balcony's low wall.

"Gareth!" Julie screamed as she rushed toward Darkbeard. She stabbed him in the neck before landing a blow with her elbow into his left kidney.

With a raspy growl, Darkbeard shoved her aside and charged the stunned Gareth, whose head and shoulders drooped over the wall. Overshooting his mark, Darkbeard sent both himself and Gareth tumbling off the precipice.

Julie watched transfixed as Gareth plummeted into the murky depths of the Wye. With tears streaming down her face, she whispered, "*Dasvidaniya*, my darling Gareth."

Then, a volley of piercing shrieks escaped from the ball of pain buried deep inside her belly.

BAD VIBRATIONS

By Rosalind Place

"I don't know, Chris. Can't the board do something? I'm thinking of packing it in."

Amy ran her fingers through her hair as she sat down, flattening half of her carefully managed curls. It gave her the appearance of a crested bird, an image reinforced by her black sweater, black jeans and high-heeled black boots, now tapping anxiously against the auditorium stage floor. She felt nauseous and angry, as she often did after one of Neil's so-called motivational meetings.

Chris didn't seem to be paying attention to her. "Do you ever get the feeling, when you come back from a break or something, that things aren't quite as you left them?" Hands on his hips, he stood staring at his bass, which was resting on its side propped against his chair. In his sweatpants, T-shirt and running shoes, he looked like he belonged on the track, not in the string section of a community orchestra. Tonight, his normally serene expression had been replaced by a frown. He crouched and leaned forward, pushing his instrument ever so slightly backward.

"No, I don't," Amy answered, growing impatient. "Didn't you hear me? I'm going to pack it in."

"You're always threatening to quit, Ames." Chris straightened, his frown replaced with a smile. "We're a community orchestra, and we've got no say. If he wants to put us in the band shell again, he can. If he wants us to play the 1812 Overture again, he can. True, he can't keep time, despite his friggin' ivory baton with the silver handle crafted by I forget who. The board doesn't care. They just want someone on the podium." He looked around. "Christ, why is it still so cold in here?" He pulled a tatty gray sweater from the back of his chair and threw it on.

The other orchestra members began to file in. Their clothes reflected their reasons for being there. Although it was only a rehearsal, some, like Amy, were serious musicians who had dressed carefully. Many were still students who hoped to move on to professional careers. Others, like Chris, were just as serious about the music, but had to juggle the rehearsal schedule with day jobs, family or other demands.

As all the players found their seats, they looked more alike than different—all silent, all downcast, focused on their instruments and on warming up. No one made eye contact.

Neil, a tall, angular man who did nothing slowly, strode across the stage carrying his baton. As always, he was dressed in a tailored black suit, white shirt and startlingly bright red tie. His thick, black hair was perfectly styled, shiny and immovable.

"I hope our little meeting inspired everyone to do their best from now on." He raised his baton. "From the top." The musicians lifted their instruments. Taking longer than necessary, he waited, and then, with a flourish, began.

***

"That was the most humiliating experience of my life!" First Flute complained. "When did the 1812 Festival

Overture become the 1812 Funeral Overture? How did he ever get hired and why don't they do something about it?"

The instruments were alone again, the players having been summoned to another room for another inspirational talk.

"Well?" First Flute demanded. She was so upset that the music stand she lay on started to quiver. Wasn't she a world-class instrument? Wasn't her owner, Amy, a talented if rather tense player, on her way up?

"They're not going to, are they?" Oboe responded. Unlike Flute, her owner was on his way out. "They either play or walk away, and none of them have anywhere to walk to. There's no 'I'm going to the Philharmonic' talk here anymore, is there?"

"So you just want to stay in this wretched auditorium forever, playing the same old repertoire over and over again, with whatever moron they decide to throw onto the podium?" Flute asked. "Don't you want more? Don't we all want more? You've heard the new music; don't you want to play *that*? Where's your ambition?

"And you, Oboe, weren't you the one who, all last year, went on ad nauseam about the Littlewood Symphony, the orchestra that started on a shoestring with a few good players and ended up in Carnegie Hall?"

Flute knew this was a very sensitive subject. Oboe's previous owner had been a talented, ambitious young musician. She had recently graduated to a semiprofessional orchestra and promptly purchased a better instrument. Oboe had been sold to Jamie, the new but definitely unambitious oboist.

"That was last year," Oboe said. "That was when Maria was here and we were all delusional. We're just a small-town orchestra, Flute. We're lucky to have a conductor at all. Amy's been making you listen to those stupid podcasts again."

"Well, maybe Jamie should spend a little time listening, too," Flute responded. "If today's rehearsal is anything to go by."

"There's no need to resort to personal insults."

"Will everyone please stop arguing?" It was First Violin, who had been happily contemplating his imminent return to the string quartet he loved so much. The audition last week had gone well, despite the fact that Evan, who suffered from performance anxiety, had been high at the time. Yes, he could see the light at the end of this particular tunnel quite clearly if everyone else would just shut up.

"Let's just get through the rehearsal," First Violin continued. "We're at the band shell next week. The 1812 is a good choice for the band shell. And we don't really mind playing there again, do we?"

Trombone jumped in. "Don't mind? Are you kidding?" The entire brass section was humming angrily.

"Let's just all calm down." First Violin realized, too late, that he had been careless. "I know we all remember what happened the last time we played the band shell. However, Neil is now our conductor. We work with what we have. Flute, laughter is not helpful at this point. Bass, you're unusually quiet."

"Yeah, Bass. Nothing to say, eh?" Flute's music stand was still quivering. "The biggest of all of us, in one piece and heavy enough to actually accomplish something. Look at me. I'm lucky if I'm not in three pieces, trapped in a case and even if I'm all put together I'm either in the air, on a music stand or on a chair. If I roll off and break a key, where would that get us?"

"Out of the 1812, at least."

First Violin attempted to gain control again as the percussion section began to vibrate. "Whoever made that comment, I am disappointed in you. It was not helpful."

Bass was barely paying attention. Chris had just started a new weekend gig with a jazz ensemble, and it had been a revelation. *That* was where he belonged, not here, in this orchestra full of unhappy instruments and unhappy players. Since Maria left, well, he didn't even like classical music anymore.

"Well, Bass?" Flute ignored everyone else. "You know what I'm talking about. And you won't even consider it? The so-called accident last year wasn't your fault. Everyone knows it but you."

"I think that is a topic best left..." It took a moment for First Violin to regain enough composure to intervene. Just the mention of the accident was enough to send the entire orchestra off the deep end. Bass was already vibrating loudly behind him, clearly very upset and who could blame him? He had been so fond of Maria.

It had been Maria, on that fateful last performance in the band shell, who had tried to save Bass when his stand gave way. As a result, Maria lost her footing, and fell from the stage. She was carried off on a stretcher and never returned.

"Yes, I know, First Violin," Flute cut in. "God forbid anyone mentions *the accident*. It goes to show, though, doesn't it, Mister First Bass, who won't do anything to help the rest of us? Easy for you, who looks down on everyone. But then, you don't have to worry so much, do you? Basses don't play in marching bands, do they?"

The woodwinds were vibrating now; in fact, the entire orchestra was starting to quiver in distress.

"You didn't know?" Flute addressed them all. "He's going to do it. Next spring. *A marching band!*"

217

"Flute! Quiet, everyone! Please!" First Violin ordered. "They're coming back. Trombone, is that how she left you? Cello, were you not facing to the left?"

***

The rehearsal ended earlier than usual, despite the extra break.

Neil slumped dramatically over his music stand, hand over eyes, then straightened up, tucked his baton under his arm and, with a flick of his wrist, told the orchestra to go home.

Chris and Amy were the last to leave.

"You know how it is when you walk into a room and everyone's been talking and they suddenly stop?" Chris said. "That's just how it feels."

He waited as Amy carefully put her flute away and slipped sheet music into her briefcase, then straightened her chair and the one next to it. She had been known to straighten all the chairs in the orchestra before leaving—a pointless exercise, since the school janitor would pile them all up the next morning to clear the stage for the school assembly.

"We don't have another rehearsal before Saturday," Amy said. She turned to Chris. "It's going to be a disaster. What kind of a conductor thinks tuning an orchestra is an unnecessary evil and when he does deign to do it, tunes to an oboe who regularly plays half a tone flat?" She glanced back at the chair she had just straightened.

"It happens every time we come back from a break, Ames. As if there were people here, whispering to each other and…moving things."

"Moving things?" Amy asked.

"It's just a feeling," he said. "I didn't say it made sense."

218

Chris watched Amy move toward the next set of chairs. "It's okay, Ames. Let's just get out of here." He touched her lightly on the arm, and she turned back to him with a small smile. "I was just saying that something feels wrong, that's all," he said.

"Something's wrong all right. We have a conductor who cannot conduct, an oboist who cannot play and a bass player who's losing it."

***

A school bus had been booked to take the players and their instruments to the fairgrounds. The musicians had been told to arrive half an hour early, leave their instruments in the bus and meet inside the school.

Everyone in the orchestra was required to wear a black jacket. The order created hard feelings among the players as they searched for the proper apparel at local secondhand stores. No one had money to burn.

When everyone had been gathered and seated in the auditorium, Neil, baton in hand, appeared on stage. He was followed by a very young woman, dressed in a long sweater and leggings, who looked tense and uncomfortable.

The conductor said, "I felt it my duty, given the importance of today's concert, to do my utmost to prepare everyone. Leanna is here today..." He paused, raised his baton and pointed it at her. The woman took a few steps back and bumped into a row of music stands not yet put away by the janitor. The stands clattered onto the stage floor.

Neil waited, baton still raised, as one of the players jumped up to help the woman. "As I said, I felt it was my duty to ensure you are prepared, and to this end I have asked Leanna here today to teach everyone some simple techniques of meditation." He promptly left the stage.

Leanna, red-faced and still recovering from her brush with the music stands, hesitantly stepped forward.

***

Bass was regretting, and not for the first time, the way Chris always chose to sit with Amy. He was now trapped at the back of the bus right next to Flute, who was getting everyone upset.

Flute's constant carping was getting on Bass's nerves more and more, and making all the instruments anxious and irritable. He would be perfectly content working weekend gigs at the bar if Chris would just give up this lost cause.

Flute, whose speechifying had been going on for some time now, was getting louder and impossible to ignore.

"Just what are you suggesting, Flute?" asked First Violin, who sounded distinctly nervous.

"There is a rumor—it's surprising what one can learn when forgotten in a conservatory hallway—that Maria has recovered and may wish to return. Neil is about to make us all a laughing stock. If we don't want that to happen, well, something has to be done. Isn't that right, Bass?"

Several instruments chimed in at the same time. "What?" "What something?" There was a definite vibration running through parts of the orchestra, and Bass could feel the tension rising around him. He wasn't happy that Flute had addressed him directly.

"All right. I'll say it, then." Flute waited, ratcheting the tension up another notch. "Neil has to go and he has to go soon. He'll never resign, not unless he gets a better offer. But who would have him? No, he has to go and the only way I can see it happening is if he were... well...unable to continue."

"Yes!" cried Trombone, who almost slid off the seat across which she had been carefully laid.

The vibration was now a hum, moving down the rows, instrument to instrument.

Oboe, uncertain and unwilling to give in to Flute on anything, would have refused to join in, but for the impossible-to-ignore thought that this could be a way to get back to where she had once been.

Only one instrument did not react. Bass remained silent and perfectly still.

***

The bus was almost halfway to the fairgrounds when the rain started. The driver had warned Neil back at the high school that the forecast had changed. Neil ignored her, so she repeated it, more loudly, as the players trailed onto the bus. The meditation lesson had left them more irritated than calmed, but all knew better than to raise a protest. They stoically watched as the sky darkened, the wind picked up and the first drops of rain splashed against the bus windows.

By the time they arrived at the fairgrounds, a full-blown thunderstorm was sending fairgoers running for cover. The chairs lined up on the band shell stage were sliding away in the wind. The temporary steps at the front of the stage that Neil had demanded—as the conductor, he couldn't possibly enter the stage from the wings like everyone else—had been pushed sideways.

The musicians waited, listening to the pelting rain and the crashing thunder, feeling the wind pushing against the bus with alarming strength.

When the sandwich board announcing the orchestra's performance fell facedown into the mud, even Neil had to admit there would be no performance.

As the bus turned around, Neil stood at the front, shouting to make himself heard above the storm, and reviewed the schedule of performances for the next three months. Unfortunately, the fall season finale would be in the same band shell during the Festival of Lights.

"Really? Outside at the end of November?" complained Jamie, the oboist. "We'll freeze our asses off." Tall and extremely thin, he pulled his ill-fitting black jacket around him and shivered as if he could already feel those chill winter winds.

The bus had arrived back at the high school just as the sun came out, and the players were returning to their cars.

"And what was it he said about a marching band?" Jamie continued.

"A marching band?" asked Jeanie, the petite trombone player. "Who said anything about a marching band?" She hefted her instrument case onto the backseat of her truck. Nightmarish memories of high school football games ran through her mind, making her a little dizzy. "You can't have heard him right."

"Oh, I heard him all right," Jamie said. "You should've seen the look on Amy's face! He'll be firing us left, right and center if he gets his way. Speaking of which, did you hear the latest?"

The small group of players who had gathered around him all shook their heads.

"Well, Maria wants to come back and got turned down," Jamie said. "The word is that there's going to be an investigation of her accident. Word is, it wasn't one."

Chris joined the group. "What's up?"

Jamie had a nasty habit of gossiping about other players that Chris wanted to quash. Amy had already stalked off to her car.

"Nothing," Jamie replied. He didn't make eye contact. Chris was impossible when it came to any kind of gossip. "We were just talking about the marching band, that's all. Nothing you have to worry about."

"Hmm." Chris nodded and turned away. He asked himself when everything had started to feel so wrong. A vision of the auditorium stage, chairs empty but for the instruments, appeared before him, and he felt a chill creep from the top of his head to the base of his spine.

"Get a grip," he muttered as he got into his car. "All that BS about phantoms moving instruments around. Amy's right. You are losing it."

***

It took about six weeks of playing outdoors in their black jackets in the summer heat, six weeks of alternating sycophantic praise and bullying from Neil, and six weeks of band shells and distant town halls before some of the orchestra members decided they'd had enough.

By the time October—with its promise of extra rehearsals for the endless Christmas concerts Neil had scheduled—rolled around, there were mutterings about going to the board. This was something of a pipe dream, as none of the players knew who the board members were, where they met or if they would be the least bit interested in what any of them had to say.

Leanna, the meditation teacher, had been replaced by Bjorn, the life coach, who had just been replaced by Ariana. No one was sure exactly what Ariana's specialty was.

So the players and their instruments found themselves in the gloomy auditorium again, on a busy weekday evening, rehearsing the 1812 Festival Overture. The Festival of Lights was fast approaching, the temperature was dropping daily and it appeared to everyone that Neil was intent on making the final concert of the outdoor season one to remember.

"Open minds, everyone. Open minds!" Neil stepped down from the podium and walked slowly around the stage. This was extremely disconcerting to any female player he paused behind, as he stood just a little too close and placed his hands on the back of her chair, making it impossible to move forward.

Neil's hands had a tendency to wander, as did his thoughts, evidenced by sudden and abrupt speechifying that left many a woman trying to ignore the moist warmth of his breath against her skin.

Tonight, however, he walked off into the wings and beckoned the players to follow. Ariana was waiting, he said, and, as long as their minds were open, she would lead them all on a spiritual journey that would bring their playing to new heights.

***

"We've been over this. How many times have we been over this?"

Flute had started to address the instruments as soon as the last player had followed Neil off the stage.

Then she turned her attention to Bass. "It's perfectly simple. Those steps were dangerous last year, and they haven't done anything to fix them. That's a sign. We are meant to do this."

"There is no 'meant to' only 'must do,' remember?" Trombone, quoting Bjorn, interjected. "And is that the royal 'we' you're using, there, Flute? I don't see that *you* actually have to do anything at all. It's Bass who has to 'move,' a euphemism if ever there was one."

Flute was annoyed by the interruption and offended by the sarcasm. "Well, I'm obviously not in a position…"

But she stopped herself from saying something she'd regret later. *Stay on point.*

She turned to the full orchestra again. "All he has to do is fall over. That is all he has to do. He's in the perfect position to do it, now that Neil has moved everyone around. Bass falls over, Neil loses his balance, and, with any luck, given the condition of those steps…well… there's a good chance he'll be laid up for a while. It gives us some breathing room, some time to…to…"

"Find a way to get rid of him?"

"Yes, thank you, Oboe," First Violin cut in. "We can always rely on you to be on the mark." He waited for the hum of nervous instruments to subside.

It had been a difficult summer for First Violin. His longed-for move to the concert world had not come to pass, despite all signals to the contrary. He had received the news on the very day that Flute had come to him. She had presented her plan in such cool, well-thought-out terms that he found himself unable to say no. "As you all know, as Concertmaster, I cannot condone this kind of action. However—"

Flute cut him off. "I was going to say, some time to consider our options." She paused, seeming to come to some certainty, then continued. "But Oboe is right. That is what we all want in the end."

When had things started to go so wrong? Bass wondered, as the arguments continued around him. They had been replaying them all summer and fall, and Flute had been haranguing him every chance she got. He had been able to stand up to her, but she was winning over the string section.

And when had Flute become so powerful anyway, powerful enough to make them all think that he would do something like this on purpose? Last year had been an accident, and they had all lost Maria as a result.

Bass could still remember the sickening feeling he had as the instrument stand snapped and he started to slide. Maria had stepped forward to try to catch him and then stepped backward into space. How *could* they expect this of him?

Bass had been sold after that accident, his player telling everyone he couldn't face playing him anymore. It was sheer luck that Chris, the best player he had ever had, had been the one to buy him.

"I think we can all agree that what happened last year was not Bass's fault," Flute said. "I think we are all familiar with the rumors. When Neil was in the orchestra, the last chair in the violin section if I remember correctly, it was clear that he had ambitions. Well, he fulfilled those ambitions, didn't he? Not through talent—we all know he has none of that—but by a nasty little bit of sabotage."

"What?" Bass could feel the vibrations building to an angry hum around him. "What do you mean, a nasty little bit of sabotage?"

"Just what I said." Flute turned to Bass, but she was addressing the entire orchestra. "Neil wanted to conduct; he made sure he got the chance. If wanting to get rid of the worst conductor we have ever had isn't enough reason for you, then think of it this way—it's time for a little payback. Come now, Bass, wouldn't you agree?"

Receiving no response, Flute continued, "It appears all concerns have been dealt with. Is that not so, First Violin?"

"Yes, Flute, yes...ah...yes, certainly...ah, I believe some of the players are returning."

***

Chris stood in front of the band shell, arms crossed, surveying the stage. Chairs were askew, and some instruments lay across them. Others, like his bass, stood neatly in their stands.

The scene was no different from that of any other performance. Yet there was that feeling again. It wasn't exactly whispering … he just couldn't put his finger on what it was.

Preconcert jitters, Amy had told him. Something he wasn't usually prone to, but then again, it was their final concert at the band shell and the forecast was for snow flurries. Neil seemed to be blissfully unaware of what the cold would do to the instruments and their players.

With all the resentment that had been building since spring, Chris didn't want to be here.

"What did you say?" Amy came up behind him. "You're talking to yourself again."

"No, I wasn't. I just…did you hear anything?"

"I know. You don't have to tell me. It's your ghosts again. Maybe the band shell is haunted, too. Probably by all the players who came before us and cannot believe what they are now hearing. *That* I would believe."

"You know, I'm a regular kind of guy," Chris said. "I go to work, I go home, I practice, I come here. This, though, is creeping me out. Look at your flute, Amy. Your flute wasn't like that when we left."

The other players began filing onto the stage, and Chris returned to his own place. He looked at Amy, who hadn't moved and was staring back at him.

"It's just bad vibrations, Chris. That's all it is."

***

It was during the break between the first and second performances that it happened.

The players had all rushed into the hall behind the band shell to warm up. The first performance had not gone well, which was no surprise given that the temperature was hovering close to zero.

Neil had said nothing to any of them, striding off alone toward the bleachers. He arrived back well before the second performance, though, and stood at the entrance to the hall. He stared at each of them in turn, a look of disgust on his face. With a flick of his baton, he beckoned them to follow him back to the bandstand.

But no one paid much attention. The musicians were past fearing the flick of Neil's silver-handled, ivory baton. No one wanted to leave the warmth of the hall, and they still had 10 minutes of their break left.

Which was why Neil was alone when he walked, fast, toward the stage. He took the first two steps in a leap, jumped again onto the third and landed heavily on the final, crucial step. No one was there to hear it give way, nor to witness him, one foot on the stage and one on the collapsing step, turn and, still holding his baton and arms flailing, fall face-first onto the ground below. There was a scream, and then nothing.

The players ran to the band shell, as did some of the audience members. They were all too late. They milled around in confusion and horror as Neil's body was lifted onto a stretcher and carried away.

No one noticed the bass. It lay where it had fallen, across the cracked steps, pointing at the bloodied, snow-covered grass where Neil had landed.

***

It was a long time before the orchestra was able to assemble again.

Two terrible incidents, one fatal, occurring within the space of a year had resulted in investigations by the police, the Department of Health and Safety, and the previously invisible orchestra board of directors. All had come to the same conclusion—that these were two very nasty, undoubtedly coincidental, accidents.

So it was months later, on an unseasonably warm March day, that the players came together again. Depositing their instruments in the still chilly auditorium, they went back outside to await Maria's arrival.

Chris, standing with Amy, couldn't help but feel that things were on the upswing at last. Those strange forebodings of last year, those bad vibrations, were gone. The cloud of guilt that had surrounded him ever since the accident had lifted with the end of the last investigation. And Amy had finally auditioned for the jazz ensemble; she was a shoo-in.

"It feels good to be back!" Amy said, slipping her arm into his. "It's going to be a good year; I can feel it!"

***

In the auditorium, no one was thinking about Maria or looking forward to the new season. The instruments were on edge, watching a familiar, unnerving scene play out in front of them, with no one to keep things under control.

First Violin had left the week before. On to better things, or so he said, though all suspected he had simply lost his nerve.

"It was murder, pure and simple," Bass declared, comfortable enough in his new stand to let himself vibrate and be heard. He was determined to get Flute to admit the truth. Then he would let it go. He had done what he had done and would have to live with it, but he was damned if Flute was going to get away with pretending it hadn't happened at all.

"It certainly was not!" Flute shot back, vibrating loudly. "How long are we going to have to discuss this?" She was sick and tired of Bass going on and on, trying to make her feel guilty. She felt no guilt and never would. The plan had been more successful than she could have imagined.

"They investigated not once, not twice, but three times," Flute said. "All three were ridiculous, and I still can't imagine how they got away with any of them."

"*I* can imagine," Oboe cut in. She had had quite enough of Flute, and was stressed out by problems of her own, namely Jamie. "It was because it was the *second time*. They probably thought Bass was some conductor-killing serial murderer."

"Oboe, don't be absurd," Flute replied. "It was an *unreliable* instrument stand. Which was perfect. Bass, you fell perfectly. If Neil hadn't held onto that ridiculous baton, he wouldn't have fallen on it, and it wouldn't have—well, you all know what happened."

A shudder went through the instruments as they remembered the grisly scene.

"It was murder," Bass said. "It was what you wanted. And you got *me* to do it."

"Excuse me! It was what everyone wanted."

Flute had had enough. She had been angry and upset all week. She still couldn't believe that Amy had auditioned for the jazz ensemble. Flute was as open-minded as any other instrument about music, but *jazz*!

No, Neil had only got what he deserved. Flute had saved them all. And she would do it again.

"As I have said many times, Bass, it's not like someone took his baton and stabbed him to death. In fact—" Flute turned to the orchestra again "—if you really think about it, it was the stairs giving way that did it. It really had nothing to do with any of us, at all."

Bass could feel the mood changing around him now. She was winning them over, and there was nothing he could do about it. He thought of Chris, the ensemble, Maria. He would just go forward and never listen to Flute again.

"We all need to think about this differently," Flute said. "Maria is back and we need to think about what we can accomplish under her." Flute felt excited, sure of herself, sure of her power. "We want to get out of this wretched high school auditorium, don't we? We want something better, don't we? Isn't that what this has all really been about?"

She had them now. "In light of what we have learned from this…"

She paused. Bass had said nothing more, was silent; in fact, the entire orchestra was silent. Yes, they were waiting for her, waiting for her to show them the way forward.

It was time. It was her time. She would not be turned back, not by Bass, or anyone.

"In light of what we have learned from this," she repeated, certain and calm now, "I, for one, see nothing wrong with a little more weeding out. Oboe, has Jamie been practicing?"

DEATH OF A CHEAPSKATE

By Melodie Campbell

Dad died years ago, but I remember it clearly. Looking back, it seems remarkable that no one but me realized it was murder.

The phone call from my sister came at night. "He's dead," Elaine said. "Finally."

There was an awkward pause. You're supposed to be upset when someone dies. It's hard to know how to behave when you're not.

"Are you coming?" my sister asked.

"Tomorrow morning. Do you know what finally did it?" *To him.* Those were the unspoken words. Because he was a tough old bugger, and it seemed impossible that anything could kill him. Not even the diabetes that had haunted him for a decade.

"The doctor said sepsis. A massive staph infection, like he had before. Tell you more when you're here. I have a shitload of organizing to do. Mom is…well, you know Mom."

Yes, I knew. Words like *helpless* and *incompetent* came to mind. She would be in a state, waiting for someone

233

else to take over, as Dad had always done, had always insisted on doing.

We all knew what Mom was like.

***

It was a three-hour journey by car to my home town, but I didn't mind. It was early May, and the day was gorgeous, like one of those perfect pictures a child will draw with the sun in the sky surrounded by fluffy clouds. I spent the time listening to Elvis on the oldies radio station, thinking about my early years.

Does anyone have a happy childhood? I suppose mine could have been a lot worse. There was always food on the table and a fairly warm place to sleep. But being thrifty can become like a religion to some people. Our dad was one who worshiped at that altar. Mom was sweet, but completely under his thumb.

There is a coldness that comes with enforced austerity that I'm not sure I can explain. It wasn't as if our dad was less successful than other fathers on our street. But they were the "spendthrift" families. We were, in some twisted way, more noble than our neighbors.

We never had family vacations. Elaine might have gotten new clothes, but I always wore her hand-me-downs. It wasn't until I could work part-time to earn my own money that I ever had anything new.

Not surprisingly, we all left home as soon as we could. Dad didn't mind. "Less mouths to feed," I heard him say once.

"Fewer," I remember mumbling to myself.

***

By the time I got to the yellow brick bungalow, Elvis had gone through his entire repertoire, and the sun had made most of its journey across the sky from east to west.

My brother John was waiting for me, leaning against the side of the house and smoking a cigarette.

I got out of my car and slammed the door shut. "Those things will kill you," I said.

It was my standard greeting. He gave the standard response. "Better that than the clap."

We both grinned and hugged each other.

"Good to see you, Mandy."

"You, too." I pushed back from his embrace. "Did Jill come?"

He shook his head. "Someone had to stay home with the twins. She won the toss."

That was too bad. I liked Jill.

"Thanks for looking after the kids when we're at that convention this summer, by the way."

"You know I love doing it," I said.

"Jill really appreciates it, too."

That made me happy. John puffed on his cigarette, and I leaned back beside him against the brick wall. It was a comfortable moment, being outside the house. It wouldn't be so comfortable inside it.

"Still bossing those third graders around?" John asked.

"That's me. Miss Bossy-pants. They're counting the weeks until school ends."

He laughed easily.

A cloud drifted over the sun, and I felt a chill.

"Elaine inside?" I asked.

"She's at the funeral home with Mom. I just got here."

I raised an eyebrow. "She didn't wait for you?"

"Nope. Left a note on the kitchen table."

I was relieved I didn't have to go with them to pick out the coffin. Elaine was much better at that sort of thing.

Elaine was better at most things. Just not actual work.

"Funeral is in two days," said John. I watched him pull on the cigarette. He looked relaxed, and healthy in spite of the smoking. The navy golf shirt suited his svelte physique, and he still had a full head of light brown hair.

Mine was a mousy color. Elaine dyed hers blond, of course. Or rather, some salon did that every three weeks. I was secretly envious.

"You look good," John said. "I like that top thingy you're wearing."

That made me smile. I liked it, too. The sapphire-blue tunic swished as I walked, and suited me now that I had lost a little weight.

But mainly, I was smiling because John hadn't changed. He had always been good to me, his little sis. It wasn't until after he left home that I realized how good.

The sun left our house that day, leaving me in shadows.

***

We didn't have to wait long for them to return.

"The visitation is tomorrow night. Funeral is Thursday at one," Elaine announced, throwing her purse on the floor of the tiny foyer.

Mom trailed in after her, wearing a new gray skirt with matching jacket. She picked up Elaine's purse and placed it on the hall chair.

She looked better than I had seen her look in a long time. Her salt-and-pepper hair had been recently cut and styled. Her face seemed tired, of course, but rather serene. I gave her a big hug and then a kiss on the cheek. It was soft, smelling of loose powder.

"That's a nice outfit," I said to her.

"Thank you, dear. Elaine made me buy it yesterday," Mom said. "For the visitation. I'll wear black to the funeral, of course."

Elaine herself was wearing separates in shades of butterscotch and caramel, clearly designer. It all coordinated perfectly with her ash-blond hair. The divorce settlement last year had not been stingy.

"What's for dinner?" Elaine threw herself into the only easy chair in the living room. I took a hard chair by the picture window.

"I have some leftovers I was saving for when your dad came home from the hospital."

I watched Mom carefully remove her new jacket and prepare to hang it up in the hall closet.

Elaine groaned. "No way. I'm not eating old leftovers. Let's go out."

"Oh, no." Mom's hazel eyes flashed in alarm. "I wouldn't feel right, going out for dinner before the funeral."

"Oh, for Crissake," muttered Elaine. She kicked off her pumps.

"She's right, Elaine," said John. "It wouldn't look good."

"Who cares?" said Elaine.

"You forget. Some of the people in this town are still clients of mine. I manage their investments," said John. "But there's no reason we couldn't order in. How does everyone feel about Chinese? My treat."

"That would be nice," Mom said. "Would you mind ordering, John? I don't...I'm not at my best today. I feel a bit weary."

"Of course you do," said John, kindly. "Go lie down for a bit, and I'll call you when it's here."

I waited until Mom left the room to ask the question that had been bothering me.

"Elaine, what were you going to tell me about how Dad died?"

She continued to examine her long red nails. "What do you mean? I told you on the phone."

"But you said you would explain more when I got here."

"Oh. Well, it was just something the nurse said to me about the sepsis. *'We can't understand why it keeps coming back.'* They seemed baffled."

"I guess we'll never know," said John.

***

By ten o'clock, Mom had gone to bed. The three of us sat around the old wooden table, in the kitchen, in our childhood places. I remembered when Dad had last refinished that table. I couldn't have been more than seven at the time. It looked pretty dilapidated now, these many years later.

The kitchen hadn't fared much better. The white painted cabinets had faded dismally. No longer could you pick out the sparkles that used to delight me in the original laminate countertop. They were dull now, discolored, as was the vinyl floor that refused to shine, no matter how much Mom tried. It was like viewing a room through soap scum.

"Good thing I was there today." Elaine lit a cigarette with Dad's butane lighter. "Old Pike would have talked her into a ridiculously expensive mahogany coffin. I told him no way, not for our dad. He would turn over in his grave. We ended up with oak. But Mom would have caved for sure if I hadn't been there."

John leaned back in the rickety chair. "You know Mom. No backbone at all. It's a miracle she can even stand upright." He chuckled at his own joke.

"That's not fair," I said, quick to defend her. "He wasn't easy to live with. You know that."

John smiled indulgently at me. "You're right, of course. Can you imagine having to nurse him, like she did for the last year? Waiting on him hand and foot, as he bossed her around all day long. Frankly, I'm surprised she didn't bop him one on the head. I would have, in her shoes."

"Good thing you weren't in her shoes, then," said Elaine.

"Her ancient shoes." John frowned. "How many times have they been resoled? I've never met anyone as cheap as him in my whole life. Remember the time we were reroofing the shed and he saved all the old nails to reuse them? Nails are a couple of dollars a box, for Crissake."

"He spent the whole winter in the basement straightening them," said Elaine. She took a drag from the cigarette. "I remember."

"I can top anyone's 'cheap' stories at work," John said, reaching for her pack. "Which reminds me. Did you know Mom wants to go on a cruise?"

"What?" I looked over in disbelief. Mom only left town to see John's kids, and then only once a year.

Elaine groaned.

John laughed. "Yeah, surprised the hell out of me. She asked me about it over the phone last night. You know that Med cruise Jill and I took last year? She's going to look into it." John snapped open the lid of the old lighter and lit the end of his cigarette.

"Well, that explains the passport," said Elaine.

"Passport?"

"I saw it in her purse, when we were shopping."

"But a cruise like that? Aren't they really expensive?" I was baffled. Mom never spent a cent on herself. Even now, she made most of her own clothes to save money.

John shrugged. "'Go for it,' I said to her. The old man has a pile tucked away. Almost a million bucks."

That got Elaine's attention. "Are you kidding me? How do you know?" She leaned forward, eyes wide.

"She told me last night on the phone."

I shook my head. "That's unbelievable. How could they have that much money?"

John waved the cigarette through the air. "Look around here. The place is a pile of crap. He wouldn't *spend* any money, is the problem. One of those guys who loved money for money's sake, not for what it could buy you. I've known a few in my time at the bank."

There was ample truth to that. The house hadn't been renovated since my parents bought it 50 years earlier.

"At least he didn't hit her," Elaine said. "Or at least, I don't think he did."

My eyes shot up in surprise.

John put his cigarette down on the glass ashtray. "Nah. Didn't have to. Just belittled her, so she didn't think she could do anything right."

The phone rang then. It was some man wanting Elaine. She pulled the coiled cord of the receiver around the corner into the hall for more privacy.

One thing niggled at me. John would know. "Doesn't it take a few weeks to get a passport?"

John gave me a thoughtful look. "Yes."

Elaine's provocative laugh drifted into the room. I seized the opportunity to claim the solitary bathroom first to prepare for bed. It had been a long day.

***

I wasn't alone with Mom until late the next morning. She was wearing another new outfit I hadn't seen before. Brown slacks with a cream embroidered top. Probably another Elaine-choice, but it suited her. I hadn't realized until now that she still had a pretty good figure.

"It's good of you to help me with this, Mandy," said Mom. "The others…well, you know."

I certainly did know. Elaine wouldn't be caught dead anywhere there was actual work to be done, and John had made an excuse to go visit an old friend. Little Mandy would help Mom, as usual. The old family history played itself out yet another time.

But I was glad to see Mom had more energy today. "What can I do?"

"Get me some bags for charity. I want to clean out these drawers."

I dutifully went down the hall to the kitchen and out the door to the garage. An open package of the cheapest green garbage bags sat on a dusty shelf. I grabbed a few. It was appropriate. Most of Dad's clothes would be garbage. I smiled at my own private joke.

Mom was standing in the kitchen when I returned. She had a small box in her hand.

"Here are some unused insulin needles. What should I do with them?"

"Give them to me," I said, determined to be helpful. "I'll dispose of them." Poor Mom. She shouldn't have to worry about things like that.

She stood staring down at the box. Hesitating, as usual.

"Can't they be used by someone? Your father wouldn't like them to be thrown out."

No, he wouldn't. I could practically hear him yelling all the way from purgatory. "Let me take them," I said.

She put the box down on the kitchen table. "There's one used needle in there. I guess no one would want it, even though it's only been used once."

I was only half listening. This room was so full of uncomfortable memories that they seemed to crowd out new thoughts.

"What do you mean, only used once?" I said absently.

"Your dad didn't believe in using things only once."

I could feel her eyes on me. It seemed important that I give my full attention to this moment.

"What do you mean, Mom?"

She turned away abruptly, grabbed a dishtowel from the holder and busied herself at the kitchen sink. "You know how your dad was, Mandy. He didn't like to throw things out that were still good."

"He had you reuse the insulin needles?" My voice was hoarse.

She stopped moving. "Until they weren't sharp anymore. Sometimes we could get four or five uses out of them. He was very proud of that."

I think the earth must have stopped spinning in that moment. I placed a hand on the counter to steady myself. *Recurring sepsis. The doctors and nurses baffled. "We can't understand why it keeps coming back."*

The passport, ordered weeks ago. DID SHE KNOW?

Now she was humming. I'd never heard her hum before. What was that song? I'd heard it earlier the other day in the car. Elvis sang it. I could hear his voice clearly in my own mind, now, singing each word as she hummed the tune.

RELEASE ME....

LET THE SUNSHINE IN

By Lynne Murphy

"Let's try 'There's a Bluebird on Your Windowsill,'" Carol, the seniors' choir leader, announced in her relentlessly cheery voice. One or two members of the audience looked hopefully toward the windows, but only the February snow was swirling down outside. "Join in if you know the words," Carol called out.

Charlotte Manners sang along with the other altos about rainbows and happy thoughts, but her heart wasn't in it. Seniors' residences were always depressing, and Sunny Ways Lodge was more depressing than most.

The residents sat slumped in their wheelchairs, heads lolling, eyes vacant. A few of them mouthed the words, others tried to tap time with slippered feet but, in general, the choir might as well have been singing to an audience of zombies.

Sunny Ways was perfectly clean and nicely furnished, even though everything was beige. Charlotte recognized the usual odor you found in these places: disinfectant, air spray and yesterday's meals. Underneath, there was the inevitable tang of ammonia.

Charlotte was mindful that good genes and a little luck meant she was singing in the choir instead of slouched in a wheelchair in the audience. She could be thankful that, at the age of 80, her back was still straight, her memory was good and she still had all her own teeth. She took a deep breath and tried to sing with more feeling.

The song came to an end and there was a little applause.

"We're going to take a break for the delicious tea Sunny Ways has generously provided," Carol announced. "Enjoy!"

Charlotte noticed that one of the residents was waving at her. She recognized the woman with the ridiculous name who had moved from Charlotte's condo building a few years earlier. Cookie. Cookie Baker. But this was a much-changed Cookie. Where was the woman Charlotte remembered with the ash-blond coiffure and the color-coordinated outfits? Now her hair was iron-gray and needed washing. And she was wearing red track pants with a hideous orange paisley top.

Charlotte walked across the room and bent over Cookie's wheelchair. "Cookie! I didn't know you were here. I thought you were living with your son and his wife."

Cookie clutched Charlotte's arm and grimaced. "I broke some vertebrae. Osteoporosis. I couldn't manage the stairs from the basement apartment. I've been here for— oh, I don't know, I guess it's more than a year now. Charlotte, I need to talk to you. Somewhere private."

Cookie said this with such urgency that Charlotte couldn't refuse.

"Of course," she said. "Where can we go? Your room?"

"They might have it bugged," Cookie whispered. "I guess if we turn on the TV—"

Oh, dear, Charlotte thought, *Cookie has lost it. And she used to be such a practical person.* Perhaps it was best to humor her.

"You direct me and I'll wheel you there," she said. "I'll tell Maisie I'm going to have a look at your room in case she wonders where I am."

"Maisie? The short one that's blind as a bat?"

"That's Maisie," Charlotte said. She briefed Maisie and then, following Cookie's directions, pushed the wheelchair out of the lounge and down the hall. Cookie's small room seemed even smaller because of the quantity of furniture—a queen-size bed, a large dresser, two easy chairs, a TV set on a stand. There were large brass or china ornaments on every flat surface. Mostly animal figures. There was scarcely room for the wheelchair and Charlotte.

"Sit down." Cookie gestured to one of the chairs. "Hand me that remote first."

Charlotte did as she was told and Cookie pressed the button. The TV set was tuned to a cooking show, and both women studied the screen for a moment. Then Cookie said, "I think someone is killing the residents in this place."

Charlotte was well aware of cases that had been in the news: murders in nursing homes by caregivers. But people were watching out for that now. Weren't they?

"Since I've been here, five people have died. And I know what you're going to say—that you expect deaths in a seniors' home. But these were some of the more alert people, and they complained all the time. Troublemakers."

"Have you talked to anyone about this?"

"I mentioned it to my son after Shirley died. She was the third. He said I was imagining things. Truly, Charlotte, I think he just doesn't want to bother. I'm here and that's that."

"What about the staff? Have you spoken to them?"

Cookie gave a wry little laugh. "How would I know who to talk to? Maybe they're all in on it."

"Do you suspect anyone?"

"There's this one nurse who comes on in the evenings. Nurse Thrasher. I call her Nurse Ratched."

"Like in that movie? *One Flew Over the Cuckoo's Nest*?"

"Yes. She's like a—a dictator."

Charlotte could hear the choir starting up again. Teatime must be over. They were singing "Open Up Your Heart (And Let the Sunshine In)." Charlotte disliked that song with its talk about the devil. And why couldn't they sing something more recent than the '50s? Something by the Beatles, or even Leonard Cohen.

"I have to go, Cookie," she said. "Carol will be wondering where I am. Do you want me to wheel you back?"

Cookie shook her head. "I'll just stay here. You aren't going to do anything, are you?"

Charlotte wished that someone from Golden Elders Condo had kept in touch with Cookie after she moved out. Maybe if they had, things would have been different. Loneliness can make a person start imagining things.

"I'll talk to the gals about it at coffee tomorrow morning," she said. "They may have some ideas. Meanwhile, be careful not to be a troublemaker."

She had meant it as a joke, but Cookie's face twisted and tears came to her eyes. Then she turned her wheelchair around so that Charlotte had to say goodbye to the back of her head. In the lounge, the choir was singing "Let a Smile Be Your Umbrella." Charlotte slipped into her place and sang along, thankful that it was the last song in their repertoire.

Driving Maisie home, she explained what had happened.

"If I remember Cookie right, she was very down-to-earth," Maisie said. "Not the kind of person to make things up. In fact, she was pretty boring."

"I know. And today she seemed really frightened. It was upsetting to see her like that."

***

After coffee the next morning, Charlotte asked Bessie, Olive and Maisie to stay behind for a few minutes. She repeated Cookie's story and, to her surprise, Olive reacted as soon as she heard the name Sunny Ways.

"I know that place," she said. "Don's cousin, Harry, was there for a while. I visited him once and there was something…creepy about it. It had bad vibes."

"Is he still alive?" Charlotte asked nervously.

"Oh, yes. It was just temporary, till the family could get him into a place closer to them. He was really jumpy, looking around every few minutes to see if someone was watching us. I was glad to get out of there."

"I think we should look into it," Bessie said. She was a big woman and used to taking charge. "You'd feel terrible if something happened to Cookie and you hadn't done anything. And she's stuck in a wheelchair. She's vulnerable."

Charlotte wished she had never gone to Sunny Ways with the choir, never responded to Cookie's wave, never brought the story to the coffee club.

"If anyone has any suggestions…" she said.

There was a pause while everyone looked at everyone else. Then Bessie said, "Respite care! Who do we know who could book in for respite care?"

The ladies turned to Charlotte.

"Oh, no," she said. "There isn't anything wrong with me. I couldn't tell lies to get in."

"I remember now," Olive said suddenly. "There was this one nurse Harry hated. She was a real bully. He said she was like a nurse in a horror movie."

"Charlotte, isn't that what Cookie said?" Maisie interjected. "You told me that yesterday."

Charlotte tried to ignore her.

"You had those back spasms, Charlotte," Olive said. "Last year? They never found anything on the X-rays, but you couldn't walk properly for days. Remember, you had to borrow a walker."

"My daughter came every day to help me. She would do it again."

Bessie banged her fist on the table. "Aren't Joanne and her husband going to Costa Rica in March? You told us about it at bridge last week. You wouldn't want your bad back to ruin her holiday."

"But my back is just fine!"

"Charlotte," Bessie said, "show a little creativity. Think of all those poor old people lying there, helpless." Bessie was 93, but she didn't consider that old.

Charlotte felt helpless herself. Here were her presumed friends, willing to send her into a situation which could be dangerous, possibly life-threatening. Just as she was about to give a definite *No*, Maisie spoke up.

"I'll do it. I wouldn't be as useful as you, Charlotte. What with my poor eyesight and everything. But it'll be easy for me to fake needing respite care."

The other women looked at Maisie with admiration, and then turned to Charlotte. She knew when she was beaten.

"Oh, all right. I'll do it. But you all have to help with the planning. I'm not good at making things up."

"Attagirl. We need to set up a spreadsheet," Olive said. She was the condo's resident computer geek, an unlikely one with her sensible shoes, tightly permed hair and pastel polyester pantsuits. "When does your daughter leave for Costa Rica?"

"The beginning of March."

"That doesn't give us much time," Bessie said. "You and I have to go see Cookie this afternoon, Charlotte, and find out everything she knows. In the meantime, Olive, think about people who can help us get Charlotte in there while her daughter is away. There may be a waiting list."

Bessie was a lifelong worker for the Conservative party, and Olive's husband had once sat in the provincial legislature as a Liberal. They were also pillars of their respective churches: Olive, the Roman Catholics, and Bessie, the Anglicans. Between them, they knew a great number of influential people.

"I can drive us to Sunny Ways if you want," Bessie said to Charlotte as they were gathering their things.

"I'll drive, thanks. I was there just yesterday so I know the best route." Charlotte had vowed never again to let Bessie drive her anywhere after a very bad experience. She still remembered the truck driver's astonished (and angry) face.

"I'll meet you downstairs at 1:30." And Bessie strode off, as well as one can stride while pushing a walker.

***

At Sunny Ways, Cookie thanked them again and again for coming. It was almost embarrassing. The three women crowded into her room, which seemed even smaller with the addition of Bessie and her walker.

"We're making a plan," Bessie said, after they had shed their coats and found seats. Charlotte had to sit on the bed. "Charlotte is going to apply for respite care here while her daughter is away in Costa Rica. She's going to have a bad back when the time comes."

"That's a great idea, Charlotte."

Bessie said, "We need to know about the staff—this nurse you mentioned, to begin with. Charlotte, you better take notes." She pulled a sheet of paper from the capacious knitting bag, which she always carried, and handed it to Charlotte.

Cookie described Nurse Thrasher. "She works the overnight shift several times a week, and she likes to be on alone, which is suspicious, don't you think? And she's a registered nurse, so she's the one who handles the medications, needles and things."

"Anyone could use a pillow to smother people," Bessie said.

Cookie looked stunned at the thought, then carried on. "Everybody's afraid of her, even the other nurses."

Charlotte shivered. She wasn't good at confrontation. How was she going to help if this woman came after Cookie in the night?

"There's Flora, who's from the Philippines. She's a PSW—personal support worker. Works days mostly. A nice little thing, always sending money home to her family. And there's Patrick, he's an RN. He sometimes does the overnight shift. He's very good to his mother, talks about her a lot. Then there's Linda, another PSW, and the day nurses, Latoya and Rhonda—"

Bessie said, "Stop. That's enough to start with. We have to leave soon. Now, Cookie, you need to start complaining. You told Charlotte it was the whiners who were being targeted, didn't you? Complain about something every day."

"Isn't that dangerous?" Charlotte asked. "Suppose it's someone with a short temper and they go after Cookie before I get here?"

"Just little things at first," Bessie said. "So she gets a reputation."

"I can do that. God knows, there's enough to complain about," Cookie said, with feeling. "I think I'll send back my soup at dinner. It's always lukewarm."

Charlotte wasn't sure they had done the right thing by unleashing Cookie's troublemaking side, but it was too late now. She and Bessie donned their coats and boots and said their goodbyes.

Bessie's last comment to Cookie as she saw them off at the front door was, "And for heaven's sake, do something about your hair."

"Well, that was a good start," Bessie said as Charlotte helped her into the car and heaved the walker into the backseat. "I wonder what Olive organized while we were away?"

"Do you think Cookie has the right idea? How is annoying the cooks going to help? They aren't likely to be killing people."

"Cooks are in the perfect position to poison people," Bessie said grimly.

Charlotte wanted to ask how they could be sure of killing just one person, but she knew Bessie would have an answer for that. She started the car, and they drove home in silence.

***

Three weeks later, Charlotte found herself in her temporary room at Sunny Ways Lodge, wondering why she had given in to this crazy plan. Every night of those three weeks she had gone to bed with a feeling of dread. And every morning she had wakened to the same feeling. But

251

every day Cookie had phoned her to report that she had filed a new complaint and she was still alive, which was something to be thankful for.

Charlotte looked around the room. It was the same size as Cookie's, but it wasn't as full of furniture. She had only one armchair, and there was no TV. Hers was too big to bring with her.

At least she hadn't had to lie to her doctor, who was an old friend. Well, only a little fib. She had explained that her daughter and son-in-law were going on holiday and they would feel better if she was in respite care while they were away. Dr. Stephens had signed the papers without any questions. And Bessie and Olive had worked their magic with the admitting process. Later today, she would phone her grandson, Justin, and ask him to tell his parents in Costa Rica where she was. He was at university out of town, so he wouldn't be coming to visit.

There was a knock at the door. Charlotte stood up, then remembered that it was supposed to be painful for her to walk and she had to save her energy. She called, "Come in."

It was Cookie. "I'm so glad you got here, Charlotte. I've come to take you down to the lounge for the sing-along before dinner."

Cookie seemed to have gained a new lease on life in the past three weeks. Her hair had been decently cut, and she was wearing a matching top and pants. And she was using a walker, instead of a wheelchair.

"I hope you don't mind. I told Keisha, the social director, that you can play the piano. We have a sing-along before dinner on Saturdays and Jenny, our usual pianist, broke her femur yesterday and is in the hospital. It won't bother your back, playing piano, will it?"

Before Charlotte could say that Cookie knew there was nothing wrong with her back, the door was flung open and a wild-haired woman appeared. She pointed at Charlotte and said, menacingly, "You're on the list!" Then she retreated and slammed the door.

"Who was that?" Charlotte asked when she got her breath back.

"Oh, we call her The Slammer. We're all used to her, though Paul Sikorski found it very frightening at first. He used to live in Russia."

"I hope she doesn't do that in the middle of the night."

"I think they sedate her. But lock your door, just in case. Ready to go?"

In the lounge Charlotte was introduced to Keisha, a plump little thing with dreadlocks, who looked all of 16. She was almost tearfully grateful to have a pianist appear in front of her.

"We're so glad to see you, Charlotte. Aren't we, everyone? Let's all say, 'Welcome to Sunny Ways, Charlotte.'" The small group gathered around the piano didn't seem terribly enthusiastic, but one or two responded. "We usually sing for half an hour or so, don't we, Cookie? The residents prefer the old favorites. There are music books on the piano. I hope you sight-read. Or if you play by ear, that's fine. Anything is fine. What would you like to sing, ladies? And gentlemen?"

Charlotte slid onto the piano bench and looked at her audience. There were murmurs of "Where's Jenny?" but no suggestions. Finally, Cookie piped up. "How about 'When the Red, Red Robin Comes Bob, Bob, Bobbin' Along'?"

Charlotte played that and then one old standard after another. Keisha had a good, strong voice, and she carried the others. Finally, she announced that it was time for dinner. "And isn't it lovely that Charlotte can come and play for us while she's here?"

"Where's Jenny?" someone asked. "Did Jenny die, too?"

Keisha ignored the speaker and called for a round of applause for Charlotte. There were a few handclaps, then the wheelchair and walker parade formed up and headed for the dining room.

"Come on, Charlotte," Cookie said. "I asked for you to be at my table. The Dougs will already be there."

"The Dougs?"

"There are two men at my table, and they're both called Doug. Tall Doug and Little Doug. The little guy is a lot of fun."

Tall Doug was tall, abnormally thin and very quiet. Little Doug, was tiny, bald and had traces of an English accent. He was one of those people who love to dwell on disasters, not Charlotte's idea of fun. He had a high, piping voice that got on her nerves after just a few minutes.

First, he wanted to talk about Jenny, the missing pianist. "Terrible thing, Jenny breaking her femur like that. They'll likely have to take the leg off now. You know she's had three hip replacements. Well, she should never have been line dancing."

"She was line dancing?" Charlotte said. Sunny Ways was not as quiet a place as she had thought.

"Yesterday evening. Gina Muzzi started it after the movie. What was the movie, Cookie?"

"*Saturday Night Fever.* Jenny loves dancing."

Little Doug went on to review the recent deaths. Shirley, who hadn't really needed to be here and did she let everyone know it! Jane, who had all her marbles and could still play a mean game of bridge. Lou, a good guy but cranky. Mabel, not the friendliest of people but she was all right if you didn't get on her bad side. And Rose, who hadn't used a cane, let alone a walker, and there you were. At some point during this speech, Tall Doug stood up, nodded to everyone and left the table.

"They'd all still be with us if they'd had proper care," Little Doug said. "Dying in their beds like that. They should have used their alert bracelets to get help. I've got mine on now."

"I have one, too," Cookie said. "You should get one, Charlotte. It's a comfort in the night if you can't get to your phone."

"I'll certainly think about it," Charlotte said. Someone should have suggested it before she got here. Suppose the killer (if there was a killer) caught on to her act and came into her room in the night? She felt in her pocket for her cell phone. It would have to do.

Little Doug left the table, promising to see them at breakfast. Charlotte didn't look forward to the meal. The food at dinner had been just short of disgusting—lukewarm soup, glutinous beef stew, lumpy mashed potatoes and overcooked gray-green beans. And Little Doug's voice had given her a headache.

She declined Cookie's suggestion that they play bingo or watch the hockey game on TV in the lounge. She said she wanted an early night, even though it was barely seven o'clock.

On her way to her room, she was accosted by a tall, handsome woman in nursing whites. "Mrs. Manners," the woman said, "I want to have a word with you before you turn in. I am Nurse Thrasher. I was busy with another resident when you arrived, so I didn't see you then. I understand that you plan to look after your own medication while you're here?" She sounded surprised, as if Charlotte didn't look capable of tying her shoes, let alone administering her own pills.

Charlotte wished that she hadn't been pushing a walker. She felt at a disadvantage.

"Yes, I do. Is that a problem?"

"It's much safer if you turn them over to us at the nursing office and we see to it. Pills can sometimes go missing from the residents' rooms."

"I only take the one prescribed pill for my blood pressure. I can handle it myself. I was a registered nurse."

Nurse Thrasher ignored that. "What about the medication for your back pain?"

Charlotte had forgotten her bad back. "My doctor said to take them only as needed. I have to have them with me in case the spasms come in the middle of the night."

"Very well," Nurse Thrasher said. "But you must keep them in the locked box that is in your room." She just missed adding, "or else."

Charlotte was glad to get away from her and let herself into her room.

After leaving a message on her grandson's phone and a message for Bessie (thank God for voice mail), she locked the door, remembering The Slammer, and crawled into bed. It took her some time to get to sleep, and she woke with a start not much later. A figure with a flashlight was moving quietly toward her bed.

Charlotte froze. Where was she? Then she remembered. She felt under her pillow for her cell phone and turned it on.

"Stop," she shouted to the intruder. "I'm calling 911."

"Mrs. Manners, it's me. Flora. I'm just checking to see you're okay."

Charlotte sat up and turned on her bedside light. She recognized Flora, the care worker who had admitted her the afternoon before.

"Oh, I'm so sorry," Flora said. "I don't mean to wake you up. I knock but no answer. You don't call me to help you get ready for bed, so we wonder if you are all right. Ms. Thrasher ask me to check on you."

As if the mention of her name had conjured her up, Nurse Thrasher appeared in the doorway.

"What is all this disturbance?" she asked. "I heard shouting."

Charlotte and Flora both quailed. Charlotte spoke first. "I'm so sorry, Nurse. Flora came in to check on me, and I woke up and didn't know where I was. I do apologize for shouting."

"I hope there won't be any more of this, Mrs. Manners. It is very disturbing for the other residents. Flora, you can go back to doing the bed checks."

"So sorry," Flora said, retreating. Nurse Thrasher sniffed loudly and went out. Charlotte heard the door lock from the outside. Of course, she realized, the staff had pass keys to all the rooms. Any of them could get in. And now she was branded a troublemaker, her first night here. She wanted to take a sleeping pill, but it seemed unwise to fall into a deep sleep.

The rest of the night was uncomfortable. She woke early, got up and dressed. Breakfast was served at 8 a.m. on Sundays, she knew. A few minutes before eight o'clock, there was a knock at the door. She called, "Come in," then remembered that the door was locked. While she was fighting with the brake mechanism on her walker, the door opened and a young, blond man in a blue nursing smock walked in.

257

"Mrs. Manners?" he said. "Or is it okay if I call you Charlotte? I'm Patrick, the nurse on duty. Welcome to Sunny Ways. By the way. I'm afraid I have some rather unpleasant news."

No, Charlotte thought, not a death the first night I'm here!

Before she could speak, Patrick went on, "There was an outbreak of tummy trouble in the night. That's why I'm still on. We've been terribly busy."

"Oh dear. That's too bad."

"Anyway, since you're new here, I thought you should know about outbreak procedure. Your visitors are restricted to family members, and they must come straight to your room. Meals are still being served in the dining room, but please clean your hands at the disinfectant stations before and after meals. And if you feel any nausea or have any other symptoms, report them to the nursing office and stay in your room. I have a printout here that outlines the rules."

He walked over to hand it to her. Up close, she realized that he was older than she had thought. She was almost sure his hair was dyed. "Sorry to dump all this on you, your first morning here."

"Thank you, Patrick," Charlotte said. "I trust no one is badly ill."

"These outbreaks can go through a seniors' residence like wildfire," he said. "I hope I don't carry it home to my mother. She's pretty frail."

"You take care of your mother? That's good of you."

"Oh, Mother appreciates it. And she never complains. Not like some of the people here." He stopped himself. "I shouldn't have said that. I'm just tired after last night."

At that point his phone rang. Patrick took it out of the pocket of his smock, looked at it and sighed. "It's Mother. She's worried because I'm not home yet. Well, better get on with things. Have a nice day." And off he went to spread the news of the outbreak.

Charlotte's first reaction was panic. Bessie had promised that she would come by after church "to check the place out" and help Charlotte make plans. Now she was going to be on her own with no one but Cookie for moral support, and she didn't have much faith in Cookie.

There was another tap on the door and Cookie appeared. "Yoo-hoo. I've come to walk you down to breakfast."

"Cookie, have you heard about the sickness going around?"

"Yes. I got one of the notices under my door. Don't worry. It happens all the time. Lockdown, I call it. Come on—pancakes or waffles this morning."

Little Doug was at the table when they arrived, but Tall Doug was missing. Charlotte hoped it wasn't the stomach virus keeping him away. Cookie and Little Doug spent the meal speculating on who was "down" with the bug and whether the lockdown would come into full force this outbreak. Then meals would have to be served in rooms. Charlotte listened with increasing gloom as she tried to eat the leaden pancakes.

After breakfast, she headed back to her room to phone Bessie and tell her about the outbreak. Bessie was briefly daunted by the news of the stomach virus, but only briefly. "You can keep us informed by phone, Charlotte. You'll be just fine. Call me back after you've had a good look around."

Charlotte started off to check the place out. Everything took so much longer when you were pushing a walker. Finally, across from the nursing station, in the main hallway, she found a small alcove with an armchair where she could sit and observe everyone coming and going, without being too obvious herself. She could also see Cookie's door from that spot. There was a large artificial schefflera that would partially mask anyone sitting in the chair. This would be her post. She could sneak down at night, when everyone else was in bed, and keep an eye on things. She would have a nap during the day so she could stay awake. If anyone found her in the chair, she would say that her back hurt so much she couldn't sleep, and she had been taking a walk to keep her mind off it.

Now that she had a plan, she felt much better. Back in her room, she tried to read but couldn't concentrate. The only break in the boredom was listening to The Slammer going up and down the hall, occasionally finding an unlocked door. It was a relief when lunchtime came.

Tall Doug was still missing from the table. Little Doug announced that he was "down" and that things didn't look good. "These tall, thin guys don't have much resistance."

When Charlotte got back to her room, she was startled to find Flora there. "Just making the bed," Flora said and she left quickly. But hadn't the bed already been made when Charlotte went to lunch? Cookie had mentioned Flora sending money home to her family. Might she be getting some of this money from residents' rooms?

Charlotte decided to take a nap. Suspecting everyone was making her unusually tired, and the atmosphere of Sunny Ways was sapping her energy. When she woke, she went to the lounge where many of the residents were sitting, looking drearily at the snow-covered windows. Charlotte asked Linda, the attendant on duty, if it was all right if she played the piano. Her own piano had gone to her grandchildren when she moved into the condo. Playing for the sing-along had made her realize how much she missed making music.

She played hymns, because it was Sunday, the hymns of her childhood, and she was touched to hear some of the residents joining in: "Shall We Gather at the River?," "Amazing Grace," and "Blessed Assurance." When Cookie called her to dinner, she felt a little better.

There were more residents missing at dinner, but not Little Doug, unfortunately. He sounded delighted as he added names to the roster of those who were "down." Cookie was just as bad, reminding him of those he hadn't mentioned. Charlotte felt as though she had entered a war zone. Would she ever get out of this place? Dinner was a choice of fish fillets or a salad plate, and, smelling the fish, Charlotte opted for salad.

After dinner, she fled back to her room. She was beginning to realize why she hadn't kept in touch with Cookie when she moved from the condo—they had almost nothing in common. Cookie liked bingo, for heaven's sake. And she had to spend two more weeks here. Unless Cookie was attacked very soon. She was horrified to find that the idea was not unwelcome.

She read for a while, then undressed for bed and set her alarm for twelve o'clock. The night nurse came on at 11 p.m. and by midnight, things might be quiet enough for her to venture out to her observation post. When the alarm went off, she was sleeping soundly. It took all her willpower to get up, put on her robe and make her way out the door, after looking down the hall in both directions. She left her walker behind—it was just an encumbrance.

She made herself comfortable in the little alcove, pulled the schefflera in front of her and hunkered down. Nurse Thrasher and Patrick were in the nurses' office.

Every so often, one of them came out and headed down the hall, apparently in answer to a summons. They would come back after an interval then head out again. There must be a large number of patients needing help. Patrick seemed to be taking frequent phone calls when he was in the hall, away from Nurse Thrasher.

Charlotte struggled to stay awake, but after a while she dozed off. The next thing she heard was a group of workers arriving, chattering in a foreign language. The kitchen staff, she assumed.

"Some security guard I am," she thought as she eased her cramped body out of the chair and shuffled back to her room, hoping no one was watching. If she spent many more nights like this, she was genuinely going to have a bad back.

Monday was a dreadful repetition of Sunday, brightened only by a phone call from her grandson and several sessions at the piano in the lounge. During the sing-along she noticed that one couple was jiving, quite nimbly, when she played "On the Sunny Side of the Street," and that cheered her up a little.

At dinner, Little Doug announced that Keisha, the social director, had caught the bug. "Young people are more likely to succumb to these plagues. Like with the Spanish flu," he said, clearly relishing the prospect. All activities had been cancelled anyway, because of the outbreak. The food continued to be almost inedible.

After dinner, Charlotte napped. Once again, her alarm woke her at midnight and she crept down the hall to her hiding place. She saw Nurse Thrasher seated at her desk in the lighted nursing office. She was alone. Suddenly, the woman lifted her head and seemed to stare right at Charlotte. She came out of the office and walked to the alcove.

"Someone moved that plant," she was saying. She bent down to slide the schefflera into place and jumped back on seeing Charlotte.

"Mrs. Manners," she said. "What are you doing up at this hour?"

Charlotte pretended to have suddenly wakened from sleep. "Where am I?" she asked.

"You're out of your room, in the middle of the night. That is against the rules."

It was lucky Charlotte was prepared for this. "My back hurt," she said. "Sometimes it helps to walk it off so I was doing that. I sat down and must have dozed off."

Nurse Thrasher frowned. "I will help you back to your room," she said. "It isn't good for someone with a bad back to sleep in a chair. And the halls are cool at night. We have enough problems with the outbreak without someone here for respite care getting pneumonia."

"I'm sorry," Charlotte said. And she truly was. Now there was another black mark against her.

On their way to Charlotte's room, they met Patrick, who must have been dealing with another sick resident.

"Charlotte!" he said. "Do you need help?"

Nurse Thrasher was quick to explain. "I found Mrs. Manners sleeping in a chair in the lobby." She made it sound as if it were equivalent to dancing naked. "Could you take her back to her room, Patrick? I was in the midst of some important paperwork when I discovered her there. Let us have no more of this wandering, Mrs. Manners."

Patrick took Charlotte's arm. "Not using your walker, Charlotte? Isn't that a bit dangerous?"

He would notice. "I must have been half asleep when I left my room. I took some pain pills earlier. My head is a bit fuzzy."

When they reached her room, he unlocked the door and shepherded her in. "I'll help you into bed. Would you like a sleeping pill? Mother always takes one when she feels wakeful."

"No thank you, Patrick. My pain pills should be enough. Please lock the door behind you." Although much good that would do with the staff able to enter at will.

As Patrick went out, his phone rang again and she heard him say, "Yes, Mother. I'm still here."

***

Charlotte slept late the next morning and missed breakfast. Cookie came knocking at her door to see if she was ill and brought her a banana, which was very welcome. When Charlotte was dressed, she phoned Bessie to report.

"I don't think I'm doing any good at all here, Bessie. Couldn't I come home? I'll say my back feels a lot better, and it's silly for me to be taking up a room here."

"But this is the perfect time to do away with someone, when they're already weak with the flu. And if you come home, you might bring the sickness with you."

Charlotte had never thought of that. "All right," she said. "I'll stay a little longer."

It was another tedious day. Then in the late afternoon, Cookie phoned to report that she was feeling queasy and had been told to stay in her room. Charlotte played for the sing-along crowd and then went in to dinner, alone with Little Doug. He was almost gleeful at the news that Cookie was "down."

Charlotte knew she couldn't go back to the alcove that night if Nurse Thrasher was on duty. But Cookie needed protection. If Charlotte got into her room and just sat there, surely she wouldn't pick up the bug. She wouldn't touch anything.

Night came, and Charlotte put on her robe and started down the hall to Cookie's room. And was stopped by Patrick, who must have seen her from the nursing station.

"Charlotte," he said, "where are you going?"

"Where is Nurse Thrasher?"

"Alas, she has succumbed to the stomach bug. She's lying down in one of the empty rooms. Are you having trouble sleeping again? Where is your walker?"

Damn and blast! He'd caught her again. "My back is so much better after a good rest today. I don't feel I need it. I was just going to check on my friend, Cookie. I heard she has the bug."

He took her arm firmly and walked her in the direction of her room. "You mustn't have any contact with Cookie. You might pick up the virus. Anyway, she was sleeping soundly when I last checked on her."

"But I'm worried about her," Charlotte said as they entered the room. Patrick closed the door behind them.

"She's lucky to have such a good friend. She's not very, well, popular here. Now, let's get you back to bed, and I'm going to give you a sleeping pill. Ms. Thrasher suggested that. We thought you might be suffering from what we call sundowning."

Charlotte found the term ominous. "Sundowning?"

"Yes. Sometimes seniors feel more active at nights and take to wandering." He took a plastic-wrapped pill from the pocket of his smock and handed it to her. "Take this right now. I see a glass of water by your bed."

She didn't want to take anything Nurse Thrasher had suggested. Nor did she trust Patrick. Maybe they were in on this together. But it was best to seem compliant. She got into bed, accepted the pill and pretended to swallow it. As soon as he had left, she spat it out and hoped it had just been a sleeping pill and not something more lethal. She hid it under her pillow in case she needed to have it analyzed later. Then she got out of bed and opened her door just a crack. She positioned her walker so that she could sit on it and see down the hall.

It seemed that hours went by before she saw Patrick, moving down the hall. Something glinted in his right hand. She opened her door wider and looked out. He was going into Cookie's room. Quickly, she slipped out into the hall and followed him. When she reached the half-open door, he was bending over Cookie. In the light from the hall she could see he was holding a syringe. She heard him say, "Die, Mother, why won't you die?"

Charlotte picked up one of Cookie's large brass ornaments, a giant peacock, and struck Patrick over the head. He dropped to his knees. Cookie sat up in bed and screamed. Patrick tried to get up and Charlotte hit him again. This time, he fell on his face and lay still.

"My God, Charlotte," Cookie said, "what are you doing?"

"I'm calling 911," Charlotte said. She took a tissue from the bosom of her nightdress and picked up the syringe off the floor. "I just hope this contains something lethal and isn't a shot to control the stomach flu."

***

The next afternoon, Charlotte sat in her own living room, telling her story while Bessie, Olive and Maisie listened, awestruck. She'd had some difficulty explaining things to the police when they arrived. Later, they had found that the syringe contained insulin. And Cookie was not diabetic.

Now that sun was actually shining and she was back in her own home, she felt human again. Cookie had called frequently with the latest news and rumors. She didn't have the stomach bug, just a bit of gas. Patrick hadn't been severely injured, and he had confessed to being responsible for the recent deaths at Sunny Ways. Police were looking into other deaths at nursing homes where he had worked. Patrick's mother had been taken into care, as there was no one to look after her. Nurse Thrasher had collapsed when she heard of Patrick's crimes and kept saying, "But he was an RN." She was on sick leave and might not be returning to Sunny Ways. Tall Doug was back for meals, though Little Doug was "down" now with the bug.

"You must be proud of yourself, Charlotte. Your name will be in all the papers," Bessie said, somewhat enviously.

"I hope not. Since Patrick has confessed, there shouldn't have to be a trial. You know, it's funny. I thought I'd never want to see Sunny Ways again, but that stay there did something for me—I found out how much I miss my piano. I'm going to get my grandson to find me a keyboard. And when this outbreak is over, I'm going to volunteer at Sunny Ways, go in once a week and play the piano for sing-alongs if they'll have me."

***

A month later, with the outbreak over, Charlotte was back in the lounge at Sunny Ways seated at the piano. Quite a crowd had gathered. Cookie and Tall Doug were there, holding hands. Charlotte opened up her songbook and launched into a tune from *Hair.* And everyone started singing "Let the Sunshine In."

GENTLE RAIN FROM HEAVEN

By Catherine Astolfo

Mersey hands the form with her ID to the policeman blocking the door. He examines the document closely, but does not look at her.

Perhaps the man does not feel a need to study the face before him. Mersey is slim and short, never described as skinny or tiny. Plain, average, gray hair, dull brown eyes. A pale woman in a mostly white world. An eyewitness would have difficulty describing her. There is no quality that makes her appearance distinctive.

Finally, the policeman raises his eyes to look at her. He has discovered the only unique thing about her.

"Mer-zee?" he asks, saying her name like the famous river.

"No. Mer-see. As in, 'The quality of mercy is not strain'd, It droppeth as the gentle rain from heaven.'"

He hands back the form, giving her a quizzical look. *Not a Shakespeare fan,* she guesses.

"Keep that on you at all times."

His voice is stern, as though she has already done something wrong.

Dusky despite the sun's rays straining to enter through beveled glass, the room is large and stark. There's a hospital bed and a plastic chair.

"The nurse is here," the doorkeeper announces, and Mersey enters the room.

More police officers huddle in a circle off to one side, voices muddy. Their sheer size smells of power. Domination.

The lone female in the group is Mersey's opposite. She would easily be spotted in a crowd. As tall as any of the men, as wide at the hips as the shoulders, she proudly carries a spare tire over her belt. Hair the color of fire at its burning peak is rolled in a bun and topped by her hat.

The group stops their mumbling. Red turns fierce green eyes on Mersey. Looks her up and down as though sizing her for an orange suit.

The nurse turns toward the bed. Her patient is hidden under sheets that glimmer with the residue of strong bleach and hundreds of washings. This is a tiny person.

At first Mersey is confused. She was told she would be accompanying an adult, not a child. She had explained to her union rep—

But no, this is not a child. On second glance, she notices bare feet. Heels a mass of calluses. Toes that have walked a lot of years. Farther along the prone body, breasts that move up and down with each stuttering breath. A tiny woman, then.

Mersey moves closer to the bed. The patient looks up at the scent of someone less threatening. Her porcelain face is framed by a mass of brownish blond waves. Her blue eyes blink and stare. Not quite robin's egg-blue, darker and more layered, they are skies full of promise. An invitation to dream.

Her unlined, flawlessly perfect skin is white, yet dusted with tan and freckles that give her an exotic look. Lips are naturally red, plump and sweet. Her tongue pokes from between teeth that should be white and dazzling, but are yellowed with the stains of life. An imperfection that prevents her from being achingly beautiful.

Mersey recognizes the tongue gesture and looks over at the bedside table. A cup and straw, hospital issue. She brings the water to her patient. The girl sips desperately.

Under the sheets, Mersey can see that the young woman's arms and chest are bandaged. The smell of burned flesh mingles with antiseptics and the acrid scent of urine.

Red barks, "Hey, what are you doing?"

"Giving the patient some water," Mersey answers in her crisp, professional voice.

"You were just hired to transport."

"Part of my job is to ensure the patient is well enough to be transferred, Constable."

"She's as good as she's ever gonna get," Red snarls.

The men snicker behind her.

"And it's Sergeant," the woman adds. Tucks her fingers in her belt. Thrusts the spare tire farther into the room.

Ah, she's in charge, Mersey thinks. *No wonder she surrounds herself with an extra layer. She needs to let the men know she can pounce at any time.*

"Sergeant, I promise I won't get in your way. Just doing my job."

Their eyes meet. Mersey sees the sudden understanding. *We don't need a catfight in front of the men.*

"Well, don't make her too comfortable."

271

Mersey hears *bitch* and something that sounds nastier. Mumbled like little kids in a playground. Their animosity is an oppressive blanket of disapproval.

The young woman's eyes fill with fear. Film with tears that can't quite flow from her dehydrated body. She reaches out and clasps the nurse's hand.

This skin is softer than anything Mersey has ever felt, other than the downy head of her baby. Warmth rushes through her blood, prickling her skin. She is smitten beyond control and—she knows this from past encounters—reason.

This young woman could be Mersey's daughter. Had Rachel been allowed to reach this age.

She gently strokes her patient's cheek, reassuring her. The sky-blue eyes clear slightly. Lock on Mersey's face. An infant discovering her parent. Her source of life. Her mother.

The girl's bandages stretch from elbow to shoulders on both sides. When Mersey lifts the sheet, she can see white gauze covering the young woman's chest. A lick of flame has scraped off the first layer of skin. A fiery brush, not enough to require skin grafts, perhaps. Time and infection prevention will heal her.

Mersey plumps the pillow and resumes holding her patient's hand.

The officers glare at her.

Mersey is astounded by the animosity. A ferocious cloud of hostility hangs over the room. They do not even attempt to be professional. Their feelings are raw and blatant.

Mersey wonders what on earth Rachel could possibly have done to deserve this level of anger. She has decided that until she knows this young woman's name, it doesn't hurt to think of her as Rachel.

The patient licks her lips. Once more, Mersey wets the girl's mouth and tongue with water.

A word that might be *mercy*, the Shakespearean one, croaks from a chest that is plainly ravaged by smoke inhalation. The kind of intake that includes melted oil products. Burnt offerings from a world that forms chairs from plastic.

Mersey brushes wisps of hair away from Rachel's forehead. Allows her long cool fingers to linger on the young woman's heated skin. The girl whimpers like a kitten being stroked and closes her eyes.

Mersey begins to sing very softly. It's an ancient lullaby that Rachel loves. Sleep. Peace. Guardian angels watching all through the night.

How ironic.

The memories always come at unexpected times. This is probably not one of those. Blond blue-eyed stunning youth is an obvious trigger. Still, Mersey doesn't like being sideswiped at work. Were she at home, she could curl up in bed, sweat out the moment. Yet here it is. She catches her breath.

Tiny body, blond hair. Fuzzy infant down along her arms. Empty blue eyes. An impossibly small coffin sucked into the wet ground under an appropriately rain-soaked sky.

The door shuts as he leaves, unable to look into her accusing eyes one more time.

Where were you at the time of death?

Sudden infant death syndrome. No-fault fatality.

We…went back to bed…

Left in the impervious look of the investigator, a stamp of images. The romp in the bedroom. So much fun, especially for him, while their baby takes her last breath right next door.

Let her sleep for once. It's been six weeks.

Sudden infant death syndrome. No-fault fatality.

Alone in her crib. Soft skin, bright-eyed smile. Mersey might have gone in and jiggled her, picked her up, embraced her cuddly body. Started that heart beating. Now her soft squirming child was cold and unyielding. Hardened with the cessation of breath and blood flow. Repellent.

I can't even stand to pick her up.

Mersey shudders. Catches the images, thrown at her with the ferocity and sting of a hardball. Thrusts them back.

This Rachel is warm. Her hand curls around Mersey's, soft as a kitten's breath. Those blue eyes, so very blue, cling to the life raft that is her transport nurse.

"Mersey," she rasps again, a throaty, grating sound that only approximates speech.

"Did you hear the policeman say my name, dear? Yes, it's Mersey, an odd title, I guess, but maybe okay for a nurse."

She smiles at the girl and studies the eyes that peer up at her. *If innocence had a face, it would be this one,* she thinks. Although the blue orbs are filmy with injury, they are fathomless. Tinged with fear perhaps, but childlike and pure.

"You rest, dear. I'm sure everything will be all right."

Mersey feels another wave of love rise in her chest, pinking her cheeks. She fights the desire to pick the child-woman up in her arms. Wishes she could whisk her away from this wall of suspicion. She continues to whisper-sing the lullaby about watching all through the night. All through the day. Mersey would never take her eyes off Rachel again.

Red swaggers up to the bed. "Nurse, I don't think singing to the patient is part of the deal here. Just shut it, will you?"

"I absolutely must do whatever it takes to ensure my patient's comfort."

Mersey uses her prim voice. The way she imagines a nun would speak.

"In fact, I am wondering why the patient does not have a morphine drip. Shall I call the doctor?"

Red leans over and breathes a foul, hot scent in Mersey's face. Her snarl is rancid.

Where were you at the time of death?

"She gets no morphine."

"Are you a doctor?"

"Don't get lippy with me. I'll have you replaced."

"Still, I think I will speak with the doctor. It's my right as the transportation nurse to ensure—"

"Fine. The line's there. Make it quick. But I can assure you, no doctor will be giving out morphine today."

Mersey, however, knows how to speak to physicians. She understands the language. The liability issues. The political overtones of transporting an injured patient.

Shortly after the phone call, the doctor, a tall man with lines of haste burrowed in his forehead, bustles into the room. He hands Mersey a package.

"Only sips, Nurse, as you know. There's enough there to last through the wait period here, as well as the ambulance ride."

Liquid morphine to avoid the drip. Easier for transportation purposes. The girl has tolerated water, and the dropper is appropriately small, so this method will be fine.

The doctor's middle-aged, kindly face tries to maintain professional neutrality, but his eyes are willful. They dart back and forth from Rachel to Mersey. Linger on the girl. Curiosity flashes like sparks on the brown layers as he blinks.

When he has gone, Mersey administers a small amount of the medicinal oil, chased with a sip of water. Mersey must remember that she is very tiny. A child-sized portion is plenty.

Rachel's eyes are huge and hopeful. The message is obscure, but Mersey knows there is one.

Finally, the girl swallows the medication and immediately closes her eyes.

Mersey hums the lullaby's tune this time. *My guardian angels will protect me, all through the night. They will not allow my sweet breath to falter.*

After a moment the girl is snoring slightly, a soft purr of relaxation. Rachel's hand does not slacken, however. Even in her angelic sleep, she continues to hold on for dear life. Mersey pats her patient's damp forehead with a cloth and readjusts the pillow.

Red sidles up to the bedside. Once again, the nurse can smell this sergeant's malevolence. The woman is literally sweaty with rage.

"Want to know what your sleeping angel has done?"

"I don't think it's appropriate—"

"Of course, it's not *appropriate*. Who gives a crap about appropriate? You didn't have the pleasure of seeing this little angel's destruction, did you? Think she's just full of innocence?"

The police officer's words are so close to the ones running through Mersey's head that she's momentarily thrown off balance. Red sees her weakness and springs.

Where were you at the time of death?

"They were side-by-side on the bed, arms around each other. Sweet little blond boys. Though you could only tell from their pictures how beautiful they were. Cute smiles, soft delicate skin, lovely giggles. Oh my God, you shoulda seen the videos, Transport Nurse! Break your heart in a second flat. So darling they were."

Red straightens up, uses her full height to flatten Mersey's defense.

"And this little piece of shit, this lovely innocent sleeping angel, turned them into twisted bits of charred ash. Frozen in one last gesture of brotherly love. She doped them and set them on fire. Said she was going to die with them, take an overdose and set the whole house ablaze. But miracle of miracles, she didn't quite get around to it. Neighbors saw the smoke and called the fire department a little too quickly. Ruined her sick plan."

Where were you at the time of death?

Red kicks the side of the bed, cheeks flushed with anger and frustration. Twisted black ash-covered bodies are imprinted on her face.

"And why did she do it? Because her man left her. As though she's the only woman in the world to be left with the kids."

Mersey sees the other layer of Red's anger. The undertow of a broken promise, a "Paradise by the Dashboard Light" kind of vow. The woman scorned who scorns any female who can't handle it.

"Transport to the detention center clinic from here, then hopefully prison for life. It's really too good for her."

Rachel jars awake. She cowers away from Red. Tightens her grip on the nurse's hand. Mersey looks into the blue sky of the girl's eyes. That face. That gaze of longing, hope. Purity.

Mersey reaches out once again and comforts the child-woman with a brush of cool fingers on her warm skin.

Red shakes her head and stomps away, preferring the mutters of angry men to ministrations of compassion.

"Mersey," the girl says again. Eyes brim with tears, but don't quite overflow. They shine with entreaty.

Suddenly the nurse understands the message. It's not Mersey she wants. It's *mercy*. That gentle rain from heaven.

Kill me, those sky-blue eyes beg her. *Give me the dark peace of death.*

Mersey feels overwhelmed with empathy. She takes out the morphine package. So easy to overdose in this oily, liquid form.

"I understand, Rachel," Mersey whispers. "You wanted to die with your babies. I understand that feeling. Oh my, do I ever."

She strokes the girl's hair. Relishes the feel of Rachel's bodily warmth. Her overheated stress. Looks into those wells of trust and hope. Clouds begin to clear from the blue skies as Rachel contemplates release. Her hand never moves from Mersey's. Soft fist. A frightened, shivering bird finally at rest.

Mersey tucks the morphine bag under the side table. Smooths the wild hairs from Rachel's forehead one more time. Swiftly lifts the small body to change her diaper. Flattens the sheets. Straightens the pillow.

"Don't worry, Rachel," Mersey whispers. "They'll put you in the Highlands Psychiatric Facility. They always do in cases like this. No mother deliberately kills her children unless she is insane."

She feels the beat of the girl's heart, the blood of being, throughout her own body. Mersey can't tolerate the thought of this daughter, this warmth, becoming cold and hard.

Not again.

"I work at Highlands part-time, Rachel. There was another girl there, like you. Her name was Ann-Marie. It was easy to spirit Ann-Marie away from there, and I know I can do it again. You'll live in comfort with me. We'll be mother and daughter."

The girl makes a mewing sound. Mersey sits down again and smooths Rachel's furrowed brow.

"This time, I'll make sure there are no sharp objects around. It won't be like Ann-Marie. We'll be together always, you and I."

"Mercy," the girl says.

"I'm here, dear," the nurse answers. "I'll always be here."

Mersey begins to sing the lullaby again, in soft, motherly tones.

You

NONE SHALL SLEEP

By Sylvia Maultash Warsh

Akmola, Kazakhstan, 1950

Galina's mistake was to tell her understudy at the Moscow Opera a stupid little joke. She whispered in the girl's ear: *When we are finally paid our wages, I will splurge and spend it all on a tin of herring.* Her understudy, recognizing the opportunity, relayed the conversation to the committee head, who informed the police. It turned out to be treason to imply that the government had not paid its artists in months, or that government-run stores were empty. Galina was sentenced to five years in a labor camp for anti-Soviet activity while the understudy was promoted to Galina's role.

Her mother and uncle wept when she was taken away. There was no one else left of her family. Her husband, a brilliant but unstable composer, had hanged himself two years earlier after a visit from the police who demanded that he write only music praising the virtues of Stalin.

She traveled the nearly 2,000 miles from Moscow in bitter November, four days by rail, sleeping on the crowded floor of a boxcar surrounded by women, then standing for three hours in an open truck. She was nearly frozen when she arrived at the camp near the village of Akmola in northern Kazakhstan.

All she could see was snow. It covered the barracks, the fields and the woods beyond, white under the gray brooding sky. Only barbed wire protruded through the snow; a guardhouse loomed above them.

Galina was assigned to a work detail with other women, sawing logs felled in the forest. She dragged herself back to the camp every evening, exhausted and hungry. She still had her good looks—shiny black hair, green eyes, clear skin—unlike the women who had been there for months and grown haggard from the labor and the cold. The male guards stared insolently at her.

One day, she was taken from the forest where she was working and brought before Nikolai Petrov, the director of special inspections for the province. He was of average height and weight with clipped mouse-brown hair receding from a high forehead. Unlike the rest of him, his eyes were extraordinary. They wanted things. They devoured people, searching to find what use he could make of them.

To Galina's surprise, he asked her to sing an aria from Puccini's *Turandot*. Though Galina had performed it on stage in Moscow, her body was worn out from labor and malnourishment, and her body was her instrument. It wasn't her best delivery; nonetheless, Petrov leaned forward, listening attentively, while she sang.

When she finished, he levelled his pale blue eyes at her. "Not as good as the great Maria Zamboni. But it will do. You will come and sing for me when my duties bring me to the camp every fortnight. I need to relax at the end of the day." He tilted his head. "You do not look pleased, Comrade Adamova."

"I will gladly sing for you, sir, as long as I can return to my barracks afterward."

"But you have not seen my suite—plenty of food, much better than what you eat in the camp. And space! You lie like sardines in the barracks. I have a nice big bed…"

"I appreciate the offer, sir, but I prefer to return to my friends at the barracks."

"I don't think you understand, Comrade. I am asking because I'm a gentleman, but if I want you to sing for me, you will sing."

"Of course, sir, only not—"

"And you will do whatever else I ask."

She still had some faith in the system, so she said, "I will report you to the commandant…"

His pale eyes darkened. He jumped up from his seat and came at her with a wooden stave in his hand. She screamed out, but no one came to help her. The first blow knocked her off her feet. She covered her head with her hands as he smashed the stave down on her arms, her chest, her back. She curled up into a ball, but felt her flesh disintegrating beneath the contours of the stave.

***

She spent the next four days in the camp hospital. Though she was battered and bleeding, Petrov had managed not to break any bones. Her bruised body looked like a horror show for three weeks.

When the surface of her skin had healed, Petrov sent for her. This time, she knew better than to refuse. His suite was a palace compared to the rest of the camp, with a leather sofa, bookshelves and an oak desk in the front room. In the bedroom he offered her apples and dates on a plate. She took nothing.

In front of the massive feather bed, she sang the aria "Tu che di gel sei cinta," or "You who are girdled with ice," the servant girl's song under torture. Though Galina's voice was a shadow of its former self, her pain gave it depth. Petrov lay on the bed and drank vodka from a bottle, stared at her with his devouring eyes. Then he switched on a turntable beside the bed and played a recording of "Nessun Dorma," or "None shall sleep," by Francesco Merli. During the tenor's aria, Petrov forced himself on her. The aria, and Petrov, concluded with the resounding repetitions of "Vincerò! Vincerò!" "I will win."

***

Her life changed after that. Every two weeks Galina entered his suite and sang the same aria, and every two weeks he violated her during the crescendo of "Vincerò." During those nights her spirit emptied out of her. Her body could not escape, but her essence, the kernel that was her, flew out the window into the freezing dark. She felt nothing.

She was reassigned from the forest to the sewing shop. She had never used a sewing machine and one of the other prisoners, a tall sturdy woman named Nadya, took pity on her, showing her how to handle the fabric and thread the machine.

Another woman expressed indignation that Galina had landed among them after prostituting herself to Petrov.

"Look at her! New boots, new jacket! Were they worth it?"

Galina wrenched off the padded jacket and threw it at the woman.

"Shut up!" Nadya said. "You're just jealous he doesn't want *you!*"

She pulled the jacket from the woman before she could put it on and returned it to Galina.

The other woman scowled but turned away.

After sneaking out of Petrov's bed, Galina would stuff an apple, some dates and rolls into her pockets and give them to Nadya as thanks.

Nadya would sit on her bunk, her wide cheekbones moving as she chewed the treats. "You would like my little brothers," she said wistfully. "They were sent to Siberia, but maybe one day you'll meet them."

Galina pictured two boys who looked like Nadya.

"Tell me again about *Turandot*," Nadya said.

Her friend was of good peasant stock, but Galina knew she keenly felt her lack of education.

"The beautiful Chinese Princess Turandot was betrayed by a man and wants never to marry. So she makes each suitor who comes for her hand answer three riddles. If they don't answer correctly, she has them beheaded."

Nadya nodded in approval. "Attagirl."

Not the usual audience reaction. She caught Nadya staring at the red worm of a scar on her forearm, a souvenir of Petrov's rage. He had never beaten her again; he didn't have to. Galina went on.

"The foreign Prince Calaf falls in love with her and answers the riddles correctly. She begs her father, the emperor, not to make her marry him. The prince gives her a riddle in turn. 'Tell me my name before sunrise, and at dawn, I will die.' Turandot accepts. Heralds call out her command: 'This night, none shall sleep! All will die if the prince's name is not discovered by morning.' Anticipating his victory, the prince sings 'Nessun dorma,' finishing with 'Vincerò!': 'I will win!'"

Not a romantic at heart, Nadya couldn't understand why Turandot fell in love with the prince at the end. "She should've killed him. Things would go better for her."

Galina had once loved the story, the unlikely tangle of love and death. How could she have taken it so seriously? All the melodramatic deaths. Real death was ugly and final. The only thing that mattered was survival. She had survived, but at great cost. In Petrov's dresser mirror, she saw that her eyes were empty.

***

In 1953, Joseph Stalin died. An amnesty was immediately declared, but it took a year of authorities dithering, uncertain about the new dogma and paperwork, before a million nonpolitical slave laborers were sent home. It took another year before political prisoners were set free.

While they waited for their freedom, Nadya told Galina, "I prayed every day for my little brothers in Siberia. Now they'll be coming home, and we'll be a family again."

Galina made the long trek home to Moscow in 1955 to find that her mother had died six months earlier. Her uncle, still a staunch Communist, had found work as an engineer in the Ministry of Industry and Trade. His faith in the old system was unintelligible to her now. The whole world was unintelligible to her.

Toronto, April, 1979

Galina examined the white tulle bridal gown on the mannequin with a critical eye. She draped a swath of lace along the too-low neckline on which the young bride had insisted. Oksana had tried on other gowns in the store, but had rejected them as too traditional or not tight enough. Galina had designed a custom dress for her after much discussion, Oksana picking and choosing features from photos. She was coming in for her first fitting tomorrow. After they finished her dress, Oksana would bring in her four bridesmaids and the whole process would start over, this time with four determined girls arguing over what they wanted.

Galina wondered how she had come to this, fabricating wedding gowns for spoiled young women who would have been her daughter's age, if she had had a daughter. But in order to have a daughter, you needed a man, and Galina had spent the past 25 years keeping a safe distance from men. She reflected, with some irony, that she had turned into the ice princess Turandot, who refused all suitors. Her boss, Nadya Makarova, the owner of the shop, knew better than to try to fix her up with a date, unlike some of the well-meaning mothers of the brides. Nadya was the only one who knew about Nikolai Petrov and his "arrangement" with Galina.

The two women had parted ways after leaving Akmola. Then five years later, after an exchange of letters, Nadya had offered to sponsor Galina to come to Toronto to work in the store. They had become close in the camp and trusted each other.

In Toronto Nadya told her the story of how she had emigrated to join her little brothers. Galina had always pictured them as tall young saplings from the protective way Nadya spoke of them. She had been the older sister, cooking cabbage rolls for them on the farm. So the first time Galina set eyes on the little brothers, Sergei and Dimitri, her jaw dropped. They were tall all right, but their waists were thick as tree trunks, their arms bulky, their necks like those of wrestlers. Their brown hair was crew-cut, making their heads look too small for their bodies. They greeted her politely, looking her over beneath their eyelashes. Nadya shook her head at them, signaling Galina was off-limits.

The brothers had helped Nadya establish the store, becoming silent partners. When Galina had asked what their occupations were, Nadya responded with vague clichés, that they were in import/export and finance. Galina didn't care about their murky business dealings and never asked again.

Nadya received regular injections of funds from a firm in the Soviet Union, more money than she made from dressmaking. It gave her the freedom to do what she loved—she set up a fancy store in Yorkville, the toniest neighborhood in Toronto, all in pristine white with a crystal chandelier, velvety broadloom, rich cream walls. She loved to serve champagne to rich customers who would never guess her peasant background.

Galina had jumped at the chance of a new start since, after leaving the camp, she had lost her voice. Not like someone loses a beloved hat or a glove on a bus. It had disappeared into her chest; some cave had opened up in her heart and swallowed it whole. She had lost the only part of herself that mattered. Her voice had saved her in the camp. But she had sleepwalked through her life ever since. Maybe she should have died there.

How did a woman whose body was her musical instrument live without music? Yet she couldn't bear to listen to it. It reminded her of what she had lost: *herself.* At 53, Galina was still a beautiful slim woman, though unrecognizable from her younger self: chin-length hair dyed blond to hide the gray, permed into waves around her pixie face. Oversized glasses with a slight tint so people couldn't see her eyes.

***

Galina glanced out the window, while she waited for Oksana. A black limousine pulled up in front of the store on swanky Cumberland Avenue. A stocky man in a black trench coat got out of the driver's side and stepped around to open the back door. Oksana climbed out. The car pulled away. Galina would probably never meet the fiancé; it was unlucky for him to see his future bride's wedding gown.

Oksana bounced into the salon in stiletto heels and a tight flowered dress, the summit of her white breasts cresting above the low neckline.

"How are you today, Miss Popova?" Galina took in the mass of platinum blond hair reaching her shoulders.

"I'm excited to try on my dress!" she exclaimed, rubbing her perfectly manicured hands.

But when Galina brought out the gown, Oksana said, "What is this *thing* on the top?" She flicked a red nail at the lacy cowl.

"I thought it would soften the neck. It's only pinned on. If you don't like it, we can take it off."

In the dressing room Galina helped the girl struggle into the tight gown. The swath of lace along the neck was the only bit of fabric that didn't cling to her body suggestively.

"Take it off! It hides my boobs. Andrei loves to see my boobs."

Galina removed the pins and the lace. The girl had no class. Yet she had snagged a rich husband, so what did Galina know? The pull of sex was strong in young men.

Though the gown hugged all her curves, Oksana found places where the fabric could be tucked in further. Galina scheduled her for another fitting.

***

Two days later, Galina peeked through the window at the sound of a car screeching to a halt. A racing-green Jaguar convertible had pulled up in front of the salon, Oksana in the passenger seat beside an older man. Was her father dropping her off? The man leaned over and kissed her on the mouth, not fatherly. Galina cringed. So this was the fiancé she needed to be sexy for, a 60-year-old man with scant gray hair and aviator sunglasses?

Oksana coquettishly removed his sunglasses, revealing an ordinary face. But his eyes! It couldn't be. Those devouring eyes!

Galina stumbled backward. She must be mistaken. The fiancé's name was Andrei. But years ago, Nadya had heard a rumour about Petrov: some important Party bosses in Moscow were looking for him after he'd stolen the fortune they had amassed for themselves. Corruption was an open secret, yet they could hardly go public. Petrov had apparently fled the country, but the Party bosses had a long reach. Galina assumed the information had come from Nadya's brothers, who seemed to have a pipeline to nefarious businesses back home. If Petrov was a wanted man, he could have come to a quiet city like Toronto, could have changed his name…

Galina composed herself as Oksana stepped into the salon.

While helping the girl into her dress, Galina asked casually, "Was that your fiancé who dropped you off?"

"Yeah, Andrei loves that car."

"How did you meet?" Galina didn't usually ask personal questions, so she followed up. "I ask all our customers that."

"Oh, we met at a dance. You know, that hall on Steeles Avenue."

She named a venue where Russian expats went to meet other Russian expats.

"I'm a good dancer, and he saw me. Picked me out right away."

Galina forced a smile. "What does he do?"

"He's a businessman. Arranges mortgages and things."

Oksana was admiring herself in the mirror. The mermaid dress, tight down to the hips then flared, flattered her hourglass figure.

"He's done well here," Galina said. "Your parents must be happy."

She made a face. "My mother likes his money, but my father says he's too old for me."

"Must be hard living at home."

She waved her hand. "Oh, no! I moved in with Andrei right away. He has a penthouse! Why would I stay at home in a tiny little bungalow?"

Galina would look up the address Oksana had written down on the form all the brides filled out.

"You need a veil," Galina said. She brought over a length of gauzy fabric and a strip of white satin. "I can make a headpiece for you."

She arranged the satin into a semi-circle and pinned it on the veil. "It will come down across the front of your hair, like a princess." She placed the satin over Oksana's hair, the veil like a cloud behind. "We'll sew on crystals and pearls to make it pretty."

Oksana smiled. "I love it."

She took the gown home in an opaque garment bag that hid its secrets. Galina watched the fiancé lay it in the trunk of the Jaguar. She recognized the way his body moved, deliberately, with confidence, only a few pounds heavier after 25 years.

She retreated to the office in the rear. Falling into a chair, she folded back the sleeve of her blouse. She wore only long sleeves so she could avoid it, but now she searched out the red worm of scar. It pulsated on her arm, relentless, dragging her back to Petrov's bed, the magnificent music, once nearly sacred to her, now polluted. She put her head down on the desk and wept.

Nadya found her there. Galina struggled to get out the words, but finally Nadya understood.

"You're sure it's him?"

Galina nodded, her eyes swollen.

Nadya picked up the phone and dialed. She spoke in Russian.

"Yes, Nikolai Petrov." She waited during a response. "He's here, in Toronto." She waited again. "Of course. Galina saw him."

Nadya listened on the phone, nodding, nodding. Finally, she looked up at Galina and gave her a crooked smile.

***

Galina painstakingly stitched crystals and pearls onto Oksana's headpiece. The next morning, she phoned the girl, offering to bring it to her home after work so she could try it on with her gown. Galina fidgeted the rest of that day, unable to concentrate.

It was twilight when she pulled into the guest parking in front of the north Toronto apartment building. She trembled, carrying the headpiece in a garment bag over her arm. She had brought her large purse, heavier than usual. Inside the front door, she punched in the code Oksana had given her.

The elevator slid up fifteen floors and opened right into the penthouse, a high-ceilinged front hall with marble flooring. Oksana appeared in tight pants and a sweater, kissing her on both cheeks. She brought Galina into the vast living room where floor-to-ceiling windows looked into the night, becoming a mirror of the room. The building backed onto a ravine. Galina noted the balcony door.

The "fiancé" sat on a white leather sofa, phone in hand. Galina held her breath.

"Andrei, this is the wonderful dressmaker who made my gown, Miss Adamova..."

He nodded and waved from his seat, engaged on the phone.

Galina understood. His fiancée's dress was of no consequence to him. A frivolous diversion. He had important business matters to deal with. He had no *idea* how important.

Oksana led her into a bedroom with red drapes and a king-sized bed covered with red silk. It looked like a brothel.

The girl closed the door before pulling the wedding gown from the closet. Galina helped her on with the dress, then placed the spectacular headpiece over her hair.

"Oh, it's gorgeous!" Oksana said, entranced with her image in the mirror.

Galina had taken special care embroidering the piece, though she knew it would never be worn.

After a few minutes, loud voices rose in the hall outside. Men were arguing. Oksana looked at Galina with alarm. Then the noise of a scuffle, someone falling heavily to the floor. Oksana covered her mouth with her hand.

"What's happening?" she cried, stepping anxiously to the door.

"No!" Galina said. "You don't want him to see the dress. I'll look."

She opened the door, took a step, then pulled back in quickly, closing the door. She shook her head ominously and whispered, "Go into the bathroom. Lock the door. Don't let anyone in but me."

Oksana's eyes widened in terror, then she ran to the ensuite and locked herself in.

Galina's heart leaped in her chest. She took a deep breath before walking out the door, carrying her purse. The yelling had stopped. The brothers Makarov, Sergei and Dimitri, had Petrov pinned against the glass door of the balcony.

He was bleeding from his nose and a cut above his eye. His expensive silk shirt was torn. He looked small beside the brothers' bulky chests.

"I'll give you money, as much as you want!" he screamed. "I have a lot of money."

"We know. The men you stole it from sent us."

"This is a mistake! You have the wrong man. My name is Andrei Zhadenko."

"Liar!" Galina spat out.

He turned his bloody face toward her. "Who the hell are you?"

One of the brothers slapped his face hard. "Respect!"

Petrov closed his eyes, then opened them, staring at her.

"You don't recognize me, do you?" She took off her tinted glasses.

He screwed up his eyes.

"I wasn't blond then."

He blinked.

"It was a long time ago. In Akmola."

He gasped. "*Ga... Galina?*"

She couldn't remember why she had been so terrified of him.

"Please, *help* me!" he sputtered.

Some men never learned.

The brothers peered at her; they were waiting for her to give the word.

She pulled a cassette player from her purse and turned on the tape. Pavarotti's immense voice began to sing "Nessun Dorma." No one sang it so well. She hadn't listened to it or any other music for years. The sound expanded in the air, filled her with memories she had almost beaten back.

Petrov's eyes grew wide. "What are you doing? I *helped* you. Don't you remember? I saved you."

She turned up the volume. The brothers looked at each other and smiled.

The song was heading toward its climax, when the prince vowed he would win the love of the ice princess, Turandot. Galina gave the brothers the agreed-upon nod. One husky man on each arm pulled Petrov away from the balcony door. They slid it open. Cool spring air rushed in.

Petrov began to scream. "Help! Someone help me!"

The music drowned out his voice. They dragged him onto the balcony. He kicked his feet against the concrete floor. She followed, noting the dark moonless sky. They were high above the ravine, nothing but a black hole below.

"I'll give it all back! Let's go to the bank now and I'll transfer it all back!"

The brothers lifted him by the legs and held him over the edge of the balcony.

Petrov howled, but the night swallowed up the sound.

Pavarotti had come to the resounding climax, the B note sustained with heroic length.

The first "Vincerò!"

The brothers let Petrov slip a bit, as if they had trouble holding on.

Galina closed her eyes, squeezing out tears for the self she had lost in Akmola.

The second "Vincerò!"

She opened her eyes.

The last "Vincerò. Vincerò!" "I will win! I will win!"

The brothers let go.

Petrov screamed into the bottomless night.

She held her breath, listening for more. But there was no more.

SOLACE IN D MINOR

By Donna Carrick

Memory…

That never-completed first draft of life, ever changing, evolving with each telling and retelling.

Still, I do remember him. He is forever blended in the mixer of my mind, images that swirl within the music. Always moving to the rhythm, the melody of sorrow.

***

As a child, I was fully aware of how special our father was. He was a superstar, the proverbial "whole package," loved by millions, and he was my hero.

Dad was a real father, one who spent time with us, as precious as that time was. He blessed us with genuine love and a unique outlook on life.

I remember the day he gave us the "talk"—the one about our family's wealth and privilege.

"Money," he said, "is a fortress. It protects us from the outside world. It shields us from the consequences of our actions.

"But never forget, girls, it's also a prison. Wealth, especially old money, can hold you in a comfortable, concrete bubble.

"Do your best to avoid that trap. Experience the outside world. Keep an open heart. Get to know people from all walks of life.

"And, above all, never be afraid of love."

***

I was eight years old when he passed away. That's what our mother called it: "passing away."

He hanged himself in the sound room one fine morning, leaving our mother to finish raising my sisters, Tara and Clara, and me within the walls of this ornate prison we called home.

Our father was born into money. All key aspects of his life were mapped out for him from a young age. He knew what kind of woman he was expected to marry. And he didn't disappoint. Our mother was raised on old money. Not as old as Dad's, but still, plentiful enough.

Calvin was a good son. He studied at the right schools. He married the right woman. He loved his family, his parents, wife and children.

In every way he strove to become a model prisoner. Every way, that is, except for one.

Our father, Calvin Bernard Chambers III, was a rock 'n' roll legend. Cal Chambers, CC to his friends.

You know his work.

In his early years, he studied at the conservatory, making a name for himself as a prodigy. Of course, he had family money behind him. Unlike most of his contemporaries, he suffered no financial risk in plunging headfirst into his passion.

Singer, musician, songwriter—Dad did it all. I loved watching him rock on stage. I stared at the TV, fascinated by the audience, those devoted faces alive with adoration.

I understood on some deep level that he was more than just "my dad." He belonged to the *world*. And the world belonged to him.

We never knew why he chose to end his life. Years later, I noted a suspicious tone in something my mother said, something about the band's bass guitarist, Marlon Troke, Dad's closest childhood friend.

Something to the effect that Dad had left behind *two* widows.

But we never *knew* his reasons. Not really.

That last morning, when my sisters and I scrambled to the studio to tell Dad that Maggie, our cook, was putting breakfast on the table, well, let's just say it was a defining moment for each of us. Until then, we'd been merely sisters, running wild throughout the corridors of our LA mansion, three mermaids swimming comfortably in an ocean of privilege.

From that moment on, we were three individuals. Our reactions to his death defined us in ways we previously couldn't have imagined.

Tara, the eldest, was changed in an instant. She became serious to the point of solemnity, helping Mom survive all the myriad death-related tasks that are heaped so cruelly upon the heads of the newly widowed.

Clara, the baby of the family, ran screaming from the studio that morning. In the chaos that followed, no one thought to look for her. It was dinner time before Maggie tracked her down, hiding inside a trunk of cast-off clothes we used for dress-up games.

Clara wouldn't speak for over a week, and when she did, it was as if Dad's suicide had never happened. No reference to the man, not to his life, nor to his death, escaped her lips for months. When she finally spoke his name, the inference was that he was away on tour and would be home any day now.

In her flighty way, Clara probably suffered more deeply than any of us. She bottled up her grief, and during her teen years she became highly promiscuous, ignoring her studies and relying, more than once, on our money to shield her from the consequences of her behavior.

Mom cried herself to sleep the night Dad died, and probably for many nights to come, although I can't say for sure.

As for me, I remember with sickening clarity staring up at his lifeless body. It hung from a cable strung over an oak beam not far from his beloved baby grand. His guitar rested on its stand, not more than a few feet away.

I recall the pungent odor, the foul emissions of a dying body. I studied his grotesque death mask, looking for some semblance of the only man I'd ever loved—a gentle, talented father and musician.

I found nothing in that mask to which I could relate.

In that moment, my lifelong obsession was born. I turned to music as my one true solace. Every night I lay in bed, headphones on, playing every song my father had loved.

At first, I couldn't bring myself to play *his* music— that would have been too much to bear.

But there were so many other gems we'd enjoyed together: opera songs, rock, jazz, blues. After his death, I would listen, often singing along in my bed, until I fell asleep to my favorite: "Time to Say Goodbye," the Andrea Bocelli and Sarah Brightman version.

Within weeks of Dad's "passing," I had abandoned any pretense of connection to the outside world. I no longer paid attention to conversations, to schoolwork, to my mother or sisters. Every waking moment was filled with the music in my head, the lyrics, the melodies that rolled constantly through the hills and valleys of my developing synapses.

Did the music bring me serenity? Peace? Joy? Maybe.

I was too young to understand the autism taking root in my personality. All I knew was that music, with its steady thrum, the rise and fall, the poetry of the lyrics, covered me in a merciful blanket of solace.

I sold my first pop song at the age of 11. By the time I was 13, my music was featured in a number of lesser-known films.

I scored my first hit movie at 15.

No doubt my father's name gave me more than a leg up in our industry.

Predictably, our wealth protected me from the ravages of my "disorder," the Asperger's syndrome of which I was only peripherally aware.

My family kept the secret of my illness away from the outside world.

Drop out of school? No problem. My mother explained it away. "Our Farah is home-schooled. Her future in music makes it hard for her to attend traditional classes."

Refuse to make eye contact or to answer when spoken to in public? "Farah's like that," my sisters would giggle. "Always has her head in the music. Earth to Farah!"

And they were right. I wasn't being deliberately rude. I had simply become, over the months following Dad's death, unable to engage, focused exclusively on the music that filled my head, my heart…my soul.

My mother did her best to drag me out of my cocoon, lining up soirées and other small events where I would play my compositions for members of our wealthy class. Of course, these events were often attended by well-known artists and musicians, ensuring my talent would be publicized to the right people.

I didn't mind. I was okay in those social situations, removed as I was from the main gathering. The audience didn't exist for me, not really.

My vocal range was passable enough for such small groups. I sang my original pop pieces, although I was under no illusions of talent in that arena. Dad's voice had been pitch-perfect. Mine, well, it was pleasing, in the right setting. That is all.

And so, the years passed. My mother aged. She never remarried. She insisted Dad had been her one true love.

Besides, she argued, she wasn't willing to risk a marriage that would diminish the inheritance intended for her children.

Prisons. No one escapes, not really.

She seemed happy, though I'm the first to admit, I'm no judge of the happiness of others. She was always good to me, that's all I really know.

My sisters recognized my illness long before I could give it a name. They covered for me publicly, and found ways to include me in social events, despite my craving for solitude.

They could well have lost patience with me. I complained endlessly. I made myself generally unpleasant whenever I was forced out of the music room—it was now *my* music room—and into the company of others. They could have given up on me, but they insisted I join them in the greater world, at every opportunity.

When my disorder made a public appearance, causing me to act out rudely to others, they surrounded me, speaking for me when necessary and shielding me from the brunt of dreaded human contact.

***

And so it happened that I found myself, flanked by my two beautiful sisters, at the wedding of a cousin. You know her. She's big in accessories.

We were all gathered at a huge church. The bride was another lovely Chambers redhead. A smidge taller than me, though not as tall as my sister, Tara.

Clara and her husband, the drummer Eddie Keats, were there.

Our eldest sister, Tara, had never married. She'd enjoyed the usual number of relationships, but ruled each out on the grounds that her suitors were smitten by the Chambers trust fund, rather than by our sea-green eyes.

My mother, two sisters and I occupied one pew in the grand church. I'd never mastered the skills of society—how to dress, smile, speak. Mom and my sisters took care of me.

Tara had chosen my silk dress, a clingy number in strokes of burnt amber that made me think of a Pacific sunset. Mom had surprised me with a delicate silk hat.

Normally I'm no fan of fashion. I won't pretend false modesty. The women in our family are good-looking, with our stature, our flaming red hair, almond-shaped green eyes and natural curves. Physical appearance was not something I ever thought much about.

But that morning, standing in front of the gilded mirror as Mom placed the tasteful deep burgundy hat atop my head, I couldn't help but think, "Damn, I look pretty good!"

"Stunning," Tara said, hugging me from behind.

"Gorgeous," Mom agreed.

303

When we hooked up with Clara and Eddie, they let out whistles of appreciation.

At 29, I'd never dated. It had never been an option for me, really. To date, you have to notice other people. You have to be aware of them, and of yourself, of your own behavior.

The lack of romance never bothered me. I had Mom, my sisters, my memories of Dad. And above all, I had music. It was what I lived for.

Tara and Clara were both charming, funny, engaging, and at the same time, they knew how to keep me safely wedged between them, to protect me from being touched by strangers.

I *hate* being touched. *Especially* by strangers. I don't shake hands. I don't hug. I don't make eye contact. For me, it's the most intimate connection between two human beings. It's a spiritual union, however brief, between people.

It's not a union in which I care to engage.

Hell, I usually don't even answer when people say hello!

In gatherings such as this, I stay inside my own head until I feel the familiar nudge from one of my sisters. That's my cue to nod, to smile, to pretend I know or give a damn about what some aging relative just said to me.

***

Henry.

We met him that morning at my cousin's wedding. His eyes were blue. His hair was angel-blond.

He was tall, close in height to our late father, although that was where the similarities ended.

Dad had been a warm man in his own way, gracious and generous to the world, to his friends and fans, and certainly to his wife and daughters. Handsome as all get-out, with his laughing green eyes and shock of red hair.

But he'd never been "charming," not in the way Henry was.

The moment Henry was introduced to us outside of the church, he clasped Tara's hand and said something so funny she almost snorted in laughter.

I didn't catch what he'd said, but I sure noticed Tara's reaction. You might say I *woke* in that moment, from a long, deep sleep.

The endless dream my life had fallen into, my supreme fugue state, was *over*.

Clara giggled at Henry's joke, and Eddie guffawed, as they each shook his hand in turn. Mom nodded and smiled. I could see she was taken with our new friend.

And then he looked at me!

His blue eyes met mine directly. All of the surrounding noise fell away, and I was suddenly aware of him, the way I hadn't been aware of another human being in a long, long time.

There were tiny crinkles at the corners of his eyes, the kind that spring from a well of laughter.

His hands, when he held mine, were pleasantly warm.

He stepped back, still holding my fingers—and oh, the charge of electricity that raced from those digits into my very soul!—to admire the silk sunset dress I'd forgotten I was wearing. I felt my cheeks burn, knowing that he found me utterly attractive.

"Henry Oulds," he repeated, as if he knew I hadn't been listening but was willing to make allowances for my previous inattention. "It's lovely to meet you at last! I'm a huge fan of your music."

This took me by surprise. Most people outside the industry wouldn't know *my* work. The singers, the artists, the performers—they are the stars, the ones who bring my art to life. They are the names and the faces, the *famous ones* adored by fans.

Me, I'm merely a conduit. That's what Mom once said, and it's true.

***

Mom didn't know I'd been listening when she said it to Maggie one morning. I so rarely listened to anyone, or engaged in conversation, that people forgot I was there.

"She's a savant," Mom said, carrying the breakfast dishes to the sink. "The music just comes out of her, complete and ready to go. It's as if she's a robot of some kind. A conduit for music, really."

"One day," Maggie said, "she may want more from life than just the music."

"I know. And God help her when that day comes."

"God help us all," Maggie agreed.

***

"F-Farah Ch-Chambers," I stammered, unable to break free from Henry's gaze.

The moment was becoming weird. We'd held each other's hands, and gazes, too long. I felt my sisters squirm, and pulled away, looking at my feet, suddenly aware of the designer stilettos Clara had purchased to match my dress.

"So nice to meet you, Mr. Oulds," Mom said, reaching for Henry's hand. Her tone was friendly, in a chirpy, socially graced way, but I could tell it was also dismissive. She was ready for Henry to move on.

"Hope to see you at the reception," he said. He waved at all of us before making his way to the long line of limousines, but I sensed that both his wave and his comment were directed at me. He found his car and

306

opened the passenger door, but before he slid into the backseat, he looked our way.

His eyes met mine once more, and my body burst into flames.

***

"I'm afraid you're moving too fast," Mom said.

Maggie plopped a pancake onto my plate. Her silence was no cover for her opinion. I could tell she agreed with Mom. Maggie had always been my protector, a gargoyle of sorts.

"Farah, there's just something about Henry," Tara said. "I don't know what it is. Please think this through."

I felt the hot sting of tears burning my eyes. It was an unfamiliar sensation. I had not wept, not even come close to crying, since the day my father died.

Any time sorrow threatened to rear its dark head, there was always the music, the relentless rhythm, the irresistible melody. I was safe behind that wall of sound.

Now, without warning, my music was no longer enough. In fact, I'd hardly worked on my current sound track, had barely even *listened* to it, since Henry had danced into my life.

"Don't you want me to be happy?" I whispered.

"Of course, honey," Tara said, "but Henry is the first man to show an interest! You have no experience in romance. You should be dating, getting to know each other."

Tara looked past me at my mother, who nodded.

"Besides," my sister added, "he may not understand about…the music."

She meant to say that Henry might not get it about my autism. About my obsession, my inability to see or hear anything *or anyone* beyond the melodies that dominated my mind.

"He understands," I argued. "He gets it. He accepts me as I am. Who else would ever accept me?"

"You're a beautiful young woman," Mom said. "You have your father's looks and his talent. Any man would be lucky to have you in his life."

"And yet," I said, spitting out the words, "Henry is the first. He's the first to notice me, to look at me, to realize there's a human being in here. All these years, not even one date! Not a single hint of romance in my life. Henry is my first, and probably my last chance for happiness."

In the end, it would be my decision. They could shield and protect me only so far. I was, after all, a grown woman.

Later that week, I received a call from Clara. My younger sister had never been one to mince words.

"I don't like him," she said. "He's *too* much. He's unbelievable. And Farah, to be honest, you've never been a good judge of character. You don't see things that other people see. You're…distracted."

Yes. *Distracted.* Good word for my illness.

She had a point. Until the day I met Henry, there had been only the music.

But thanks to him, my long interlude was over. I was awake, clear-eyed, aware in a way I'd never been.

They all thought I was *blind*, that I couldn't see Henry in a realistic light. But they were wrong. I could see him perfectly, in all his splendid appeal. I could see him to the exclusion of everything and everyone else. I had committed his laughter, his countenance, his every turn of phrase to memory.

He was my *magnum opus*!

Besides, Clara was in no position to judge me. She'd married that headbanger *Eddie*, for Pete's sake, a drummer who'd once trashed a hotel room so thoroughly that his entire band was barred from entering any Hilton facility for life. Eddie was a goon, true to the drummer stereotype.

Still, he did seem devoted to Clara. And why not? Despite her troubled teenage years, my baby sister had grown into a fine lady, beautiful and down-to-earth. She'd make a great mother one day.

Mother. Good God! Did I dare consider the possibility of my own motherhood?

No! Push that thought aside. I was awake, but I was not miraculously cured, not ready by a long shot to toss aside all my emotional crutches and claim sweet freedom!

I had many miles to go before I could entertain the idea of *motherhood*.

Thank God, Henry understood. He was in no rush to have children.

***

Our wedding was small, by Chambers family standards. My mother planned the service and reception. I'm not capable of things like that. My sisters decorated the church in dangling silver treble clefs, instead of wedding bells. I thought they did a beautiful job.

My dad's childhood friend and former bass player, Marlon Troke, walked me down the aisle. Whatever suspicions Mom might have harbored about Marlon, he'd remained a close friend of the family, helping Mom whenever he was able.

My dress was lovely.

The guests were lovely.

The church was lovely.

It was all lovely.

I'm sure it was. But to tell you the truth, I had eyes only for Henry.

He stood there, near the minister, flanked by groomsmen on his right (close cousins of mine) and bridesmaids on his left (my sisters and a cousin).

Henry had no close family of his own.

I floated toward him, mindful of my six-inch, silver-plated heels. The shoes were a nightmare—sterling silver mesh uppers that wrapped around my Parisian ivory lace stockings. Heels any red-blooded fashionista would die for.

Heels that I, if I wasn't careful, might die on!

The minister blathered on. The rings were exchanged, the organ played. None of it penetrated my consciousness. I was fixated on those playful blue eyes, watching me with their sparkle of humor, affection and a hint of lust.

I blushed all the way from my silver clad toes to the roots of my red hair!

Mom had asked repeatedly why we'd rushed this wedding. I was surprised she couldn't guess the reason. It was no mystery. I was a *virgin*, for Pete's sake!

Since I'd maintained an involuntary virginal state for 29 years, Henry and I agreed we might as well wait until our wedding night before exploring our lust. After all, I'd come this far. He made no secret of his own sexual experience, and once or twice he pressed me to go further, but in the end, he respected my wishes. He assured me that, so long as it was not a long engagement, he would wait.

I had no intention of allowing the engagement to drag on!

Finally, the ceremony was over.

Tara and Clara stayed close to me as the after-wedding throng gathered on the church grounds.

Somehow, we all survived the chaos of photos and greetings, hugs and kisses.

When you are blessed with social standing, Mom reminded me, you also have certain obligations. So, while the wedding itself was not large, the reception afterward was a real barn burner. So many social debts to be repaid.

Marlon had arranged for his band to perform, complete with a hot new singer to fill Dad's lead role.

They performed one of Dad's early pieces, a poignant love song, which was perfect for the first dance.

Like me, Dad had a soft spot for D minor. A fair portion of his work fell into that key. "Yours Until Sunset," one of his earliest hits, flowed through my veins. It haunted me, but in a beautiful way. When my new husband danced me onto the floor to that sweet music, I felt as if Dad was smiling down, congratulating me for breaking free at last from my personal prison.

He rained his ghostly blessings onto my head, as only a father can.

***

I was exhausted. Anyone would be, after a day like that, but it really took a toll on someone with my emotional issues.

Still, as tired as I was, I could not take my eyes off my husband. He was my new obsession. I could not believe he was mine!

My eyes searched the darkened dance hall and located Henry speaking to one of my relatives, Aunt Phyllis, my father's oldest sister.

He leaned in, said something to her, and she instantly lit up, breaking into genuine laughter. Then he glanced my way, nudged Aunt Phyllis and pointed at me.

My dear Henry. Such love burning in those eyes! Such husbandly pride!

Suddenly I was overrun by a gaggle of cousins. I surprised myself by engaging in a conversation. Marriage to the most handsome man in the world filled me with confidence. I joked with my relatives, they laughed, and I thanked them for coming. You know, spoke to them the way a normal person would. And they spoke to me.

Who would have thought it possible? Not me!

The reception had been fun, and long. The band was packing up. It was almost time to leave. I'd lost sight of Henry about 20 minutes earlier. Fatigue was getting the better of me.

"Go to your room," Tara said. *Ordered*, actually.

Henry and I had booked a room in the hotel. We'd be leaving for Barcelona in the morning.

"I'll tell Henry where you are," she assured me.

"Okay," I agreed. "I just need the ladies' room before I go up."

Tara laughed. "Good luck using the bathroom in that dress!"

"Actually, it's not so bad," I said. "But these shoes!" I lifted the dress and poked a silver toe out onto the carpet.

"Well, I'm going to take Mom home," Tara said. "I'll be surprised if she doesn't pass out in the car."

"Good night, Tara," I said, kissing my sister on the cheek. "Thank you for everything. Really, for everything."

Her eyes were wet with tears at my rare display of love. "I'd do anything for you, Farah," she said. "I hope you know that. We love you, Sis."

I knew she loved me. I supposed I'd spent my life soaking in their unconditional love, taking it for granted. But those days were over. Henry had opened my heart, taught me the importance of returning love for love.

"I love you too, Tara. Please give Mom a good-night kiss for me."

With that, she was gone. The hall was thinning out. A few hangers on watched drunkenly as the band helped roadies move their equipment.

"Marlon," I said, "thank you. That was a super performance. Truly wonderful."

"I'm so glad you enjoyed it, dear. Remember, you will always be my family. If you and Henry need anything, just say the word."

Henry. Where was my dear husband? It was getting late. Even the roadies looked like it was past their bedtimes.

"Have you seen Henry?"

Marlon pointed to a side exit, a small door near the stage. I wasn't sure what was beyond, but I assumed the caterers had used that door.

"Good night, Marlon," I said. "I'll call you and Brian when we get back from Barcelona."

I leaned in to give him a kiss, something I'd never done before, despite having known him all my life. I was going for broke, becoming a new woman. Reaching out to show people how much they meant to me.

All thanks to Henry.

Marlon held my hands for a moment, planting a kiss on my forehead, the way my father used to when he tucked me in.

"Good night, dear."

On the way to the side door, I removed my shoes. I could not take five more steps in those brutal heels. I set them on the stage, along with my lace wrap and the tiny silver clutch that held my cell phone and a tube of lipstick.

Floating on stocking feet was a great relief, after so many hours of trying to stay erect on those gorgeous medieval torture devices!

And so I floated, my wedding dress fluttering silently, my red hair swept up and bound at the top of my head. In my mind, I heard my father's song, "Yours Until Sunset," and my heart danced as I went in search of my one true love.

***

They didn't hear me pass through the swinging door. The caterers had long since gone home for the night, their leftovers packaged and shared among the staff, their dishes washed and neatly stacked into the cupboards.

The young woman looked familiar. I'd seen her at the church, although I hadn't paid her much attention. I'd thought her dress was lovely, although she wore it awkwardly, like a woman unaccustomed to fine garments.

She was a pretty girl. Not tall, but not so short as to appear insignificant.

Henry's face was in shadow, turned away from me.

"Do it soon," the woman said.

"Patience, Janice."

"Patience my ass!"

"There's no point, until we can deal with her mother."

"So, deal with her mother."

"I will. As soon as we get back from Barcelona."

"Doesn't it make more sense," Janice said, "for Mama to pass on while you're overseas? You know, gifted with an unquestionable alibi?"

Henry angled his face into the light and looked directly into Janice's eyes. The love I saw there took my breath away. I almost fainted on the spot, from the sheer shock of it. Finally, he said, "Clearly you have an idea."

"I do," she said. "Leave it to me. I can handle the mother. A day or two before you're due to come home, she'll have a nasty fall. You'll receive a call."

"Are you sure?" Henry asked. "Have you thought it through? It has to be perfect."

"Don't worry your pretty head about that." Her laughter was sweet, not the sort you'd expect from a villain. "I've worked out every detail. Right down to the moment you receive the call. All you have to do is act surprised. Can you do that?"

"Hmm…yes. I can act."

"Indeed," she agreed, "that you can. Actually, the best scenario would be to get rid of the sisters, too."

"That's nuts," Henry said. "Greed is always a mistake. Besides, Farah's inheritance is more than enough."

"Never forget, my love," she said, "that *greed* is the cornerstone of our relationship." They both laughed. "But," she added, "I agree. It would be stupid and unnecessary to screw with the sisters. Having said that, don't waste any time on Farah. I want her gone as soon as you get back. I'm not into sharing my man."

"Oh for God's sake! Don't tell me you're jealous of Farah?"

"Jealous of a mental spaz? I don't think so. Just the same, hear me loud and clear. That bitch dies a *virgin*. Got it?"

"Got it. She won't be able to live without her mother. I promise you, within a week Farah will hang herself, just like her father did. No one will be surprised."

Janice took his face into both of her hands and kissed him deeply, passionately. She was clearly *not* a virgin.

For a second, I was unable to move. The cold, sharp hook of reality jabbed me in the chest. I understood what I had just witnessed. Henry and his lover were planning murder.

My mother's murder.

My murder.

I slipped quietly through the swinging door, just as I heard Henry murmur, "Not now. I have to go. She'll be looking for me."

I grabbed my shoes, purse and wrap from the stage and ran toward the main exit. Made my way to the ladies' room down the hall. Hid in a stall till I managed to get my heart rate under control.

***

People outside the music industry have no idea what it takes to create a masterful composition. They think you can just sit at a piano or some other instrument, and the music will flow effortlessly from your mind through to your fingertips, and all you need do is to record it.

Not so.

Even for someone like me—an emotional cripple, a musical savant, a mental spaz, an autistic genius, as some have said—the art of creating beautiful, accessible music is *never* easy.

We may make it *look* easy, I'll grant you that. But it takes many years of internal struggle and turmoil to forge something unique out of a few errant electrical impulses flying around in the brain.

It takes plotting, planning, discipline of the highest order.

It takes focus.

These are skills my father and I both possessed in abundance.

Henry would be the first to "pass on." I wasn't sure how he would die, but by the second day of our honeymoon, he would meet an untimely fate. Most likely a poison-induced heart attack.

The doctors in Barcelona would be baffled.

I would be heartbroken.

My money would take care of any inconvenient details.

Making sure Mom was safe would be more difficult. I'd have to conjure up a plan to protect her until I could return home.

Marlon would help. He thought of me as a daughter. He'd loved Dad, and he would do anything I asked him.

I reached into the tiny silver purse for my phone.

He picked up on the second ring.

"Marlon," I said, "are you home already?"

"No. Brian and I are in a cab."

"Head over to the house. I have a bad feeling about Mom. She's looked after me for so long, I'm worried about her there, all alone in that big house. There was something she said...I have a feeling she might hurt herself. Please, Marlon, don't leave her alone, even for a second, till I get home."

"Is Tara with her?"

"No. She was planning to drop her off. Please don't tell Tara unless you have to. I may be imagining it. But I can't live with myself if I fly off and something happens to Mom. I can't go through that again."

"What if she argues? Your mother doesn't like a lot of fuss."

"You can blame me. Just tell her I went into one of my fits. I made you swear you wouldn't take your eyes off her."

"Don't worry, hon. We're turning the car around now. We'll spend the week with your mom."

"Thank you, Marlon. And remember, stay with her. Don't take no for an answer."

Killing Janice would be a challenge. I didn't even know her last name. I'd have to do some research, and not the kind you could trace on a browser history.

Patience was the key. I knew nothing about Janice, or her connection to Henry. For all I knew, he might have grown up next door to her.

She couldn't die immediately. There could be no connection drawn between her death and Henry's. I'd need time to plan a suitable end to her existence.

Let her wallow in her grief. Let her wonder what really became of her lover.

Then, when sufficient time had passed, move in for the *kill*.

Nothing fancy. Simple and elegant. A fall in front of a train would fit the bill.

No weapons, no witnesses. Nothing that could connect me to that evil bitch.

***

It's been a year since I lost Henry to a heart attack in Barcelona. He went for a morning swim, leaving me to breakfast in the hotel dining room, and died alone in a chlorine sea.

In the depths of my silent rage, I never realized how much I would miss him. I missed the way he looked at me, as if he really saw me.

Like I was a human being, and not just some emotionally challenged freak, some trained chimpanzee on a string, churning out music for money.

Oh, yes, the music returned to me with a vengeance. With Henry's "passing," it slid back into my consciousness, reclaiming its crown as my one true obsession.

I've been on a roll, in fact, unleashing new hits like a demented Babe Ruth. And the money is pouring in again. Not that we need it. We still have more old money than I can count. But it's nice to earn my keep again.

***

I pull the white silk duvet up to my chin. I've slept in this very room for as long as I can remember. Mom peeks in, blows me a kiss. I smile and wish her good night.

The headphones are soon in place, and Andrea Bocelli is once more paired with Sarah Brightman. I allow myself to drift away on an ocean of perfect harmony.

"Time to Say Goodbye."

My very own solace, in D minor.

I whisper, "Good night, Dad," at the ceiling, thinking how some prisons are, indeed, comfortable.

I'll rest for a couple of hours, then I'll sneak out the back way. Earlier, I disconnected the security cameras, so I won't be seen leaving this fortress we call home.

Enough time has passed. I've been patient, careful.

Tonight, I have a date with Janice. I know what time she catches the train to Pasadena.

Greed and malice, I will vanquish thee!

Then I'll grab a cab back to Beverly Hills, pay in cash and walk the short remaining distance home.

Money can be a fortress, or a prison.

But music, well, *music* is always my comfort.

I'll return to my soft, warm bed, set my headphones over my ears and let the melody lift me into the sweet release of my dreams.

***

It was never for the money, our music. My father and I had plenty of money.

It was for the dark comfort, the relentless rhythm, the undeniable solace of a haunting melody.

THE BALLAD OF WILL ROBINSON

By Ed Piwowarczyk

My name is Will Robinson, same as the kid on that '60s TV show *Lost in Space*. My fictional counterpart had a robot who warned, "Danger, Will Robinson, danger!" Too bad that robot wasn't around when Rose Connelly entered my life.

Maybe I wouldn't have been beguiled by her beauty. Maybe I would have steered clear of her. Maybe we'd both be alive.

Perhaps the robot would have cautioned me to temper my passion for collecting traditional folk music, lest my obsession be the death of me—literally.

But there was no robot for *this* Will Robinson.

Instead, I'm looking up at the stars from a shallow grave, playing out the final verse of my personal murder ballad.

***

I was born in 1940, the only child of middle-class parents, and grew up as rock 'n' roll took hold on the record charts and a folk music revival blossomed. Most teenagers my age listened to Elvis Presley, Jerry Lee Lewis and Buddy Holly, but my musical heroes were Woody Guthrie, Pete Seeger, the Weavers, Leadbelly, the Kingston Trio, Peter, Paul and Mary, Joan Baez and, of course, the young Bob Dylan.

Listening to and delving into the history of songs of economic hardship, disasters, civil rights, union struggles, war and love became my obsession. With an eye toward someday opening my own shop, I worked at Anderson's, one of the city's downtown record stores—part-time as a student, then full-time once I'd earned my arts degree. What better way to save money while learning about the record business?

Then came July 25, 1965, when Dylan switched from acoustic guitar to electric at the Newport Folk Festival. Up-and-coming singers and songwriters followed his lead, and the music I loved faded from the mainstream. But I continued to work and save, determined that my store would keep those traditional sounds alive.

Then in 1974, my parents died in a car crash. I was left with a modest inheritance and some insurance money. Along with my own savings, there was enough for me to open my dream record shop.

I rented a small-town, main-street storefront in a town of about 6,000 souls, about an hour's drive from the city. It included a two-bedroom upstairs apartment with a separate entrance at the back, perfect for a bachelor like me.

And voilà—Robinson's Records was born. I specialized in folk music and blues, and carried strictly vinyl.

I tracked down concert posters and artists' publicity photos to adorn the shop, and ordered records that reflected my personal tastes. Gradually, folk and blues devotees began to seek me out when they were looking for hard-to-find LPs, singles or imports.

I also checked out estate sales, yard sales and auctions. You never know when a rare recording might turn up, something that might interest a customer or something for myself. I was building a private collection of first pressings and out-of-print recordings.

The rarest 78s, 45s and LPs I kept under lock and key in a custom-built wooden cabinet in my inner sanctum, which I dubbed The Conservatory. I had turned the spare bedroom into a record library, complete with high-end hi-fi equipment. I kept my favorite albums, books and record guides on shelves lining the walls.

I rarely had guests. Once in a while, I'd invite a neighbor or a good customer up for a drink, but when I did, I'd entertain them in my living room.

I had just turned 40 and settled into a comfortable groove with my life when Rose Connelly came along.

***

One spring day in 1980, I was reading *Goldmine* magazine, a publication for record collectors, behind the counter when I heard the door open and close. I looked up to see a slender woman, dressed in a sleeveless white top that accentuated the curve of her breasts, a tan miniskirt showcasing long, shapely legs, and brown suede ankle boots. She was in her mid-20s, I guessed, and stood about five foot six. She had auburn hair in a pixie cut, a straight nose, heart-shaped lips and sapphire eyes.

She flashed me a smile. "Mr. Robinson?"

I was momentarily dumbstruck, then collected myself. "Call me Will." I stepped out from behind the counter. "How can I help you?"

"My name is Rose Connelly." She extended her hand, and I enfolded her smooth, delicate fingers in mine.

"I'm looking for...well, I'm not really sure." She grinned sheepishly. "I'm trying to earn a master's degree in music and thought I'd do my thesis on folk music."

I waited for her to continue.

Then she laughed. "Folk music. Now *that's* narrowing it down. I must sound foolish, but I don't know where to start. I hope you can help."

"Hmm." I stroked my chin as I admired her figure. "Do you want to focus on a particular singer? A certain style? A period? Who are your favorites?"

"There's Dylan, of course, and Baez, Joni Mitchell, people like that. I suppose *everyone's* done papers on Dylan."

"Your adviser should know. Who is he, by the way?"

"It's a woman. Dr. Barbara Grayson. In fact, she steered me to you. Are you familiar with her work?"

The name gave me a jolt. *Barbara!* "I've read her book on Appalachian ballads."

"You know her?"

I did, once. Intimately. "We've met."

Barbara Grayson and I had been lovers.

***

The first time I saw Barbara was in a music history class in my final year of university. She was a willowy blonde with shoulder-length hair, long legs, and green eyes. One day, she caught me staring at her, but rather than turning away, she grinned and winked at me.

It took me a couple of weeks to summon up the nerve to ask her out. I was bracing myself for a rejection, but she accepted my invitation to a campus hootenanny.

The sing-along evening eliminated the need for small talk on our first date. We discovered our mutual love of folk music, and soon we were regulars at coffeehouse performances and concerts.

I was living in a room in residence, but Barbara had her own apartment, courtesy of her wealthy parents, close to the campus. Soon I was spending more and more time there. Evenings consisted of eating take-out food, drinking cheap wine, listening to albums and talking about our futures. Her goal was to pursue a career as a musicologist, while mine was to own a record shop.

At the time, that seemed far away. What consumed us back then was our heated lovemaking. Nothing seemed quite as important as our sex life.

After graduation, we shocked our families by moving in together without getting married. Barbara went on to postgraduate studies, while I worked my way up to management at Anderson's and started building my record collection.

About six months after moving in together, Barbara's bedroom ardor began to wane, and our lovemaking became more perfunctory than passionate.

One night, as she rolled over to go to sleep, I asked, "Is there someone else?"

She turned and propped herself up on one elbow. "What?"

"You heard me."

"No, there isn't anyone else. I've had offers for afternoon quickies but I've never accepted. If I had, would you have noticed? Or cared?"

"How can you say that? What we have is…is…"

"What we *had* was good, but people change. I keep waiting for you to grow up, but you don't."

"Haven't I encouraged your studies?"

"Yes, you have. The concerts and records, they're part of my education—an important part. But I want to study the musical past, not be a prisoner to it like you. I want something more out of life."

"Like what?"

"Like a family, maybe?"

Suddenly it hit me. "You're *pregnant*?"

"Yes." Her voice grew gentle. "I was waiting for the right time to tell you. I thought you'd be happy." She put a hand out to touch me, but I turned away. "It'll be tough at first, but we can make it work. My parents will help, and—"

"No!" I was confused and...terrified. "We're not ready." Then I lashed out. "You get your baby—"

"*Our* baby!"

"—and your doctorate, but I don't get my record store. That's not fair."

"Listen to yourself! You love your records more than you love anything or *anyone*, including me."

"That's ridiculous."

"Is it?" She paused for a moment. "What if I and your records suddenly disappeared? Which would you miss most?"

I hesitated. And in that moment, I lost her.

Her eyes flashed with anger. "You have to *think* about it?" She held up a hand. "Don't say anything. I have my answer." She turned her back to me. "Don't touch me."

She turned off the bedside light. "Someday, you'll regret choosing vinyl over flesh and blood."

The next day, Barbara was gone.

***

Rose waved her hand in front of my face. "Hello. Mr. Robinson. Will. Are you okay?"

"What?" I emerged from my reverie. "Yes, I'm fine. Where were we?"

"We were about to discuss narrowing my focus."

"Right." I thought for a moment. "Well, you could examine a particular period, going back decades or even centuries. If you're interested in musical styles, there's bluegrass, country blues, Delta blues, ethnic songs, Appalachian ballads, spirituals…it all comes down to your tastes."

Her shoulders sagged. "It seems so…daunting. Maybe I'd better forget about it."

"No, don't give up." Call it what you will—midlife crisis, loneliness, romance, lust—but I was bewitched by Rose. "Let me think." Then an idea came to me. "I know. Let's enroll you in Will's Folk Music 101. Follow me."

She looked at me quizzically, but trailed behind me as I headed for the bins. I started pulling out albums—recordings by Woody Guthrie, Pete Seeger, the Weavers, Leadbelly and Odetta. "Listen to these and see what you think."

She reached into her shoulder bag, but I held up my hand. "No charge. If any of these appeal to you, come back and see me, and we'll talk some more."

I handed her the albums, and she kissed me on the cheek. "I really appreciate this," she said, clutching the records to her chest. I opened the door for her, and she gave me a little wave as I watched her get into a red Corvette across the street.

As she drove off, it occurred to me that the Corvette was somewhat…flashy…compared to my modest gray Chevette. I assumed a student—even a postgrad student—would drive something more economical.

***

A week later, she was back. "Will, those albums, they were great. But that makes it even harder to find a focus for a thesis. Any other suggestions?"

I tried to hide my excitement at seeing her again. "Sure." I plucked out more selections from the bins: Doc Watson, the New Lost City Ramblers, Bill Monroe, Tom

Paxton, Dave Van Ronk. Once again, I waved off her offer to pay.

"You've been such a help," she said as I bagged the records. "Surely there's something I can do to thank you."

Here's your chance, Will. I cleared my throat. "How about having dinner with me sometime?"

"It's a date. But let *me* treat *you*. I insist."

"Okay. How's Italian sound? Antonio's down the street has great lasagna."

"Perfect. Let's say next Saturday. Six o'clock?" She turned to go.

"Wait!" I was so excited that I reached under the counter for a special compilation. "There's probably no better primer than this."

It was the multi-LP *Anthology of American Folk Music*, released in 1952. The cover of the first release—I had one locked away in The Conservatory—featured an ancient instrument called a monochord, while the 1960s' reissue, also in my collection, had a photograph of a Depression-era farmer. It was a distinction that would likely only be noted by a collector.

Whenever I came across the reissue, I snapped it up, notified enthusiasts and sold it to whoever made the best offer. This one had been put aside for one of those select few, but the customer hadn't picked it up or paid for it yet. So I gave it to Rose.

I told her the *Anthology*, a collection of songs originally recorded between the late '20s and early '30s, was a touchstone of the Greenwich Village folk scene and introduced artists such as the Carter Family, Mississippi John Hurt, Uncle Dave Macon and Sleepy John Estes to wider audiences.

"You've been holding out on me, Will," Rose chided. "Naughty, naughty." Then she chuckled. "Just kidding. See you on Saturday."

Once she had gone, I phoned Daniel "Ole Dan" Tucker to advise him that the *Anthology* I'd earmarked for him was no longer available. Born into a wealthy family, Tucker had made millions more in enterprises as varied as construction and pharmaceuticals. The combination of money and rumored Mob connections gave him a fearsome reputation. Now he had become a collector, aggressively seeking out and bidding on art, antiques and records.

I'd expected an angry blast for letting the *Anthology* go, but to my surprise he was unperturbed. "Someone came along with a better offer, then." I didn't contradict him. "That's disappointing, but I'll have it in good time."

Although I had never invited Tucker up to my apartment, he suspected I owned more than what was for sale in the shop. Whenever he made a purchase, he offered to buy my private collection. Which I always denied having.

"I'm a man who gets what he wants, whatever it takes," he said. "I can wait for you to sell, but not indefinitely." Before I could protest, he said, "Look, why not show me your collection? We can make a deal. You can name your price—within reason."

"There is no collection."

"If you say so. Just remember, the time may come when you'll regret not taking my offer."

Then he hung up.

***

The streetlights were on when we left Antonio's.

"That was wonderful, Will," Rose said as I walked her to her car. "Thanks for suggesting Antonio's. You won't find anything better in the city, not even in Little Italy."

"Glad you liked it. Although it was a little far for you to come for a bit of pasta."

She smiled. "It was worth the drive."

Dinner at Antonio's couldn't have gone better. We had "dressed up" for the occasion, me in a black tie, blue plaid shirt and jeans, and her in a red miniskirt, a white, off-the-shoulder top and black high heels. We got off to an awkward start, but some Chianti loosened us up. Before long, the wine and the conversation were flowing.

After I'd sketched out my background, she gave me hers. Her parents divorced when she was six, and after the split, her mother developed a drug problem. Rose ended up being raised by an elderly aunt and uncle, now deceased. After graduating with a bachelor of arts degree, she landed a job as an executive assistant. She wouldn't say to whom or what she did. "My boss likes to keep everything hush-hush."

I poured more wine. "What about the Corvette? How can a working girl afford a car like that?"

"It was a gift from my boss. That's all I can say." Before I could ask more, she added, "Next subject."

As for her thesis, "I'm working on my master's part-time," she said. "When I met with Dr. Grayson, she suggested I visit your shop." She sipped her wine. "And here we are."

As we approached her car, she groped in her purse for her keys and stumbled slightly. I caught her by the elbow to steady her. "Rose, you seem a little...tipsy. Do you think you should drive right now?"

She put her hand to her forehead for a moment, then stood straight. "I...I guess not." She handed me her car keys. "Can you take me to a motel?"

In the car, I became emboldened by the wine. "Look, don't waste money on some fleabag. Crash at my place."

I thought she would politely turn me down, but instead she gave me a coquettish smile. "Why, Will Robinson," she drawled in a mock Southern accent, "would that be...proper?"

"I'm not trying to hustle you. There's a sofa bed, and—"

"Enough already." She leaned in and kissed me on the lips. Hard. "Let's go."

I parked the Corvette behind the store, led Rose upstairs and ushered her into the living room. "Home sweet home," I said. The room was modestly furnished—a television, an armchair, a couple of lamps on end tables, a stereo, record shelves and the sofa bed. Folk festival and record posters covered the walls. "A nightcap?"

"Why not?" She kicked off her shoes, leaned back on the couch and closed her eyes.

I placed an Irish whiskey in front of her on the coffee table. Then I sat in the armchair, sipping mine as I watched—no, *ogled*—her.

She must have sensed me staring at her. Raising her head and looking straight at me, she picked up her drink and downed it in one shot. Then she patted the seat beside her. "Come here, Will." As I sat beside her, she put her hand behind my head and gave me a long, sensuous kiss. Then she drew back. "Well?"

I grabbed her by the waist, tugged her into me, nuzzled her neck, then gave her a passionate kiss.

"Mmm," she purred. "Where should we do it? Here, or—" she pointed to my bedroom door "—in there?"

I tried to contain my excitement. "Definitely there." I pulled her up from the couch and led her into the bedroom.

Our lovemaking was frenzied at first, leaving us panting. Then we settled into a gentle rocking rhythm. I hadn't been so aroused and so sated since Barbara left me.

***

Sunlight streaming through the bedroom window roused me from my slumber. Yawning, I rubbed the sleep from my eyes and rolled over to face Rose. But the space beside me was empty.

"Rose!" I threw on my bathrobe. "Where are you?"

"In here."

Where was *here*? Then it hit me—The Conservatory! I hurried in to find her sitting on the couch, sipping a mug of coffee. She was wearing nothing but one of my shirts, unbuttoned in the front.

"Will!" She put the mug on the coffee table, rushed over and threw her arms around me. "I hope you don't mind me borrowing this." She tugged at the shirt.

"Not at all. You look…sexy." I summoned up a wan smile.

She frowned. "What's wrong?"

"Nothing." I kissed her on the forehead. "It's…this room."

She glanced around. "What about it?"

I sat her down on the couch and looked her straight in the eye. "I've never taken anyone to this room. No one's been in here but me."

"Until now."

I nodded. "Promise you won't tell anyone."

"My lips are sealed." Her hand made a zipping motion across her mouth. "But why?"

"There's valuable stuff in here," I said solemnly. "If word got out, collectors would pester me to sell. And I might become a target for thieves." Tucker suddenly came to mind.

She looked around the room again, then turned back to me. "Why is one of these records worth more than another?"

"It depends on a number of factors. The artist, the condition of the record, the cover, the rarity, the pressing—"

"Okay! I get the picture." She pointed to the cabinet. "What's in there?"

Now she knew about The Conservatory, but did she have to know *all* about it? My reluctance evaporated as she looked into my eyes.

"They're my most prized records," I finally said. "Some 78s by old bluesmen like Elmore James and Charlie Patton, 45s from the '50s and '60s, LPs like Dylan's *The Freewheelin' Bob Dylan*—"

"How is *that* rare?" Rose cut in. "I've seen plenty of copies."

"Yeah, but the earliest pressings were a mistake, and those are the ones that are rare," I explained. "Just before its release in 1963, four songs were replaced with newly recorded tracks. I don't know why. Somehow, someone at the pressing plant used the old version of the album instead of the new masters to put out an unknown number of LPs."

"That's incredible," she said. "So how much are all of these worth?"

"Hard to say. Some might be worth a couple of hundred bucks, while others might fetch a few thousand."

She scanned the room. "Is this some sort of investment?"

"*No!*" I snapped. "This isn't about *money*. I'm not going to *sell* anything here. Don't you *get it*?"

She drew back from me. "No, I don't. These are just...*things*."

I inhaled deeply. "To me, they're priceless, even sacred." I struggled to find the right words. "All of this is *me*. If I lost anything here, it would be like losing a piece of my soul."

She was silent for a moment. "Now I understand. I'm sorry I intruded."

She was about to rise, but I pleaded, "Don't go. Please." I hung my head, then looked back up. "I'm just...confused...at the moment. It's been so long since—"

She put a finger to my lips. "Don't explain." Then she gave me a soulful kiss. "You *do* want me in your life, don't you?"

"Yes," I said hoarsely.

"Then show me."

She peeled off the shirt. I slipped out of my bathrobe.

***

Dinners at Antonio's, attending auctions and yard sales looking for collectibles, drives in the countryside, lovemaking that swung between frenzied urgency and rhythmic rocking—weekends with Rose couldn't arrive soon enough.

She quickly made herself at home in my apartment. About two weeks after our first date, she arrived with a small suitcase. "Just something to leave here." She stuffed some clothes in a dresser drawer and cleared some closet space in my bedroom. "This way, I don't have to pack in a rush after work." She hung up a black negligee, then turned to me. "I'm sorry. I should have asked." She gave me a mock contrite look. "You don't mind, do you?"

Picturing her in that negligee erased whatever misgivings I might have had.

The following Friday evening, Rose was late for our weekend rendezvous. She arrived just after midnight.

"Sorry for keeping you up, Will," she said. "I didn't expect to have to work late tonight. I was going to phone, but the only number I have is for the store. Is there another number?"

"No," I replied. "I should've told you. My business number is also my home number. The phone up here is an extension." I handed her a glass of the wine I'd poured while I'd been waiting for her. "You could probably use this."

"It *has* been a long day." She sat on the couch and sipped the wine. "There's going to be more of them, I'm afraid. There's a special project at work, and—"

"You still haven't told me what you do," I interjected. "Or who you work for."

"My boss is very secretive. Sorry, I can't tell you, Will. Can you live with that?"

"Guess I'll have to."

"Anyway, with this project, he wants to be able to reach me at any time," she continued. "I hate to ask this, but…do you mind if I give him the number?"

I was annoyed, but tried to hide it. "I suppose not. Maybe your boss wants to buy a few records."

She beamed. "You're a sweetheart. Thanks for understanding."

As we finished breakfast the next morning and I was about to head downstairs to the store, Rose asked, "Will, can I have your keys?"

I automatically dug into my jeans pocket for my key ring, fished it out and was about to hand it over when I stopped. "Why?"

"I want to get a set cut for myself at the hardware store," she said.

I stood there speechless.

"Don't you see?" she said. "We can avoid what happened last night. Next time, I can phone ahead, and you won't have to wait up. I can let myself in and join you in bed."

"I'm…I'm not sure…"

"Look, I'm also going to get a set of *my* keys made for *you*." She tore a sheet of paper from a notepad and scribbled on it. "There." She handed it to me. "My address and phone number in the city. I know you don't go in often, but when you do, I'll be waiting. Drop in anytime."

I stood there, staring at her.

"Don't you trust me?" she asked. "We're making a *commitment* to each other with our keys. Or don't you want that?"

I swallowed hard. "You're right." I took her hand. "C'mon. I have to open the store first." Once that was done, I tossed her my keys.

She threw her arms around me. "That wasn't so hard, was it?" She gave me a quick kiss before heading out.

***

That night, we were listening to music in The Conservatory when she pointed to the cabinet. "You know, I've never heard any of the music you've got locked away in there. How about playing something now? Please?"

Her request caught me off guard, and I wavered for a moment. "Sorry, but no."

"Not even for me?" She pouted. "Why not?"

I took a moment to gather my thoughts. "Some of them, the 78s, are shellac records, not vinyl. They're brittle and can break easily. Sometimes the spindle hole size won't fit modern players. Others may be—"

"Stop!" she interrupted. "I don't want a long-winded explanation. Keep it short."

I took a deep breath. "Okay. I'm afraid they'll be broken, damaged, lost or stolen when they're not locked up." I paused. "I don't know what I'd do if something happened to them."

"Let me see if I understand," she said. "The cabinet is like a safe-deposit box, a place to store your musical valuables, but that you open only occasionally."

I nodded.

"Not often, then. Hmm. That's interesting." She quickly continued, "Anyway, I guess I'll never see the point of having those records if we can't listen to them."

"I wish I could explain better."

I was expecting her to press me more about the collection, but she said, "Don't worry about it." She leaned in and gave me a deep kiss.

***

The next morning, Rose slid out of bed and put on her negligee. She looked sexy as hell. "Go back to sleep," she whispered and kissed me on the cheek.

I mumbled, rolled over and pretended to doze. Once she was out of the bedroom, I got into my bathrobe and tiptoed down the hall.

"I just had to tell you." Her voice was low but excited. "I've got them....Yes, I'll have something for you soon....Be patient. If you're satisfied, there'll be more....Gotta go. Bye."

As she hung up, she turned and saw me standing in the living room entrance.

She yelped. "Will!" She put a hand to her chest and breathed deeply. "You startled me."

I sat down beside her on the sofa. "What was that all about?"

"I just remembered something I had to tell my boss," she said. "I had to make a quick call."

"Couldn't it have waited?"

"Afraid not." She threw her arms around my neck and gave me a long kiss. "I hope this doesn't happen again, but I can't promise it won't. Try to understand."

"Okay," I grumbled.

The negligee fell from her shoulders. "Let me make it up to you."

***

On one of our drives into the countryside in early August, we parked at the side of the road near a bridge. We strolled along the bank of a fast-flowing river, and our ambling soon brought us to a willow tree, its branches drooping low over the water.

"It's lovely," Rose purred, then turned to me. "Like a Monet painting, don't you think?"

"Yeah. Makes for a romantic picture."

Before long, we were lying in each other's arms beneath the tree. We dozed as a breeze rustled the branches above us.

When I finally stirred, I glanced at my watch. "We'd better get going. It's almost six."

Rose sat up and rubbed her eyes. "Do we have to?"

"You said you had to leave early, remember? A morning meeting."

"Right." She sighed. "We should go." She slowly looked around before we started to leave. "This spot is so idyllic. I want to come back and spend the day." She clapped her hands. "I know! We could have a picnic. Let's do it, Will. Don't you dare say it's corny. How about next weekend?"

I smiled. "Sure thing."

As we strolled back to the car, clouds drifted by overhead, casting shadows on our path. My mood shifted from contentedness to melancholy. Songs of lovers, willows and rivers started to swirl in my head. None of them ended happily.

***

Once Rose was on her way back to the city that evening, my disquiet led me to The Conservatory. Surveying my musical shrine calmed me, but something niggled at the back of my mind. Then I did what I hadn't done since I'd been seeing Rose—I unlocked the cabinet.

The cabinet had three shelves, each divided into six compartments. The top two shelves were in order, but the bottom one was empty.

I swayed and bent over, as if I'd been punched in the gut by a prizefighter. I lurched to the washroom, expecting to vomit, but only dry-heaved.

I felt as if my heart had been ripped out. No one but Rose could have done this. I cursed her and my own stupidity.

What she'd said when I overheard her on the phone was no longer cryptic. *I've got them.* My key ring, which included the key to the cabinet. *I'll have something for you soon.* The first batch of stolen records. *Be patient.* Her boss wants results—soon. *If you're satisfied, there'll be more.* She was cherry-picking the collection for her boss.

Then I recalled one of her fleeting remarks. *Not often, then. Hmm. That's interesting.* Another instance of my stupidity—I'd admitted that I rarely opened the cabinet.

I cursed. Rose would pay for this, I vowed. I breathed deeply to calm myself. I looked at my watch; it was 10:30. My anger-addled brain decided it would be a good time to pay Rose a visit.

The city was only an hour's drive away. I could be at her place by midnight, burst in on her...but then what?

Slow down. Think. Then it came to me. *See where she goes, who she meets. Find out who her boss is.*

I grabbed a few hours of restless sleep before heading to the city for my early-morning stakeout.

***

Around 6 a.m., I found the three-storey apartment complex where Rose lived and her Corvette in the adjacent tenants' parking lot. I parked a few doors down the street to keep an eye on the building's entrance.

Three hours later, Rose emerged, holding a black record carrier case. *Damn it! What's in there is mine!* She wore a strapless, knee-length white sundress and brown gladiator sandals, an outfit that would turn men's heads. But not mine—not anymore.

She wasn't alone. Accompanying her was a slim woman in a beige top and long denim skirt. Her hair was tucked under a wide-brimmed straw hat, and her face was obscured by dark glasses.

What the hell? Rose never mentioned a roommate.

When they reached the Corvette, Rose stashed the case in the trunk. Then the women exchanged a long embrace before parting. As Rose drove off, the mystery woman headed my way. I started up the Chevette and drove off, turning my face away as I passed her, hoping she hadn't seen me.

I thought I'd lost Rose a few times in the city traffic, but the Corvette's red exterior allowed me to pick up her tail quickly enough. Before long, I followed her into Tuxedo Heights, home to the city's upper crust.

She parked in the driveway of a Tudor mansion, retrieved the case from the trunk and approached the front door. I cruised by as she waited to be let in, noted the address and then accelerated down the street.

I drove to the public library's central branch, and looked up the address in the city directory. Daniel Tucker's name jumped out at me.

My last conversation with Tucker took on new meaning. *I'm a man who gets what he wants.* He wanted my records. *Whatever it takes.* Having Rose seduce me was a means to an end. *The time may come when you'll regret not taking my offer.* He'd have the records he wanted and I'd be left with nothing.

The "gift" of the Corvette was a down payment for Rose's services, and there was likely more coming her way.

To Tucker, the records were just *things* to own for the sake of owning them. They meant so much more to me.

What could I do? Call the police? They'd find no signs of a break-in, and I couldn't prove anything had been stolen. Confront Tucker? He'd simply laugh. Again, no proof.

Then I realized Rose didn't know that *I* knew about the stolen records. How could I take advantage of that? Fury consumed me as I drove home.

***

As I sat in The Conservatory fuming over Rose, I pulled out a 1958 Everly Brothers album, *Songs Our Daddy Taught Us*, and "Down in the Willow Garden," a murder ballad, caught my ear.

A murder ballad is a story song—rooted in Appalachian, Irish, Scottish and English ballads—of a violent death based on a mythic or real crime. The song tells listeners who the victim—often a woman—is, describes how the killer lures her to a remote murder site, depicts the murder itself—frequently stabbing or drowning—and recounts the killer's capture, escape or execution.

"Down in the Willow Garden" is believed to have originated in Ireland in the 19th century and later found its way into Appalachia. There have been various versions, including one by a bluegrass musician, Charlie Monroe, which the Everly Brothers sing on the album. In the song, a woman meets her lover in a willow garden, where he gives her poisoned wine, stabs her with a saber and throws her into a river. At the end of the song, the murderer is facing the gallows; his father—who put him up to it, the lyrics hint—has been unable to buy his freedom.

The name of the victim in the song? *Rose Connelly.* I could have kicked myself. Why hadn't I twigged to that earlier?

Then I seized on an idea. Why not follow the lead of the song's killer?

Poison in Rose's wine? Its taste or smell might tell her the drink had been tampered with. Better to spike it with tranquilizers crushed into powder to knock her out.

Then there was the saber. I opted to substitute a chef's knife, like the one used in the shower scene in *Psycho*.

I drove to the city to make my purchases away from the eyes of curious townsfolk.

***

A light breeze stirred the branches as we spread a blanket beneath the willow. Rose dropped her picnic hamper beside the tree, and I followed suit with my knapsack, which held the wine, the sleeping powder and the knife.

She kicked off her canvas sneakers and lay on her back. "Come here, Will." She patted a spot next to her and turned onto her side. "What's wrong?" she asked when I joined her. "You've been on edge since we left your place."

"I'm just a little tired. I haven't been sleeping well lately." What had me tossing and turning was wondering whether I had the resolve to carry out my plan.

"Maybe I can perk you up." She drew my head to hers, giving me a deep, lingering kiss, one that I returned with equal fervor. Soon my lips were exploring her sun-kissed neck and shoulders above her tube top, while my hand stroked the sleek legs beneath her denim shorts.

Then guilt over what I planned to do overcame me, and I eased away from her. "Sorry. I just can't."

She sat up. "What gives?" When I didn't reply, she said, "Maybe we should forget about this."

"No! It's such a beautiful day, and…and…I've got the cure for the blues right here." I dragged over the hamper. "Here we have—" I started to put out bread, cheese, cold cuts and olives "—all this. Not to mention—" I raised a bottle of wine from my knapsack "—this. We don't want to let this go to waste."

Her expression softened. "No, we don't." She smiled. "How about some wine?"

"Coming right up." I turned my back to her as I uncorked the wine, slipped a generous dose of the powdered tranquilizer into a white plastic cup and handed it to her. "Bottoms up!"

As we snacked, she drank more spiked wine. After a while, she murmured, "I'm…feeling…kind of…drowsy."

Her head bobbed. "Will…what's…happening?" She moaned, tried to stand, but collapsed on the blanket. Her eyes closed, and she lay still.

I sat watching her for I don't know how long, letting my anger over her deception simmer. Finally, I got the knife from my pack and knelt beside her. I raised the blade above my head, then froze.

Focus, damn it! I stared at her bare midriff. *Do it!* I gripped the knife's handle with both hands and held it above me, as if I were making a sacrifice. *Do it!* I pictured blood blossoming around her navel. *Do it!* For a moment, I thought I saw Rose staring up at me wide-eyed.

343

Impossible! Closing my eyes, I plunged the blade into her abdomen. Then again...and again...and again....

The killing frenzy left me gasping. I slowly opened my eyes, flinching as I gazed at Rose's bloody body. We had driven here in the Corvette, so I fished her keys out of her shorts and put them into mine. I staggered to my feet, then dragged her corpse to the riverbank. I rolled it into the water, and watched as the current carried it downstream.

When it had disappeared from sight, I hung my head but shed no tears. I had become a monster.

***

I got off an overnight Greyhound bus at the town's terminal around two o'clock the next morning. I figured at that hour and in the dark, none of my neighbors would notice my late arrival home, but I kept away from the streetlights.

As I climbed the steps to my apartment, I went over what I had done to cover my tracks.

After stuffing the bloodstained knife and blanket, the hamper and Rose's sneakers into a black plastic garbage bag that I'd tucked away in my pack, I drove to our rural garbage dump. By then, the sun was setting, and no attendant was in sight. Spotting a couple of bears pawing through the landfill, I heaved the bag onto a pile of trash near them. I envisioned them ripping it open and strewing the contents among the waste.

Next, after I'd parked the car in the alley behind my place, I showered and changed my clothes. My bloodstained T-shirt and shorts went into a garbage bag that I planned to drop off at the dump the next day.

Then I headed into the city to ditch the Corvette. I parked it at a metered space downtown, where I was sure it would to be ticketed and towed. I hoped this would befuddle the police when Rose's body was found.

344

Rose had stashed her handbag under the front passenger seat when we'd set off for our picnic. I found it and searched for my duplicate keys. *Not here!* But if they turned up later, so what? They were part of my relationship with Rose, something I wasn't going to deny when the police came calling.

I wasn't worried about my fingerprints on the Corvette—the car, with Rose behind the wheel and me seated beside her, had become a familiar sight around town—but I wiped the steering wheel clean anyway. Then I locked the car, dropped Rose's keys down a sewer grate, and caught the overnight Greyhound bus to town.

What had I missed? As I entered my apartment, I remembered that Rose had come up to use the washroom before we left. "Meet you downstairs," she'd called out and closed the bathroom door. No longer trusting her, I'd hidden at the top of the stairs to find out what she was up to. I heard her scurry into the living room and place a furtive phone call. "We're heading out now….All clear for the day….Bye." She dashed back to the washroom and flushed the toilet. "Coming!" she yelled as I scrambled down the steps.

Then it dawned on me. *The duplicate keys! She'd given them to someone, and her call had rolled out a welcome mat for a thief.* I ran to The Conservatory, unlocked the cabinet and yanked the doors open. *Empty!*

I knelt on the floor in front of the cabinet, staring at the space that had once held my prize possessions. I couldn't summon up any rage; I felt nothing inside.

***

Five days later, I read a newspaper account of Rose's body being found—Fishermen Snag Corpse, the headline read. Anglers had found her about halfway between the town and the city, well away from our picnic spot.

Rose's roommate, or Tucker, or both, would point the police in my direction, so I decided to call the cops first. I explained my relationship with Rose and expressed my shock at her death. I invited investigators to question me at the store, and I showed them where we'd had the picnic.

If they had hoped to make an arrest, they left disappointed. Her clothes in my apartment? She often stayed overnight. The ground around the willow? No sign of anything suspicious. When was the last time you saw her? The day of the picnic. Had there been a lovers' quarrel? No. Weren't you worried when you didn't hear from her? No, we generally saw each other only on weekends. How do you explain her body being found in the river and her car in the city? I can't. Neighbors recalled seeing us together around town and in her Corvette, but as to the last time, they couldn't be sure.

The police had nothing to tie me to Rose's murder. With no progress in the investigation, the media soon lost interest in the case.

***

It was early October, and I was heading home after dinner at Antonio's. The last time I'd been there was with Rose, so I was hesitant to return, but my craving for good Italian food overcame that. The staff expressed sympathy for my loss and provided a complimentary bottle of wine.

It was dusk, and the streetlights had just started to come on. As I approached my building, I froze. A black Lincoln Town Car, with two shadowy figures in the front seat, was parked across the street. A light glowed in my living room window.

What's going on?

I dashed around to my back entrance, crept up the stairs and peeked into the living room. There on the sofa sat Barbara, wearing a gray sweatshirt and faded jeans. Her blond hair hung loosely on her shoulders, her eyes were closed, her legs were tucked under her, a glass of wine was in her hand. She looked as good as ever.

Struggling to keep my composure, I eased into the armchair across from her and cleared my throat. "What are you doing here, Barbara?"

Her eyes blinked open. "Will Robinson!" She fixed her gaze on me, prompting me to shift in my seat. "After all these years, that's all you can say?" She swung her legs out, reached for the bottle of wine beside her and poured me a glass. "Don't worry. It's not poisoned, like in those murder ballads." She refilled her glass and took a swig. "See?"

I downed the glass and rephrased my question. "Why are you here?"

"I'll get to that, but first, let's have a toast." She filled glasses again. "To the past. To the people we once were and the love we lost."

We both drank before Barbara continued. "As for my visit, I wanted to talk about us."

"What's there to talk about? That ended years ago when you walked out."

"Not for me." Her eyes welled with tears. "I was still in love with you when I left. I hoped you felt the same and would come after me. But there was no phone call. No note." She wiped her eyes. "You knew I was pregnant. I thought, at the very least, you'd want to know about our baby. But nothing."

I fumbled for something to say. "So was it a boy or—"

"A boy. Stillborn. Complications during delivery." Her voice softened. "Umbilical cord prolapse, they call it. It's rare. The cord becomes compressed and cuts off the baby's oxygen supply." She paused. "I needed your

347

shoulder to cry on, but you weren't there." She inhaled deeply. "Anyway, I got on with my studies and my career."

I felt guilty and ashamed. "I…I'm sorry about the baby."

"Not really. You're too self-absorbed." Her words cut me to the quick.

Then she reached into a shoulder bag by her feet. "I also came to return these." She tossed something to me. *A ring with my duplicate keys!* "I don't need them anymore."

I stared at the keys, then at Barbara. "Where did you get these?"

"From Rose, of course."

"Why would she give these to her thesis adviser?"

Barbara grinned. "There is no thesis. That was a ploy to get Rose in here, stroke your ego and libido, and get the records."

"*You* were behind this?"

"There were three of us," she replied. "Dan Tucker wanted your records; he got them. Rose wanted money; she got the Corvette and cash. As for me, I wanted to get back at you; I had the satisfaction of seeing you stripped of what you held most dear."

I was stunned. "What about the roommate?"

"What roommate?"

"One morning, I parked near Rose's apartment. I saw her and a woman leaving—"

Barbara chortled with glee. "Dark glasses? Straw hat? That was *me*! So it *was* you in that little car." She chuckled. "I thought so."

She refilled our glasses. "You're wondering about Rose and me, right?"

"If you weren't student and teacher, or roommates, you were…friends?"

"We were *lovers*."

I was dumbstruck.

"Can't believe it, can you?" Barbara asked. "It just...happened. Tucker had Rose get in touch with me. An afternoon coffee led to dinner, then to after-dinner drinks and then to bed. I let myself go, and she aroused me like no one ever had. We've been lovers since then."

Barbara and Rose? "If she was so in love with you, why was she so hot for me?"

"Rose was bisexual. Going to bed with you was a game to her."

"Her and me—it didn't bother you?"

"I had my reservations," she conceded. "But Rose told me you were just another notch on her bedpost. Now I see I needn't have worried. Paunchy, graying hair, receding hairline—you've gone to seed."

The words stung. I gulped down the rest of my wine.

She continued, "Once Rose had your keys, I wanted to clear out your collection. But she wanted to stretch things out to get more money out of Tucker. And have a bit more fun with you.

"But when I suspected that was your car outside the apartment, I worried that you were on to her. I urged her not to go back, but she couldn't resist one last score. 'Let's finish it with our picnic,' she said.

"That day, I followed her in my car to the town bus terminal and waited by the pay phone for her all-clear call. I had your keys, so as soon as you two were gone, getting the rest of your collection was a cinch. But Rose never came home."

Barbara finished her wine. "That's why I'm here, Will. You murdered Rose. She gave me another shot at love. When you killed her, you took that away. You have to pay."

Her calmness rattled me, and I shifted in my seat. "What makes you think it's me, and not some hitchhiking maniac?"

"It's the ballad imagery," she replied. "Remember, I wrote a book about this. The willow tree, the river, the stabbing—it all fits. And only you would use a murder ballad as your modus operandi."

"*That's* your proof?" I scoffed. "You'd be laughed out of court."

"I'm the judge and jury here," Barbara snarled, "and I say you're guilty."

Grabbing her shoulder bag, she went to the window, looked out and gave a wave.

What's she up to? I joined her at the window as the Town Car pulled out of its parking spot.

"Who are they?" I asked.

"Associates of one of Tucker's connections," she said. "He lost a valuable asset, as he put it, when Rose was killed. He arranged for Nick and Marco to help me, in exchange for the rest of your collection."

"They're Mob goons." A shiver ran through me. "What are you going to do?"

"Once we meet them out back, the four of us are going for a ride."

"And if I refuse?"

"Then we'll have to persuade you," she answered. "If we're not at the back entrance in a few minutes, they'll come up for us. There's no way out."

I had only one chance to escape. I shoved Barbara to the floor and bolted down the stairs, hoping to reach the back door before the hoods arrived. But as I flung it open, two figures, their features obscured by shadows, loomed in front of me.

I started to run, but one of them tackled me. The other slugged me in the jaw as I turned around, leaving my head spinning.

What happened next was a blur: I had a rag stuffed into my mouth, was rolled onto my stomach, and had my hands tied behind my back. I felt the jab of a syringe, and everything went black.

***

When I came to, I was groggy. I heard the rush of water and the crackling of a campfire, and smelled wood smoke. My wrists were still bound behind me, but now I was kneeling. I felt heavy hands pressing down on my shoulders to hold me in place.

Opening my eyes, I tried to get my bearings. Night had fallen, but by the light of the fire, I saw the silhouette of a tree before me. *The willow where I'd killed Rose.* But directly in front of me was a rectangular hole—about four feet deep, three feet wide and eight feet long, I estimated. Two shovels were stuck in the mounds of dirt beside it. *My burial plot.*

Clutching a record carrier case, Barbara stepped out from the shadows behind the fire. She set the case down, crouched beside it and gestured to the hole. "Nick and Marco spent hours digging this. It's your final resting place." I squirmed, but the mobsters' grips remained firm. "There's no getting away, Will."

I slumped. "Why didn't you just kill me back at my place?"

"I wanted symmetry," Barbara replied. "What could be more appropriate than your dying where you murdered Rose?"

"How did you find this spot?"

"Rose told me about the road, the bridge and the river," she said. "Those I found on a map, and a short walk brought us to the willow." She reached into the carrier case. "Let's move on."

She pulled an album from the case and held the cover in front of me. "Recognize this?" She tossed it into the hole and grabbed another. "Or this?" I was speechless as she pitched LPs, one by one, into the hole. "Still nothing?"

I stared at the albums in the hole. "Will's Folk Music 101," I said. "The albums I gave Rose."

"It's a royal send-off," Barbara said. "A pharaoh buried with his treasures." She paused. "Now we come to the finale."

Her hand dug into the case and came up holding a chef's knife.

"Since you followed the lead of a murder ballad, I figured I'd do the same," she said. "I chose 'Pretty Polly.' Remember it?"

I nodded. Another centuries-old song, "Pretty Polly" tells of a woman, lured into a forest by a boyfriend, fiancé, sailor or gambler, depending on the version. She grows more fearful the deeper they go into the woods. When they arrive at a shallow grave, the man tells her he dug it for her. Polly pleads for her life, but in vain. He kills her and flees.

"And the name of the killer?" Barbara asked.

"Willie," I said softly. *Will.*

"And what did Willie do?"

"He stabbed Polly and her heart's blood did flow."

"What happens to Willie?"

"Depends on the version of the song."

"Pick one."

Dread crept over me. "Some lyrics say there's a debt to the devil that Willie must pay."

"Continue," Barbara ordered. "What's the debt for?"

I swallowed hard. "For killing pretty Polly and running away."

"I knew you'd get it," she said with a smirk. "But I've come up with my own variation." She cleared her throat. "A debt to the devil that *Will* must pay, for killing my *Rose* and running away."

She tightened her grip on the knife. "Tonight, the devil is coming to collect." She thrust the blade into my chest and pulled it out. "Go to hell!" Then she stabbed me again. The third time, she drove the knife into my gut and left it sticking in me.

At first, I felt as if I'd been punched. There was a dull throbbing, and I stared down at the knife handle and my bloody shirt. Then panic and pain set in, and a chill ran through me.

Barbara stood and took a step back. I was hoisted up, spun around and tossed into the pit, landing on my back on top of the records.

***

I groan as I look up at the stars and the quarter moon in the night sky. I'm weak from loss of blood. Shovelful after shovelful of dirt is thrown on me.

As my lifeblood oozes out, another murder ballad pops into my head. The music just won't leave me alone.

This time, it's the Kingston Trio's "Tom Dooley." In that song, the eponymous killer meets a woman on a mountain, stabs her and flees. But his escape is thwarted, and he's destined to hang.

Then I see the connection between Dooley and me, and it's not just that both of us murdered our lovers. Dooley laments that he'd have gotten away if not for a man named Grayson. Similarly, I might have gone unpunished for Rose's murder except for another Grayson—Barbara.

How amusing. I laugh, close my eyes and begin to hum "Tom Dooley."

I AM THE VERY MODEL OF A MODERN MYST'RY SCRIBBLE'ER

By Cheryl Freedman

One of the best known, popular and probably most parodied of Gilbert and Sullivan's patter songs is Major General Stanley's "I Am the Very Model of a Modern Major General" *from* The Pirates of Penzance. Hence this, my version of the song, because just as Major General Stanley was acquainted with all "matters vegetable, animal, and mineral," mystery writers as a group can deliver stories about (almost) any subject a reader might be interested in.

I Am the Very Model of a Modern Myst'ry Scribble'er

(to the tune of "I Am the Very Model of a Modern Major General")

I am the very model of a modern myst'ry scribble'er:
I've ways of killing people that would never raise a quibble, or
A doubt that I have knowledge of so many ways of offing folks,
Like guns and poison, knives and bombs, and even puns and killer jokes.

I know not of equations, whether simple or quadratical
Because I am a writer, not a genius mathematical.
But I know how people talk, including period profanity,
And I can diagnose your illnesses or even your insanity.

I've memorized *Chicago's* on most everything grammatical;
I've stories of Bill Johnston, an Ontarian piratical.
I can write of ghosts and witches or of authors and librarians
And reading clubs with members who are octogenarians.

I play French horn and viola and can sing in perfect harmony;
Arrest you—or defend you—when you do commit a felony;
I can walk with you through neighborhoods in every part of Canada,
And read dramatic roles in every period of theatah.

If you want to read of dogs and cats and ferrets, well, just
    come to me,
And I can discourse on your gods from Zeus to
    Christianity;
Cooking, quilting, painting, dancing: I'm an expert on them
    all,
And I'll expound on far-flung planets, cops and crooks, and
    volleyball.

The in and outs of publishing from writing books to selling
    them
I know, as well as government and hospital and biz admin.
I set my crimes in wineries or concert halls or high schools,
    while
You have your choice of gravitas or books that simply
    make you smile.

I'll enlighten you with thinking from political philosophy,
Or quote you words from *Batman* (the old series that was
    on TV);
Create a website or a blog, I certainly have what it takes,
And don't forget the creepy-crawlies: bugs and slugs and
    rats and snakes.

Then there's hist'ry from the years BC up to the current
    century,
And almost every continent, let's say I know geography;
I'm familiar with photography and academe and Northern
    Lights
And outré things like Fundy tides, exotic teas,
    hermaphrodites.

Belly dancing, fairy tales, luxury hotels, and more,
Journalism, puppetry, computer crime, running a store:
In short, you must admit that you can never raise a quibble, or
Deny I am the model of a modern myst'ry scribble'er.

Meet the Mesdames and Messieurs

Catherine Astolfo is an award-winning author, mainly in the mystery genre. In both 2012 and in 2018, she won the Arthur Ellis Award for Best Crime Short Story. Catherine has also written five novels, two novellas and four screenplays. A Derrick Murdoch Award winner, she is a past president of Crime Writers of Canada, and a member of the Writers Union of Canada and Sisters in Crime. Twitter: @CathyAstolfo

Rosemary Aubert is an internationally published author of 20 books, including poetry and short-story collections, romance novels and crime fiction. She is a two-time winner of the Arthur Ellis Award. Rosemary's other endeavors include 25 years' hands-on work in the Canadian criminal justice system and a distinguished teaching career. She lives in Toronto with her husband, well-known artist Doug Purdon, whose art classes inspired "The Beethoven Disaster."
http://www.rosemaryaubert.com/

Born and raised in Toronto, **Jane Petersen Burfield** and her family have lived in a family home similar to the one in "Requiem." Its garden, old-fashioned paneling and oak floors still inhabit her dreams. Jane won the Bony Pete Award in 2002 for her first attempt at a short story. In 2018, she was a finalist for the Arthur Ellis Best Short Story Award. Jane loves the mystery world, and enjoys fellowship and fun with her writer friends.

www.mesdamesofmayhem.com

A long-standing member of Crime Writers of Canada and Sisters in Crime, **M. H. Callway** cofounded the Mesdames of Mayhem in 2013. Her thriller, *Windigo Fire*, was short-listed for the Debut Dagger, the Unhanged Arthur and the Arthur Ellis for Best First Novel. Her short crime fiction has appeared in several anthologies and zines, and has won or been nominated for many awards. The *Globe and Mail*'s Margaret Cannon called her "a writer to watch."

http://mhcallway.com

Called the "Queen of Comedy" by the *Toronto Sun*, **Melodie Campbell** has won the Derringer, Arthur Ellis and eight other awards for crime fiction. She has shared a literary short list with Margaret Atwood, and was a Top 50 Amazon best seller, sandwiched between Tom Clancy and Nora Roberts. Melodie teaches fiction writing at Sheridan College, and is a past executive director of Crime Writers of Canada. *The Goddaughter Does Vegas* is her 15th book. www.melodiecampbell.com

Donna Carrick is an award winning thriller author, host of the Dead to Writes podcast, an Indie publisher, (Carrick Publishing,) former treasurer of Crime Writers of Canada and a long-time member of Sisters in Crime. Her novella *The Noon God* and novels *The First Excellence* and *Gold And Fishes* have all, at various times, topped Amazon's Bestselling Thriller charts. Her story "Watermelon Weekend" (*Thirteen*) was a finalist for the Arthur Ellis 2014 Best Short Story Award. www.donnacarrick.com and www.carrickpublishing.com

Catherine Dunphy is a retired, award-winning journalist. Her book, *Morgentaler, A Difficult Hero*, was nominated for the Governor General's Award in 1997. She is the author of two books of young adult fiction for the Canadian television series, *Degrassi High*. Always a mystery reader/addict, she wrote screenplays for the Canadian television series, *Riverdale* and created a four-part *CBC* radio mystery series called *Fallaway Ridge*. She is presently at work on a literary novel.
https://mesdamesofmayhem.com

Lisa de Nikolits is the award-winning author of nine novels, including *The Nearly Girl, No Fury Like That, Rotten Peaches* and *The Occult Persuasion and the Anarchist's Solution* (Inanna). *No Fury Like That/Una furia dell'altro mondo* was published in Italian by Edizione Le Assassine. Her short fiction and poetry have appeared in several anthologies. She is a member of Sisters in Crime and International Thriller Writers.
https://www.lisawriter.com and
http://www.lisadenikolitswriter.com

Cheryl Freedman was executive director of Crime Writers of Canada for 10 years and was awarded the Derrick Murdoch Award for outstanding service to Canadian crime writers. She headed the board of directors for Bloody Words, Canada's national mystery conference, and together with Caro Soles founded the Bony Blithe Award for Light Mysteries. She edits manuscripts ranging from nonfiction to history to crime fiction, and in her spare time writes crime and fantasy fiction.

www.mesdamesofmayhem.com

Marilyn Kay began as a medievalist, then morphed into a freelance journalist, communications officer, webmaster for WSIB and policy "wonk." Her debut short stories were published in *13 Claws* (Carrick Publishing) and the Bouchercon anthology, *Passport to Murder.* Currently, she is editing the manuscript of her first novel, a police procedural set in Toronto. Marilyn also serves on the executive board of Sisters in Crime Toronto.

https://marilynkay.me

Blair Keetch is the winner of this anthology's contest for emerging crime writers. He is an avid fan of mysteries from Christie to Connelly. His work history includes serving as an airline project manager, overseeing a pet event center and promoting Ontario tourism. A self-proclaimed procrastinator (becoming a father for the first time at age 55), "A Contrapuntal Duet" is his first published story. He is currently working on his first mystery novel, *Flight Risk*. Twitter: @BlairKeetch

Born to Holocaust survivors, **Sylvia Maultash Warsh** is the author of the Edgar Award-winning Dr. Rebecca Temple mysteries. Project Bookmark Canada chose her fourth novel for a plaque installation. She has published a novella and many stories, two of which have been short-listed for the Arthur Ellis Award and one for the Derringer. Sylvia is working on an historical/paranormal mystery. She also teaches writing to seniors. http://sylviawarsh.com/

Rosemary McCracken writes the Pat Tierney mysteries. *Safe Harbor*, the first novel in the series, was a finalist for Britain's Debut Dagger. It was published by Imajin Books in 2012, followed by *Black Water* in 2013 and *Raven Lake* in 2016. "The Sweetheart Scamster," a Pat Tierney story in the collection *Thirteen*, (Carrick Publishing) became a Derringer Award finalist. Jack Batten, the *Toronto Star*'s crime fiction reviewer, calls Pat "a hugely successful sleuth figure."
https://rosemarymccracken.wordpress.com/

Lynne Murphy is a retired journalist whose short stories have appeared in *Thirteen*, *13 O'clock*, and *13 Claws*, (Carrick Publishing) as well as *The Whole She-Bang* anthology series published by Sisters in Crime. Many of her stories feature the comic adventures of a group of elderly ladies who reside in the same condo building. She is a founding member of the Toronto chapter of Sisters in Crime, which is still going strong after 27 years.
www.mesdamesofmayhem.com

Ed Piwowarczyk is a veteran journalist, who has worked for the *National Post*, *Toronto Sun* and the *Sault Star*. He has edited Harlequin manuscripts, and is currently a freelance editor. A lifelong fan of crime fiction, he is also a film buff and plays in the Canadian Inquisition, a Toronto pub trivia league. His short fiction has been published in Mesdames of Mayhem and Toronto Sisters in Crime anthologies. www.mesdamesofmayhem.com

An interpreter by profession, **Rosalind Place** is a writer of short stories. Most recently, her story "The Garden Door" was chosen for publication in the anthology, *The County Wave, 21 Stories by Prince Edward County Writers*. A lover of mysteries, Rosalind's first foray into the genre was "Dana's Cat," which appeared in *13 Claws* (Carrick Publishing.) She is thrilled that "Bad Vibrations" will be included in the Mesdames' anthology, *In the Key of 13*. www.mesdamesofmayhem.com

Madona Skaff has published several SF and mystery short stories, including the 2014 Arthur Ellis Award finalist "First Impressions" (*The Whole She Bang 2*). Her short story "Backbone" appears in the anthology, *Nothing Without Us* (Renaissance Press, Fall 2019). Her debut mystery novel, *Journey of a Thousand Steps* (Renaissance Press), is the story of a young woman recently disabled by MS who turns sleuth to find her missing friend. www.madonaskaff.com

Caro Soles' novels include mysteries, erotica, gay lit and science fiction. She received the Derrick Murdoch Award from the Crime Writers of Canada, and has been short listed for the Lambda Literary Award, the Aurora Award and the Stoker Award. Her latest mysteries, *A Friend of Mr. Nijinsky* and *People Like Us*, will be followed in 2019 by MARLO'S DANCE, a debut police procedural series set in the world of the pleasure-loving hermaphrodites of Merculian. www.carosoles.com

Kevin Thornton is a seven-time finalist for the Arthur Ellis Award and winner of the 2016 Buffy Literary Award. He specializes in short stories (which means he can't get a book published) and poetry. A former soldier, military contractor, gadabout and ne'er-do-well, he lives in Northern Alberta where Fahrenheit and Celsius meet frequently at -40°. www.mesdamesofmayhem.com

Also by the *Mesdames of Mayhem*:

Thirteen

13 O'Clock

13 Claws

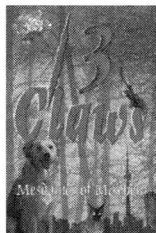